Sea Rose Lane

Center Point
Large Print

Also by Irene Hannon and available from Center Point Large Print:

Deceived
Thin Ice

**This Large Print Book carries the
Seal of Approval of N.A.V.H.**

Sea Rose Lane

A Hope Harbor Novel

Irene Hannon

CENTER POINT LARGE PRINT
THORNDIKE, MAINE

This Center Point Large Print edition is published in the year 2016 by arrangement with Revell, a division of Baker Publishing Group.

The text of this Large Print edition is unabridged. In other aspects, this book may vary from the original edition. Printed in the United States of America on permanent paper. Set in 16-point Times New Roman type.

ISBN: 978-1-68324-033-4

Library of Congress Cataloging-in-Publication Data

Names: Hannon, Irene, author.
Title: Sea Rose Lane : a Hope Harbor novel / Irene Hannon.
Description: Center Point large Print edition. | Thorndike, Maine : Center Point Large Print, 2016. | ©2016
Identifiers: LCCN 2016014164 | ISBN 9781683240334
  (hardcover : alk. paper)
Subjects: LCSH: Large type books. | GSAFD: Love stories.
Classification: LCC PS3558.A4793 S42 2016b | DDC 813/.54—dc23
LC record available at http://lccn.loc.gov/2016014164

To my niece, Catherine Hannon,
as she graduates from eighth grade.

From day one, you have been
a blessing in my life,
adding sweetness, joy, and sparkle.

May your high school years be filled with
fun, friendship, and infinite possibilities
as the world opens its doors to you.

Sea Rose Lane

—1—

He was going to hit that pickup truck.

As the vehicle in front of him screeched to a halt, Eric Nash flung his cell toward the passenger seat, clenched the wheel, and jammed the BMW's brake to the floor.

Too late.

A bone-jarring thud reverberated through his body, accompanied by the crunch of compressing metal and the explosive tinkle of shattering glass.

This was so not the way he'd envisioned his arrival in Hope Harbor.

Before his car even stopped shuddering, the driver-side door of the truck flew open. Shapely legs clad in snug denim swung out. In one smooth, lithe motion, a slender woman slid out of the cab, the coastal Oregon wind tossing her mane of blonde hair.

Nice . . . except for her stormy expression and taut posture.

Better forget her appearance and focus on an apology.

She paused to give the back of her pickup a cursory sweep, then marched to his door and glared at him through the window, fists jammed on her hips.

Oh, brother.

This was not going to be pretty.

Bracing himself, he pushed his door open and stood.

"Sorry about that." He tipped his head toward her truck.

She slammed her arms across her chest, leaned sideways, and homed in on the phone resting on his front passenger seat. "In case you didn't know, it's illegal to use a cell while driving in Oregon."

Of course he knew that. He'd know it even if he wasn't an attorney. The controversial law had received a serious amount of press.

But he was almost at his destination, and Hope Harbor wasn't exactly Portland. The only real traffic here was at lunchtime—*if* Charley's was open and *if* there was a run on his fish tacos.

However . . . it wasn't yet noon and he wasn't anywhere near the wharf-side stand.

"I'm aware of the law. But making a quick call on a quiet backstreet should have been safe."

"It wasn't."

"Look, I said I was sorry. My insurance will cover any damage."

Her eyes narrowed. "Money doesn't fix every problem."

Sheesh. Talk about attitude with a capital *A*.

"It will fix your truck." He surveyed the muddy vehicle. "Not that it will be easy to tell what damage I caused versus what might already be under the dirt." If she could be nasty, so could he.

She bristled, and tiny pieces of . . . something . . . drifted out of her hair. Squinting, he shaded his eyes against the late-morning sun high in the sky on this early July day. Was that . . . sawdust?

"It rains a lot here, okay? I have better uses for my time than washing a vehicle that will be muddy again tomorrow. And not that it's any of your business, but I prefer to spend my money on more important things than a hunk of metal."

"Obviously." He gave the truck another dubious once-over.

"Hmph."

With that pithy retort, she stalked back to the front of his car.

He trailed after her. "Why did you stop so suddenly, anyway?"

"A dog ran in front of me."

"I didn't see a dog."

"You didn't see me brake, either. If you'd kept a few car lengths between us—and been paying more attention to the road—you could have stopped in time." She bent to inspect her truck again. "Lucky for me, this baby's sturdy. I don't see any serious damage." She shifted her attention to his car. "Your wheels, however, are going to need some work."

For the first time, he gave the BMW his full attention. The left front fender was crinkled, the broken glass from the headlight glinting on the pavement.

Great.

Wasn't it enough that his career was in shambles and his future in limbo without adding a smashed-up car to his list of woes?

He wiped a hand down his face. Some homecoming this was turning out to be.

"There's a body shop in Bandon."

At least the woman's tone was a shade less hostile now.

"Yeah. I know. Marv's."

"So . . . you want me to call the police, file an accident report? The chief can get here fast. I passed her a few blocks back."

And have Lexie read him the riot act, maybe even cite him for using his cell while driving?

Not a chance.

"Why don't we just exchange contact information?"

"I don't need yours. I won't be calling my insurance company. But ah'll give you mine." She rummaged through her pockets, the faint hint of a southern accent lingering in the air. "I thought I had some business cards with me . . . but this will work." She pulled out a dog-eared receipt and scribbled on the back with the stub of a pencil.

Eric skimmed the slip after she handed it over. No name. Just a phone number—with a local area code. "I take it you live around here?"

"Yeah." She retreated a step and tucked her fingers in her front pockets. "You want to see if your car is drivable before I leave?"

He examined the BMW again. It wasn't listing, and the tire was holding air. "I think the damage is mostly cosmetic. I don't have far to go. I'll be fine."

"Suit yourself." She strode back to the cab of her truck, stopping at the door to skewer him with one final scowl. "And do yourself a favor. Ditch the cell while you're driving."

Without waiting for a response, she swung up behind the wheel, started the engine, and drove off, spewing noxious fumes in her wake.

Eric turned away from the billow of reeking exhaust, shoved the slip of paper with her number in the pocket of his jeans, and sighed. After psyching himself up during the five-hour drive from Portland to share the bad news with his father, he'd been as ready as possible for that conversation when he drove past the Welcome to Hope Harbor sign. Had even tried to call his dad seconds before the fender bender to alert him of his approach. Softening the surprise of this unexpected visit with a few minutes' warning had seemed like the considerate thing to do.

But since his dad hadn't answered, and since the accident had totally *un*psyched him, why not take a walk on the beach, past the soaring sea stacks, before he headed home? The salt air and sea breeze had always given him a lift . . . helped clear his mind . . . calmed him . . . when he needed it most.

And he could use some calm about now.

Trudging back to the driver-side door, he tried to look on the bright side. His life might be a wreck, but the car was fixable and no one had been hurt.

There was one other plus too.

This day couldn't get any worse.

BJ Stevens flicked on her left-turn signal, swung onto Eleanor Cooper's street, and tuned out the rumble in her stomach. Fixing a stuck door hadn't been on her lunchtime agenda—but what could you do when a kindly eighty-eight-year-old woman called to say she couldn't get out of her bathroom?

As she pulled into the driveway of Eleanor's Cape Cod–style house, BJ scrutinized the modest structure. The paint was flaking on the shutters. The stepping-stones winding toward the front door were rippling. The edge of one of the wooden steps leading to the small front porch showed signs of rot.

This house needed help.

A lot of it.

But so did the houses owned by many of the older Hope Harbor residents. Upkeep had simply become too much for them. Yet none wanted to leave the place they'd called home for most of their lives.

Understandable—as she well knew.

A pang echoed in her heart . . . followed by a surge of all-too-familiar guilt.

Gripping the wheel with one hand, she jerked the gearshift into park with the other. This was not the time to dwell on the past . . . or on regrets. She needed to rescue Eleanor from the bathroom and fix that recalcitrant door.

After grabbing her toolbox, she followed the uneven pavers to the porch and felt around under the wicker planter of geraniums until her fingers encountered the key Eleanor had promised would be there. Ten seconds later, she cracked the door and peeked in, scanning the shadows in case Methuselah was crouched on the other side, waiting for a chance to escape.

No sign of the cantankerous cat.

She slipped inside and moved toward the hall bath. "I'm here, Eleanor." Her raised voice bounced off the walls. "I'll have you out of there in a minute."

"Oh, bless you, sweet child!" Relief infused the older woman's muffled words. "I'm sorry to bother you during the workday."

"Don't worry about it. I was on my lunch hour." BJ set her toolbox on the carpet beside the gold-and-black-striped feline who'd taken up sentry duty outside the bathroom door. "Hi, Methuselah."

She stroked his soft fur, earning her a mellow meow. "How long has the door been giving you trouble, Eleanor?"

"Six or eight weeks, I imagine. It's been getting worse—but I never thought it would trap me inside. A firm tug has always done the trick if it gets stubborn."

BJ tested the door.

Definitely stuck.

"Let me give it a push. Can you back away from the door?"

"Yes. I'm tucking myself into the corner now . . . all set."

BJ positioned her shoulder against the wood and shoved. The door shimmied but didn't release its hold on the frame. She tried again, putting more muscle into the effort. This time it gave way.

Instantly Methuselah wove around her legs and disappeared into the bathroom.

Once the door swung open, she turned her attention to Eleanor. The older woman's trademark neat chignon had loosened, releasing wisps of soft white hair. Her cheeks were flushed, and there was a bruise forming on the back of the hand she lifted to smooth down the wayward tendrils.

"How long were you stuck in here?" BJ edged back to let Eleanor escape the confined space, Methuselah meowing at her heels.

"About an hour. I tugged on the door, rested a bit, tugged on it some more. Thank goodness I had my phone with me. I thought about calling 911, but that seemed extreme." She paused in the hall to adjust her glasses and fuss with her hair, gripping her walker with one hand. "I imagine I look a sight."

"No, but you do have a nasty bruise on your hand." BJ gently touched the aging skin.

Eleanor flexed her fingers and studied the black-and-blue splotch. "I lost my grip on the knob during one attempt and banged my hand against the vanity. No harm done, though. This old skin bruises if you breathe on it. I'll be fine. Now what do you suppose is wrong with that door—aside from humidity?"

BJ gave the hardware on the doorframe a quick inspection. "Humidity doesn't help, but some of the screws in the hinges are also loose. That can cause a door to sag." She pulled out a screwdriver and tried tightening a couple, but they were stripped.

Of course. A simple fix would be too easy.

She rooted among her tools, found a longer screw, and replaced the one closest to the center of the jamb, tightening until it dug into fresh wood.

"Let's see if this helps." She straightened up and tried the door.

It opened . . . but under protest.

"That's a big improvement." Eleanor patted her arm encouragingly.

"Not big enough. I don't want you getting stuck

again." Once more she dug around in her toolbox, withdrawing a few toothpicks and some wood glue.

"What are you doing now?" Eleanor leaned closer to watch while Methuselah nosed into the box.

"I'm going to coat the toothpicks with glue and shove them into the screw holes. Once they dry, it will be like new wood and I can reset the screws. That should fix the problem—but if not, I'll try shimming one or two of the hinge mortises."

"My. You certainly know your stuff."

BJ grinned. "You're easy to impress."

"Not at all. I just recognize talent. LA's loss was Hope Harbor's gain when you moved here last year."

"It was a positive change for me too." BJ continued to work with quick efficiency as she spoke. If she finished fast, she might still be able to swing by Charley's and grab an order of tacos on her way back to the job site.

"You know, there's one thing I can't understand." Eleanor's tone grew thoughtful.

"What's that?" If the older woman wanted a lesson in carpentry, BJ was happy to oblige.

"With all your talent and beauty—plus your kind, caring heart—I can't believe some smart, handsome man hasn't wooed and won you by now."

BJ's fingers spasmed on the glue bottle. A spurt

of white paste shot out, coating the toothpick and her fingers before dripping onto the tile floor . . . and Methuselah.

The cat yowled and sprang back.

"Oh, mercy!" Eleanor's hand flew to her chest. "I must have distracted you. Let me grab some paper towels."

While she trundled down the hall as fast as her arthritic knees allowed, Methuselah in her wake, BJ stared at the sticky mess on her fingers.

Sticky mess.

Yeah, that about summed up the state of her LA romance.

But she had a new life now. One that was calm, fulfilling—and blessedly romance-free. If she hadn't been on edge from the accident, she wouldn't have overreacted to Eleanor's comment.

BJ secured the cap on the wood glue with more force than necessary. She should have called the police and let them throw the book at that guy in the BMW. Maybe a ticket would have taught him not to drive with his cell pasted to his ear, paying more attention to conversation than the road.

Although—in fairness—he *had* been contrite.

Not to mention good-looking.

Oh, for pity's sake!

She grabbed a wad of toilet paper as more glue leaked through her fingers onto the floor. You'd think she'd be immune to the stereotypical charms of tall, dark, and handsome after—

No! She was not going to even *think* his name. He wasn't worth it.

She wiped her fingers as best she could with the flimsy tissue and took a calming breath. That fender bender had really done a number on her peace of mind.

But it shouldn't have, BJ. Your truck emerged unscathed. The other guy's the one who has to deal with repair hassles. That's not why you're tense.

"Oh, shut up." She ripped off flecks of tissue that had stuck to her fingers, trying to stifle the annoying little voice in her head.

"Did you say something, dear?" Eleanor's query wafted in from the kitchen.

"Just . . . uh . . . talking to myself."

"You're too young for that. I'll be back in a jiffy. I'm trying to clean up Methuselah, who isn't inclined to cooperate."

Hooking a piece of wayward hair behind her ear, BJ slumped back against the doorframe and faced the truth. Much as she might want to blame her agitated state on the accident, the little voice in her head was right. The BMW owner—and her visceral reaction to him—was the culprit. Like it or not, the instant her gaze had connected with those brown eyes, a bolt of electricity had sizzled through her.

The very kind of ill-advised attraction that could lead a woman astray if she followed her heart instead of prudently listening to her brain.

And she wasn't making that mistake again.

Still . . . it hadn't been fair to jump all over the guy because she was annoyed at herself. He *had* apologized. Offered to make restitution. His eyes had held sincere remorse . . . plus some other emotion, now that she thought about it. Melancholy, perhaps? Dejection? Despondency? Hard to pinpoint. But there had been a sadness in them that seemed unrelated to the accident. As if his day had gone down the tubes long before their unpleasant encounter . . . and he hadn't needed any more grief.

She blew out a breath.

Wonderful.

Now she could add a heaping serving of guilt to whatever she had time to scarf down for lunch.

"Here you go. Let me know if you need more." Eleanor pushed the walker down the hall and thrust a handful of paper towels at her while Methuselah kept a wary distance.

"This should do it." She used half of the towels to wipe the globs of glue off the tile, then dampened the rest and swiped up the residue.

"Do you want me to get rid of those?" Eleanor held out her hand again.

"Thanks." She passed them over. "I'll fill the last couple of holes while you do that."

BJ finished up as fast as she could, packed away her tools, and waited for Eleanor near the front door.

When the older woman reappeared, a foil-wrapped bundle rested on the tray of her walker. "Thank you again for coming to my rescue."

"No problem. And I'll be back tomorrow or the next day, after the glue is dry, to reset those screws. Could you leave the bathroom door open until I finish the job?"

"Certainly. I only close it out of habit. It isn't as if there's anyone here to disturb me, other than Methuselah—and at his age, he spends most of the day sleeping in the sun." Her smile drooped for a moment, then brightened again as she picked up the plate and held it out. "A little thank-you treat."

"That's not necessary, Eleanor."

"I disagree. Besides, I like to bake—and I know you're partial to my fudge cake. Have it for dessert after lunch."

At this point, with the clock ticking, it might *be* lunch—not that she needed to share that with Eleanor.

"I'll do that—and enjoy every bite." BJ took the offering. "I'll call before I swing by to finish the job."

"No need. I'm always here. You won't be interrupting anything."

The older woman's tone was upbeat, as usual, yet a faint thread of loneliness wound through her words.

Most people would miss that subtle under-current.

Not BJ, though. She was tuned in to such nuances these days—which did *not* help restore her peace of mind.

"Is everything all right, dear?"

"Yes." She switched gears and hefted the plate. "I'm looking forward to this."

"Enjoy, sweet child. And don't work too hard."

She let that pass as she left the house. Working too hard was part of her DNA . . . but if she couldn't dial back her work ethic, at least the work she did in Hope Harbor—on *and* off the clock—was worthwhile and satisfying.

And it might become even more so if the plan she was formulating came to fruition.

After carefully stowing the cake on the seat beside her, BJ glanced back toward Eleanor's planter-filled porch. With a final wave, the older woman picked up a watering can and began tending her abundant container garden.

BJ put the truck in reverse and checked the clock on the dash. No time for a swing by Charley's. But her appetite had disappeared anyway, thanks to the unsettling conversation with Eleanor about romance . . . and a disturbing encounter with a good-looking stranger.

Which was dumb.

She was *not* in the market for a relationship, especially with someone of the tall, dark, and handsome variety.

Maybe someday—some very distant day, far

down the road—she'd entertain the notion of love again.

Maybe.

But for now, her quiet, simple, peaceful—uncomplicated—life suited her just fine.

And she had no intention of changing it.

His childhood home was a construction site.

As his BMW limped toward the two-story hybrid Victorian/Craftsman hilltop house where he'd spent his youth, Eric gawked at the saw-horses, stacks of lumber, and . . . a toilet? . . . strewn over the front yard.

What in the world was going on?

He parked on the street, opened the door—and was greeted by the muffled banging of hammers.

A moment later, the grinding, high-pitched whine of a buzz saw sliced through the air.

Seconds after that, the snarl of ripping wood further sullied what should have been a tranquil summer day in Hope Harbor.

It sounded like the guts were being wrenched out of the one place he'd thought would never change.

The saw kicked back in, and his stomach twisted.

Apparently his career wasn't the only thing in a shambles these days.

But why hadn't his father mentioned during one of their frequent phone conversations that he was having work done on the house?

It didn't make sense.

The modicum of calm he'd achieved during his walk on the beach evaporated.

Was there *anything* in his life he could count on to remain the same?

Psyching himself up for whatever chaos lay inside, he circled the car. Ironic that he'd been worried about surprising his dad, when John Nash obviously had surprises of his own to—

Eric froze as a dirty pickup truck turned the corner.

A familiar dirty pickup truck.

It rattled down the street and swung into his dad's driveway while he stood rooted in place.

The truck door opened and the same jeans-clad legs he'd admired earlier appeared. No loose, flowing hair this time, however. The blonde's long tresses had been secured in a ponytail and tucked through the back of a baseball cap. She gave him a quick, cool perusal, folded her arms, leaned against the door . . . and waited.

As if she was daring him to approach.

Eric drew himself up to his full six-foot-one height. The two of them might not have gotten off to the best start, but he'd apologized and her truck hadn't sustained any apparent damage. There was no reason they couldn't be civil.

Besides, this was his house. Or his dad's. He wasn't the outsider here, even if she did have some role in whatever destruction was taking place inside.

He strolled toward her, stopping six feet away. "We meet again."

All at once, recognition dawned in her eyes. "You're John's son, aren't you?"

Dad and this woman were on a first-name basis? "Yes."

"Hmm." She gave him another quick appraisal. "He's got family pictures around the house—mostly from your younger days. You've changed a lot, but I see the resemblance now." She pushed off from the truck and began to walk away.

"Hey!"

She paused and looked over her shoulder.

"What's going on here?" He waved a hand toward the house.

One of her eyebrows rose. "Your dad didn't tell you?"

"No."

"Huh." A few uncomfortable beats ticked by. "Anyone passing by can see construction is in progress." She gave him another scan. "Then again, I guess you haven't passed by lately."

At the hint of censure in her tone, he stiffened. "I'm sure my father mentioned I'm an attorney—and the practice of law is very demanding. But I talk to him often."

"Funny he didn't tell you about this, then."

No kidding.

"So you want to enlighten me?"

Before she could respond, his dad appeared in

the doorway. Did a double take. "Eric?" He hurried down the steps, his expression morphing from surprise to concern.

"I think I'll let the two of you work that out." The woman moved aside as his father strode toward them and pulled him into a hug.

"What are you doing here in the middle of the week?"

"Long story." Eric returned the hug, then swept a hand around the yard. "What's going on?"

"Also a long story." His father smiled at the blonde. "Have you two met?"

"Not officially." The woman cast a wry glance at his dinged-up car.

"Then let me do the introductions. BJ, my son, Eric. Eric, meet BJ Stevens, the best architect, contractor, and construction manager in the state of Oregon."

After an infinitesimal hesitation, she stuck out her hand.

Eric closed the distance between them, assimilating this new information. With all those titles, this woman wasn't just involved in his dad's project; she was in charge of it.

However, once he gripped her slender fingers, once he got an up-close view of her intelligent green eyes and the faint freckles dusting her pert nose, assimilation gave way to admiration.

BJ Stevens might not be the warmest or friendliest female he'd ever met, but she was the prettiest, hands down—even if her palms were callused, her nails unpolished, and her face free of makeup. There was something intriguing about her, some compelling quality he couldn't quite identify, that sucked him in. Strength . . . character . . . integrity . . . whatever it was, it scored high on his appeal meter.

Her lips parted slightly as he continued to hold her hand, and a flash of . . . fire? . . . sparked in those emerald-color irises.

One second ticked by.

Two.

Three.

All at once, a sizzle of electricity zipped through the air, so strong it—

"BJ! We have a question."

At the summons from some guy in shadows inside the front door, she jerked her gaze from his and tugged her hand free. "I'll be right t-there." Clearing her throat, she spoke to his dad. "If you have an hour or two, we ought to visit the show-room later this afternoon to pick out hardware and lighting fixtures. The plumber wants me to place the bathroom order this week, if possible."

"That works."

With a dip of her head, she took off toward the porch.

Eric watched her until she disappeared through the door.

"Nice woman. Talented too. I was lucky to get

her for this job. Smart and pretty is a winning combination, don't you think?"

He turned to find his father watching him with amusement, and his neck warmed. Instead of responding, he asked a question of his own. "What job would that be?"

His father transferred his weight from one foot to the other, a distinct uneasiness replacing his amusement. "You're not going to like it."

Uh-oh.

Eric shoved his hands in his pockets and clenched his fists. "Go ahead and lay it on me."

"I'm converting the four bedrooms upstairs into two suites."

"Why?"

"Because I'm going to open a B&B."

"A B&B." He tried to wrap his mind around the notion as he said the words. "As in . . . bed and breakfast?"

"Yes."

"But . . . but why do you want to let strangers stay in our house?"

"They won't be strangers once I meet them." His dad flashed him a quick smile, then grew more serious. "It's a big house, Eric. Too big for me. But you and your mom and I made a lot of great memories here, and I didn't want to leave. So I figured, why not let other people make great memories here too? Plus, this will give me a chance to put to use those culinary courses I took in Coos Bay after I retired. I'm going to call it Seabird Inn. Great name, don't you think?"

The question registered on only a peripheral level as Eric tried to picture his dad—a man who'd never prepared a full meal until his wife died six years ago—cooking a gourmet breakfast for strangers every morning.

It wouldn't compute.

"I thought you . . . that you valued your privacy. You always said that much as you loved people, your home was your sanctuary."

"It still will be. I added a small extension to the family room, and the whole back of the first floor will be innkeeper's quarters. My private domain if I want to escape my guests—but I plan to mingle a lot." He clasped his hands behind his back, and his tone grew melancholy. "The truth is, since I retired it's been a little lonesome around here. And too quiet. It would be nice to hear laughter ring through the rooms again."

A sharp jab prodded Eric's conscience. If he'd carved time out of his schedule to come home more often, maybe his father wouldn't have decided to shake the foundations of his life—literally.

He exhaled. "You wouldn't have done this if I'd been around more, would you?"

"Hey." His dad gripped his arm. "I'm not trying to lay a guilt trip on you. You call me more than most kids check in with their parents, despite your busy life. I know that job of yours keeps you hopping. Which brings me back to my original question. What are you doing here in the middle of the week?"

The hammering picked up in the house—and in his heart. So much for his plan to share the news over cups of coffee around the table in the quiet, homey kitchen where most of the important events in his life had been discussed.

Finally his father spoke again. "You want to ride down to the beach, take a walk?"

At the gentle prompt, Eric shook his head. "I already did that."

"Then I'm guessing this is serious."

"Yeah." Retirement hadn't dulled his dad's keen intuitive abilities one speck.

Silence fell between them as his father gave him space, waiting until he was ready to share his news.

But he'd never be ready—and postponing the inevitable was pointless.

Summoning up his courage, Eric spit out the foul-tasting words. "I don't have a job anymore."

His father stared at him. "They . . . they fired you?"

"Not according to my boss. That term isn't PC these days." Despite Eric's attempt to coax up the corners of his mouth, they refused to budge. "He said we were being laid off as part of a strategic repositioning in a difficult economy. But a rose by any other name . . ."

"I can't believe it." His father seemed as stunned as Eric had been yesterday afternoon when his boss dropped the bomb.

"Me neither. I knew a lot of law firms were struggling, that the market for high-end legal services was shrinking. Corporate clients are beefing up their in-house legal staffs, outsourcing routine work to less-expensive contract lawyers, sending legal research overseas, and capping fees . . . but I thought we were doing okay."

"You should have been. Your firm is one of the largest in Portland. They have offices all over the country . . . all over the world."

"Ironic, isn't it?" A touch of bitterness etched his words. "I always assumed going with a large, established firm was a guarantee of job security. I guess the joke's on me."

His father laid a hand on his shoulder, compassion softening his features. "I don't know what to say. Your whole life, you did everything right. You knew what you wanted, and you went after it with single-minded determination."

Yeah, he had. He'd excelled in high school; been accepted by a great college; attended a prestigious law school; graduated at the top of his class; and landed a job in a solid firm where he'd planned to become a partner and stay until he retired.

And now, instead of realizing that dream, he

was unemployed, his well-plotted career in ruins.

Pressure built in his throat, and he blinked to clear his vision. "Doesn't seem fair, does it?"

"Not even close." His father drew in a lungful of air. Let it out. "Days like this can make you wonder what the good Lord is thinking."

"That's an understatement. In fact, I . . ." Eric stopped. Someone with a rock-solid faith, who prayed daily, wouldn't take kindly to negative comments about the Almighty.

"Don't be mad at God, son." His father's tone was gentle.

Mad? Hardly. He'd been too fixated on building his career to give God more than a passing thought over the past decade. Truth be told, the Almighty was so far off his radar he hadn't connected this whole fiasco with him until his father mentioned it.

"I'm not." It was an honest answer, if incomplete.

"Glad to hear it. Because bad as this whole situation smells now, I'm guessing he has a new direction in mind for you. That a better path lies ahead."

"It would be nice if he let me in on it." Eric didn't try to mask his skepticism.

"He will—in his own time. And you've come to the perfect place to hear his voice. There's nowhere better than Hope Harbor for clearing the mind. How long has it been since you had a real vacation . . . and I don't mean a long weekend?"

"I can't remember." When had he had a spare minute, let alone a week? Billable hours were the key to a partner slot . . . and you could never log enough of them.

Not that all those sixty-plus-hour weeks had helped him in the end.

"Then you need to stay awhile. Unless you have other plans?"

"I don't have any plans, period." Which felt weird. He'd always operated from a meticulous game plan.

"You know, that might be for the best." His father's demeanor grew pensive. "Sometimes good things come our way when we're open to new opportunities."

That was possible—but there wasn't much chance any great opportunities would find him here. For all its charms, Hope Harbor didn't offer many career options for those with ambitious aspirations.

Nevertheless, hanging around for two or three weeks couldn't hurt. With six months' severance and benefits, he could afford to chill a bit.

"You certain you have room for me in that construction zone?" He swept a hand toward the house.

"There'll always be room for you here. I can't offer you the plushest accommodations yet, but the sleeper sofa isn't bad. And I'll whip you up some gourmet breakfasts to compensate for the makeshift bed. I've been honing my skills on the very appreciative work crew. You might be surprised what your old man can do with a few eggs and assorted other ingredients these days."

"Sold. I'll grab my bags from the car."

He started to turn away, only to have his father once again take his arm.

"Can I tell you one more thing?"

"Sure."

"When I spotted you out here a few minutes ago, I was terrified. This is where your mom stood the day she came home with a fistful of orders for all kinds of tests after what we assumed was a routine doctor's visit. You know the rest of that story." His Adam's apple bobbed. "I realize this is a blow, but it's not the end of the world. You'll find another job; you can't find another life."

Leave it to Dad to restore his perspective. Dark as the past thirty-six hours had been, there were bigger tragedies than losing a job. They'd both lived through one as they'd watched cancer consume his mom, leaving an empty shell of the vibrant woman whose sunny smile had brightened their days.

"Thanks for the reality check."

"Part of a father's job description." His dad patted his shoulder. "Now go get your bags and let's get you settled in."

Eric returned to his car and popped the trunk,

their conversation replaying in his mind. Was it possible good would come of his career disaster? Would a stay in Hope Harbor give him clarity and new direction? Did God have a better path in store for him?

Suitcase and laptop in hand, he closed the trunk and approached the childhood home that looked the same as always from the outside but was undergoing a transformation inside. Finding a new purpose.

If his father was right, maybe the same would happen to him while he was here. Maybe the job debacle would lead to unexpected opportunities. Maybe Hope Harbor would live up to its name and steer him in a new, better direction.

But for a man who preferred definites to maybes and facts to fancies, leaving tomorrow to the whim of fate—or God—was downright scary.

"I bet you're hungry, aren't you?" Eleanor spread a spoon of tuna salad on a piece of toast while Methuselah fixed his amber eyes on the bowl of chunks she'd set aside.

He meowed, whiskers twitching.

"My sandwich will be ready in a minute, then we can eat together. How's that?"

Another meow—except this one sounded a bit cross.

"Patience isn't your strong suit, my friend. You're becoming a grumpy old cat."

He swished his tail and lifted his nose in the air.

"See what I mean? But who am I to point fingers? I'm becoming an eccentric old woman who talks to cats."

She finished making her sandwich, placed it and the tuna chunks on the tray of her walker, and shuffled over to the table. After setting her plate beside a glass of milk, she lowered the tabby's dish to the bench seat beside her that ran the length of the table.

Methuselah gave her a doleful look.

"Sorry, my friend. My bending-down-to-the-floor days are over."

With a resigned snuffle, he slowly climbed up on the box she'd put there for his use and hauled himself up to the bench.

His old, arthritic joints must be as stiff as hers today.

She lowered herself into her seat and twined her fingers together. "Thank you, Lord, for this food, for the flowers that brighten my days, and for my feline friend here. Thank you, too, for the kindness of people like BJ. Please keep me healthy enough to stay in this house until you call me home. Amen."

As usual, Methuselah was halfway through his lunch by the time she finished the simple prayer. She knew the drill by now. Once he scarfed down the last morsel, he'd pad into the living room and claim his usual spot in the circle of afternoon sun streaming through the front window, leaving her alone to finish her meal.

The tick of the old-fashioned clock over the sink was loud in the quiet house as she tackled her lunch. Perhaps this afternoon she'd give Rose or Anna a call and have a chat. Or invite them to stop by and share a piece of fudge cake.

No. That wouldn't work. Anna was busy with that cranberry cake business she'd gotten involved in, and since it was Wednesday, Rose would be tending the flowers in the planters along the wharf with her crew of volunteers.

A crew Eleanor had been part of until her knees gave out.

The bite of sandwich lodged in her windpipe, and she took a long swallow of milk . . . but she couldn't dislodge the feeling of uselessness that plagued her these days.

Methuselah finished the last of his tuna, licked his lips, and stretched.

"I see you beat me again."

In response, he hunkered down and slid to the floor, his leaping days long past—as were hers. All she could do was hobble along in an old-lady shuffle behind that obnoxious walker. But after the dire warning her doctor had issued about broken hips following her little tumble in April, refusing to use it would have been foolish.

Her crotchety companion disappeared through the door into the living room, and she pushed her plate aside, a wave of melancholy sweeping over her. Lord knew she tried to keep up a happy front in public. Complaining about your lot in life, dragging others down, was wrong. And she did an excellent job presenting a cheery facade to the world. Not a soul in Hope Harbor would guess that sweet old Eleanor Cooper, with her perennially sunny smile, waged a fight against darkness every day.

One that grew harder to win with every passing week.

It was the evil one at work, no doubt about it. He was always on the lookout for weaknesses to exploit.

This, however, was one battle he wouldn't win. Her faith was strong. She might not see much purpose in her life anymore, but God must or he'd have called her home long ago. Hadn't Reverend Baker said last Sunday it was easy to row a boat toward shore in calm water but much more difficult to stay the course when seas got rough?

No one knew that better than her.

Shoulders slumping, she pushed herself to her feet. Waited until her unreliable body adjusted to the new position. Trundled the walker over to the fridge and slid her half-eaten sandwich inside.

Once it was stowed, she lingered over the photos secured to the door with magnets. Most were old and yellow now, crinkled around the edges, showing signs of their age—just as she was.

But the memories they brought back were still sweet and fresh.

Stan and her at the Eiffel Tower on their twenty-fifth anniversary. The two of them stacking canned goods in the food pantry at church. On stage at the awards banquet where she'd been honored for her behind-the-scenes volunteer work with Birthright. Hosting a party for friends from church who were leaving for Africa on a mission trip.

If there were no children in the photos—well, that had been God's design too. But he'd blessed them in many other ways, mitigating that deep sadness.

She reset the magnet on a photo that was slipping. No, she had no complaints about her past. For the most part, her days had been happy —and rewarding. She'd made a difference. Her life had mattered.

Not anymore, though. Now she was a taker instead of a giver. Relying on the kindness of others to keep her in her house, get her to church, do her grocery shopping . . . even liberate her from her own bathroom.

A film of moisture further blurred her diminished vision. Maybe it was time to admit defeat and move to that senior living center in Coos Bay. She'd had the brochure for months, and they called on a regular basis. A friendly young woman had even picked her up, taken her on a tour, and treated her to lunch in the dining room. It was a pleasant place.

But it wasn't home.

She examined the cozy kitchen. This might not be the house near the harbor where she'd been raised. Or the spacious two-story she and Stan had shared in Seattle for most of the thirty-nine years of marriage God had granted them. But it had been home for the twenty-three years since she'd returned to the town that held all her cherished early memories. How could she leave?

Hope Harbor—and this house—were her world.

Her knees began to ache, and she turned away from the photos. Better get to her recliner before one of the joints gave out.

Methuselah was in his favorite spot in the living room, curled up in a sunbeam, satisfied and happy, when she plodded past.

Too bad she couldn't find contentment as easily.

She lowered herself into her chair and picked up the large print book BJ had retrieved for her from the library. The suspense novel by one of her favorite authors would help her pass a few hours of the long, empty afternoon stretching ahead. Perhaps she'd nap a bit, too, like Methuselah.

And pray that God would give her the strength to endure until he called her home.

"Hey, stranger! Long time no see."

Shading her eyes against the sun, BJ pulled the nozzle out of her gas tank as an older-model Civic drew up at the pump across from her. Tracy Campbell—no, Hunter now—waved at her through the driver-side window.

Oops.

"I know I owe you an update on the house plans, but a few delays with the B&B project put me a little behind schedule on your job." She stuck the nozzle back in the pump while Tracy climbed out of her car.

"That, plus doing home repairs for lots of the older folks in town who call Helping Hands for assistance. And that's not counting all you do for Eleanor."

"I don't mind volunteering my skills for charity." Of course Tracy would know about the stuff she did through Helping Hands. Her husband was director of the charitable organization and she was active in the group herself when cranberry farm duties allowed. But who'd clued her in about Methuselah's owner? "As for Eleanor—I don't do that much for her."

"That's not what I hear."

"From who?"

Tracy swiped her credit card in the pump and grinned. "It's a small town, remember? Everybody knows everything and is only too happy to share news. However, in this case my scoop came from the source. I took her a loaf of cranberry nut cake last week, and she sang your praises during my visit. I'm feeling a tad displaced."

"Don't be. Eleanor sings your praises to me too. But she told me she didn't want to bother the blushing new bride. Her words."

"Mmm. I can't say I mind having an extra hour or two a week to spend with Michael—though Helping Hands keeps him hopping. And speaking of that, he told me you're on the agenda for Saturday's board meeting."

BJ sidestepped the implied question. She wasn't ready to share her proposal publicly. For all she knew, the board would shoot it down.

"Um . . . yeah. I had an idea I wanted to run by them."

"Not talking, huh?"

"It's too early for that."

Tracy grinned. "Got it. I'm just giving you a hard time." She lifted the nozzle from the pump and inserted it in her gas tank. "In terms of the house plans—no worries. We aren't in any hurry. How's the B&B project going?"

"Great overall, aside from the few delays I mentioned. It's fun to be the one turning blueprints into reality versus turning them over to a construction firm."

"So you're liking your new gig in our little town?"

"Loving it. No big city blues for me."

"Glad to hear it. I can't wait to take a tour of Seabird Inn once you're finished. By the way, I heard John's son, Eric, is back in town."

Wow. Tracy hadn't been kidding about word traveling fast around here.

"How did you know that? I think he just arrived a couple of hours ago."

"I told you—it's hard to keep a secret in this town. Bear that in mind if you ever plan to do anything scandalous."

BJ snorted. "Not my style."

"I know. I'll never forget the night that guy tried to pick you up during one of our girls-only dinners while we lived in Phoenix. Man, you gave him an earful." Chuckling, she coaxed a final gallon of gas into her tank and pulled out the nozzle. "So did you meet Eric yet?"

"Uh . . . yeah." And she did *not* want to discuss it. "Who told you he was back?" BJ tucked her credit card into her wallet.

"No one. I passed him on the road to Bandon. The mashed fender and broken headlight were hard to miss. I wonder what happened to his car?"

BJ rubbed at a speck of mud on her truck. She could let the rhetorical question pass—but if

Tracy's take on the small-town grapevine was accurate, everyone would find out about the accident sooner rather than later. Then her friend would wonder why she'd remained mute.

Better not to raise any red flags.

"Actually . . . he ran into my truck."

Tracy's eyes widened. "Seriously?"

"Yeah." She gave her the topline, leaving out the part about him being on his cell.

"Huh." Tracy folded her arms and leaned back against the car. "That doesn't sound like him. He's always been the careful, cautious, focused type. And it's odd he'd visit midweek. According to his dad, he works horrendous hours at that big law firm he's with in Portland. Did he say why he was here?"

"No. We . . . uh . . . didn't have that kind of conversation."

"I guess not." She pushed off from the fender. "From what I could tell through the windshield, he hasn't lost his swoon-worthiness."

BJ tried for a nonchalant shrug. "If you like that type."

"Most of the girls in my high-school class did."

"I'm not a teenager anymore." Stomach knotting, BJ snatched her receipt from the pump. "And I'm not interested in hot-looking guys who have no qualms about clawing their way up the corporate ladder, leaving carnage in their wake."

"Whoa!" Tracy held up her hands, palms out.

"Sorry. I didn't mean to dredge up bad memories."

Of course she hadn't. All she'd done was comment on the man's appearance.

BJ exhaled. The last thing she wanted to do was alienate her friend. "I'm the one who should apologize. It's just been kind of a . . . strange day. First the fender bender, then Eleanor brings up my love life, and to make matters worse . . ." She stopped. Admitting her unwelcome reaction to the good looks Tracy had mentioned would open a big, messy can of worms.

"To make matters worse . . . what?"

"A story for another day."

Tracy cocked her head. "Why do I think it involves Eric?"

"No comment."

"Hmm." Tracy jingled her keys. "If you're not talking, I'll leave you with a comment of my own. I have no idea why he's back. Whatever the reason, I doubt he'll hang around long. But for the record, he's a good guy. Reliable. Trustworthy. Hard working. Conscientious. Which proves that not all eye-candy men fit the same mold." She opened her door. "Let me know when you're ready to go over the house plans and I'll corral Michael."

With that, she slid behind the wheel and drove off.

BJ retrieved her own keys and watched the car recede in the distance. Maybe her friend was correct about Eric. Maybe not. But she wasn't aiming to test that theory anytime soon.

Swinging back up into the truck, she pushed Tracy's comment to the back of her mind and gave a more urgent priority center stage. Food. Her stomach was *not* happy about the lunch she'd skipped—and scarfing down the fudge cake on the seat beside her instead of eating a healthy meal was a bad idea. She would *not* let a stressful incident or two resurrect bad habits. However, she did need a nutritious, filling dinner—fast— or she might end up succumbing to temptation.

A little comfort food wouldn't hurt, either, after the unsettling day she'd had.

And she knew just the place to find it.

Eric parallel-parked his rental car on Dockside Drive and did a slow sweep of the marina across the street. Boats bobbed in the gentle swells. A gull soared over the white gazebo that occupied the small park where the two-block-long, crescent-shaped frontage road dead-ended at the river. Colorful flowers spilled from planters that served as a buffer between the sidewalk and the sloping pile of boulders that led to the water.

He let his gaze drift farther afield. Past the long jetty on the left and the pair of rocky islands on the right that tamed the turbulent waves and protected the boats in the marina. Across the cobalt water that sparkled as if strewn with diamonds. All the way to the indigo line where sky met sea.

Peace seeped into his soul, and the tension ebbed from his tight muscles.

He drew in a lungful of the fresh, tangy sea breeze, letting it chase out the drywall-dust-laced air he'd ingested at the house. Not that he'd lingered there after he'd stowed his stuff. The tour his father had offered could wait until the construction crew—and its chief—departed for the day, along with all their headache-inducing noise. Plus, he'd needed to get his car to Marv's and deal with a different headache.

Talk about a rough thirty-six hours.

But a fish taco from Charley's would help soften the edges.

Ignoring the quaint row of shops adorned with bright awnings and overflowing flower boxes to his right, he homed in on the white truck perched at the edge of the tiny wharf-side park, near the gazebo.

At least that hadn't changed.

The colorful letters spelling out "Charley's," the serving window on one side, and the man behind the counter with long gray hair pulled back in a ponytail—all were exactly the same as they'd been for as far back as he could remember.

He left the rental car behind and followed his nose toward the enticing aromas emanating from the small stand, a town fixture that had been grandfathered into its location on the wharf years ago.

Charley Lopez greeted him with a smile, weathered skin creasing at the corners of his eyes, white teeth gleaming in his latte-colored face. The man didn't appear in the least surprised to see him.

"Hey, Eric. It's about time you came home. We've been waiting for you."

Waiting for him?

Odd.

No one here had been waiting for him . . . even his dad. Everyone in town knew his life was in Portland.

But Charley had always had a penchant for making inscrutable remarks.

"I'm just here for a visit."

"Uh-huh." Charley picked up a spatula. "The tacos are exceptional today, if I do say so myself. You still partial to avocado?"

"Yeah."

"I'll put in extra."

"Thanks. How's the painting career?" He leaned a shoulder against the truck as the man opened a Styrofoam cooler and pulled out a ziplock bag of chopped red onion.

"No complaints."

His usual answer—and no doubt very true. Charley might dabble in tacos for fun and social interaction, but his real money came from art. The fortunate tourists who stumbled on his modest stand would never guess the best taco maker in the state—maybe on the West Coast—was also a respected artist whose work drew top dollar in prestigious galleries around the country.

"Glad to hear things are going well."

"They usually do if you do what you love."

Not necessarily.

Eric swallowed past the sudden thickness in his throat and remained silent.

"The real challenge is discovering what that is." Charley tossed a handful of the onions on the griddle. "Why don't you stop by the studio soon? I'm working on some interesting pieces."

"I might do that." Why not? He'd hung around there plenty during his teens, watching the man work. Dabbling at art himself. Those had been some of his happiest hours.

But art paid the bills only for a very privileged few—and leisure pursuits were a luxury partner-track attorneys couldn't afford.

Turning aside, Eric scanned the curving side-walk. The wharf was a popular spot this evening. Every bench was occupied except the one closest to the taco stand. "I'll go toss my jacket over there to save my seat while you get my order ready."

"No need." Charley dug some fish out of another cooler behind him. "Floyd and Gladys will guard it for you."

Eric looked again. No one was anywhere close to the bench.

"The seagulls." Charley slapped the fish onto the grill, eyes twinkling. "Nice couple. They hang around here a lot."

He checked again. Two nondescript gulls were pecking around the base of the bench.

Another thing that hadn't changed—Charley's eccentricity.

A middle-aged couple fifty feet away paused in their stroll down the wharf. The man spoke to the woman, gestured to the vacant bench, and they ambled toward it.

No way was he giving up that seat.

"I'll be back in a minute, Charley." He broke into a half jog. "I need to go grab that . . ."

As the couple approached from the opposite side, the two seagulls rose a few feet into the sky and, with much wing-flapping and squawking, hovered over the bench.

The pair stopped. Eyed the screeching birds and the flying feathers. Circled around the bench, giving it a wide berth, and continued on their way.

"See? Your bench is secure." Charley sprinkled some kind of spice on the sizzling fish.

Eric returned to the serving window and gave the birds a cautious inspection. "What makes you think they're going to let *me* sit there?"

"Give it a try." Hope Harbor's taco chef began

chopping an avocado. "You can come back for your tacos after you claim it."

Eric weighed his options. Continue the strange conversation with Charley or take his chances with the birds?

The birds won. He wasn't up for riddles today.

As the aroma of grilling fish set off a rumble in his stomach, Eric warily approached the seagull sentries. They continued to hunt and peck for food scraps at the base of the bench until he drew close . . . then hopped aside with nary a peep.

Weird.

Eric laid his jacket across the seat while Charley grinned and gave him a thumbs-up.

He wasn't even going to try and figure out what had just happened. Not with all the other stuff he had to sort through.

Rather than make more confusing small talk with his personal chef for the evening, he stayed by the bench and checked his voicemail. Most days, keeping up with messages was a challenge. Now? He dispensed with the four that had come in during the course of the afternoon in two minutes.

Charley waved at him, and he slid the cell into his pocket while he walked back to the window.

"Here you go." The man set a bulging brown bag on the ledge. "I put two waters in there. The tacos are on the spicy side today."

"I like spicy." Eric pulled out his wallet. "I don't suppose you're taking credit cards now."

"Nope."

"You ever put in Wi-Fi at the house?"

"Nope."

Eric counted out some bills. "Tell me you finally got cable."

"Nope. I'd rather watch live action from here. Hope Harbor has it all, you know—better than any TV show. Drama, comedy, joy, sorrow, laughter, tears . . . love. This town is full of stories." He passed over some change.

"If you say so." Eric pocketed the coins and moved aside as another customer approached the window.

"Enjoy—and come back soon." Charley gave him a jaunty salute.

The delicious smell wafting upward kick-started his salivary glands, and he hurried back toward the bench. Man, he was starving. Except for that bout he'd had with the flu two years ago, he'd never gone this long without a real meal.

But he'd had little interest in food after the termination news. Other than that half bag of potato chips he'd ingested during the long, sleepless hours last night while he'd prowled around his condo trying to recover from his shock, he hadn't eaten a bite since noon yesterday.

You couldn't beat Charley's tacos for a fast-breaker, though.

He wolfed down the first one so fast he wasn't certain he'd even stopped to breathe.

Rummaging around in the bag for the next one, his fingers encountered three more wrapped bundles.

Huh.

Had four become the new standard order?

He shifted sideways and peered at the price board. Three was still the magic number. Charley must have lost count while they chatted.

Not surprising. Their conversation had certainly kept *him* off balance.

Whatever the reason for the bonus taco, he needed to pay for it.

Eric rose—just as Charley rolled down the aluminum window on the serving counter.

He hustled over and caught Charley as he emerged from the door in the back. "You gave me one too many tacos, Charley. Let me pay you for the extra one."

The man dismissed the offer with a flip of his hand. "Consider it a welcome home present. Save it for later if you don't want it now . . . or share it with someone." The man began to walk away.

"Are you closing already? It's dinnertime."

"No, it's painting time. My muse is calling." He lifted a hand in farewell. "See you soon."

Shaking his head, Eric watched the tall, thin man fade into the distance. Same old Charley, letting the weather, the catch of the day, his mood, the current painting project in his studio—and who knew what else?—set the always unpredictable hours for the taco stand.

Good thing he hadn't dallied at the house or he'd have had to wait another day to get his taco fix.

He settled back onto the bench, dug out the second taco, and dived in.

Halfway through, his hunger somewhat appeased, he slowed his pace and gave his surroundings some attention.

The scene was nothing like his usual setting for dinner in Portland. There, he typically grabbed a to-go order from the café on the corner and ate dinner alone at his desk in the sleek, ultra-modern, glass-and-chrome environs of the high-end firm where he'd spent most waking hours.

This quaint harbor, with weathered boats gently rocking in their slips and gulls cavorting on the rough boulders that sloped down to the water's edge, was about as far from sleek and modern as you could get.

He wasn't alone, though. Floyd and Gladys continued to lurk nearby. They weren't much on conversation, but their antics were amusing.

Picking up his taco again, he took a deep breath. Exhaled. More tension seeped out of his wired body.

Maybe his dad was right. Spending two or three weeks in Hope Harbor might be smart. If he gave himself a chance to clear his mind, relax, it was possible he . . .

A familiar dark blue pickup truck swung onto Dockside Drive farther up the street.

Oh no.

Sinking down on the bench, he averted his head and angled away. BJ Stevens might be pretty and appealing and the kind of woman he'd like to get to know better under different circumstances, but given their rocky start, she wasn't likely to be thrilled to cross paths with him again today—and he wasn't up for another sparring match.

After a minute, he risked a peek over his shoulder. If he was lucky, the truck would be gone.

But luck wasn't on his side today.

Not only was the truck still on Dockside Drive —it was parked directly behind his rental car.

Even worse, his father's architect was dashing across the street toward Charley's shuttered taco stand.

As she drew closer, however, she slowed. Stopped. Shoulders drooping, she pulled off her baseball cap and massaged her forehead, her posture spelling disappointment in capital letters.

The savory aroma of the taco in his hand tickled his nose . . . reminding him he had an extra one in the sack on his lap.

Save it for later . . . or share it with someone.

Charley's words echoed in his brain, nudging his conscience.

He crimped the bag closed and shut out the man's voice. He was *not* going another round with the willowy blonde today.

The breeze picked up, ruffling her ponytail, and she put her cap back on. After one last sweep of Charley's stand, she turned away.

Yes! He was safe.

Yet as she trudged away, clearly tired and hungry and let down, unbidden words tumbled out of his mouth. "Would you like to share mine?"

She halted and swung toward him, looking as surprised as he felt.

A few silent seconds passed before she spoke.

"Thanks, but I . . . I can't take your dinner."

Reprieved! No matter what had prompted him to make that foolish offer, she'd refused. Now he could enjoy the rest of his meal in peace.

"I have extra. Charley miscounted."

His fingers crumpled the edge of the bag again. What was he, a ventriloquist's dummy? His lips were moving, but someone else seemed to be speaking.

Again she hesitated.

More alien words bubbled up and spilled out. "I have an extra water too. And there's plenty of room on the bench, unless Floyd and Gladys claim the other half."

Faint furrows dented her brow as she glanced around the area and gave him a quizzical look.

"The seagulls." He indicated the two birds pecking away at crumbs a few yards away.

"You have . . . pet seagulls?"

"No. Charley introduced us earlier. They're friends of his, apparently."

Her brow smoothed, and one side of her mouth quirked up. "That I can believe." She wiped her palms down her jeans. "I did have my heart set on a fish taco, so if you're sure . . ."

He was in too deep to back out now.

Resigned, he scooted over to give her extra room.

She approached him as cautiously as he'd approached the seagulls earlier and perched on the far edge of the bench.

He passed her the extra bottle of water and one of the remaining butcher-paper-wrapped bundles from the bag. "They're great tonight."

"Charley's tacos are always amazing." She set the water beside her and began unwrapping the white paper.

"You eat here often?"

"Uh-huh."

"Not into cooking?"

"Not much time for it."

Silence fell between them. He took a few swigs of water while BJ put a healthy dent in her taco. "You must have been hungry."

"Yeah. I missed lunch." She dived back into her taco.

He joined her.

As he polished his off, his taut muscles began to ease. again. The woman beside him seemed more inclined to eat than snipe tonight.

That could change once her stomach was full, however.

He gave her a surreptitious glance. Some sauce leaked out of her taco, onto the corner of her mouth. His gaze strayed there—and got stuck on her full, soft lips.

". . . close for the night?"

With an effort, he tuned back in to the conversation. "Sorry. I got distracted for a minute. Floyd and Gladys are . . . uh . . . leaving." He motioned toward the two seagulls waddling away. Lame excuse, but it was the best he could do. "What did you ask me?"

"When did Charley close for the night?"

"Oh." He pulled a napkin out of the bag. "A few minutes before you arrived." He held out the white square and tapped the corner of his mouth with his free hand. Too risky to look at hers again. "Some of Charley's secret sauce escaped."

She dabbed at it, then wiped her hands. Though she continued to hug the edge of the bench, her posture had relaxed a hair. "Thanks. That was perfect."

"Do you want to split the last one?"

"You're probably still hungry." She gave the bag a covetous glance.

Yeah, he was—but he could always raid his dad's refrigerator later . . . and while he'd hoped at first to escape her notice, now he didn't want her to leave.

Go figure.

"They're pretty filling. Why don't we share?" He dug out the last one and gave it to her. "I'll let you do the splitting honors."

She took it, unwrapped it partway, and tore it in half.

He took the section she held out and bit in.

"So did you venture upstairs at the house yet?" She kept up with him bite for bite.

"No. I thought I'd save that for tonight. How close are you to being finished?"

"Barring any glitches, we should be done by the middle of August. Your dad wants to be open for the cranberry festival in September, so that will give him a chance to furnish and decorate."

"You have a large crew?" It might not hurt to find out a bit more about the architect his dad had hired. She wasn't a Hope Harbor native, that was for sure.

"Me, plus two full-time workers. I subcontract electrical and plumbing."

"Have you been in town long?"

"A year." She finished off her taco.

"You're from the South, aren't you?"

She hesitated. "Not originally, but I moved to Tennessee when I was eight. Most people don't notice the slight southern drawl anymore."

"We had someone from Georgia in our firm. Her accent was similar to yours. You're a long way from home."

"This is home now." She wadded the white paper in her hand and stood abruptly. "Thanks for sharing your tacos."

"You don't have to eat and run." He adopted a teasing tone, but he wouldn't mind if she stuck around for a few more minutes.

"Yes, I do. I've got another commitment tonight. I'll see you around your dad's while you're here, I guess."

"That would be a safe bet."

"Well . . ." She squeezed the crumpled paper into a tight ball. "Have a nice evening."

Without waiting for him to respond, she swiveled around, tossed her trash in one of the receptacles along the wharf, and strode back to her truck.

Prickly thing.

And not too anxious to talk about personal stuff, apparently.

Why?

He watched her climb into her truck, put it in gear, and pull away.

Who *was* BJ Stevens? Where had she lived before coming to Hope Harbor? What had brought her here? Why didn't she want to talk about her past? And on a professional level, what kind of credentials did she have? There wasn't a lot of work in a town this size for an architect. If she was licensed, she'd make a much better living in a larger city.

Eric stuffed his trash in the empty brown bag. His dad might be able to answer some of his questions—but he'd have to be careful how he asked or the elder Nash might incorrectly assume he had a personal interest in the woman. Attractive as she was, and despite her intangible appeal, he couldn't afford to be more than friends, at best. If she was new in town and in the process of building a business here, there wasn't much chance she intended to leave anytime soon.

And his stay was very temporary.

He rose, tossed the bag into the trash container, and ambled toward his car, yawning. After his night of pacing, the long drive from Portland, and all the surprises this day had held, he might turn in with the sun tonight. A cup of coffee, two or three Milano cookies from the bag his dad always had on hand, a quick tour of the upstairs, and he'd be ready to call it a night.

His fact-finding mission about a certain blonde builder could wait until tomorrow.

But no matter what he discovered . . . no matter the sizzle of electricity that had zipped between them as they'd shaken hands . . . BJ Stevens was off-limits. She might be willing to settle for Hope Harbor—but with rare exception, if you wanted to earn enough money to provide the kind of security he was after, you had to leave the town behind.

He pushed the autolock button as he approached the rental. No reason not to put his stay to profitable use, however. Lay out a game plan for his future.

And long before Seabird Inn was ready to open, he'd move on to wherever that future took him.

— 4 —

BJ lifted her mug of java . . . inhaled the fragrant aroma . . . and took a sip.

The perfect way to start a day.

Or it *would* be perfect in less than thirty seconds.

Balancing her brimming mug in one hand, she pushed through the back door, strolled across her small patio, and gave the sea a slow sweep. Sea Rose Lane might not be in Hope Harbor's toniest neighborhood, but the setting? World-class. You couldn't beat a double lot that abutted the sea and offered an unobstructed view of open water, vast sky, and Little Gull Island. She might be mere minutes from the heart of Hope Harbor, but this spot felt a world removed from civilization.

She drew in a lungful of the fresh briny air, so different from the smog-laced LA haze she'd breathed for seven years—and had expected to breathe for the rest of her life. Yet just shy of her one-year anniversary here, this last, tiny rental cottage on this tiny dead-end street in this tiny town felt more like home than LA ever had.

Best of all, very little these days could resurrect the tension she'd shed over the past few months.

Eric Nash, however, had managed to accomplish that feat—drat him. Thanks to the distracting attorney, for the first time in weeks she'd spent a night tossing into the wee hours.

Steam tickling her nose, she took a fortifying sip of coffee and skimmed the rocky shore of Little Gull Island, searching for the mottled silver-white harbor seal that had taken up residence a few weeks ago. No matter her worries, the playful little fellow always managed to distract her.

She spotted him tucked into a crevice, his impish face turned toward her.

"Morning, Casper." She cupped her free hand around her mouth and aimed the greeting his direction. At six-thirty, it was too early to yell at full voice across the water and risk waking her neighbors.

As usual, he flapped a flipper.

The corners of her lips rose. There wasn't much chance his response was directed at her, but whatever the reason for it, he exhibited the same behavior every morning, as reliable as the sun that crested the hill behind her.

It was nice when life unfolded in a predictable pattern.

Unfortunately, it sometimes threw curves—like Eric Nash.

Her smile faded. So much for distraction.

As if Casper realized she'd lost interest in him, he bounced over to the edge of the ledge, dived into the water, and disappeared.

Too bad she couldn't make thoughts of the Portland lawyer vanish as easily.

But it was going to be a whole lot tougher to do that after her dumb decision to share a cozy dinner with him on the wharf last night.

She took another sip of coffee, gripping the mug with both hands while a tufted puffin—its orange, parrot-like bill a beacon in the morning sun—dived for his breakfast.

The little guy must be hungry . . . as she'd been last night.

Hmm. Could she blame her appetite—plus her craving for Charley's tacos—on her ill-advised lapse in judgment?

Only if you're trying to fool yourself.

She sighed. No sense denying the truth. She'd known when she accepted Eric's invitation that no matter how much distance she kept between them on the bench, sparks would fly. On her end, anyway.

And that was bad news.

Because while Tracy might praise his integrity and reliability, Eric Nash wasn't going to hang around Hope Harbor—and getting involved with a man who was passing through would be foolish.

She took a gulp of her coffee, then waved a hand in front of her mouth as the hot liquid burned a trail down her throat. Just the way she could get burned if she let herself fall under the spell of another good-looking guy.

Not happening.

Turning away from the wildlife show, she marched back inside. It was going to be hard to avoid him, since she was spending her days at his father's house. But if fate was kind, his visit would be brief. Based on what Tracy had said, his firm wasn't likely to grant long vacations.

She drained her coffee, rinsed the mug, and eyed the remaining half piece of fudge cake from Eleanor. She ought to save it for tonight. A bowl of oatmeal would be much more nutritious.

But for once, she broke all her rules about healthy eating. Quashing the red alert strobing across her mind, she grabbed a fork, ripped off the aluminum foil, and scarfed down the decadent cake.

Yum.

Yet the instant she finished . . . even before the last bit of rich chocolate flavor dissolved on her tongue . . . regret left a sour taste in her mouth.

And once again, John Nash's son was to blame.

She wadded up the foil, rinsed off the fork— and tried to sustain her annoyance. Holding him responsible for her own decision to eat the cake might not be fair, but it was less disconcerting than admitting she could still be vulnerable to dark good looks and impromptu invitations from smooth-talking men.

The sooner he returned to his briefs and

depositions and court dates in Portland, the better.

Except . . . try as she might, she couldn't muster much enthusiasm for that verdict.

Huffing out a breath, she grabbed her keys and stomped toward the door. She did *not* need this disruption in her life. She'd come to Hope Harbor for a new beginning. One that didn't include romance—or even attraction. She had a business to build and people to help. Those were her priorities for the foreseeable future.

So if Eric Nash wanted to organize any more cozy taco parties with his seagull friends, he'd better look elsewhere for female companionship.

Because from now on she intended to keep her distance.

Bang, bang, bang, bang, bang.

At the sudden hammering above him, Eric jerked awake, squinted at his watch, and pulled the covers on the sleeper sofa over his head.

The flimsy cloth barrier didn't muffle the obnoxious din one iota.

He groaned. Much as he hated the shrill, piercing beep of his alarm clock in Portland, ear-splitting pounding was a far worse wake-up call. Besides, it was too early to have to endure noise this high on the decibel meter.

Giving up any hope of further shut-eye, he threw the sheet back and peered at his watch again.

Oh.

It was seven, not six—and most days he rose at five-thirty.

He'd zoned out for nine hours?

His sleepless night on Tuesday had to be the culprit.

A faint haze of drywall dust hung in the air, the motes drifting lazily in the ray of sun peeking around the window shade, and his nose began to tickle. A sneeze was coming. Or two. Or three.

Once he finished ah-chooing, he swung his feet to the floor and stood. Sleeping in was obviously not going to be an option during his stay.

He pulled on his jeans, finger-combed his hair, and opened the French doors that led from the living room to the foyer.

All at once, the banging upstairs stopped. A few seconds later, a lean, fortyish man with olive skin appeared at the top of the stairs, lugging one end of a beam. As he descended, a skinny thirty-something guy, sporting the bad-boy stubble popular in Hollywood these days and wearing a black bandana around his longish hair, emerged from the shadows behind him, holding the other end. Neither gave him more than a cursory glance as they passed.

Where on earth had BJ found this motley crew?

And were they qualified to be ripping his dad's house apart?

Better find out.

He watched them disappear through the front

door, then padded barefoot toward the kitchen in the back of the house, following the rattle of clattering pots.

His father turned from the stove as he pushed through the hall door into the kitchen. "Good morning. I didn't realize you were planning to sleep late or I'd have warned you last night about the early reveille around here."

"That's okay." He surveyed the pots on the burners, the pan of English muffins on the counter, the eggs in a bowl. "What are you making?"

"Eggs Benedict. This is the hollandaise sauce." His dad tapped the pot he was stirring. "I haven't mastered it yet, but I'm getting closer. Want to give it a try in a few minutes?"

"Sure. I guess." He edged closer and lowered his voice. "Listen . . . I just saw your construction crew. Are you certain those guys are qualified to be tearing out walls?"

"BJ hired them, and I trust her implicitly. From what I've observed, Luis is very competent. Stone's younger and less experienced, but he's a hard worker."

Eric narrowed his eyes as his father removed the sauce from the stove and put a lid on it. Stone . . . or stoned? The long-haired guy looked like a refugee from Hell's Angels.

His father opened a cabinet, gave it a swift scan, and hustled toward the dining room. "I need to grab some place mats."

Eric trailed after him as the two-man crew traipsed back upstairs to wreak further destruction.

"Dad . . ." He followed his father across the room. "Does your architect have liability insurance?"

"Yes."

"Did you get a lien waiver?"

"Yes."

The banging resumed, and he increased his volume. "What about the Hispanic guy? Is he a citizen?"

"Calm down, Eric. Everything's fine."

"Dad . . . you have to be careful about hiring illegal aliens. If he's from Mexico, he needs to have a green card or work permit."

"He's not Mexican."

Eric swung around. BJ stood at the foot of the stairs, fire shooting from her green irises.

And it wasn't the pleasant kind he'd seen yesterday during their introductory handshake in the front yard.

"He also has a green card." She shifted toward the stairs. "Luis!"

His father darted him a disgruntled look before he addressed the architect. "That's not necessary, BJ."

She strafed Eric with her gaze, and he tried not to squirm. "I wouldn't want your son to have any doubts about the legality of my operation, him being an attorney and all."

The fortyish man came back down the stairs, gave the assembled group a quick sweep—and froze.

BJ crossed to him and touched his arm. "Luis, John's son would like to see your green card. Would you show it to him, please?" Gone was her snippy manner, replaced by a conversational, dismissive tone—as if she wanted to assure this man he had nothing to worry about.

The fear tightening his features didn't diminish, however. He groped in his pocket for the requested document, pulled it out, and passed it to BJ with quivering fingers.

She stalked over and thrust it at Eric, resting her other hand atop the lethal-looking hammer hanging on her tool belt.

Eric wanted to sink through the floor. "I didn't mean to make a big deal out of this."

"I can understand why an attorney would want to be certain all the i's are dotted and the t's crossed." Her voice was pleasant. Her expression wasn't.

But only he could see her face from this angle.

He took the card. Two things registered at once. The man's full name was Luis Dominguez, and he was Cuban, not Mexican. As far as he could tell, the document was authentic.

"Thank you." He handed it back.

BJ dug around in her own pocket and pulled out a business card. "If you have any other questions or concerns when I'm not around, feel free to call my cell."

In other words, don't bother her crew.

Message received—loud and clear.

"I'm making eggs Benedict this morning. I need some taste testers." His father's tone was a tad too upbeat, as if he was trying to atone for the younger Nash's gaffe. "Luis, I hope you and Stone are up for the job. You too, BJ."

No mention of his son joining them, despite the invitation a few minutes ago in the kitchen.

BJ planted herself next to Luis. "We, uh, have a lot of work to do this morning."

Eric caught her quick venomous glance. Interpretation? Him being part of the breakfast party was a deal breaker.

Since he was the cause of all the tension in the room, there was only one honorable course of action. "Dad, if you could put a serving in the oven for me, I'd like to take a walk on the beach before I eat."

"Excellent idea. Some fresh sea air might clear your head." His father gave him The Look. The one he'd used during Eric's teen years to express his displeasure over some transgression that disappointed him.

It had as powerful an impact now as it had then.

He exited as fast as he could, closed the French doors to the living room behind him, and rubbed his temple, where an ache was beginning to throb.

Barely seven o'clock, and this day had already bottomed out.

And if things didn't improve quickly, this might end up being a much shorter visit than he'd expected—even if the thought of returning to his noise-and-dust-free condo in Portland held zero appeal.

"All fixed, Eleanor." BJ gave the bathroom door one final test swing, tucked her screwdriver back in the toolbox on the floor, and stood.

"Bless you, child. I'm sorry to be such a bother."

BJ stroked Methuselah and hefted the toolbox. "You're not a bother. I'm happy to help."

"Well, the least I can do is offer you dinner. I have enough pot roast left from last night for both of us. Would you like to join me?"

BJ hesitated. She could see the yearning for companionship in the woman's eyes, and Methuselah wasn't much of a conversationalist.

But she couldn't swing it tonight. Her schedule was too tight.

"I wish I could, but I promised to work on sets tonight for that fundraising show for Helping Hands."

"My goodness." Eleanor tut-tutted. "Do you ever have a free moment?"

"When I'm sleeping." BJ winked at her and moved toward the front door, dodging Methuselah.

"I have a feeling that's not a joke."

"I like being busy."

"That B&B project you're working on seems like it would keep you plenty busy. Which reminds me, have you met John's son, Eric, yet?" Eleanor trundled after her down the hall.

BJ kept her expression neutral. "Yes."

"Nice young man, from what I recall."

Not in her experience.

BJ's fingers tightened on the toolbox as this morning's encounter replayed in her mind. Who was he to question the legitimacy of her work crew? This was his father's project, not his—and the elder Nash had been satisfied with their credentials.

However, it might have been better to handle the situation with more discretion. Luis had clearly been upset, and none of her reassurances later had erased his distress. She should have reined in her temper and left him out of it.

Still, if Mr. Big Shot Attorney wanted proof her employees were legal, that had been the best and fastest way to provide it.

On the plus side, the incident had dimmed the luster of Eric Nash's appeal. The only electricity she'd felt this morning had been a charge of anger. If this kept up, she wouldn't have to worry about trying to avoid him while—

". . . lost his job."

BJ tuned back in to Eleanor. "What did you say?"

"Oh, dear." The older woman bit her lip. "I don't mean to be talking out of school. I thought you already knew, working at the house and all."

"Knew what?"

"About Eric losing his job."

The legal eagle had been fired?

"What happened?" The question popped out before she could stop it.

"Well . . ." Eleanor adjusted her grip on the walker. "I don't know the details. Rose ran into him in town. He mentioned downsizing and changed the subject. I'm guessing he got caught in one of those corporate realignments that are all over the news. Poor boy. That must have been quite a blow. He was always such a conscientious, hardworking young man."

The same words Tracy had used to describe him.

BJ's stomach twisted. No wonder he'd seemed dejected when they met. And he had to be stressed out. To make matters worse, his homecoming had been less than placid—and she'd played a big role in that.

"Do you have a headache, dear?"

Yeah, she did. But not the kind the older woman meant.

"No. It's just been a long day."

"And it's not over yet. I don't want to delay you, but why don't you let me fix you a plate to go? You could warm it up later at home."

BJ grasped the doorknob. "To tell you the truth, I'm not that hungry. John was in a cooking mood today. We had eggs Benedict for breakfast and chicken crepes for lunch. He's spoiling us for every future job. Most people don't offer coffee, let alone food."

"Rumor is he's becoming quite the chef."

"He gets high marks in my book, that's for sure." She pulled the door open, keeping tabs on Methuselah. She didn't have time to go chasing after an escaped feline.

"If you get a chance, give Eric my best, would you? And tell him I'm praying for him—not that he'll remember me after all these years. But perhaps it will help to know others care. It must be a terrible blow to lose your dream job. And starting over is never easy."

No. It wasn't.

"I'll pass that on if I run into him . . . and I'll take a rain check on dinner too, if I may." She pushed through the door.

"Anytime, sweet child. It's always a pleasure to see you."

BJ strode down the path, hopscotching over the uneven stepping-stones. After her tension-filled day, it would have been nice to pop a can of soda on the patio, put up her feet, and let the sea breeze whisk away her tension.

Not on her agenda tonight.

But banging nails was also an excellent stress

reliever—and there was a high school scene shop full of them waiting for her.

This wasn't how he'd expected his life to end.

Luis stared down into the dark, roiling water from his perch on the cliff high above the sea. The tide was in, the crash of surf against the huge, irregular sea stacks booming through the night under the three-quarter moon.

His gaze lingered on the luminous orb.

Elena had loved the moon.

Pressure built behind his eyes, and the distant, dark horizon blurred.

Yet no tears came.

He had none left to shed.

Curling his fingers around the rosary he'd carried since the day he set out on the hope-filled journey that ended in tragedy, he fingered the familiar beads. Praying had always been part of his life—but it was hard now. The words were dry. Empty. Rote. Often it felt as if the Lord had tuned him out, leaving him to fend for himself in this foreign place.

Like today.

Despite BJ's assurances that there was no reason to worry, the lawyer's suspicion said otherwise. Although he'd seemed embarrassed about creating a scene, it was clear he had doubts about having a Cuban working under his father's roof—and men like him had power.

Luis's fingers sought the crucifix that dangled at the end of the rosary. Held on tight. Despite the green card bearing his name, one misstep and he'd be sent back to the land he'd paid such a steep price to escape. Even if this man didn't cause him trouble, others might.

And he was tired of living in fear.

Tired of living in a place where he didn't feel welcome.

Tired of living alone.

Gripping the cross, he dropped his head into his hands. Father Murphy wouldn't approve of what he was about to do—but the priest had no idea what it was like to be a stranger in a strange land, with a burden of grief that sucked the life out of you day after day.

There was nothing for him here.

He needed to be with Elena again.

And if this was a sin, as his faith taught, he'd have to trust that God, in his mercy and wisdom, would understand and forgive a desperate choice driven by desolation and loneliness and despair.

Luis folded his hands into the classic position of supplication, rosary twined through his fingers. Raised his face toward the heavens. And began his final prayer.

Oh my God, I am heartily sorry for having offended thee . . .

Taking a cliff-top walk at eleven-thirty at night while the moon played hide-and-seek with the clouds wasn't his most brilliant idea.

But after tossing for an hour on the sleeper sofa in the living room, it had been worth a shot to see if some fresh air would unscramble his brain and chase away his tension.

Eric shoved his hands in the pockets of his jacket.

So far, the trek was a bust.

In fact, listening to the thunderous waves booming in the blackness below was more unsettling than relaxing—as was the litany of messes from this disaster of a day that continued to loop through his mind.

The estimate on the BMW repair, an expense that would eat up the entire high deductible he'd taken a chance on after compiling a flawless driving record that was now toast.

His father's annoyance. The elder Nash hadn't brought up this morning's incident again before heading to some church committee meeting tonight, but he'd left Eric to forage through the fridge for his dinner. Meaning he remained miffed.

The evil eye BJ had directed his way every time their paths crossed.

Stone's animosity. The guy had looked as if he'd like to use a crowbar to administer some corporal punishment as payback for hurting his buddy's feelings.

A brisk breeze whipped past, and Eric flipped up the collar on his jacket.

Tomorrow had to be better—because if he got much lower, he'd be down there with the worms in his father's garden.

An analogy he suspected BJ would deem apt.

A movement to his left caught his eye, and he slowed. Angled toward the horizon. Was that . . . ?

Yes. It was a person. Standing close to the edge of the cliff.

Too close.

He veered off onto the spur path that led toward the edge of the rocky outcropping high above the sea, gaze riveted on the figure.

The person's jacket flapped in the wind again, but the body remained deathly still.

Eric suppressed a shiver.

No one should be standing alone on the brink of an abyss this late at night.

Pulse picking up, he followed the path for a couple dozen yards. Though the person was turned away, the build suggested it was a man. His head was tilted back, his hands clasped, his body rigid.

When he dipped his chin and swayed toward the void, the air whooshed out of Eric's lungs.

Every angle of the man's posture, every vibe radiating from him, telegraphed his intent.

He was planning to jump.

Eric lurched forward again, erasing the distance between them as fast as he could—and the closer he got, the more certain he was that he hadn't misread the situation.

The man teetering on the edge of the cliff didn't intend to see another day.

Eric continued forward, any noise from his footfalls masked by the crash of the waves below.

Ten feet away, he halted. Now what? If he got close enough to make a grab for the guy before he spoke, he might frighten him. The man could lose his balance, fall over the edge. Yet if he stayed back, quietly alerted him to his presence, the guy might jump anyway.

If only there was time to call 911! Those people were trained to handle situations like this.

The man lowered his hands . . . swayed toward the cliff . . . and Eric knew he had mere seconds to act.

Panic short-circuiting his lungs, he sought help from the only available source.

God, please give me the words that will keep this son of yours safe.

The moon came out from behind a cloud, bathing the landscape in an ethereal silver light. The jumper noticed it too. He lifted his face toward the glow, offering a clear view of his profile.

Dear Lord!

It was the Cuban guy on BJ's crew.

Eric sucked in a breath. The man had been upset this morning by the green card incident, but surely . . . *surely* that wouldn't have driven him to this. There had to be more to his story.

But perhaps that incident had been the proverbial last straw.

Eric's gut clenched. If that was the case, he shared some of the blame for whatever had driven the man to a cliff high above the churning sea in the black of night.

Another cloud shrouded the moon, plunging the world back into darkness . . . and Eric knew his time had run out.

He had to act.

Now.

"Amazing view, isn't it?" He didn't quite pull off his attempt at a conversational, shoot-the-breeze tone. How could he when fear had a choke hold on his windpipe?

Luis spun around—and Eric's muscles coiled, ready to spring into action if the man tottered and lost his balance.

He didn't.

"Sorry to startle you." Eric prepared to lunge for the man if necessary. "I like night walks myself." He extended his hand, praying the guy would take it. "We met this morning, but we haven't been formally introduced. Eric Nash."

An eternity ticked by while the Cuban immigrant studied Eric's fingers.

Please, God . . . if you give me his hand, I promise I won't let it go.

At last, shoulders slumping, the construction worker stepped toward him—away from the edge—and took his hand. "Luis Dominguez."

Eric gripped his hand and moved a few feet back toward a flat rock, drawing Luis with him. He motioned toward it. "I was going to sit for a few minutes. Want to join me?"

"It is late." The man's heavily accented words were tinged with a soul-deep weariness.

"Yeah, I guess it is. But I couldn't sleep, and I thought a walk by the sea might relax me."

"The sea, she is . . ." Luis seemed to search for a word, resorting in the end to Spanish. "*Potente.*"

Powerful.

Eric knew enough of the language to recognize the term—but he couldn't tell whether the man's comment was positive or negative.

No matter. He had another priority at the moment.

"Would you like to walk back up to the main path together? Safety in numbers and all that."

Silence once more stretched between them.

Eric waited him out. If Luis refused, he'd find some excuse to stick close. No way was he leaving him here alone, steps away from a very bad—and very final—decision.

After what felt like an eon, Luis dipped his head. "I will walk with you."

Thank you, God!

Eric started up the path, and Luis fell in beside him.

As they left the precipice behind, Eric gave voice to the regret that had plagued him all day. "I'm glad I ran into you tonight, Luis. I wanted to apologize for making an issue of the green card." He felt the man glance over at him but kept talking. "I should have known my father would verify everything was legal. It was none of my business. I'm sorry for embarrassing you."

Eric thought he heard Luis sigh, but he couldn't be certain in the brisk wind.

"You did only what many others have done." There was a world of hurt and pain in his words, of resignation and deep sadness. "Bad things happen. They are part of life."

Yes, they were—but *bad* was too mild a word for what this man must have endured if it had propelled him to the edge of a cliff.

Whatever the reasons for that decision, however, the key goal now was to ensure he didn't follow through on it later.

When the spur trail intersected the main path, Eric stopped. "Did you park around here somewhere?"

"No. I walked."

"Do you live close?"

"Not far. Outside of town." He mentioned the area.

Eric frowned. That was on the *other* side of town—a very long walk.

Though maybe not so long if you weren't planning to make a return trip.

"Look, why don't I give you a lift home? I parked in the lot at the top of the hill."

The man eased back. "Thank you, but I can walk."

Perhaps back out to the cliff.

Not happening on his watch.

"I have a feeling it might rain any minute. You'll be soaked before you get home." That was no lie. On the Oregon coast, sudden rain was always a possibility.

"I do not mind getting wet." The man turned and began to walk away.

"Luis." There was a hint of desperation in his voice—but he didn't care.

The man halted. Angled back.

"Please let me do this. Consider it an apology for what happened this morning."

Luis hesitated. Cast one final look at the cliff top. Exhaled. "A ride would be welcome, if it does not trouble you."

The knot in his stomach loosened. "It's no trouble at all."

They hiked to the car in silence, and despite Eric's attempts to draw the man out with a few questions during the short drive, Luis offered little more than directions.

After a while, Eric stopped trying. If his passenger didn't want to talk, that was his prerogative. At least he was safe. For now.

Once on the other side of town, Eric followed the rutted drive Luis directed him to and pulled up in front of an apartment building that had once been a low-end motel. The one-story kind, with access to the units through flimsy exterior doors. The kind where rooms had often been rented by the hour rather than the night.

It was hard to tell, given the lack of exterior lighting, but unless the place had been seriously spruced up since he'd last ventured down this road a few years ago, it was a total dump. Why the county hadn't condemned the eyesore long ago was beyond him.

Living in a rathole like this would almost be sufficient reason in itself to take desperate action.

"Thank you for the ride." Luis reached for the door handle as Eric slowed across from the entrance to the original motel office.

"Do you want me to drop you in front of your unit?"

"No. It is near." He waved a hand to his right and opened the door.

"Wait."

Luis shifted back toward him.

What to say now? The truth—that he was afraid to abandon him in such an awful place, where the shadow of desperation would no doubt swallow him up again—wouldn't do.

"Will you . . . uh . . . be at the house tomorrow?"

Inane—but it was the first thing that popped into his mind.

"Yes. There is much work left to do."

"That's true." He gripped the wheel. "Listen . . . is this place . . . are you okay here?"

Luis gave the ramshackle structure a slow scan. "It is not what I hoped for in America—but I have slept in much worse spaces. Good night, Mr. Nash."

"It's Eric. I'll feel old if you call me Mr. Nash."

"If you wish." He swung one leg out of the car.

Again, Eric stopped him. "You know, I think my dad is planning to make cranberry waffles in the morning. I saw the recipe on the counter. Will you join us?"

Trying to coerce Luis into a commitment for breakfast was stupid. Even if he accepted the invitation, he could hustle straight back to the cliff the minute the car disappeared down the drive.

But Eric had no other ideas, short of tethering himself to the man for the night.

"Your father . . . he is a good cook."

"Does that mean you'll come?" Eric's knuckles whitened on the wheel.

The man hesitated too long to suit him. "Yes."

"Is that a promise?"

You're pushing, Nash.

Tough.

"Will you be there?" Luis's features were shadowed in the dim light.

"Not if you don't want me to be."

"It is your house."

"It's my father's house. And I can eat later if you prefer."

"No. It is not a problem. I will eat John's waffles. It is a promise. And . . . thank you for tonight." He slid from the car, closed the door, and walked away.

Eric waited until he stopped three units down, fitted a key in the lock, and disappeared inside. A few seconds later, a light illuminated the dingy shade in the window.

The man was safe . . . for the moment.

And he'd promised to show up tomorrow morning.

But as Eric put the car in gear and maneuvered around the potholes in the drive, he wasn't convinced that promise would be kept.

He glanced in the rearview mirror. The light in Luis's room was visible from here. Why not pull off to the side and wait until it went off? Be certain the man wasn't planning to venture out again tonight? Anyone leaving the sleazy apartments had to pass this way. If the light went off—and stayed off—for half an hour with no further activity, it should be safe to go home.

Besides, given the late hour, what difference did another forty or fifty minutes make? He wasn't going to clock a lot of sleep this night, anyway.

And he'd get even less shut-eye if he didn't make sure Luis stayed put.

Why was he still alive?

Luis examined the bleary-eyed stranger in the cracked bathroom mirror, face lined far beyond his years, wings of silver streaking his black hair.

Had God had a hand in tonight's aborted plan—or was it simply due to three freak, back-to-back coincidences?

A motorbike that wouldn't start, forcing him to walk to the site he'd chosen. Giving him a chance to reconsider.

The song blaring from the radio of a passing car as he'd trudged along, its lyrics about hope and brighter tomorrows following him down the dark road.

Eric Nash wandering by at the pivotal moment, appearing out of the blue in that wild, deserted area late at night.

One of those might be a fluke—but three in a row?

Hard to believe they were all due to chance.

He turned away from the mirror, wandered over to the lumpy bed in the furnished unit, and sat. The place was a dive—yet he and Elena hadn't expected five-star accommodations. They'd been too old for starry-eyed dreams, had known it would be a struggle to get established, to learn the language and the ways of this country. But freedom and opportunity . . . those were worth every sacrifice and hardship. Hand in hand, they'd been ready to face whatever challenges their new life threw at them.

Facing those challenges alone, however? Much more difficult.

Too difficult.

Eyes stinging, he pulled the dog-eared photo from his shirt pocket and tilted it toward the light on the nicked bedside stand.

Elena smiled back at him, innate goodness and sweetness radiating from her. The juxta-position of softness and strength in her features, of humor and compassion and conviction, had captivated him from the instant they met. Theirs had truly been a match made in heaven, as his grand-mother had predicted early on in their relation-ship.

But she'd left him too soon.

And he bore much of the blame.

Luis squeezed his eyes shut, gritting his teeth against the pain. They could have waited to undertake the journey. In time, they might have found the money for a safer option.

Yet . . . they *had* waited. Far longer than expected. So long that their dream of creating a family had begun to crumble. Thirty-eight wasn't too late for Elena to have children—but the risk grew exponentially after forty.

So in the end, they'd decided to put their trust in God, pray for his protection, and take the next chance at freedom that came along.

Except God hadn't protected Elena, despite their prayers.

Ah, Luis, my dear one . . . do not blame God.

The gentle admonition echoed in his heart, hard as he tried to shut it out.

"But he did not protect you, *mi amor*." His whispered reply came out hoarse. Broken.

There was no response.

Yet he knew what she'd say if she were here.

What happened might not have been our plan, Luis, but it was God's. He brought you safely to this land, gave you the opportunity and freedom we were seeking. You are here for a reason—and that is why God intervened tonight. He is offering you a second chance to do what you are meant to do.

Could that be true?

And if so, what *was* he meant to do?

It was hard to discern the truth these days, with grief and despair muddling his mind.

He heaved himself to his feet, stripped off his sweatshirt, and pulled back the covers on his bed. Perhaps Elena was right; perhaps not. Either way, he wasn't going back to the cliff tonight.

He'd promised Eric Nash he'd show up for breakfast, and he never broke his word.

Weariness weighing him down, he sank back onto the bed. Pulled up the sheet. Stared at the water spots on the ceiling as he considered all that had happened this night.

John's son might not have spoken about what he'd observed, but he was a smart man. You had to possess solid instincts and sound insights to become a respected attorney. He'd understood what was happening out there on the cliff.

Yet he hadn't said a word about it or probed for explanations.

For a man who seemed to like answers, that was surprising.

Even more unexpected, though, was his remorse —and humility. He'd appeared to be genuinely sorry about causing a scene and inflicting distress. And he'd prolonged his departure as much as possible, as if he was worried the poor lost soul who worked for BJ might wander back out to that cliff as soon as he left. Eliciting a promise to show up tomorrow had been an obvious ploy to try and guarantee a certain Cuban immigrant was still around in the morning.

A crack of thunder boomed overhead, rattling the windows and heralding the rain Eric had predicted. A storm was coming.

Yet thanks to the young attorney, he'd escaped a different kind of storm tonight.

Funny how help sometimes came from people you'd least expect.

The kindness of Father Chaviano in San Antonio and Father Murphy here in Hope Harbor, who'd worked together to help him find a job far from the Mexican border, hadn't surprised him. Clergy were supposed to aid the downtrodden and those in distress.

But Stone owed him nothing—yet in his own rough-around-the-edges way, he, too, had shown compassion and benevolence.

As for BJ, she'd made the biggest leap of all, taking a chance on a man she didn't know and doing everything she could to make him feel welcome and needed.

It was a short list of good Samaritans. But that was understandable. After all, he kept to himself . . . and it was difficult for people to befriend someone who didn't speak their language.

His English had improved a lot, however. He was becoming less self-conscious about engaging in conversation. Soon it would be much easier to communicate and connect—if he had the heart for it.

And that was a big if.

Because his heart was cold and empty these days.

Eric's kindness and compassion tonight might have warmed a tiny corner of it—as had the kind gestures of BJ and the priests and Stone—but the warmth always faded.

Spirits sinking, he leaned over and clicked the light off as depression once again shrouded him.

No matter how he felt in the morning, though, he'd show up for breakfast, as promised. Put in a full day's work for BJ.

After that—hard to say. Looking ahead was too disheartening. It was better to take life hour by hour.

But if the days to come were as bereft of laughter and love and hope as the ones he'd already endured in this new country, the cliff remained a very real option.

— *6* —

Bang, bang, bang, bang, bang.

At the earsplitting, staccato wake-up call, Eric jerked his eyelids open, bolted upright on the sleeper sofa, and tried to read the numbers on his watch.

Hard to do after five hours of twitchy slumber.

But if BJ and her crew were at work, it had to be seven o'clock.

However . . . was all that racket being produced by two people—or three?

He dressed as fast as he could, shoved his feet into his shoes, and pulled the French doors open.

His father smiled at him from the dining room on the other side of the foyer. "Good morning."

"Morning." At least his dad wasn't still holding yesterday's faux pas against him. "The crew all here?"

His father pulled a small glass pitcher out of the china cabinet. "Far as I know. BJ has a key. They let themselves in. I was in the kitchen long before the noise began. By the way, when did you leave that note on the counter? It wasn't there last evening."

"Late."

"Must have been. How did you manage to invite everyone to breakfast?"

"I . . . uh . . . ran into Luis last night. I thought it might help smooth things out after yesterday's . . . incident."

"Works for me. For the record, though, the crew is always welcome for breakfast. Lunch, too, if I'm testing brunch recipes. It's a standing invitation on days I cook."

"Nice gesture."

"More on their part than mine." His father grinned and closed the cabinet door. "They're my guinea pigs—and they've paid the price with a few of my less-successful culinary experiments. Would you run up and tell them the food will be on the table in about ten minutes?"

The perfect excuse to do a head count.

"Sure."

While his father moved toward the kitchen, Eric ascended the stairs two at a time, pausing at the top to take in the unfamiliar view. It was hard to believe this was the same house he'd called home for his first eighteen years.

But he had to admit the new layout was nice. Two large suites with sitting areas and posh bathrooms now flanked a spacious center hall, where wainscoting and intricate crown molding were being installed.

He peeked into the suite on the right. Empty. The hammering that had jolted him awake must have come from the room on the left.

As he strode toward the door to the second suite at the far end of the hall, BJ's voice met him half-way.

"Let's get this sheet of drywall set. You want to grab the other end?"

A man's deep rumble responded, too muted to identify.

Eric arrived at the door as BJ and Stone hefted the drywall into position and began to screw it in place.

He shoved the plastic drape in the doorway aside and scanned the rest of the room.

No one else was there.

His pulse skittered.

"Where's Luis?" The question echoed loudly in the empty room, ricocheting off the bare walls as he pushed through the plastic.

Both screw guns fell silent, and BJ and Stone turned toward him.

The architect's eyes narrowed, and her chin rose. "Why?"

No problem interpreting her body language. She thought he was here to cause more trouble.

But that wasn't on his agenda today—or in the future.

"Look, just tell me where he is, okay?"

Faint puckers appeared on her brow as she assessed him. It was obvious she was trying to decipher his mood . . . and his intent.

He couldn't discuss either, however. Luis's late-night trip to the cliff was the man's secret to share, if he chose to.

At last BJ relented. "He's not here yet."

"Why not?"

"I have no idea. He doesn't own a cell. Something must have delayed him." She lifted her chin. "For your information, he's a very responsible—"

"Is he late often?"

She blinked at the terse interruption. "Never."

Not what he wanted to hear.

A flicker of apprehension flared in her eyes. "What's going on?"

"Nothing." He backed toward the door, already digging for his car keys, mentally outlining his game plan. He'd try the man's apartment first. Hope he'd overslept. If he wasn't there, he'd drive back out to the cliff and . . .

The faint sputter of a motorbike in need of a tune-up rattled in through the open windows.

"That's him now." BJ waved her drill toward the front of the house, expression wary. Like she was still expecting more trouble.

He edged toward the door. "Dad wanted me to let you know breakfast will be ready in about ten minutes." He fled into the hall.

The front door opened, and before he could escape, feet clattered up the stairs.

He and Luis met in the center of the hall.

The man gave him an apologetic look. "My

bike . . . she did not want to begin this morning."

Eric shoved his trembling fingers into his pockets. "I'm just glad you're here."

Luis's gaze never wavered from his. "I do not break promises."

"I can see that." Eric managed to coax up the corners of his mouth. "The waffles are almost ready."

"I will enjoy."

Eric shifted aside to let Luis pass—and found BJ watching the scene from the doorway of the suite.

She arched an eyebrow at him.

He ignored it and continued down the hall. If she wanted to give her tardy employee the third degree, that was up to her. His lips were sealed.

The important thing was that Luis had shown up.

But the man hadn't promised anything beyond today—and that was worrisome.

Big time.

Frowning, Eric descended the steps while the screw guns whirred back to life. It was going to be difficult to stop Luis from taking another late-night cliff walk unless he could figure out what had prompted the first one.

He needed more information.

Unfortunately, Luis didn't seem inclined to enlighten him.

But BJ might know some details about his

background. She'd come to his defense yesterday, hadn't she? He worked for her, had earned her loyalty. If the man was going to share his story with anyone, she was the obvious choice.

Not that she'd pass it on to her client's son, though, given their combative relationship to date.

Nevertheless, it couldn't hurt to ask.

So as soon as he could maneuver it, he'd corner her for a little chat.

BJ pulled the knife along the drywall tape she'd secured to the seam, smoothing it out from the center, going through the familiar routine by rote as she pondered the question that had been on her mind all morning.

What was up with Eric?

He'd turned on the charm at breakfast, even managing to coax a smile from taciturn Stone.

Then he'd offered to tinker with Luis's motorbike, see if he could get it running better. And he might succeed, despite its decrepit state. According to his dad, he'd always had a knack for mechanics.

Finally, he and Luis appeared to have made their peace, though when that might have occurred she couldn't fathom.

In any case, this was not the same man who'd blundered into town two days ago.

She finished her seam, closed up the joint

compound, and checked on her crew. Across the room, Luis was concentrating on his own drywall seam, Stone assisting. "Lunch break."

"Is John cooking today?" Stone gave her a hopeful look.

"Not that I've heard."

"Bummer."

She grinned and dropped her drywall knife into a bucket of water. "Hey, we hit the jackpot on this job with food. Count your blessings." She picked up a damp cloth. "I have to run to the hardware store over lunch. You guys want me to pick up some food for you?"

"No, thanks." Stone took a swig of the sludge he lugged to work from home every day, which he claimed was coffee. "I brought lunch."

"Luis?"

"No. The waffles, they full me up."

Meaning he was going to skip the noonday meal again—because every spare dime he could eke out went back to his ailing father-in-law in Cuba.

"You can have my extra sandwich, Luis." Stone finished his coffee. "No way I can eat two after that breakfast, and I don't want to throw it out."

She telegraphed him a silent thank-you. They both knew how tight money was for their co-worker, but Luis refused to take anything he deemed charity—even the government assistance that was available to Cuban refugees.

"Wasting food is bad. If you cannot eat, I will take it."

"You'll be doing me a favor."

BJ wiped her hands on the rag. "Now that we've settled our lunch plans, I'm off. I'll see you guys in about an hour." She pulled off her baseball cap, tossed it next to the bucket, and headed out.

Her errand at the hardware store went faster than she'd expected, and she tooled around the block to see if Charley's was open.

No luck today. The window was rolled down.

Bummer, as Stone would say.

Takeout from the café around the corner would have to do . . . but chowing down on The Myrtle's Friday stir-fry special wouldn't be a hardship. For a tiny town, Hope Harbor had more than its share of excellent culinary options.

She circled the block, pulled into an empty parking place, and slid out from behind the driver's seat.

A Nissan Sentra pulled in behind her, and she gave it no more than a passing glance—until the driver emerged.

Eric Nash?

Very suspicious.

She crossed her arms tight over her chest. "Did you follow me?"

"Yes. Are you eating here?" He motioned toward the café.

"I'm getting takeout. What's with the tail?"

"I'd like to ask you a few questions."

Sheesh. Did all attorneys have a third-degree gene—or just him?

"About what?"

"Not here. After you get your food, would you meet me back at the wharf? I spotted a couple of empty benches as we passed. I won't delay you long, but it's important."

Must be, if he'd been following her around town.

The notion of sharing a bench with him again set off a red alert—but the intensity in his brown irises overrode it.

"Fine. Give me ten minutes. Takeouts usually come up fast."

"I'll save a bench." He retreated to his car.

BJ propped her hands on her hips and watched his taillights disappear down the street.

What could he possibly want to talk with her about?

Hard as she wracked her brain, not a single topic came to mind.

But for sure she'd have to watch her step around this kinder, gentler Eric.

Because the new and improved version could be very, very dangerous.

Had she stood him up?

From the wharf-side bench he'd claimed, Eric watched the corner where BJ's truck should have appeared. She ought to be here by now.

Considering the stupid stunts he'd pulled since his arrival, though, he couldn't blame her if she'd hightailed it in the opposite direction.

But he hoped she showed. He needed information.

Another minute ticked by.

Two.

Three.

This wasn't promising.

As two seagulls waddled over in search of a handout, Eric stood. No sense lingering. BJ had said ten minutes; twenty had passed. She wasn't coming.

The birds edged closer.

"Sorry, guys. No food today."

He started to circle the bench . . . and all at once, the two gulls rose into the air, squawking and flapping their wings. Like Floyd and Gladys had done the other day.

Could these be the same two gulls?

Hard to tell. They all looked alike to him.

He tried again to circle around them.

Feathers flew, driving him back toward the bench.

This was ridiculous.

Jaw clenched, he glared at the gulls. He was not going to be held prisoner by two wacko birds.

He feinted toward them, then dodged around the other side of the bench toward freedom . . . just as BJ's truck came around the corner.

The birds fluttered back onto the pavement and wandered away.

Odd.

Eric glanced toward the taco stand. No sign of Charley—but the man's seagull friends had saved his bench for him the other day. Today, it was as if they'd been trying to delay him so he wouldn't miss . . .

He cut off that line of thought. How nuts was that?

Besides, he had more important issues to deal with.

BJ nosed into a spot directly across from the bench, in front of Sweet Dreams Bakery, and emerged from the cab a few seconds later carrying a large plastic carryout container and a white bag.

"Sorry I'm late." She called out the apology as she sized up the traffic, then rushed across the street, a becoming flush pinkening her cheeks. "They had some kind of disaster in the kitchen that delayed all the orders. I thought you might leave."

"I tried to, but I was . . . forcibly detained."

"Huh?"

"Trust me, you don't want to know. Can I take one of those?" He reached for the large white bag.

After giving the area one more puzzled inspection, she relinquished it. "That's yours anyway."

"What do you mean?" He sat beside her after she claimed a spot on the bench.

"Did you have lunch yet?"

"No."

"That should hold you until dinner. Since I didn't know if you were a fan of stir-fry, I went the safe route—The Myrtle club. Unless you're a vegetarian?"

"Never have been, never will be." He dug out the sandwich and two bottles of water, passing one to her. "You didn't need to do this. I had a big breakfast."

"You treated me to tacos. I always repay my debts. And you only ate half a waffle this morning. The other guys chowed down two apiece—plus a cinnamon roll."

"I had a lot on my mind." He unwrapped the sandwich.

"Understandable."

He gave her a guarded look. Had Luis told her about their encounter last night?

"What do you mean?" Better not to make assumptions. It was bad policy in law—and in life.

Dropping her gaze, she made a project out of extracting her plastic fork from its wrapper. "I heard about your job. I'm sorry."

Oh.

He'd forgotten how fast news traveled around here. The only person he'd told was Rose—after she cornered him on the street.

But if BJ knew about it, of course she'd think that was front and center in his mind. Losing a partner-track position was a big deal.

Yet after last night, his problem seemed petty in comparison to the ones Luis must be facing.

"Thanks. But to be honest, that's not why I was distracted. I was thinking about Luis."

She stabbed a bite of chicken in her stir-fry but didn't eat it. "Why?"

"It's . . . complicated."

"In other words, butt out."

"It's Luis's story to tell."

"Okay. I can accept that. We all have our secrets." She speared a piece of carrot. "What do you want to know?"

"Anything you can tell me about his background."

She froze. "Is this about his green card again?"

"No."

"Hmm." She ate another bite of stir-fry. Took a sip of water. Focused on the boats in the harbor.

He could almost hear the gears whirring in her brain.

Since pushing wasn't apt to help his cause, he ate his sandwich and waited.

He was a quarter through his club, and she'd put a significant dent in her own lunch, before she spoke again.

"I've been hearing positive comments about you."

The non sequitur threw him for a minute—but BJ struck him as intelligent, clear-thinking, and focused. Her comment must have a connection to their previous line of discussion.

Best to go with the flow.

"From who?"

"Tracy Hunter, for one. You would have known her as Tracy Campbell."

"From the cranberry farm, right? We went to high school together. How do *you* know her?"

"We both lived in Phoenix for a while. Her first husband was from there, and I was in town for an extended period to oversee a major project for my firm. Not this firm." She motioned toward her truck. "The one I worked for in LA."

So BJ was a big-city girl.

That raised some interesting questions.

But she didn't give him a chance to ask any of them.

"Eleanor Cooper also thinks well of you."

Eric tried without success to place the woman. "The name is familiar, but otherwise I'm drawing a blank."

"She said you might not remember her. She's eighty-eight and moved back to Hope Harbor twenty-some years ago."

A vague image of the older woman materialized in his mind. "Okay. It's coming back. I do recall seeing her around town on occasion."

BJ creased the napkin in her lap. "She wanted

me to tell you she was sorry about what happened with your job and was praying for you."

"I appreciate that."

Except he knew someone who needed the woman's prayers more than he did. Someone he wanted insights about—if BJ ever got this conversation back on track.

As if she'd read his mind, she moistened her lips—a major distraction he did his best to ignore—and brought her digression full circle. "I mention all this for two reasons. First, I want to apologize for being a bit . . . irritable . . . with you. Had I known about the job situation, I would have cut you some slack. Second, hearing people I respect praise you tells me your concern for Luis is genuine and that I should be able to trust you to keep our conversation confidential."

"It is, and you may."

"So what would you like to know?"

He chose his words with care. Getting the info he needed without giving away the reason for his concern required finesse. "Why did he emigrate, and how did he end up in this tiny town?"

BJ poked at her stir-fry, faint creases marring her forehead. "Let me preface this by saying that Father Murphy at St. Francis—better known around town as Father Kevin, as you probably know—told me most of this when he came to me four months ago and asked if I'd be willing to give Luis a job. John had just signed the contract for the Seabird Inn project, so the timing of the request couldn't have been more perfect."

"You agreed to hire him without ever meeting him?"

"After I heard his story, yes. He also came with strong credentials and experience, as well as an excellent recommendation from his boss in San Antonio."

"How long has he been in the US?"

"Ten months, the first six in Texas."

"So he crossed the border from Mexico?"

"No." BJ closed the top on her plastic container, a fourth of her lunch uneaten. "Do you know anything about Cuban emigration?"

"Not specifically—but there are stories about *Hispanic* emigration all over the media."

"That's a whole different ball game, as I learned from Father Kevin. Unlike other immigrants from Latin countries, once Cubans set foot on American soil, they're protected as refugees. They get green cards, have access to government benefits, and within a year can become permanent legal residents."

Translation? They had an easy in.

But if things were rosy for Cubans in the US, why had Luis been seeking a permanent escape last night?

"You seem confused." BJ took a sip of water.

"Processing." He wrapped up what was left of

his sandwich and tucked it back in the bag to finish later. "So Luis jumped to the front of the line and waltzed into the US. No sweat."

"I didn't say that." BJ rested a hand on the back of the bench and angled toward him. "Getting in was easy. Getting here wasn't."

This must be the story he was seeking.

Eric tuned out everything around him—the squawk of the gulls, the clang of boat bells, the chatter of passing tourists—and gave the woman beside him his full attention. "Tell me."

"The first thing you should know is that Luis is a physician."

Shock reverberated through him.

The carpenter who lived in the third-rate apartment was a *doctor?*

"Your ears aren't playing tricks on you." BJ set her water bottle beside her. "And I had the same reaction."

"But . . . why isn't he practicing medicine?"

"Easier said than done. I'll get to that in a minute. Let's start in Cuba. The country has two currencies, one for locals, one for tourists. Residents are paid in the local currency, which has little value. As a doctor, Luis earned the American equivalent of twenty-five dollars a week."

Eric tried to wrap his mind around that number. "Twenty-five dollars?"

"Yes. His wife, Elena, was a teacher. She made

less. Luis drove a taxi in his free time to keep food on the table. He and Elena wanted a family, but they also wanted to raise their children in a land of political freedom and economic opportunity. America offered both. They planned their escape for years."

Since Luis's wife wasn't part of his life in Hope Harbor, Eric was already getting a sense where this story was heading.

"They saved as much as they could for close to a decade but never managed to accrue the kind of money needed for a safer overland trip through South America. Luis's father-in-law has been in poor health for years and needed their financial support—as well as scarce medications only available on the black market. That ate up a lot of their savings. Time was running out for having children, so in the end they chose the only other option."

"Boat?" He'd read a few stories about Cuban refugees arriving by sea.

"That would be a generous term. Father Kevin told me it was a patched-together craft of plastic foam and metal rods wrapped in tarp, powered by an engine adapted from a lawn mower. The trip is ninety miles across open ocean filled with sharks, strong currents, and oppressive heat . . . and they had no navigational tools."

Eric tried to imagine being desperate enough to undertake such a risky journey.

Couldn't.

"The trip should have taken two or three days. It took eighteen. A storm came up. They got lost. Ran out of provisions. Three of the people on the boat died and were thrown overboard. Elena was one of them." BJ's voice broke, and she took another drink of water.

Eric felt as if someone had punched him in the gut.

How did a person survive that kind of trauma for one day, let alone ten months?

A full minute passed before BJ picked up the story again. "Once they landed near Key West, Luis was processed and got on a bus for San Antonio. A Cuban he knew worked for a construction company there and had promised to help him get a job if he ever escaped."

"Why didn't he stay there?"

"He was uncomfortable. As you might imagine, due to their favored status, Cubans aren't all that popular with other immigrants. There can be lots of friction—even though Luis didn't take any of the government aid available. He talked to his priest, and Father Chaviano contacted Father Kevin. The two of them had met at a retreat and kept in touch. Father Kevin told me the story, I offered Luis a job, he came . . . and now you know as much as I do."

Although his mind was struggling to absorb all BJ had told him, there were some obvious gaps.

"But if Luis is a doctor, why choose a hammer over a scalpel?"

"I wondered about that too—especially after I learned he was the director of emergency services for a large hospital in his previous life. But I did some research and discovered there are huge hurdles for Cuban doctors who emigrate. They can't prove they're doctors, because Cuba won't release transcripts for defectors. They have language issues, making test-taking difficult. The accreditation exams themselves are expensive and require months of prep. Plus, resident spots at hospitals tend to go to younger doctors."

"Wow." His mind was reeling.

"Yeah. And on top of everything, defectors are viewed as traitors, so Luis can never go home."

No wonder the man had been standing on the cliff last night.

BJ twisted her wrist. "I need to get back to work. I'm already late. But for the record, Luis is a skilled carpenter. His father was a builder, and he worked with him from the age of eight or nine until he went to medical school. Your dad's project is in capable hands."

He waved the reassurance aside. "I'm not worried about that."

"Good to know." She rose. "Thanks for working on his motorbike."

He stood too. "It's a paltry gesture after all he's been through."

"Simple acts of kindness can have a far-reaching impact, though. And I know he appreciates the help. The bike's been giving him problems from day one—and it's his only transportation. He rides it to our job sites rain or shine."

"Given the climate here, that must mean he often arrives wet."

"His heavy-duty slicker keeps him pretty dry—but I wish he could afford a car."

And a better place to live.

But he kept that to himself. There was no way to reveal he'd been there without explaining why.

"Maybe once he gets settled here he'll be able to put some money aside for things like that."

"Not if he continues to work for me. Your dad's job requires a full-time crew, but most of my projects are smaller. I'm still building my business. My guys have always filled in with odd jobs when I don't need them—but I don't know how much success Luis will have rounding up work once we finish at your dad's. He doesn't know many people in town."

Another worry that must plague the man.

"About the bike—I may not have it finished by tonight. Tell Luis I'll give him a lift home if it's not ready."

"I can take him."

"Let's compromise. I'll do chauffeur duty tonight, you can pick him up Monday morning."

"Sounds like a plan." She edged away. "See you around."

He watched her stride away, then sat back on the bench, setting the remains of his lunch beside him. His appetite was gone.

The tale BJ had shared was the saddest story he'd ever heard.

And it wasn't likely to get any better, given how life had played out up to this point for Luis.

But it didn't have to have a dark end. There had to be a way to improve his situation. The problem just needed some time and attention.

As it happened, he had plenty of both to offer at the moment.

Besides, last night on the cliff, he'd promised God that if the man took his hand and stepped back from the edge, he wouldn't let go.

And Luis wasn't the only one who kept his promises.

— 7 —

"Sorry for the delay, BJ, but an urgent request for assistance took priority. We're ready for you now."

At the summons from Michael Hunter, BJ's palms began to sweat.

This was it.

Based on the verdict of the Helping Hands board members awaiting her presentation, the proposal that was near and dear to her heart was either going to soar—or crash and burn.

Please, God, let it soar . . . in memory of Gram.

Gripping her small portfolio, she followed Michael into St. Francis's conference room. Many of the faces around the table were familiar— and most were smiling, despite the early hour on this Saturday morning.

She hoped that was a positive omen.

After Michael introduced her, she accepted a water and took the seat he indicated at one end of the long table.

"I know I speak for the entire board when I say your teaser piqued our interest, BJ. Helping seniors has been an important part of this organization's mission since our two clergymen here got the group rolling. We're open to any ideas that will allow us to better serve them."

Michael leaned back in his chair, posture open and relaxed. "The floor is yours."

Tamping down her nerves, she folded her hands on top of the portfolio, thanked everyone for their interest, and plunged in. "As most of you know, I've been a Helping Hands volunteer for about a year. Many of the people I assist are seniors who are having trouble keeping up with day-to-day chores—things like housecleaning, cooking, shopping, grass cutting. Eventually, that burden can force them to sell their home and move into a retirement center."

Her knuckles whitened, and she took a deep breath. "That's what happened to my grandmother. Not only did the house become too much for her, but she grew lonely after health issues restricted her mobility. Friends came by and called, but for the most part, she spent her days alone. In the end, she moved to a retirement center, hoping it would provide the companionship and social interaction she missed. I'm sure many of you have faced similar situations with family members."

Several board members nodded.

"In my grandmother's case, the move didn't work out as she'd hoped. She missed her home—and the feeling of being useful, of having a purpose in life. Plus, she missed being part of a neighborhood where all ages and stages of life were represented. All her neighbors at the retirement center were in failing health. Just taking up space, she used to say, while they waited to pass on. She withered away, and in less than two years she died."

Pressure built in her throat, and BJ took a swig of water, praying her voice would remain steady.

"I know my grandmother would have lived longer if she'd been able to stay in her home—with a companion. Someone to share meals with, to take her to the grocery store or out for a cup of coffee, to help her coordinate upkeep on the house." She opened the portfolio and extracted a small stack of handouts. "I'll leave these with you to review, but essentially I'm proposing that Helping Hands establish a companion program."

One of the board members furrowed his brow as the handouts were passed around. "Aren't there already similar programs out there?"

"Yes—and they're expensive. According to my research, on average home companions charge twenty dollars an hour."

The board member adjusted his glasses. "Wouldn't insurance or government assistance help with that cost for those with limited incomes?"

"Some help is available—but even with financial aid, very few people could afford 24/7 coverage. My idea is to create mutually beneficial relationships. To pair seniors with companions who would live with them and offer assistance that would be delineated on a case-by-case basis. In exchange, the companion would receive room and board."

"You mean . . . they wouldn't be paid?"

"No."

The man gaped at her. "Who would possibly be interested in such an arrangement?"

She'd expected that question. "College students, for one—and Coos Bay could be an excellent source of candidates. There's also a culinary school there. Single people who have a job might also welcome a homey atmosphere and free room and board in exchange for companionship. Older people aren't the only ones who get tired of solitary meals. I believe the pool of candidates could be quite large."

"It's an interesting idea, BJ." Reverend Baker rested his elbows on the table and steepled his fingers. "Very innovative."

"I agree." Michael took a handout and paged through it. "It appears you've done your homework. Why don't you give us all a chance to review the material? Once we've done that, I'll get back to you with a verdict—or we might reconvene if there are questions that need further discussion. Sound reasonable?"

"Yes." BJ zipped her portfolio closed.

"As far as you know, has this ever been tried anywhere?" Another question from the crank.

He could be a problem.

"Not that I could find in terms of an official program." She did her best to maintain a pleasant, professional tone. "However, I expect people have worked out similar arrangements on their own. But that takes a great deal of effort—and carries a bit more risk for both parties. The beauty of this is that Helping Hands would screen both the older residents and the candidates and do all the coordination. I'm not certain how many residents might be interested in a program like this, but I don't think we'd be dealing with an unwieldy number."

"Anna Williams set up something along these lines last summer." Reverend Baker tapped a finger on the table. "It worked out splendidly."

"She might have gotten lucky." More negatives from the grump. "And I heard that arrangement was only for a week or two. This is much more complicated."

The doom monger seemed determined to quash the idea before he even read her proposal.

How had such a wet blanket gotten on the Helping Hands board?

"It might be best if we defer further discussion until we've all reviewed the material. I have a feeling many of the questions and concerns being raised are addressed." Michael leaned forward. "Is there anything else you'd like to add, BJ?"

"Just a request that you all give this careful, prayerful consideration. I know it will require administrative time, and there will be minor costs involved. But it could make a huge difference in the quality of life for some of our seniors."

"Thank you, BJ." Michael rose and gave her another encouraging smile. So did the clergymen and most of the board members.

A couple didn't.

And it took no more than one or two naysayers to deep-six an idea like this.

Holding tight to the portfolio, she stood and walked out the door. Closed it behind her. Sagged against the wall. At least she'd given it her best shot. The polished, professional written proposal represented hours of research and thought. Her verbal presentation had been fine too. To-the-point and articulate.

The outcome was in the hands of the board.

But a final entreaty to a higher power couldn't hurt.

Please, God, let them decide to give this a chance. I know I failed Gram, but with your help, maybe I can give some Hope Harbor residents a brighter future than I gave her.

The studio, like the man, looked the same as it always had.

Eric paused at the rear of Charley's modest clapboard cottage to examine the rectangular, weathered-wood structure fifty yards beyond the house. Except for the large expanse of glass

124

that covered the top half of the north wall, it could be mistaken for a tumbledown storage shed.

But once you entered, there was no question about its purpose.

And if fate was in his corner today, Charley would be inside, seated at his easel. It was too early on a Saturday morning for the taco stand to be open, and if the artist wasn't cooking, he was usually here.

Eric strolled over to the door, admiring the expansive view of the sea from the secluded acreage two miles outside town. The primo location, however, was the only indication he was standing on high-end real estate. Charley might be able to afford more upscale digs, but he'd always steered clear of elaborate trappings, preferring a simple life.

"Come on in, Eric." The artist's muffled voice percolated through the wooden door.

He grinned at the summons. That, too, was like the old days—though he had no more idea now than he had years ago how Charley had always been able to detect his presence.

Eric opened the door, entered the spacious studio, and did a slow sweep.

Natural light spilled into the high-ceilinged structure from the north window, providing the consistent illumination prized by artists. The familiar scent of oil paint mingling with the faint, piquant smell of solvents tickled his nose. As always, the walls were bare except for shelves brimming with well-thumbed art and philosophy books, records, and painting supplies. Canvases in various stages of completion were propped against the far wall, below a small octagonal window that afforded a glimpse of the sea. Music poured from the vintage turntable, filling every corner of the room. Ravel's *Boléro* today.

Eric inhaled. Slowly exhaled.

It was great to be back.

"I wondered when you'd get around to paying me a visit."

At Charley's comment, he regarded the artist. The man was sitting where he always sat while painting, angled so the light from the expanse of glass above him spilled over his left shoulder, palette in one hand, brush in the other, a half-finished canvas on an easel in front of him.

It was like stepping into a time warp.

"I only arrived Wednesday." He strolled over to examine the work-in-progress. It was in the early stages, but there was sufficient paint on the canvas to see that the finished piece of weathered fishermen watching a foreboding squall form on the horizon would be a powerful, evocative character study rather than one of the bright, playful scenes of whimsy and innocence Charley sometimes favored.

"What do you think?"

"Impressive, as usual."

The artist dropped his bristle brush in some solvent and leaned back. "You paint at all these days?"

"No."

"Why not?"

Eric shrugged. "I was on the partner track at my firm. That meant sixty-plus-hour weeks. A schedule like that doesn't leave much time or energy for anything else."

"Hmm." Charley stood. "Want a soda?"

"Sure." He trailed after him to a small refrigerator near the bookshelf. In the old days, Charley had always kept a few Dr Peppers on hand for him, though the artist's preference was Coke.

"Let's see what's in here." The man bent down to rummage through the contents.

"Whatever you have will be . . ."

Charley swiveled around and held out a Dr Pepper.

"I didn't think you liked these." Eric took the cold can.

"I don't—but you do."

"You were that certain I'd come by?"

"It never hurts to be prepared." He ambled over to the record player and lifted the arm from the vinyl disk. Silence descended.

"You know . . . technology has advanced beyond that." Eric waved his can toward the turntable.

"Newer doesn't necessarily mean better." The

man popped the tab on his drink. "Take Coke. After a hundred years, some genius decided he could improve the taste. Disaster ensued, and the classic formula was resurrected. Moral of the story? Never tinker with perfection."

A pall crept over Eric as the events of the past few days looped through his mind. He took a swig of soda and tried to shake it off. "Very few things in life are perfect."

"Was your job one of them?"

Where had *that* come from?

"Is any job perfect?"

"Some are closer than others."

Naturally he'd say that, given how life had worked out for him.

"That's true—but most people don't get to follow their passion, like you did."

"Why do you think that is?" Charley strolled back to his work-in-progress.

The man's tone was curious rather than confrontational, yet for some reason Eric's defenses kicked in. "Because people need to eat. It can be hard to earn a living doing what you love."

"There are ways to make it work, though."

"If your paintings sell for thousands of dollars."

Charley studied the canvas, then turned to Eric. "Mine didn't always bring in big bucks. The early years were lean—although running a taco stand did keep me from being a starving artist." One side of his mouth hitched up.

The man's attempt at humor didn't alleviate the sudden tension knotting Eric's shoulders. "But your work eventually caught the attention of the right people. You were lucky."

"Or blessed."

Eric took another drink of his soda. Odd. While Charley had always struck him as a spiritual person, they'd never discussed faith. Nor did the man attend church, as far as he knew.

"You attribute your success to God?"

Charley finished off his Coke. "What do *you* attribute it to?"

"I've never really thought about it. Talent, I suppose."

"Which was given to me."

By God.

Charley didn't say the words, but the implication was clear.

Strange that he'd never talked of this in all the hours they'd spent together in the studio.

"But how did you know in the beginning that you were gifted enough to paint for a living?" Eric swirled the liquid in his can.

"I didn't. That's where trust comes in. Besides, while my art provides a comfortable living, I'm not rich by most people's vaulted definition of that term."

That was news to Eric. "In that case, don't you

ever worry about tomorrow? What if . . . what if people stopped buying your paintings? What would you do?"

"Sell more tacos." He offered a gentle smile. "There are always options. One lesson I've learned —worry doesn't change tomorrow, it only robs today of its joy." He sat back on his stool. "Why don't you take a few supplies with you, dabble a little? You enjoyed playing with paints as a teenager."

Eric finished his soda and crumpled the empty can in his fingers. "I'm too old to play."

"No one's ever too old to play. I do it every day. It refreshes the soul and opens the mind to creative possibilities."

"For artists, maybe."

"For everyone." He retrieved a sable brush from the container of solvent. "I always hoped you'd finish that." Charley pointed the brush toward the far corner.

Eric stared at the canvas angled slightly away from them. It had been more than a decade since he'd seen it, but he had no problem recognizing the seascape. The water was bathed in the rosy hue of sunrise, a lone gull soaring overhead, a solitary figure in the distance looking toward the horizon. The colors, the composition, the perspective—all spoke of hope and joy and bright tomorrows.

It was the last painting he'd dived into the

summer before he'd left for college—and he'd never completed it.

How had he not noticed it during his initial scan of the room?

"You've kept that all these years?"

"It showed great promise. I always hoped you'd finish it one day."

"Not likely."

"A pity." Charley picked up his brush. "Would you start the music again as you leave?"

He was being dismissed.

In silence, Eric crossed the room, tossed his can in the recycle bin, and set the needle back on the vinyl disc. Once again, Ravel's powerful *Boléro* filled the lofty space.

At the door, Eric looked back. Charley was already absorbed in his work, his attention riveted on the figures coming to life on his canvas. If he realized his visitor was still there, he gave no indication of it.

Eric slipped outside. The sun had vanished, and a spatter of rain struck his cheek as he wandered back to his car. Appropriate. The dreary skies fit his mood.

Yet this wasn't at all how he'd expected to feel after his visit. In the past, an hour or two . . . or three . . . in the studio had given him comfort and peace. Now, he felt unsettled. Charley's manner might have been easygoing and non-judgmental, but Eric sensed he'd disappointed the man who'd always welcomed him to this place. Who'd taken the time to instruct an amateurish teen in the finer points of painting. Who'd encouraged him to experiment with color and form, to let his imagination run free and follow where it led. Who'd always counseled him to trust his instincts and let his brush go where his heart took it.

Those heady hours in Charley's studio had been addictive. Nothing else he'd ever done had given him such a rush—or as much gratification.

But no matter how Charley might romanticize painting, it wasn't a practical career. It was important to have a job you could count on to pay the bills and provide security.

Ironic how in the end, law had proven less reliable than Charley's painting.

Still . . . he'd find another position. With his experience and credentials, it wouldn't take long once he began sending out feelers on LinkedIn and through his network of contacts. Perhaps not with a firm as prestigious as the one in Portland, but a solid company with excellent salary and benefits.

First, though, he'd take the vacation his dad had suggested. Walk on the beach. Sleep in . . . on weekends, anyway. And see what he could do to help a bereft Cuban immigrant find new purpose in life—a far bigger challenge than anything he'd tackled during his career as an attorney.

And he had a feeling that if he succeeded at that, it would provide more satisfaction than any case he'd ever won in the field of law.

White bag in hand, BJ pushed out of the door of Sweet Dreams Bakery. The cinnamon roll was a splurge, but after this morning's Helping Hands board meeting, followed by hours in the high school scene shop constructing flats for the benefit show, she deserved a treat.

As she circled her truck, gearing up to head home and work on the design for Tracy and Michael's house, the window on Charley's taco stand rolled up.

She hesitated. All the fixings for a chicken Caesar salad were in her fridge, but why not have that tomorrow and indulge in an order of tacos today? Fish was healthy, and all the other ingredients Charley stuffed into those corn tortillas were nutritious—for the most part.

Besides, it was providential he was opening up the very minute she was getting ready to leave. Was it a stretch to think the timing was more than coincidence?

Maybe.

But she wasn't going to overanalyze her good fortune.

After depositing the white bag in the truck,

she crossed the street and hustled toward the stand.

"What's your rush?" Charley arched an eyebrow as she drew close.

"I didn't want that window to roll back down in my face."

"I just opened."

"True—but I wasn't taking any chances. Your hours aren't exactly predictable."

"They keep life interesting, though. You eating alone?"

"Yep. At home, on my patio, with my feet up while I enjoy the view."

"Sounds like a perfect Saturday."

"The second half will be, anyway. I had other commitments this morning—including some work at the high school. I finished constructing the flats, so whenever you're ready to . . ." Her voice trailed off as he pulled back his right sleeve to reveal a bandage around the lower part of his arm and his wrist. "What happened to you?"

"Long story. It won't slow me down much with my regular work—but all the wrist action needed to paint that huge backdrop?" He shook his head. "That could be tough. I was going to call you later."

BJ caught her lower lip between her teeth. It wasn't that she was unsympathetic to Charley's plight. But she'd only agreed to be in charge of sets and scenery after securing a promise from him that he'd paint the backdrop.

"I'm sorry to have to back out, BJ."

"It's okay." Not really, but what else could she say? It wasn't Charley's fault he'd injured his wrist. "I'll have to ask around, see if I can find someone else to help. I'd do it myself, but while I might be able to draft a mean set of AutoCAD blueprints, I have no artistic talent . . . and I'd hate for this to be amateurish after all the work being put into the show."

Charley pulled some fish out of the cooler with his left hand. "There have to be other options."

"Do you think I could round up a few of the art students from the high school to take over the job?"

"That's a possibility."

"Any recommendations?"

"I know most of the kids, but I can't speak to their painting aptitude. The majority of them take art because they think it's an easy elective. The most talented student I ever knew was . . ." He stopped tossing the vegetables around on the griddle. "You know, now that I think about it, you've probably met him at his dad's house. Eric Nash."

BJ blinked. Eric the attorney was also an artist?
"Are you certain he paints?"

"He used to."

"I don't think he'll be hanging around long,

though." Even as she responded, her mind was racing. Was there a remote chance she could convince him to take over for Charley?

"Doesn't take long to paint a backdrop if you have talent."

"You think he could handle this?"

"Not as well as I could, of course." Charley winked at her and flipped the fish. "But you know the old saying about beggars."

"I suppose I could ask."

"Couldn't hurt." He pulled out three corn tortillas, set them on the counter beside the griddle, and went to work filling them, his back to her.

While she waited, she leaned a shoulder against the side of the white truck and lifted her face. The morning rain had given way once again to blue sky, and warmth seeped into her pores. It was a perfect moment.

If only it could last.

But now, instead of being able to soak up the sun on her patio while she gave Tracy's design project her undivided attention, she had a new worry on her plate.

"Here you go." Charley set her bag on the counter. "Enjoy."

She dug out some bills and passed them over. "Thanks."

"And don't fret too much about that backdrop. I have a feeling Eric will come through for you."

"I hope you're right."

He gave her a thumbs-up with his left hand and greeted a group of tourists who were about to get their first taste of the world's best fish tacos.

Bag in hand, BJ returned to her truck. It was possible the new Eric would agree to help out—although painting a backdrop was a much bigger commitment than fixing a motorbike. Meaning she'd have to come up with a compelling plea. Fast. Who knew how long he planned to hang around Hope Harbor?

She pulled into the flow of traffic and aimed the truck toward home. She wasn't going to change her afternoon plans; she owed Tracy and Michael some preliminary designs.

But while she worked on those, she'd also work on the pitch she planned to make the next time she and Eric met.

Was that *BJ?*

Eric tried not to stare as he and his father slipped into a pew at Grace Christian for the Sunday service—but it was hard not to. The woman seated three pews ahead of them, on the other side of the aisle, was stunning.

He craned his neck.

Yep . . . it was BJ.

Except the worn jeans, T-shirt, tool belt, and baseball cap had been replaced by a silky dress that draped oh-so-nicely over her slender curves. Gone, too, was her customary ponytail. Today, her hair hung full and loose, the blonde strands shimmering in the rays of sun peeking through the windows that lined the walls. When she shifted in her seat to greet a new arrival, he also caught a touch of lipstick and whisper of blush.

Boy, did she clean up nice.

"Eric."

At his father's nudge, he retracted his neck like a turtle. "What?"

"Would you hand me a hymnal?"

"Oh. Sure." He fumbled for one of the books at the end of the pew and passed it over as the organ struck up the opening song.

"Aren't you going to join in?"

"Uh . . . yeah. I guess."

He picked up a book for himself and opened it to the correct page, but the melody was unfamiliar. Some new song that must have been introduced in the past few years, after he stopped attending services.

No matter. He'd just move his lips and keep peeking at BJ.

Halfway through the hymn, almost as if she could sense his scrutiny, she looked over her shoulder.

A sizzle of electricity zipped between them, supercharging the air.

Her eyes widened . . . and her head whipped back to the front.

Eric's fingers crimped the edge of the hymnal.

Wow.

Potent was the only word to describe that searing whoosh of attraction.

And that was *not* an appropriate thought during Sunday service.

Exerting every ounce of his willpower, he transferred his attention to the sanctuary—and for the next hour and fifteen minutes tried as hard as he could to pay attention to the Scripture readings, Reverend Baker's sermon, and the music.

It was a monumental struggle.

So once the organ finally launched into the last chorus of the closing hymn, he conceded the fight and moved on to his next priority—figuring out how to finagle a few minutes in the company of this spit-and-polished BJ.

As it turned out, no finagling was necessary. She approached *them* as his father joined him in the aisle.

"Morning, BJ." His dad smiled at the architect.

"Good morning." She transferred her attention to Eric. "I was hoping to talk with you, if you can spare five minutes."

His dad looked between the two of them. "No problem from my end. It's doughnut Sunday, and I'm in the mood for a sugared jelly. You can find me in the church hall, Eric." Without waiting for a response, he dived into the throng surging toward the door.

"Let's get out of the line of traffic." Eric gestured to an empty pew.

She eased past, close enough for him to catch a whiff of some fresh, pleasing fragrance.

He wrapped his fingers around the edge of the pew and held on tight.

"This won't take long." She sat, leaving a large gap between them.

"No problem. The sole item on my afternoon agenda is a motorbike repair." He claimed the corner of the pew. "Is this about Luis?" Maybe she had a few more pieces of information to add to the story she'd shared during their impromptu lunch. Why else would she waylay him?

"No."

So much for that theory.

She smoothed a hand down the silky fabric of her dress. Tucked her hair behind her ear. Moistened her lips.

His gaze dropped to them . . . and got stuck.

Look up, Nash. Forget her mouth.

Right.

He shifted his attention higher—to the cute sprinkling of freckles spanning the bridge of her nose—and waited for her to continue.

"I hate to bother you with this . . . but I need a favor." She did the lip thing again.

He wedged himself into the corner of the pew to put a bit more distance between them.

It didn't help much.

"Shoot." The word came out rough, and he cleared his throat.

"Do you know anything about Helping Hands?"

"No."

"It's an organization that does what the name says—offers a helping hand to anyone in the community who has a need. It began about six years ago as a joint effort between Grace Christian and St. Francis. Tracy's husband is the director, but everyone else is a volunteer."

"Including you?"

She lifted one shoulder, rippling the silky fabric of her dress. "I help a little. Right now I'm in charge of sets and scenery for a musical being staged as a fundraiser for the organization.

Building the sets is easy. Unfortunately, I have no talent for painting scenery. Charley promised to handle the backdrop, but with his wrist out of commission, he suggested I ask you to take on the job."

Eric tuned in fully to the conversation. "Charley's hurt? What happened to him?"

"I have no idea. I stopped for an order of tacos yesterday around noon, and his wrist was bandaged."

Only a couple of hours after he'd dropped by the studio.

Suspicious.

Was this an attempt by the painter to get him to pick up a brush again, since he'd refused the man's offer to take some supplies?

"Listen, I'm sorry to impose. I know you're dealing with a lot of other challenges and—"

"No." He touched her arm. "Don't apologize for asking someone to help out in a pinch when you're doing charitable work." As far as the legitimacy of Charley's injury was concerned . . . who cared? If he wanted a chance to get better acquainted with the woman beside him, the taco maker had given him the perfect opportunity. "Tell me what's involved. I haven't done any painting in years."

He listened as she described how the backdrop needed to capture the mood and geography of Oklahoma, with a weeping willow, a golden haze on the meadow, and corn as high as an elephant's eye.

"How big are we talking?"

She gave him the dimensions.

"Whoa." He did a slow blink. "I've never painted anything bigger than a sixteen-by-twenty canvas."

"According to Charley, it's the same principle but on a larger scale. He's never done a backdrop, either. I know he planned to rough in the scene on the flats before he started painting."

"Did he do any preliminary sketches?"

"Not that he shared with me, but I doubt it. I think he likes to go with the flow."

That sounded like their resident taco chef.

"What's your time frame?"

"The show's later this month. I already built the flats, mounted them on wheels, and prepped them, so they're ready to be painted. They're in the scene shop at the high school. I'm there most evenings building the sets, but we could arrange to give you access during the day if you decide to take this on and prefer to work then."

"Evenings are fine for me." Especially if that's when she was there.

"Does that mean . . . is that a yes?"

Was it?

Eric glanced toward the sanctuary. He'd come to Hope Harbor to regroup and chart a new course for his law career—not to paint sets for a show . . .

or paint, period. Nor had he planned to get involved with a despondent Cuban immigrant. Or meet a beautiful, intriguing woman.

Nothing on this trip had gone as he'd expected.

Yet what had his father said the day he'd arrived? Some trite phrase about good things coming your way if you were open to new opportunities.

Given all that had happened in the past few days, perhaps the saying was more true than trite.

And since he didn't exactly have a packed agenda, why not lend a hand? If he researched backdrop painting techniques, he ought to be able to pull this off—while clocking some one-on-one time with the woman beside him.

If there was a downside to the scenario, it eluded him.

He turned back to her. "It's a yes—but I'm no Charley. Don't expect miracles."

"It's miracle enough there's someone else in town who's willing—and able—to tackle this job." Her eyes lit up, illuminating her face and enhancing her already considerable beauty. "And I trust Charley. He wouldn't have recommended you if he didn't think you could handle the job."

"Let's hope he's right." The church had grown quiet, and he swept a hand around the empty pews. "We appear to be the laggards here."

"Everyone else made a beeline for the doughnuts."

"Can I interest you in one?"

"No thanks. I have some errands to run—and I try to avoid high-fat food. It's bad for the arteries . . . and the waistline."

He gave her a swift perusal. "You don't look as if you need to worry about the latter."

"That's because I do." She rose—leaving him no choice but to do the same.

"I'd like to see the flats ASAP, get a visual sense of the scale."

"No problem. I'll be diving back into the sets this afternoon about two, if you want to swing by."

"That works."

She followed him out of the pew and struck off for the back door.

Hard as he tried, he couldn't think of a single reason to delay her departure.

"I'll see you this afternoon." She kept walking as they emerged to a fine mist and a sky more gray than blue. It seemed the clouds had won in their earlier game of hide-and-seek with the sun.

"Count on it."

After flashing him a quick smile, she hurried down the steps and veered off toward the parking lot.

Once she disappeared from view, Eric wandered toward the church hall. There might be a few of the sugared confections left. He was in the mood for a sweet treat.

Of course, that would be waiting for him later at the high school if he missed out here.

Grinning, he ducked back inside to escape the mist, pretty certain BJ would *not* appreciate that thought.

As for the ambitious project he'd agreed to take on . . . his grin faded and his pace slowed. The town's resident artist might think he could pull off a backdrop, but he doubted the finished product would be up to the professional standards of a Charley original. Whatever talent he might once have had could have decayed from years of neglect.

Too late now to back out, however.

He stopped by the door to the sanctuary . . . debated for a moment . . . then slipped back inside to ask the Almighty for a little assistance.

And pray he wasn't getting in way over his head.

It felt odd to skip Sunday Mass—and Elena would be disappointed in him.

But how could a man who was still considering taking a walk off a cliff go to church . . . and face God?

Luis lowered himself to the edge of the lumpy bed where he spent more nights tossing than sleeping. Wiped a hand down his face. He'd kept his promise to Eric Nash. Shown up for work on Friday, eaten the breakfast John had prepared. There was no reason he couldn't follow through on his interrupted plans from Thursday night. He'd be undisturbed in rainy weather like this.

Except—Eric had spent all day Friday . . . and probably a large part of his weekend . . . working on the motorbike. Going out of his way to atone for the green card incident, to show kindness to a stranger. If Luis followed through on his plan now, would the man wonder if the green card incident had been the catalyst for disaster?

Perhaps.

And guilt was a terrible burden to bear.

Stomach twisting, he touched the photo of Elena he'd set on the nightstand. He knew all about guilt. Add in grief and despair and hopelessness . . . who could be expected to persevere in the face of all that?

Even God seemed to have deserted him.

Pressure built behind his eyes, and moisture seeped out the corners. Wrong as it might be, when only an empty future stretched before you, escape tempted with a seductive, powerful appeal.

Swiping away the dampness with the back of his hand, he stood.

It was time to take a walk.

He grabbed his jacket off the foot of the bed, started for the door . . . and froze as the putt-putt-putt of a well-tuned motorbike seeped in through the sliver of open window.

Jacket in hand, he crossed to the blinds and tipped one of the working slats.

Eric was tooling up the drive on his motor-bike.

Frowning, Luis let the slat drop back into place. What was going on? The plan had been for him to retrieve his bike tomorrow at John's, after work.

A knock sounded on his door, but Luis didn't move. He was *not* in the mood for company.

"Sorry to disturb you, Luis." Eric's voice came across loud and clear through the hollow-core door. "I don't mean to intrude, but the bike's ready and I thought you might like to have it back today. I don't want to leave the key in it."

He spoke as if he knew the apartment was occupied.

And he probably did if he'd noticed the slat on the blinds opening and closing.

Sighing, Luis raked his fingers through his hair. It was stupid to ignore the man. He could get rid of him fast. How long would it take to say thanks and accept the key?

He trudged to the door, flipped the lock, and twisted the knob.

"I apologize for showing up unannounced." Eric smiled and held out the key. "I finished the bike and did a test run. I don't think it will give you any more trouble. I was afraid it might be the carburetor or your fuel injection pump, but she just had a blown fuse and some fouled spark plugs. I cleaned all the plugs, replaced one of them, and put in a new fuse. You're good to go."

Luis tried to follow the explanation but stumbled over all the unfamiliar words.

One thing he did understand, though—this repair had cost some money. New parts weren't free.

He reached for his wallet. "Thank you. How much is the cost?"

"No charge. I enjoyed tinkering with the bike, and the body shop that's repairing my car gave me the parts I needed while I was there yesterday getting an update."

"They give you the parts?" Would a business be that generous?

"For what my repair is costing, they can afford to throw in a few freebies." A gust of wind whipped past, and he angled away from the billow of mist that enveloped him. "I'd suggest you take a spin, but given the weather, you might want to wait until later."

All at once, Eric's damp state registered. A sheen of moisture had glossed his hair, and his T-shirt was clinging to his chest. "Did you ride here in the rain?"

"It wasn't raining when I left." He shrugged, and one side of his mouth hiked up. "That's the Oregon coast for you."

Luis scanned the deserted parking lot. "Are you walking back to town?"

"No. My dad's going to swing by in about ten minutes to pick me up."

A second wave of mist surged toward the door —and Eric. If this kept up, he'd be drenched long before John arrived.

Luis expelled a breath. He didn't want to invite the man into his room, but what other choice did he have? After all Eric had done, it would be wrong to leave him standing in the rain.

Stepping back, he pulled the door wide. "You can wait in here until he comes."

"Thanks." Eric entered at once and moved to the center of the room, giving it a quick but thorough scrutiny.

Although his expression remained neutral, Luis knew what he was thinking: the efficiency apartment might be neat and as clean as possible, but the place was a dump.

And his unexpected visitor's conclusion was spot on.

Not that he *had* to live in a place like this. He could afford a slight upgrade if he didn't send as much money to his father-in-law. But as long as there was breath in his body, he'd honor his promise to Elena. The one that had erased the final stumbling block to their escape.

The one he now regretted making.

Pressure built in his throat again. Perhaps if he'd balked at her request, she would have refused to leave. They might not have realized their dream of creating a new life in America, but they'd still have a life together.

Reining in his emotions, he indicated the sole upholstered chair. "You will sit?"

Eric eyed it, then crossed to the straight-backed chair beside the bed. "This is fine." He dropped into it, glancing at the photo on the nightstand. He didn't speak, but Luis heard the implied question.

"That is . . . was . . . my wife, Elena." He perched on the edge of the bed. "She die ten months ago. While we come to America."

"I'm sorry." The words were rote, but they were laced with compassion.

Luis gently picked up the photo and cradled it in his hand. "It has been hard." His words rasped.

"Too hard at times, I imagine."

At Eric's soft comment, Luis sighed. No sense denying what they both knew. This man had stood beside him on the cliff. "Yes."

Eric clasped his hands together and leaned forward. "America is a great place, Luis. And Hope Harbor is special. People here care about one another. They watch out for each other. You'll make friends. Life will get better. Not every day will be gray and depressing, like this one." He waved a hand toward the window.

Ah. Now he understood why Eric had delivered the motorbike in such dicey weather instead of waiting until tomorrow. Their client's son had been afraid today's dreariness would induce BJ's Cuban carpenter to finish the job he'd begun that night on the cliff.

Luis looked down at his clasped hands. "Some days, I am not certain that is true." The soft admission, never before spoken, hung heavy in the somber room.

"I know." It was clear they were both through pretending. "But I don't want you to have any more of those days. Tell me how I can help."

Luis furrowed his brow, trying to fathom the man's motivation. "Why do you care?"

"Because I believe in the golden rule."

Based on the evidence, that was true—and it was commendable. Few people sought opportunities to get involved in someone else's problems.

"I am grateful for your offer." He left it at that.

After a few beats of silence ticked by, Eric spoke again. "But . . . ?"

But there is nothing anyone can do.

He watched the rain streak down the window. Elena was gone. His medical career was gone. He was a refugee in a foreign land, where he would live out what remained of his life alone—a doctor eking out a living as a simple carpenter who yearned for the woman he loved and a dream that could never be.

This man, however, knew none of that. Nor was he likely to understand how dark the world could be for someone who'd risked everything— and lost.

"Luis . . ." As Eric said his name, he shifted his

attention back to his visitor. "Please let me help."

"It is enough that you offer. You cannot fix all the broken things in my life."

"I might be able to fix some of them."

The attorney had persistence—and determination. He didn't seem inclined to leave without some assurance that a positive outcome was possible.

"Let me think on this." It was the best he could offer.

Parallel grooves dented Eric's forehead. It was clear he wanted to push—and also clear he didn't want to provoke. Luis understood that dilemma. He'd dealt with many young doctors on ER rotations during his medical career who wanted answers to questions that had none. Who toiled for outcomes that were impossible to guarantee and beat themselves up if they failed, unwilling to accept that not every problem was fixable.

Eric spoke at last. "Will you make me another promise?"

"Breakfast tomorrow?" Somehow Luis managed a small smile.

"No—but you're welcome if my dad is cooking. I just want you to promise that if you decide to . . . to do anything more than think . . . you'll talk to Father Kevin."

The same advice Elena would offer if she were here.

But talking to a priest . . . that would be difficult.

He was not a man who shared his emotions with other people.

Except Elena.

"I do not know if I can promise that."

The clipped beep of a horn sounded outside, and a flash of panic whipped across Eric's face. "That's my dad. Look . . . if you won't call Father Kevin, call me, okay?" He found a pen in his pocket, pulled out a scrap of paper, and jotted down some numbers. "We'll go out for coffee or . . . or something. Anytime, day or night. I could use a friendly ear myself after losing my job."

Luis stared at him. "I did not know that."

"I'll work it out. I'm more worried about . . . other things."

Like the Cuban refugee toiling in his father's house.

In light of that, how could Luis refuse the man's request?

"I will call."

Relief chased the tension from Eric's features. He rose and held out his hand. "Thank you. If the bike gives you any more trouble, let me know."

"I will. And thank *you*." He grasped the man's fingers and returned his firm shake.

At the door, Eric stopped. "I'll see you tomorrow."

"Yes. I will be there."

After one more quick appraisal, he dipped his chin and plunged into the foul weather.

Luis remained where he was until a car door slammed. Then he walked over to the blinds and lifted a slat. John Nash's car had reached the end of the drive and was accelerating onto the main road. A few moments later, it disappeared in the mist.

He let the slat fall.

There would be no walk to the cliff in his immediate future, after all.

He wandered back to the bed and sat again. Funny how an unwanted visit from a man he hadn't known a week ago could alter his plans so dramatically—and stir up the embers of warmth in his heart once again.

And for some strange reason, he had a feeling that maybe, just maybe, the warmth might linger this time.

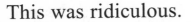

— 9 —

This was ridiculous.

Huffing out a breath, BJ jammed the lid back on the lipstick and shoved the tube in the pocket of her jeans. She *never* wore makeup while working on a construction project.

And she wasn't going to start today.

Jaw set, she grabbed her hammer. If Eric hadn't promised to stop by the high school this afternoon to check out the flats, she wouldn't even have brought the stupid lipstick—a mistake from the get-go. Impressing the out-of-work attorney was *not* on her agenda.

Even if he'd turned out to be nicer than she'd expected after their first less-than-cordial encounter.

Even if he'd bailed her out on the backdrop for the show and fixed Luis's motorbike.

Even if sparks had been flying this morning in that pew faster than a puffin diving for dinner.

Not all tall, dark, and handsome men were cast from the same mold as her LA beau, of course—but it was too early in the game to be certain about Eric. And an ace attorney who'd been on a partner track wasn't going to hang around a town the size of Hope Harbor long enough for her to get a solid read on his character.

Yet another reason to walk a wide circle around him.

Getting involved with someone who was just passing through would be a disaster.

And she was done with disasters.

She pounded a nail into the farmhouse façade—and kept pounding until she heard the door behind her open fifteen minutes later.

Her hammer missed its mark . . . and barely missed her thumb.

Squeezing the handle, she kept her back to the door and closed her eyes.

Chill out, BJ. Play it cool. In five or ten minutes, he'll be out of here and you can get back to work without any distractions.

But when she swiveled around, one honking big distraction wearing worn jeans, a chest-hugging T-shirt, and a killer smile was walking her way.

Oh, mercy!

She restrained the urge to fan herself.

"Hi." He skirted some sawhorses, dodged an unpainted set of shutters, circled a crude table and stool that were destined for one of the set pieces, and stopped a few feet away.

"Hi." Her greeting came out in a squeak, and she swiveled around to wave toward the flats for the backdrop—and hide the surge of warmth on her cheeks. "There's your canvas."

"I knew the dimensions, but seeing it in person

157

is . . . intimidating." He strolled over to the blank backdrop.

She stayed where she was.

Distance was good.

"A backdrop doesn't have to have a lot of fine detail. No one in the audience will be closer to it than twenty, twenty-five feet." She wiped the damp palm of her free hand down her jeans. "If you'll put together a list of supplies, I'll pick them up for you. The high school said we could use the drama department's tarps to protect the floor."

"I can get what I need." He continued to examine the expanse of white, his back to her.

"Okay—but keep your receipts. Helping Hands will reimburse you."

"Paint and brushes don't cost a lot. Consider it my contribution."

"Your contribution is your talent."

"Are you handing in all *your* receipts?" He pivoted toward her.

He would ask that.

"I have lots of spare stuff from jobs."

"That's what I figured." He ambled over to inspect her work-in-progress. "What are you building?"

"The façade of a farmhouse. Also the interior of a smokehouse." She motioned toward another large set piece.

"Are you doing this alone?"

"Stone stops by if I need extra muscle. Other than that, it's a one-person job—and I enjoy working by myself."

"Mmm." He held up a sketch pad she hadn't noticed until now. "I might be inspired if I sit in front of that vast empty expanse for a few minutes. I don't want to disturb you, but would it be okay if I hung around for a while and did some doodling?"

Having him nearby would disturb her plenty—but that wasn't a thought she cared to share. And there was no other reason to deny his request.

"As long as hammering and sawing won't bother you."

"I'm getting used to that, after living in a construction zone." An engaging dimple dented his cheek, spiking her pulse again.

She took a step back and swept a hand toward the flats. "Then have at it. There are some folding chairs stacked in the corner if you want to sit."

"I'll be fine."

With that, he retreated to the canvas and dropped onto the floor to sit cross-legged.

BJ watched him for a moment, then continued assembling the porch on the front of the farm-house—although twice in the next five minutes she gave him a quick peek over her shoulder. Both times his head was bent, his arm moving.

At least one of them was engaged in the job at hand.

To eliminate the temptation to steal any more glimpses, she released the brakes on the rolling scenery wagon and rotated it, blocking her view of the man on the floor.

Better.

She reset the brakes and went back to work.

Forty-five minutes later, he peeked around the side of the house. "I thought I'd lost you."

She pushed her safety goggles to the top of her head. "I, uh, swivel sometimes to get the best light." True . . . but not in this case.

"Want to see what I have?" He held up the sketch pad.

"Sure." She stowed her drill under a sawhorse.

"I set up two folding chairs by the flats." Without waiting for her to respond, he disappeared around the farmhouse.

She held back. A cozy tête-à-tête sitting shoulder to shoulder might give her legs a break, but it was going to play havoc with her respiration.

Still, what choice did she have?

Bracing herself, she followed. He'd already reached the chairs and picked up a can of soda. There was one resting on the seat of the other chair too.

"Where'd you get these?" She bent and picked up a Diet Sprite.

"A machine in the cafeteria. They must keep it stocked through the summer. I hope that's all right." He tapped the side of her soda. "I noticed you always seem to have some of these on hand at Dad's."

The man paid attention to her preferences?

Another mark in his positive column. Todd had never been able to remember from date to date whether she liked her lattes with or without whip, and he . . .

She frowned.

That was peculiar.

For months, she'd been blocking the jerk's name from her mind. Why had it popped up now . . . and with nary a blip on her stress meter?

"If you'd prefer a different kind, I can—"

"No. This is fine." She released the tab. "Thank you."

"Then on to the unveiling." He circled his own chair while she sat. "First requirement, though—if these sketches stink, you have to tell me straight up. Agreed?"

Her lips twitched at his bluntness. "I doubt they're going to stink."

"They might. And you won't hurt my feelings. I've been away from art for years, and I'll be happy to start over if these aren't what you envisioned."

"Are *you* happy with what you have?"

He lifted one shoulder. "Artists aren't always the best judge of their own work. I think these are on the right track—but they're rough."

"So are those." She lifted her can toward the

three-dimensional set pieces. "I don't mind rough. I may not be able to draw, but I can visualize."

"An aptitude that will come in handy with these." He jiggled the pad, a twinkle sparking in his coffee-colored eyes as he sat.

Whew.

This guy was seriously hot.

She wrapped her fingers around the cold can, hoping she didn't overheat the contents. "I have a feeling you're underselling your skills."

"Don't bet on that." He set his soda on the floor, flipped back the cover of the sketch pad, and positioned the page so both of them could see it.

At first glance, she concurred with his assessment. The drawing was rough. But it did contain all the requisite elements they'd discussed—the willow, the suggestion of a haze, the fields of tall corn.

The closer she examined it, however, the more she saw. A weathered, split-rail fence; fluffy clouds; a small pond in the distance; some grazing cattle; the hint of another outbuilding. All his enhancements added to the charm of the scene. And despite the sketchiness of the drawing, it was clear the man had talent. The perspective, scale, shadows . . . all were spot-on.

"It's not what you were expecting, is it?" Eric's teasing tone was at odds with the hint of uncertainty rippling through his words.

Her stand-in backdrop painter honestly didn't realize how talented he was.

BJ turned to him. "No—it's a thousand percent better. Don't tell Charley I said this, but no way could he have beat this. I love all the extra elements you added."

"Would you like to see a few more? I roughed in some detail sketches too. A lot of audience members won't catch the smaller touches, but those who do will get a kick out of them."

"Absolutely."

He flipped through the next few pages in silence, and BJ found herself smiling at his whimsical embellishments. A scarecrow in the distance wearing a Helping Hands T-shirt stuffed with straw. A nest in the willow filled with hatchlings, their beaks open and awaiting the next meal. A cat sleeping on a sunny rock, a butterfly perched on his nose. Saddlebags hanging on the fencepost, the leg from a pair of long johns trailing out.

Every sketch was amusing and fanciful—and not at all what she'd expected from a high-end attorney who spent his days litigating on behalf of international corporate clients.

Eric closed the tablet. "That's a first pass, anyway."

"First and final. I wouldn't change a thing."

"Nice to hear. My ego thanks you. Do you need to get approval from anyone else on these?"

"No, but I'd like to share them with the director. I know he'll be as thrilled as I am. May I keep them until tomorrow?"

"Sure." He handed her the sketchbook. "And speaking of tomorrow, you don't need to pick up Luis in the morning. I finished his motorbike and delivered it this afternoon."

Another nice gesture.

The man was full of surprises these past few days.

"You didn't have to do that."

"I didn't mind. It's not far." He stood. "I better let you get back to work. Assuming your director doesn't have any issues with my sketches, I'd like to dive into the flats tomorrow evening. Will you be here?"

"That's the plan." She stood too. "The cast needs the set pieces for dress rehearsal week, so I'll be here every night until they're finished."

"What time?"

"No later than seven, unless I get delayed. I can verify that tomorrow before I leave your dad's."

"That works. In the meantime, I'll round up some supplies. Finished with that?" He reached for her can.

"Yes. Thanks."

"Good luck with those." He tipped his head toward the two large set pieces. "Better you than me on that project. I might be able to simulate three dimensions on canvas, but creating real three dimensions? Not my talent."

"In that case, we should make a great team."

His eyes warmed. Darkened. "I think you might be right."

Her heart skipped a beat. He was talking about creating theatrical sets—wasn't he?

Of course he was. They'd only met five days ago, for crying out loud. And they were both too old to allow a little electricity to short-circuit common sense.

"Well . . ." She eased away. "Back to work for me."

"Until tomorrow." He hefted one of the empty cans in salute and headed for the exit.

She waited until he disappeared, then sagged against the smokehouse. It shifted behind her, and she scrambled to maintain her balance. Her own fault. She must have forgotten to set the brake on the wagon.

And that was a prudent reminder.

Because unless she put the brakes on the magnetic attraction she felt for Eric Nash, she could very well lose her balance and fall flat on her face.

Again.

Squaring her shoulders, she leaned down and locked the brakes on the wagon with more force than necessary. There would be no more starry-eyed disasters for her. If she ever decided to dip her toes in the waters of romance again, she would take it slow and cautious.

So until she got a better handle on the real Eric Nash—and his plans for the future—she'd stay a safe distance away from the appealing attorney.

Strange how quickly a person could be forgotten.

Eric rested his elbow on the kitchen table and scanned the screen on his laptop. Not a single new email. True, it was Sunday . . . yet in Portland, dozens of messages had come in each day— including Christmas. For partner-track attorneys, every day was a workday.

But he wasn't a partner-track attorney any-more.

Tamping down a surge of melancholy, he closed his email and googled scenic backdrops. Perhaps some research would distract him and chase away the blues.

"Am I interrupting anything?" His dad entered and retrieved a mug from the cabinet.

"Nope. I'm just googling. Before that, I was checking email."

"I bet that takes awhile." His dad shook some coffee into a filter.

"Not anymore. My inbox was empty, which is different. I used to be drowning in messages— 90 percent of them tagged *urgent*."

"Were they?"

"Depends on your perspective, I guess."

His dad held up the bag of coffee. "Want me to add some for you? It's decaf, if you're worried about sleeping."

"Sure." He rose and got a mug for himself.

"How's your perspective now that you've been home for a few days?" His father poured water into the coffeemaker.

"I'm still too wired to give that a fair answer."

"I expect it will take some time for you to decompress." His father leaned against the counter and folded his arms. "You know, I have to confess I've been worried about you these past couple of years. You've been so intent on making partner I was afraid the rest of life was passing you by."

Eric opened the fridge and removed the half-and-half. "It was—but that's par for the course if you're on the partner track."

"Well, maybe you'll have a chance to do a few different things while you're here. Broaden your perspective."

"Funny you should say that. I've already been sucked into a painting project, thanks to your architect. I was researching it when you came in." He gave his dad a quick overview.

"Now that sounds like fun—and right up your alley. You've loved art since you were a tyke. I thought you might even pursue it as a career. You sure spent a lot of hours in Charley's studio as a teen."

"For fun, not to pay the bills. Law is a much more stable career . . . or so I assumed."

The coffee began to sputter, and his dad held out a hand for his mug. "It should have been. But medicine should be too—and look where Luis ended up. I don't know that it's common knowledge, but he was a doctor in Cuba."

"I heard."

"From who?" His dad filled the mug and gave it back, curiosity etched on his features.

Uh-oh.

"Um, BJ told me—but I'd appreciate it if you'd keep that to yourself. It was shared in confidence."

"Is that right?" His dad filled his own mug, eyes glinting with interest. "I didn't know you two had gotten chummy enough to be sharing confidences."

Backpedal, Nash.

"We haven't. I wanted some history on Luis, and she provided it."

"You're not still stuck in that green card rut, are you?" His dad's tone suggested he better not be.

"No. I had another reason for wanting to know." He busied himself diluting his coffee with the half-and-half. "How did *you* find out about Luis's background?"

"He told me. I ran into him in town one Saturday and introduced him to Charley's tacos.

We had a long chat on a bench by the wharf. He's had some tough breaks."

"I know."

"It appears BJ told you quite a lot about our Cuban friend."

He passed the half-and-half to his dad. "Enough to know he's been through a lot." Time to get this conversation back on track. "Speaking of Charley . . . I dropped by the studio yesterday."

"I didn't think it would take you long to wander out there. Are you planning to do any painting while you're here—other than the backdrop?"

"No. What's the point?"

"You have talent—and you enjoy it."

"Once I connect with a new law firm, I'll be back on the sixty-hour-a-week schedule. No sense starting something I can't continue."

His dad added a smidgen of sugar to his coffee. "How do you feel about returning to that grind?"

He shrugged. "It's what I do."

"That's not an answer."

Eric mulled over the question while he took a sip from his mug. He'd never thought much about his brutal schedule. Long hours were expected, so he clocked them.

Yet all at once, the notion of diving back into a whirlwind of activity that left no time for anything . . . or anyone . . . didn't hold a lot of appeal.

Not an insight he was ready to admit to his father—or perhaps even to himself.

"It is what it is, Dad. Law is what I do."

"It doesn't have to be all-consuming, does it?"

"If I want to be a partner somewhere, yes—and I've been working toward that goal since the day I entered law school."

"A goal is different than a dream."

"Dreams don't put food on the table."

"Always practical and prudent." His dad gave him a gentle smile. "You know, sometimes you sound just like your mother."

"Is that bad?"

"Not at all. The world needs practical, prudent people to balance the dreamers—as does every marriage."

"Are you suggesting Mom was the practical one in your marriage?"

"Without question."

"What about that nine-to-five job you had in Coos Bay for thirty-five years, directing HR for a very stable company? The one that gave you a regular paycheck, generous benefits, and a nice retirement? You never did anything that was impractical or risky."

"Doesn't mean I didn't want to." His father sat at the kitchen table.

Eric gripped his mug with both hands and joined him. This trip home continued to be fraught with surprises. How could he not know this about the man he'd shared a house with for eighteen years?

"What are you talking about?"

"I had dreams, Eric."

"And Mom didn't let you follow them?"

"No—that's not what I meant. Don't ever think I held one smidgen of resentment toward your mom. She was a wonderful woman, with the biggest heart of anyone I ever met. The love we shared was . . ." His voice choked, and he swallowed. "All I can say is, I hope someday you're blessed enough to find someone who will fill your life with joy the way your mother filled mine."

"Then what *did* you mean about having dreams?"

His father leaned back, cradling the mug in his hands, his expression wistful. "Many years ago, when you were eight or nine, a piece of property came on the market that I'd been eyeing for years. I wanted to buy it and build a small inn. The hospitality industry had always appealed to me. I couldn't think of a better way to spend my workday than creating happy memories for guests, and I was certain I could make a go of it."

"Mom didn't share your optimism?"

"She liked the idea, but her impoverished background made her risk averse. Security was important to her. To pull off my dream, we would have had to cash in the nest egg we'd been building as a cushion for our retirement. She was afraid to take such a speculative chance—and she was right. I had a wife and young son and a mortgage and bills to pay. Those needed to be my first priorities. The dream was fine; the timing was wrong."

But now it wasn't.

Suddenly, the impetus behind the B&B project became clear.

"I'm glad you're finally getting to realize a piece of it."

His dad smiled. "So am I." He finished his coffee and stood. "And since the work crew will be here bright and early to continue bringing that dream to life, I'm going to turn in."

"I won't be far behind you."

"You want me to rinse out the pot, or would you like another cup?"

"I'll finish it off. You always did make great coffee."

His father moved to the sink and washed out his mug. "Let's hope my future B&B guests agree."

"They will."

After a quick inventory of the fridge, his dad crossed to the door of the new addition that housed his bedroom and office. At the threshold, he stopped. "I know this has been a rough week for you, son . . . but it's possible what happened isn't the disaster it first appeared to be. In fact, it might be a gift. I have every confidence that with your credentials, another partner-track spot will open up for you—if that's what you want. But if you have any desire to alter your course, you've been given the opportunity to consider that. Don't waste it."

He closed the door behind him, leaving Eric alone in the silent kitchen—more confused than he'd been in years.

Could his dad be right? Was this an opportunity rather than a disaster?

And if it was, what was he supposed to do with it? Prudence and practicality had led him to law, and that career was an excellent fit for his skills. He'd never second-guessed his choice.

But truth be told, he'd never had the same passion for law that he'd had for painting. It was interesting, and he was proficient at it, but the excitement he'd felt in the scene shop this afternoon as he'd faced that blank canvas . . . there was nothing like creative energy to juice the joy and make a person feel fully alive.

The coffeepot sputtered, and he rose to refill his mug, emptying the pot.

Too bad he couldn't channel that creative energy into a career.

And too bad he didn't have his father's adventurous spirit. The mere thought of taking a leap in a brand-new, untried direction scared him silly.

Still . . . other people did it.

Like BJ.

After shutting off the coffeemaker, he wandered

back to the table. What had compelled her to give up a position with an architectural firm in LA and move to a tiny town to launch her own business? That must have required a huge leap of faith.

He sat, set the mug beside him, and googled her name. The web might offer some answers.

A scroll through the meager hits did give him some new information—the name of her boutique firm, which worked with an impressive array of prestigious clients; a promotion notice in a business column; a press release about her winning an award from the local American Institute of Architects chapter.

But none of those explained why she'd left.

He leaned back and steepled his fingers. It took a lot of years and a lot of hard work to become an accredited architect. Based on the information on his screen, BJ had been on a career track similar to his, rising through the ranks in her profession toward a top slot.

Had she been downsized, like him? Pushed out?

Possible—but not likely. From all indications, her firm was thriving.

Meaning she must have chosen to leave.

He tapped his index fingers together. Might her reasons for making that choice help him sort through his own situation?

Maybe—but would she share them if he asked?

Downing the last of his coffee, Eric sat forward

again. From what he'd observed, BJ was a very private person. Getting her to open up about her past could be a major challenge.

But perhaps during the hours they'd be spending together in the scene shop, she'd loosen up—especially if he did a stellar job on that backdrop.

His next order of business.

He googled the subject, prepared to prep for this project as diligently as he'd prepped for any of the cases that had landed on his desk in Portland. Winning BJ's favor was a goal worth pursuing with singular focus.

For reasons that were both professional . . . and personal.

— *10* —

BJ picked up the last piece of gingerbread trim for the porch of the farmhouse, positioned it in place, and felt around in the pouch on her belt for another screw.

Empty.

Expelling a breath, she clumped down the ladder and scrounged around in her toolbox. This had *not* been her most productive session— thanks to the man on the other side of the set piece, who was roughing in the scene he was going to paint on the flats.

It should have been easy to forget about the charming attorney. She couldn't see him. She couldn't hear him. She couldn't smell that sophisticated aftershave he wore, with its subtle hint of sandalwood.

But boy, could she sense his presence. It was almost palpable—and heady enough to be illegal.

Her fingers closed over a screw, and she stood, resisting the urge to check on his progress. Getting an eyeful of him would only rattle her more.

Instead, she ascended the ladder and squeezed the trigger on her screw gun to secure the trim.

Done.

At least one unit was ready for painting.

And if all went well in the next couple of hours,

she'd make decent headway on the smokehouse before this Monday ended.

She descended the ladder and eased toward the edge of the house. Could she cross the open territory between here and the other unit without Eric noticing her and flashing that killer dimple of his?

Better get the lay of the land before sneaking out, even at the risk of elevating her heart rate.

She peeked around the farmhouse.

Hmm.

Not bad for a first foray into backdrop painting.

In the two hours since they'd arrived, he'd roughed in about half the scene.

As for him noticing her . . . unlikely. He appeared to be engrossed in his work.

She gathered up a few tools and tiptoed toward the smokehouse—only to have her phone trill halfway across the expanse.

Drat.

Eric turned toward her at once.

Double drat.

"Sorry to disturb your concentration." She set the tools on the floor and pulled out her cell.

Michael Hunter's name was on her screen.

Could this be a verdict from the Helping Hands board already?

Pulse accelerating, she strode toward the far corner of the scene shop and put the phone to her ear as they exchanged greetings.

Please, God, let this be good news.

Michael got straight to business. "I heard from all of the board members about your proposal. Do you have a few minutes?"

"Sure." She rested a hand on the edge of the faux stone bridge that had been used in the high school's production of *Brigadoon*—and prayed her dream wasn't about to vanish like that mythical Scottish town.

"Everyone liked the concept and agreed it has a lot of merit. We all know a number of seniors in town who might be interested in a program like this."

The words were positive; the subtle undercurrent wasn't.

Her stomach kinked, and she squeezed the cell. "I sense a 'but' coming."

"There *were* some concerns."

No doubt instigated by that grump who'd been such a naysayer the day she'd made her presentation.

"Serious ones?"

"Serious enough. There was general concern about liability for the organization if Helping Hands facilitates a match that goes south. What happens if there's a theft, for example? Or an accident with injuries?"

"Background checks would have to be part of the screening process, as I noted in my proposal—and both parties would have to verify their insurance policies were up to date."

"I agree background checks would be mandatory—but unfortunately, they don't guarantee a person's character. In terms of liability issues . . . insurance, as well as the contract you recommended, could cover some of those. But the board also raised issues of administrative time and costs, including legal fees."

She couldn't argue with the admin issue. The program would require management.

As for costs—background checks were inexpensive, but if the board wanted an attorney to not only develop the basic contract but review the section that would be personalized for each pairing, that could get pricey.

Unless . . .

"We might be able to find a lawyer who would be willing to develop the boilerplate contract and review individual contracts gratis." She sent a speculative glance toward Eric—and found him watching her.

He turned away immediately and went back to work.

She swiveled around too. What a dumb idea. The man was a short-timer in town.

"Did you have someone in mind?" Michael sounded hopeful.

If only.

"No."

"No one on the board could come up with a

candidate, either. Rick Jenson was a competent lawyer, and he might have been willing to volunteer for the job if he hadn't gone to live with his daughter in Utah after he retired. The closest attorneys now are in Coos Bay, and they have no vested interest in Hope Harbor. It may be hard to find a volunteer unless they have a connection to the town."

She gave her scene-shop neighbor another surreptitious scan. Even if he might be willing to help while he was here, they needed someone who would commit long term. Who knew how long he'd hang around—or where he'd end up? He might accept a job with a firm on the other side of the country. A task like this could be managed long-distance—but it didn't sound like the sort of work he did allowed much, if any, free time.

He was *not* a solution to this problem.

Turning aside, she responded to Michael's comment. "I could make some cold calls. I might be able to round up someone who'd be willing to donate a few hours a month. Once the boilerplate contract is developed, the customized section for each new arrangement is all that would have to be reviewed . . . and it isn't as if we'll be doing a dozen of these a year."

"That's true—and cold calls might be worth a try. But there was one other concern that's a bit more difficult to overcome."

BJ braced. This was the biggest stumbling block; she could feel it in her bones.

"I know you searched for examples of programs similar to the one you're proposing, and there don't appear to be any. A number of board members aren't comfortable implementing a project that has no track record anywhere, especially in light of the other issues that were brought up."

BJ rubbed her forehead, where an ache was beginning to throb. "If everyone felt like that, nothing new would ever be tried."

"I agree—and I personally think your idea is worth pursuing. If you'd like to talk with the board members again after you think about their feedback, I'll be happy to put you on our agenda."

What was the point? She had nothing new to offer that might convince them to give the program a chance.

"Let me think about that."

"Consider it a standing invitation. And I want you to know your efforts on behalf of Helping Hands are much appreciated. Every single board member asked me to express their thanks for all you do for the organization."

"I'm happy to help where I can. The group does wonderful work."

"And we're always open to suggestions for new opportunities to serve. That's why I'm not letting go of your idea yet. I intend to give the whole notion a lot more thought—and I hope you will too. There has to be a way to put some legs under the concept."

At least Michael wasn't writing it off.

Too bad the rest of the board had.

And getting the foot-dragging members to change their minds could be an insurmountable challenge.

After they said their good-byes, BJ remained in the corner of the scene shop, her back to the room. All those hours of thinking and research, of developing a program that would benefit some of Hope Harbor's longest-term residents—with nothing to show for it.

The wall in front of her blurred, and she leaned against the bridge. The program *could* work. She was certain of it. Yes, there was some risk despite all the screening she'd suggested, but that shouldn't be a deal breaker. There was risk in everything.

If only she could convince the board of that—or better yet, find a similar program somewhere with a demonstrated track record.

Neither of those seemed likely, however.

Meaning that unless she was hit with a blinding bolt of inspiration, her idea was dead in the water.

It looked like her call was over—and BJ was not a happy camper.

Eric roughed in another stalk of corn, keeping

one eye on the architect. Gone was the feisty woman who'd confronted him the day he'd hit her truck, and who'd taken him to task for badgering Luis. On those occasions, sparks and spunk had been pinging off her. Now, every angle of her wilted posture suggested defeat.

Whatever news she'd received must have been very bad.

He added some leaves to the stalk with a few long strokes, keeping her in sight. Should he ignore her obvious distress—or step in and risk a rebuff?

As he debated that question, she turned toward him . . . and once he caught the shimmer in her eyes, the decision was a no-brainer.

He wiped his hands on a rag and moved toward her, stopping a few feet away. "You okay?"

"Yeah."

That was a lie. She looked as if someone had kicked her in the stomach.

"I don't think I'm buying that."

She dipped her chin and tucked her phone back in its pouch on her tool belt. "I'll be fine. Listen, if you're getting tired, you don't have to hang around. It's been a long night."

Was she being considerate—or trying to ditch him?

"You've got to be more tired than I am." He kept his tone conversational, trying to gauge her intent. "You put in a full day of physical labor.

All I did was go to the paint store and take a walk on the beach."

She lifted one shoulder. "I'm used to it. The stuff I'm doing here is easy." She ran her fingers over the faux stone on the bridge. "To be honest, though, I'm kind of beat. I usually hang around until about ten, but I think I'm going to call it a night. Can you be ready to leave in about five minutes? I need to lock up."

"No problem. Sketching doesn't generate a mess to clean up like painting does."

She started to walk away—but this was *not* how he wanted their conversation to end.

Throwing caution aside, he touched her arm as she brushed past. "Look, I don't want to overstep, but I have a feeling that phone call was bad news."

He left it at that. No question, just an open-ended comment. If she blew him off, he wasn't going to push and risk raising her ire.

And with each silent second that ticked by, he was more certain she was going to snub his overture.

In the end, however, she surprised him.

"It wasn't the best news I've ever had." The last word hitched, and her green irises began to shimmer again.

His gut clenched, and he had a sudden, totally inappropriate urge to wrap her in his arms, hold her tight, and promise he'd do whatever he could to fix the problem.

Instead, he shoved his hands in his pockets to keep them out of trouble.

"Do you want to talk about it?"

"Talking won't change anything."

"Maybe not . . . but it can make you feel better—or even spark ideas. I learned that over many a conversation with my dad at our kitchen table through the years." Like the one last night that continued to replay in his mind—though that exchange had unsettled more than clarified.

"It's a long story."

"If that's a kind way of saying butt out, I'll respect your wishes. If it's not—I don't have any other commitments tonight, and long stories are a specialty of lawyers."

The barest hint of a smile whispered at her lips. "You make a convincing case, counselor."

"Plus, I have a very sympathetic ear." He tugged on one lobe.

After a brief hesitation, she exhaled. "Okay. It would be nice to talk with someone about this. Usually, I'd seek out my best friend in town—but given the situation, that would be awkward." She motioned to a bench she'd constructed for one of the scenes. "In the show, one of the characters sits there to churn milk. Since my stomach is churning, that would be an appropriate place to talk."

"Sounds logical."

He followed her over and claimed the opposite

end of the sturdy bench, giving her his full attention while she described the proposal she'd developed, then filled him in on tonight's call.

"Bottom line, unless I can convince the board this isn't a high-risk undertaking, it's history."

"Hmm." He stretched his legs out in front of him. "As a guy who lives and breathes litigation every day, I can understand their caution. However, I think they're overinflating the risk."

"Tell me about it."

"The way I see it, liability can be covered with insurance and a bulletproof contract. Admin time should be minimal once the program is up and running, and it sounds like Michael Hunter is a supporter. My guess is he'd do the leg-work on that score if the other problems went away."

"That's my take too."

"Which leaves legal expenses and no proto-type. I could help you out with the boilerplate while I'm here. Developing the kind of contract you'd need wouldn't be that difficult."

She smiled, and the warmth of it seeped straight into his heart. "That's a very generous offer."

He shifted on the bench. "Not really. We're not talking about that many hours."

"Enough to rack up some serious expense if we were on the clock." Her mouth flattened. "But the board thinks we need ongoing legal support for the customized section of each contract, and you won't be here forever. You might even end up out of state."

That was true.

Is it, Eric?

He frowned. Where had that disconcerting little question come from?

"My plans *are* in flux at the moment." Strange. The words that came out weren't the definitive answer he'd intended to give.

"I could always cold call a few attorneys in Coos Bay. Someone might be willing to take this on pro bono."

"I may be able to help with that. One of the guys in our office was from there. He might know of a few local attorneys. I'll reach out to him."

And if that didn't work, he could always consider volunteering himself. In the age of instant communication, distance was inconsequential. Time, however? Different story. A partner-track position at a new firm would be even more demanding for the foreseeable future than the familiar job he'd left behind.

"That would be great. Thank you." Her smile reappeared for an instant, fading again as she toed a piece of scrap wood. "That leaves the lack of a model program with demonstrated success."

"Well . . . solving three out of four problems

isn't a bad start for a Monday. Why don't we both think about this for a few days? Maybe one of us will have a brainstorm."

She didn't look optimistic. "Prayer might be more productive at this stage."

"I'll think. You pray."

Her eyebrows rose. "You don't pray?"

"Not much." Like, not at all in recent years.

"You were at church Sunday."

"My dad expected it. To be honest, once I left Hope Harbor, life got too busy for church and . . . stuff."

"Like God?"

There was no good answer to that question.

"I haven't stopped believing or anything." His response came out more defensive than he'd intended, and he took a deep breath. *Keep it light, Nash. Inject a touch of humor.* "It's been so long since he's heard from me, I doubt he'd recognize my voice."

"The shepherd always knows his sheep."

Her tone was gentle—yet the words stung.

He stiffened. "Are you suggesting I'm lost?"

Contrition etched her features. "No. I'm sorry. I didn't mean to preach. I just can't imagine how a person survives big setbacks without relying on God for strength and guidance."

The hint of fervor in her words suggested that was more than a platitude. "It sounds as if you're speaking from experience."

Her toe stopped playing with the wood, and she went very still. "I've had some . . . challenges . . . but nothing like the troubles other people have had—including some of the older folks in town who would benefit from a program like the one I proposed."

She was shifting the conversation back to an impersonal topic.

Or was she?

He did the math. A strong, tearful reaction to the thumbs-down, plus a churning stomach, plus a poignant sadness in the depths of her eyes. That didn't add up to mere disappointment over a charitable program gone south.

It added up to a stymied personal agenda.

There was backstory to her proposal—and he wasn't going to let her off the hook without one more attempt to ferret it out.

"Where did the idea for that come from, anyway?" He put a touch of casual curiosity in his inflection, keeping the query as non-threatening as possible.

A flicker of . . . pain? . . . whipped across her face, so fast he wondered if he'd imagined it.

"I volunteer for Helping Hands beyond this." She waved a hand around the scene shop. "A lot of the people I assist are older and struggling to remain independent. Like Eleanor Cooper. I mentioned her to you the other day."

"I remember. But you've only been in town a year. I would think you'd be too busy settling in, launching your business, to have much time to volunteer for anything, let alone develop an ambitious program."

BJ bent down to retie her shoelace, hiding her face from his view. "You can always find time to do things that are important to you."

He waited until she sat up again so he could watch her while he made his next comment. "You know, I get the feeling you have a personal stake in the outcome of your proposal."

Shock flattened her features.

Bull's-eye.

"Why would you think that?"

He restrained the impulse to twine his fingers with hers. "I'm used to dealing with people in depositions and courtrooms, watching reactions, tuning in to vibes. And the disappointment I'm picking up from you is out of the normal range for this kind of situation."

Her breath hitched, and when she brushed back a stray strand of hair, the subtle quiver in her fingers validated his conclusion even before she confirmed it.

"You're right. I do have . . ."

Her phone rang again, and he stifled a groan. Could the timing be any worse?

She fumbled for it and skimmed the screen. "This is Reverend Baker. I need to take it.

Excuse me for a minute." She sprang to her feet and darted away, ending their conversation.

Would she pick it up again after she returned—or succumb to cold feet?

He hoped it was the former.

Because the more he hung around BJ, the more he wanted to know what made her tick. And if she trusted him with her story tonight, who knew where that might lead?

He was ready to find out.

But was she?

— *11* —

"Tomorrow's fine, Reverend Baker." BJ angled sideways and peeked at Eric.

He was watching her . . . probably waiting for her to come back to the bench and finish the admission she'd had no intention of making.

Her stomach clenched. She'd never told anyone about the burden she carried over Gram's situation —including a close friend like Tracy. It made no sense to even *consider* sharing her secret with a man she'd known less than a week.

". . . if that works for you."

Uh-oh. She'd totally lost the thread of her conversation with the minister.

"I'm sorry . . . I missed part of that. Cell reception can be so unreliable." True . . . though not in this case.

He chuckled. "I hear you. Mine's always popping in and out. I said about five-thirty would be ideal, if that works for you."

"Sounds fine." She looked back at Eric.

He was still watching her.

"I'll see you then. Enjoy the rest of your evening."

"Thanks. You too."

Reverend Baker ended the call, but BJ kept the phone pressed to her ear as she mentally ticked off her options. She could gather up her tools and deflect any follow-up questions Eric might lob at her, blow him off with the same quick summary she'd given the Helping Hands board about Gram . . . or spill everything.

The fact that option three remained on the table shook her to her bones. Why bare her soul to a man she barely knew?

Oh, come on, BJ. You know why.

Propping a shoulder against the front of the fake farmhouse, she closed her eyes and faced the truth.

Like it or not, she was attracted to Eric Nash.

And truth be told, she kind of liked it. Yes, there were similarities between him and Todd. Both had movie-star looks. Both generated high-voltage electricity. Both had been relentlessly climbing the corporate ladder.

But not every ambitious ladder-climber pushed other people off on his way up—and everything Eric had done since he'd arrived in Hope Harbor spelled good guy in capital letters. The man radiated dependability and integrity.

She swiveled toward him again.

He was sitting in the same spot, his posture open, relaxed—and somehow telegraphing that she . . . and her story . . . would be safe with him.

Dare she take the plunge and trust him?

The temptation was strong—and keeping all her emotions bottled up inside wasn't healthy.

Perhaps a fresh perspective might help her find the elusive closure that kept her awake more nights than she cared to count.

Yes or no?

Slowly, she lowered the phone and tucked it back in the pouch on her tool belt.

Go for it, BJ. If you change your mind part-way into the story, you can always back off and keep the rest to yourself.

That was true.

Plus, she could ease in. Test the water with a few questions, see how he reacted to the first part of the story. If she got bad vibes, she could pull back.

If, on the other hand, positive energy was flowing . . . and if she could summon up the courage to admit the regret that weighed down her soul . . . maybe this man who had come so unexpectedly into her present could help her put the past to rest.

She was going to talk to him. Eric could see the resolve on her face as she returned to the bench.

And she wasn't going to regret that decision. Guaranteed.

"Sorry to keep you waiting." She sat beside him. "Grace Christian is thinking about remodeling the offices, and we were setting up a bid appointment." Her words came out fast and choppy.

The lady was very nervous.

Don't push, Nash. Let her take this at her own pace.

"Sounds like business is booming."

"It is." She wrapped her fingers around the edge of the bench and locked gazes with him. "You said before my call that you had a feeling I might have a personal stake in the outcome of my Helping Hands proposal. I do . . . and there's a story behind it, if you'd like to hear it."

"I would."

"Why?"

The direct question threw him for a moment—but it fit the personality of this no-nonsense woman.

"You want me to be honest or coy?" If she preferred to play this exchange straight, he was game.

"Honesty is always best."

"But not always comfortable."

"Agreed. However, I'll take it over sham and pretense any day." Her nostrils flared, and anger sparked in her green irises.

What was *that* all about?

She didn't seem inclined to elaborate—but it couldn't hurt to assure her he wasn't in the deception camp.

"For the record, I don't do sham or pretense."

The tension in her features relaxed a tad. "Nice to know."

"And the answer to your question is simple. I want to know more about you because I think you're an interesting woman, and I'm attracted to you."

She blinked.

"Too candid?"

"No." She cleared her throat. "But we . . . we barely know each other."

"We may be new acquaintances, but I like what I've seen so far. And the electricity is potent . . . on my end, anyway."

She blinked again.

He grinned. "Shall I cull back the candor?"

"No. I just . . . I'm not used to guys being that straightforward."

"Maybe you've been hanging around with the wrong guys."

If he hadn't been watching her closely, her tiny flinch at his teasing remark would have escaped his notice.

He frowned. "I think I hit a nerve."

Her expression shifted into neutral. "No problem. It's history."

Not ancient history, though. Her reaction felt too . . . fresh.

He fisted his hands and came to the obvious conclusion: some guy had hurt her in the not-too-distant past.

That did *not* sit well.

"Look . . ." She fidgeted on the bench. "I

thought you wanted to hear the background on my Helping Hands proposal."

Frustration coiled in his gut. He did . . . but he also wanted to hear the background on the jerk who'd hurt her. However, BJ's stiff posture, narrowed eyes, and crimped fingers were sending a clear back-off message. If he pushed, she could shut down and leave him in the dark about both the Helping Hands proposal and her love life.

Better to stick with the former tonight; she seemed willing to talk about that.

"I do."

She bobbed her head. Brushed some sawdust off her jeans. Inspected a broken fingernail. "For the record, I . . . I haven't told the whole story to anyone else."

BJ was going to share a piece of her history with him that no one else knew?

That was the best news he'd had all day . . . all week . . . all year.

And it wouldn't hurt to reassure her that her trust wasn't misplaced.

"Whatever you tell me will remain between us."

"I know. Otherwise I wouldn't be doing this."

Yet she hesitated.

When the silence lengthened, he spoke again. "Something else is holding you back."

"Yeah." She exhaled and looked over at him. "Since you were honest with me, I'll be honest with you. That electricity you mentioned? It's not one-sided. I'm not ready to deal with it at this point, but . . . I don't want it to go away, either—and I'm afraid it might fizzle out on your end once you hear what I have to say."

She felt the sizzle as strongly as he did?

More good news on this Monday night.

"I don't think you need to worry about that. I can't imagine anything you could say that would change the chemistry."

She scrutinized him. "There's some risk, though."

"Like there is with the program you want to launch. Does that mean you should back off on it too?"

Her mouth flexed. "I'll bet you don't cut witnesses any slack in a courtroom."

"Most of my cases get settled out of court—and this isn't a cross-examination. You talk, I'll listen. If I ask a question you don't like, don't answer it. You're in charge." He couldn't create a safer environment than that.

"I like those rules." She knitted her fingers in her lap. "You need to know some context first."

"Context is always helpful." He leaned against the wall behind him, stretched out his legs, and crossed his ankles. "Ready whenever you are."

She took a deep breath. "I'll try to condense the first part as much as possible. I grew up in a military family. My father was—is—in the army. He's stationed in Europe now, but when I was eight, we lived in Japan. My mom died not long after he was transferred there, and my dad didn't feel equipped to raise an eight-year-old girl alone."

"No other siblings?"

"One brother ten years older, who was away at college. We went through a series of nannies the first few weeks after we lost Mom, none of whom worked out for various reasons. Dad finally sent me to live with my maternal grandparents near Memphis. His rationale was that he wanted me to grow up in a more normal environment."

The man had shipped a grieving eight-year-old halfway around the world to live with virtual strangers? How could a father do that? Being overwhelmed in the beginning was understandable . . . but couldn't he have adjusted to the new normal instead of ceding his parental duties?

He toned down that reaction, though, keeping his inflection sympathetic and nonjudgmental. "That transition had to be tough."

"You know, it wasn't after the first couple of weeks. Of course I missed Mom and grieved for her for months. Dad . . . not as much. I didn't see a lot of him, anyway. An army career isn't always conducive to family life. And Gram and Gramps wrapped me in love. To say they were the salt of the earth would be a gross understatement."

Were. Past tense.

"Are they both gone?" He gentled his voice.

"Yeah." Her breath hitched, and she swallowed. "Gramps died eight years ago. I lost Gram two years ago."

"I'm sorry." He touched her knee.

She inspected his hand resting on the worn denim of her jeans, and for a fraction of a second he thought she might lay hers on top. Instead, her knuckles whitened and she slid her twined fingers an inch farther away.

"Thank you. It's still hard after all these months. I email my father and brother—who lives in London with his wife—and talk to them on occasion, but Gram and Gramps were my family." She shot him a quick glance. "I'm getting to the hardest part."

"Take your time."

He left his hand on her knee, giving her his full attention while she told him how her grand-mother had suffered a broken hip that left her with a bad limp and kept her housebound.

As she recounted the older woman's struggle to remain independent, it was obvious the situation had been hard on *both* of them. He and BJ might be new acquaintances, but there was no doubt in his mind that she'd fretted constantly over the state of affairs back in Tennessee.

When she paused, he massaged her knee through the sturdy denim. "Being far away must have been hard for you."

"It was." She focused on the flats he'd been working on, where a pleasing, peaceful landscape was taking shape on the blank canvas. "I stayed with her for two weeks after her surgery and squeezed in as many quick weekend trips back as I could manage. I also tried to convince her to relocate to LA—but Tennessee had always been her home and she didn't want to leave. She ended up selling the house and moving to a retirement center, which was a disaster . . . as I told the Helping Hands board."

He listened as she repeated the story she'd shared with the board.

"So that experience gave you the idea for the Helping Hands program. Since you couldn't help your grandmother, you're trying to help some of the older residents here avoid her fate."

"Yes." She leaned forward, every muscle taut. "But you're missing the key point. It wasn't that I *couldn't* help Gram. I chose not to."

He furrowed his brow. "You went home for her surgery. You made weekend trips back. I'm sure you talked with her often. What more could you have done from the West Coast?"

"That's just it! I didn't have to stay on the West Coast. Memphis might not be as glitzy as LA, but there are architectural firms there. I could have moved back in with Gram and gotten a job at one of those. It would only have been a forty-five-minute commute to the city. Or I could have done what I ended up doing here in Hope Harbor—started my own business. But I was too enamored with my life in LA, and making a name for myself in a prestigious big-city firm, to consider that possibility."

He stared at her. She felt culpable because she hadn't thrown away everything she'd worked for to go home and play nurse?

"Do you honestly think your grandmother would have wanted you to make that kind of sacrifice?"

"No. There wasn't a selfish bone in her body. But the point is, it shouldn't have been a sacrifice. Gram and Gramps took me in when I needed a stable, loving home. They put me first. Always. No parent could have lavished more love on a child. Yet in Gram's hour of need, I wasn't there for her. If I had been, I know she'd be here today."

She blamed herself for her grandmother's death?

Whoa.

That was heavy.

But as far as he was concerned, her guilt was misplaced.

"BJ . . . I think you're being way too hard on yourself. You'd invested years building your career. Walking away from that would have been . . ."

"The right thing to do."

"That wasn't what I was going to say."

"It's true, though. Especially since I ended up leaving LA and starting over in a small town less than a year after she died, anyway. I could have done that a couple of years sooner and been there for Gram."

"So coming to Hope Harbor had nothing to do with her situation?"

"Not directly." She edged away, forcing him to remove his hand from her knee and sending a clear message: her rationale for relocating to this town was not a topic she intended to discuss tonight.

One more missing piece in the intriguing puzzle that was BJ Stevens—and he wanted that piece too.

Let it go for now, Nash. Tomorrow is another day . . . and another set-construction session.

Prudent advice, even if it taxed his patience.

"I still think you expected more of yourself than anyone else would—but I do admire how much you cared for your grandparents. I also understand why this program is important to you . . . and I have to believe there's a way to get it off the ground."

Her posture relaxed a hair.

Smart choice to leave a discussion about the reasons behind her relocation for another day.

"So what I told you about failing Gram. . . it didn't change how you . . . there's still electricity?" An anxious note crept into her voice.

"Oh yeah." He smiled. "Lots of it. But . . ."

She searched his face. "But what?"

Good question.

"You're different than anyone I've ever met." He chose each word with care. "I never expected to find a woman like you living in Hope Harbor. To be honest, it's kind of knocked me off balance. My plan was to spend two, three weeks here regrouping, then plunge back into the legal fray. Now . . ."

"You're confused?"

"To put it mildly. That's why I want to go slow and easy. You're in the midst of getting your business established here, and I don't want to barge into your life, make a connection—and leave. Until I know where I'm headed, it's safer if we play this hands-off while we get to know each other. I could end up taking a position on the other side of the country . . . and I don't want either of us to get hurt."

Her eyes began to glisten again, and she dipped her chin to fiddle with a pouch on her tool belt. "Thank you for being honest . . . and considerate."

She didn't have to say it for him to know the last guy she'd been involved with hadn't been either—and this woman deserved better.

"Can I make you a promise?"

She lifted her chin. "What kind of promise?"

"A simple one. No matter where I end up, we'll still be friends." Even if ignoring the electricity between them killed him—which it might. Holding back when every instinct in his body was urging him to pull BJ into his arms was taxing his self-control to the limit. But loving—and leaving—wasn't the path to friendship.

"Thank you for that." She laid her fingers on his hand. "It means a lot to me."

Their warmth seeped into his skin, up his arm—and into his heart.

"You're welcome. But don't tempt me, okay?" He flicked a glance at her hand.

She snatched it back. "Sorry."

"Don't be. I liked it. However, while I have great discipline, I'm not Superman." He rose and took a step back from temptation. "You ready to close up?"

"Yes." She stood too. "Let me gather up my stuff. I'll meet you at the door."

He crossed to the light switch, waited until she joined him, and plunged the room into darkness.

Outside, the last lingering rays of sun faintly illuminated the western sky.

"I guess I'll see you tomorrow at your dad's." BJ stopped beside her truck.

"Yeah—and here again tomorrow night." He shoved his hands in his pockets. "Listen . . . I want you to know how much I appreciate you trusting me with your story. And I'm going to give your Helping Hands program some serious thought. There has to be a solution." He hitched up one side of his mouth. "I may even say a few prayers."

"It couldn't hurt. Where two or three and all that."

She reached for her door, but he beat her to it. "You aren't going to slug me if I try to use the manners my mom taught me, are you? Some women are insulted by niceties these days."

"No." She climbed up into the cab. "I appreciate courtesy. See you tomorrow."

He waited until she backed up and pulled out of the high school parking lot, then ambled over to his rental car. It was far too early to go to bed, and his dad was having dinner with a friend tonight. The house would be empty and quiet and . . . lonely.

Why not take advantage of the little remaining light and go to the beach for a while? Some of his best ideas had come to him there. It was possible a solution for BJ's problem would pop into his mind as he contemplated the towering sea stacks that had been shaped by ferocious storms but had never succumbed to them.

Besides, if nothing else, some beach time would give him a chance to unwind after the last turbo-charged half hour.

And if watching the waves crash against the sturdy stacks didn't help him regain his equilibrium, a dip in the chilly water should cool him down and clear his head.

At least until the next time he found himself in the presence of the most attractive architect on the Oregon coast.

— *12* —

"You're welcome to ride along if you want a change of scene, Stone." BJ grabbed the truck keys off the sawhorse in the second-floor suite.

"No, thanks." He eyed the beam of light streaming through the drywall-dust-streaked window. "I'm planning to sit outside and soak up some of that sun while I eat my sandwich."

"I don't blame you." Especially in light of his history. "Enjoy."

He acknowledged her comment with a wave and went back to work on the baseboard he was fitting into position.

"You ready, Luis?"

"Yes." He brushed some sawdust off his jeans and followed her down the stairs.

BJ peeked into the living room and dining room as they passed. No sign of Eric. And since John hadn't cooked this morning, she'd had no opportunity to spend any time with his son.

But she'd wanted to.

And that wasn't smart.

Eric had been right last night in the scene shop when he'd suggested they proceed with caution.

Problem was, she could see potential for a lot more than friendship between them—and she wanted to explore it.

Now.

Even though she'd known Eric for only a week.

Even though she'd bumped romance down to the bottom of her priority list—particularly where charismatic high achievers were concerned.

Even though she'd been burned once by moving too fast with one man who fit that description.

Swiping back some rebellious strands that had escaped the French braid she'd fussed with this morning, she lengthened her stride. This was ridiculous. She was thirty-four! Too old to let electricity or hormones or silly daydreams undermine her judgment. Eric's slow-and-easy plan was much more prudent than rushing into a relationship. Where would she be if she let herself fall for him and he left town for greener pastures . . . as he surely would?

The answer strobed across her brain: bereft and brokenhearted. And that was *not* in her plans. Been there, done that—and once had been plenty. She needed to . . .

"Are we not taking your truck?"

At Luis's puzzled question, she jolted to a stop. Spun around. He stood by the passenger door ten feet behind her.

Blast.

This was the reason she needed to rein in her emotions. Romantic fancies might be fine in fairy tales, but they could throw you totally off course in real life.

She marched back to the truck and climbed

behind the wheel. Thank goodness this errand was nothing more than an excuse to get Luis to Charley's for lunch rather than some task that required her full concentration—like the work she'd done last night on Tracy's house plans, after sleep had proven elusive.

Hmm.

She puckered her brow, put the truck in reverse, and backed out of the driveway. Better recheck those measurements tonight—and make certain she hadn't put the water pipes in the closet instead of the bathroom.

For the next few minutes, however, she needed to concentrate on her noonday mission.

"Would you mind if I swing by Charley's before we hit the building supply center, Luis? I'm getting kind of hungry, and . . ." Her cell phone rang, and she pulled it off her belt.

Eleanor.

Odd. The woman usually didn't bother her during the workday. Unless . . . could it be another emergency? Had the bathroom door gotten stuck again?

With a quick glance in the rearview mirror, she signaled and pulled over to the shoulder. "This shouldn't take long, Luis."

"I am in no hurry."

As she braked, she put the phone to her ear. "Hi, Eleanor. Your name came up on my screen. Is everything okay?"

"N-no. I can't . . . I think it's . . . I fell and I . . . I can't get up."

BJ's pulse skyrocketed. "Did you call 911?" She punched the speaker button, shoved the cell at Luis, and peeled off the shoulder in a spray of gravel.

"No. I don't want an ambulance. They'll haul me to the h-hospital, and I might never c-come home again. Like Sarah."

BJ had no idea who Sarah was, but it didn't matter at the moment. "Why don't you let me call them? It would be better if the paramedics checked you out."

"No. I'm not hurt. I just c-can't get up, thanks to this aggravating arthritis. I'm sorry to bother you during the workday, but if you could possibly swing by and help m-me up, I'll be fine."

Arguing about 911 over the phone would be counterproductive. Based on the quaver in the woman's voice, she was already upset. Delaying the decision five more minutes couldn't hurt.

She hoped.

"I'm on my way, Eleanor. Take some deep breaths—and don't move."

"I couldn't even if I tried. You remember where the key is, don't you?"

"Yes. Hang in there."

"There's not much else I *can* do."

The line went dead.

Luis returned the phone. "Who is this Eleanor?"

Zooming around a motorist with an out-of-state license plate who seemed to be more interested in taking in the sights than reaching a destination, BJ gave him the basics.

"Falls are bad. Does she take a medicine to thin the blood?"

"I have no idea. Why?"

"In a woman her age, a break here"—he indicated his hip—"is possible. They can cause bleeding inside if the blood is thin."

BJ's heart skipped a beat, and she pressed harder on the accelerator.

Four minutes later, she pulled into the driveway, slammed on the brakes, and sprinted for the planter filled with geraniums.

Once she had the key in hand, she opened the door and strode toward the living room, where the two occupants of the house spent most of their waking hours.

On the threshold she paused. Eleanor was sitting on the floor, eyes closed, her back propped against her recliner. She was a bit paler than usual but otherwise appeared to be in decent shape. Methuselah was curled up beside her, chin resting on her leg while she stroked his fur.

"I'm here, Eleanor." She spoke softly. The woman didn't need someone startling her after all the trauma she'd already been through.

The older woman opened her eyes. "My. You must have flown."

Her voice sounded stronger now, and less shaky. That had to be a positive sign.

Didn't it?

BJ crossed the room and dropped down beside her. "I wasn't far away. Are you hurt?"

"No. It was a silly little accident. Methuselah ran in front of me, and I stopped too suddenly and lost my balance. I didn't go down hard, so that ugly walker served a useful purpose. If you could give me a hand up . . ."

"Please . . . may I come in?"

BJ swiveled on her heels. Luis stood on the threshold of the living room.

Of course! The perfect person to evaluate this situation.

"Yes." She pivoted back to the older woman. As far as she knew, Luis had told only a few people he was a doctor, and it was his choice whether or not to share that information. This would have to be handled delicately. "Eleanor . . . Luis works with me. He's great at construction, but he also knows a lot about medicine. It might be smart to let him assess your condition."

The older woman adjusted her glasses and peered at the stranger in her home. "Have we met?"

"No ma'am." Luis entered the room and knelt on her other side. "I have only been in Hope Harbor four months."

"He's been an excellent addition to my crew,

Eleanor." Better jump in before the woman began asking questions Luis might not want to answer. "And he knows a lot about . . . first aid. He may be able to evaluate whether you need medical attention. I wouldn't feel comfortable leaving without someone checking you out—but I could call the paramedics if you'd rather."

As she'd hoped, that subtle threat did the trick.

"No, no. I don't want them to come. Let's see what this young man has to say."

He indicated her hand. "May I hear your heart?"

"Yes." She held it out. "But my ticker's fine. The knees are the problem. And my eyes and ears aren't what they used to be, either."

Luis acknowledged her comment with a small smile and pressed his fingers to the inside of her wrist.

Fifteen seconds later, he removed them. "You were right. Your heart is strong and steady. Does anything hurt?"

"Only my pride."

"Did you hit your head or go black?"

"No."

"We will do a few checks anyway, yes?"

BJ edged back as Luis put Eleanor through some easy physical drills. He watched her carefully, asking questions as they progressed—including ones about her prescription medications. The simple chitchat he interspersed with the medical queries sounded conversational . . . but BJ had a feeling he was using those exchanges to assess her mental function.

The man had a great bedside manner.

As far as she could tell, Eleanor passed all the tests with flying colors. None of the areas Luis examined exhibited swelling or tenderness, the older woman was as sharp as always, and she seemed calm and comfortable.

Finally, Luis sat back on his heels. "I would like to see the pressure of your blood, but . . ."

"It's always 130/80—or thereabouts." Eleanor stroked Methuselah, who was glued to her side.

"That is very good. And I do not see any problem. Are you ready to get up?"

"More than." After one more pat, she eased the cat away. "You can sit on my lap after I get back in my chair, Methuselah."

The tabby gave the two interlopers a skeptical once-over but moved aside.

"You will help me, yes?"

As Luis directed that query her way, BJ scooted closer to the woman. "Yes. Tell me what to do."

"Eleanor . . . I may call you that?" Luis touched her arm.

"Merciful heavens, yes. I'm very grateful to you, young man."

"I am happy to help. Please to bend your knees as much as you can and put your feet flat on the floor. I will go behind and lift from under your arms. BJ, if you will hold her feet so they do not slip, that will smooth the lifting. After she is up, we will help her to her chair."

She followed his instructions, and on a count of three Eleanor was on her feet. BJ rose, and with their assistance, the older woman was able to use her walker to get to her chair and sit.

"My. That was enough excitement for a month of Sundays." She leaned down toward Methuselah, who was meowing at her feet, but Luis bent and picked up the cat, gently depositing him in her lap.

"You have not fall before, have you?" Luis dropped down on his haunches beside her chair.

"Never."

"Do you ever get . . ." He faltered, then circled his finger in the air.

"Dizzy? No. Methuselah is 100 percent to blame for this unfortunate incident." He meowed loudly, and she stroked his fur. "All right, I'll take some of the blame too. I should have been paying more attention to where you were." She directed her next comment to Luis. "Don't worry about me, young man. I'm not a faller. This won't happen again. But I'm very grateful for your assistance."

"I did not do much."

"You saved me from a trip to the hospital. I know how those paramedics work. They'll trundle you off to the ER at the slightest opportunity—

and I do *not* need to be in a hospital. BJ, I baked a chocolate fudge cake yesterday. Please cut a nice, big piece for yourself and Luis. It's not much of a thank-you, but I hope you'll both enjoy it."

"That's a given." BJ smiled at Luis. "Eleanor's fudge cake is the best in the world." She touched the older woman's shoulder. "Can I bring you anything from the kitchen while I'm out there?"

"A glass of water would be nice, dear. Thank you."

"I will help." Luis stood and followed her to the sunny room at the back of the house.

Once out of the older woman's earshot, she turned to him. "Is she really all right?"

"I think so—but without tools it is hard to be sure."

"Should we try to convince her to go to the ER?"

"She does not want to do that."

"I know . . . but do you think it's safe for her to stay here alone?"

"Could someone be with her for a few hours?"

"A friend, maybe. I could ask her to call Rose."

"That would be good."

"Let's see if we can convince her of that."

BJ cut the cake while Luis filled a glass with water, but when they returned, Eleanor shook her head at their suggestion.

"I'm fine. I wouldn't think of asking anyone

to come babysit an old woman on a fine day like this." She waved a hand toward the sunny window, then tapped the cell phone on the table beside her. "I'll keep this within reaching distance and call for help if I begin to feel poorly—but that's not going to happen."

The stubborn tilt of the woman's chin told BJ that winning this argument was a lost cause. She looked over at Luis and lifted her shoulder in a what-can-you-do shrug.

"In that case, I'll stop in after work." She held up her hand as Eleanor started to protest. "You're on my route, it's not an imposition, and I'll only stay three minutes."

"You drive a hard bargain."

"The health of my cake supplier is a top priority." She winked and hefted the fudgy treat.

"Don't worry. I expect a lot more cakes will be coming out of that kitchen. But if you want to stop, that's fine. I do appreciate your concern, BJ. And yours too, young man."

Luis gave a slight bow.

"You're quite knowledgeable about medicine." Eleanor regarded him. "How did you learn so much?"

BJ telegraphed her employee an apology—but he handled the question with diplomatic aplomb and brevity.

"Since I am a boy, I am always wanting to learn many things—how to build houses, how to take care of sickness, how to fish in the sea. It is important to never stop learning, yes? But now we must get back to work."

"Yes, Stone will be waiting for us." BJ took his cue and walked toward the door. "I'll put the key back in its place."

"Thank you, my dear. I'll look forward to your quick visit later."

Luis followed her out, waiting while she slipped the key back under the wicker planter of geraniums.

"Since our mission of mercy ate up a big chunk of the lunch hour, I'll pick up the supplies later—but I want to swing by Charley's and grab some food." She led the way back to the truck. "Can I tempt you with a taco? My treat for helping with Eleanor. I'd have had no clue how to evaluate her and would've resorted to 911—which she would not have appreciated." If she positioned the food as a thank-you rather than charity, he'd be less inclined to say no.

"It was very easy for me, this kind of care. You do not have to buy me lunch."

She pointed the truck toward the wharf. "But I hate to eat alone."

"Yes. I understand." He sighed . . . and nodded. "I will eat some tacos with you."

Mission accomplished—as long as Charley was cooking today.

She rounded the corner to Dockside Drive . . .

homed in on the white truck . . . yes! The window was up.

"We're in luck." She swung into a parking place.

As they approached the counter, Charley smiled at them. "Two orders?"

"Yes." BJ sniffed. "Mmm. That smells wonderful—as usual."

Charley opened a Styrofoam container, pulled out some fish, and gave Luis his full attention. "How are you doing, my friend?"

Some curious vibe passed between the two of them, and Luis sent the man a cautious look. "I am okay."

"Glad to hear that. It's hard being a stranger in a new town. But Hope Harbor is a fine place to put down roots. People here take care of each other." He held Luis's gaze for a couple of beats before turning to her. "You, for example, have become Eleanor's guardian angel."

BJ stared at him. How could he know about the helping hand she often lent the older woman?

The painter flashed his white teeth. "People talk, I listen. You learn much more by opening your ears rather than your mouth. How is she doing these days?"

"Funny you should ask that."

Or was it?

The man always seemed to have a sixth sense about unusual activities in the town.

"Is there a problem?" He swiped at a speck of sauce on the counter.

BJ gave him a topline recap of the emergency run to the woman's house.

"That's too bad. She's a nice lady." Charley tossed some red peppers on the sizzling griddle. "It's a shame there aren't any children in the picture who could help care for her."

Except having children—or grandchildren—was no guarantee of assistance, as she well knew.

Her appetite faded. "That would be ideal—but I do what I can."

"I know." Charley spread out some corn tortillas on the counter and flipped the fish. "That's what I mean about Hope Harbor. You may be new in town, but you fit right in to the one-for-all mind-set." He transferred his attention to Luis and began assembling the tacos. "You do too. I'm sure Eleanor was grateful for your expertise."

"I did not do much." The Cuban immigrant gave him another wary appraisal.

"Providing someone with peace of mind is a priceless gift." Charley deftly assembled the tacos despite the bandage on his wrist, wrapped them in white paper, and fitted them into a brown bag. "Between you and me, the secret ingredient today is homemade mango salsa. Enjoy."

BJ counted out the cash and pushed it across the counter. "That goes without saying. See you soon."

"I'll be here."

Luis didn't speak until they were back in the truck, the aroma of the tacos filling the cab. "Did you tell Charley I was a doctor?"

"No." BJ passed him the bag and buckled up. "I thought maybe you had."

"I have told no one except you and John and Stone. How does Charley know about my medical skill?"

"Maybe Stone or John mentioned it." She pulled into traffic and aimed the truck toward the B&B-in-the-making. "Then again, Charley's always had uncanny intuition. It's like he can sense things about people. Don't ask me to explain it, because I haven't a clue how he does it—and from what I've heard, he's always been like that."

"It is a special gift."

Mysterious was more like it, as far as she was concerned. But every town had a few eccentric characters—and if Charley was Hope Harbor's, his quirkiness was more than offset by a heart of gold.

They finished the short drive in silence and found Stone still soaking up rays in the side yard.

He rose as they walked toward him, but BJ waved him back down. "We'll join you for a few minutes. We just grabbed these and ran. I'll get us some water."

"I can do that," Luis offered.

"No. I've already usurped too much of your lunch hour. Go ahead and dig in." She gave him the bag and escaped to the house.

Once inside, she leaned a shoulder against the wall and took a slow, deep breath—but it didn't produce the hoped-for calm. The incident with Eleanor had hit far too close to home. How many times during her final months in the house had Gram needed help, as Eleanor had today? And who had she called?

BJ's throat thickened, and she pinched the bridge of her nose. It was fruitless to keep asking those kinds of questions. What was done was done. It was too late to help Gram, and she needed to accept that.

It wasn't too late to help people like Eleanor, however—and she didn't have to accept the Helping Hands board's decision as final. Michael had left the door open, and he was on her side. So was Eric.

She straightened up. Today's incident might have been distressing for Eleanor, but the episode had served an important purpose.

It had given BJ's resolve to keep fighting a much-needed boost.

— *13* —

I don't understand why I'm still here, God.

Methuselah meowed, and Eleanor gave him a pat. Had she spoken out loud? It was possible. Some old people did that. She never had, as far as she knew. But things were changing—and not for the better.

She shifted in her recliner, wincing at the tenderness in her . . . ahem . . . hindquarters. There must be a doozy of a bruise back there. Nothing was broken, though. All the parts moved, even if they were creaky and slow. She was just sore from that stupid tumble.

Thank heaven she hadn't been injured and carted off to the hospital—and then to one of those rehab places, never to emerge again.

That day, however, might be coming.

A suffocating dread filled her, and she sucked in air, trying to fill her lungs. Lucky that young man who'd come with BJ wasn't here now—and able to monitor her blood pressure. It had to be well over 130 . . . and climbing.

She stroked the cat's soft fur. Usually the rhythmic motion calmed and soothed—but today it was working better for Methuselah than for her, based on his contented purr.

At least one living creature was glad she was around.

But cat-petter wasn't exactly a vital job. It didn't contribute to the world . . . or even to Hope Harbor. Neither did baking an occasional cake, much as BJ might enjoy them.

Why, oh why, didn't the good Lord call her home to join Stan in heaven? What was he thinking, letting her languish here, serving no useful purpose?

For my thoughts are not your thoughts, nor are your ways my ways, says the Lord. As high as the heavens are above the earth, so high are my ways above your ways and my thoughts above your thoughts.

As the verse from Isaiah echoed in her mind, she sighed. Scripture had an answer for most every question. Whatever God's reason for leaving her alone in this quiet house with only a cat for a companion and no worthwhile role to play was beyond her—and always would be, as far as she could see.

Giving up her attempt to understand the mind of the Almighty, she leaned over and grasped her walker. Nothing much in the fridge appealed to her, but it was past lunchtime and she needed to eat. Maybe she'd warm up that leftover mac-and-cheese casserole—

The phone beside her rang, and she hesitated. She wasn't in the mood for conversation—but it could be that sweet BJ checking up on her, and she'd caused the girl enough worry and trouble for one day.

Resigned, she picked up her phone and peered at the unfamiliar number on the screen. Not BJ.

A solicitation, perhaps?

No. The exchange was local.

Expelling a breath, she pushed the talk button, put the cell to her ear, and said hello.

"Greetings, Eleanor. This is your favorite taco man."

She blinked. "Charley?"

"Bingo."

Her eyebrows rose. Although the two of them had enjoyed many a chat back in the day when she'd been more mobile and had frequented the taco stand, he'd never called her before.

"What can I do for you?" She continued to stroke Methuselah.

"Not a thing. Just the opposite. I have an order of tacos no one's claimed, and rather than have my excellent cooking go to waste, I thought you might enjoy them. I could drop them off in a few minutes, on my way to the studio. Otherwise they're going to end up in the garbage."

Charley's tacos relegated to the garbage?

Sacrilege!

"Are you certain no one wants them?"

"One hundred percent. I've closed the stand for the day and the wharf is deserted."

"Well, if you're sure you don't mind a slight detour . . ."

"Not at all."

"Let me give you my address. It's—"

"No need. I know where you live. It's a small town, remember? Is there a key outside I could use to let myself in?"

"Yes." She told him about the geranium pot. But how had he known she wasn't up to answering the . . .

"I'll be there in five."

A click sounded on the other end of the line.

As she set the phone down, Methuselah sent her a quizzical look.

"This has been a day filled with surprises, hasn't it, big guy?" She scratched behind his ear.

He meowed his agreement.

"However, I'm not going to complain about a delivery of Charley's tacos. I can almost taste them already."

By the time the key turned in the lock four minutes later, her appetite had come roaring back. A fresh fish taco was much more enticing than reheated mac and cheese.

"It's me, Eleanor." His voice sounded muffled.

"I'm in the living room, Charley. On your right."

The man appeared in the doorway a few seconds later, brown bag in one hand, a tall cup in the other.

He hefted the beverage as he moved toward her,

illuminating the room with one of his wide smiles. "The lemonade you always used to order. And the tacos today—one of my better batches, if I do say so myself."

"I've never had a bad taco from your place." She inhaled. "They smell wonderful."

Even Methuselah had perked up and was sniffing the savory aroma wafting across the room.

He set the bag on the table beside her and pulled out a handful of napkins.

"My word, what did you do to your arm?" She inspected the gauze dressing that covered the upper part of his hand and continued halfway to his elbow.

"A long, boring story. Short version? Accidents happen." He handed her the napkins. "Would you like me to get you a plate from the kitchen? My tacos may be tasty—but they're on the messy side."

"That would be wonderful. Thank you."

While he was gone, she arranged several napkins in her lap as insurance. On more than one occasion in the past she'd come home from a trip to the stand wearing the sauce of the day.

When he returned, he unwrapped one of the tacos and set it on the plate. "Enjoy."

She secured her lunch in her lap, took a bite of the taco . . . chewed slowly . . . aaahhh.

Heaven.

And that was the perfect word to describe Charley's tacos. They were food worthy of celestial beings.

"This is spectacular, Charley."

"I'm glad you like it. As I told BJ and Luis earlier, I tried a new mango salsa today."

"Did they tell you about my . . . incident?" That might explain his out-of-the-blue offer to come by—and his question about a key outside so she wouldn't have to answer the door.

"Only that Methuselah here caused a misstep."

The cat gave him the evil eye.

"Well, it *was* your fault, you know." Charley grinned and tweaked the tabby's ear. "You should be more careful in the future."

In response, the cat lowered his head and covered his eyes with his paws—as if he was embarrassed.

Eleanor's lips twitched. How funny was that? As if Methuselah could understand one word Charley said.

"Is that why you brought me lunch?" She took another large bite of the taco.

"No. As I said, I had an order no one claimed. When BJ mentioned what happened, I knew these had your name on them. It's been quite a while since you've been down to the stand."

"This thing . . ."—she kicked the walker with her toe—"slows me down—and the arthritis in my knees, plus vision that isn't as sharp as it used to be, keep me close to home too." She crumpled a napkin in her fingers and dabbed at some wayward sauce on her chin. "You want the truth? Getting old stinks."

Even as the words left her mouth, shock rippled through her. She never, ever complained to anyone about her lot in life. People didn't want to hear about someone else's problems; they all had plenty of their own. It was better to present a cheery front to the world.

But if Charley was surprised by her out-of-character candor, he gave no indication.

"You sound like my grandmother." He gestured to the straight-backed side chair beside the couch. "May I?"

Mercy! She hadn't invited the man to sit! How rude.

"Of course."

He repositioned the chair closer to her, folded his long, lean frame into it, and unwrapped another taco as she finished the first one. "My grandmother taught me to make these. The mango salsa is one of her recipes."

Eleanor bit into her second taco. In all the years she'd known Charley, he'd never mentioned his past. Curious that he'd bring it up today. "She must have been a wonderful cook."

"Yes—and a wonderful person. She raised me, you know. Leaving her behind was one of the hardest things I ever did."

"Why did you?"

"Opportunity. There was nothing for me in the small town in Mexico where I grew up. She thought I had talent and encouraged me to pursue it. I took her advice, and that quest ultimately led me to Hope Harbor."

"Strange that you ended up here. Oregon is very different than Mexico."

"True—but people are the same everywhere. As my grandmother told me long ago, appearance and speech and customs may differ, but underneath all hearts feel the same emotions."

"I suppose that's true."

"No question about it. My grandmother was a very wise woman. And on my last trip home, she used the same words you did about growing old. I'd had a sudden urge to go, and I'm glad I followed my instincts. That turned out to be our final visit."

"Was she ill?"

"She had some health issues in her later years—but they never stopped her from living a full life. Until the day she died, she took in foster children. Nine-, ten-, eleven-year-olds who were in desperate need of love and affection . . . which she was happy to provide. In all honesty, though, I think she benefited from the experience as much as they did."

"I imagine so. Helping others, making a contribution . . . that's the best medicine." Eleanor swallowed the last bite of the taco and washed it down with a cold drink of the excellent lemonade. No need to get maudlin during Charley's visit. She could save that indulgence for later, when she was alone—and lonely.

"She used to say that too. You two would have found a lot of common ground."

"But not everyone is able to have such an impact on other people's lives."

"Oh, I don't know. Look at me—a simple taco maker who plays with paint. But the smiles on the faces of my customers are worth more than gold. Changing a life for the better is a wonderful deed, but brightening someone's day, adding a touch of joy when a person might need it most . . . that, too, has great merit. And everyone can do that."

Eleanor carefully wiped her fingers on one of the napkins. "Assuming you have contact with other people, that is."

"Or make contact."

She peeked at him. Was he suggesting she be proactive about changing her isolated life? But what was she supposed to do, with poor vision that kept her from driving and bad knees that wouldn't carry her even as far as her neighbor's house?

"There's another one in the bag." Charley held up the sack. "Shall I unwrap it or put it in your fridge for a snack later?"

"The fridge, thank you. I'm too full to eat another bite."

Silence fell while he retreated to the kitchen, and Methuselah climbed onto her lap—with an assist.

Charley returned less than a minute later and paused in the middle of the room. "Is there anything I can do for you before I leave?"

"No. You've done more than enough. I enjoyed your company as much as your food—and that's saying a lot."

His eyes twinkled. "In that case, we might have to do this again soon. In the meantime, take care . . . and you, Methuselah, watch where you walk." He strolled into the hall, and seconds later the door clicked shut behind him.

Eleanor adjusted her recliner to raise her feet and settled back to watch a ray of sun peek through the blinds. Methuselah spotted it too. He wiggled off her lap and made a beeline for the beam of light on the floor, curling up in the warmth with a satisfied purr.

She could relate. Warmth was a compelling draw for cats—and humans.

But it had been missing from her life for a long while.

Yet she'd felt a brief wave of it while Charley was here. Some of his comments might have been a bit unsettling, but there was an aura of . . . peace . . . about him. There always had been, from the first day she'd visited his stand twenty-three years ago. Being in his presence had always left her with a God's-in-his-heaven-all's-right-with-the-world feeling.

Strange that she'd never thought to invite him to her home before. Friends had often picked up an order of tacos for her since she'd become less mobile, and she always asked about him. Why had it never occurred to her to simply invite the man for a visit?

She puzzled over that for a few minutes, until her eyelids began to drift closed. A tasty meal, pleasant company, and a lingering feeling of contentment always had a relaxing effect on her. Why not sleep for an hour or two?

And while she did, her subconscious could ponder Charley's comment about adding meaning to life by offering touches of joy to the lives of others.

Where was BJ?

Eric rattled the door at the high school gym again, then propped his hands on his hips. She'd been at the house this afternoon when he'd left to retrieve his repaired BMW—and to run an errand he'd shared with no one. If there'd been a change of plans for the evening, she would have told him.

After more fruitless knocking, he dug out his cell, tapped in her number, and walked back to his car.

On the third ring, it rolled to voicemail.

Frowning, he weighed the phone in his hand. Might she be dealing with more problems at Eleanor's? According to Luis, who'd given him the scoop after they'd met at the garbage can behind his dad's house, BJ had planned to stop there on her way home.

He scrolled through his memory, searching for the woman's last name. Carson . . . Coolidge . . . Cooper? Yeah, that was it.

A quick google search pulled up her number, and he put the call through.

Eleanor answered at once, sounding hearty and chipper—suggesting she wasn't the reason for BJ's no-show at the scene shop.

He introduced himself and explained the reason for the call. "I'm guessing she's not still at your house."

"No. She wasn't here more than a minute and stayed in the doorway of the living room. She said she was feeling under the weather—and she did look rather peaked. I assume she went home after that—but I can't imagine why she isn't answering her phone. It's always glued to her hip. Do you think someone should check on her? I could give you her address if you'd like to run by."

"Not a bad idea. I'll call once more, and if she doesn't answer, I'll pay her a quick visit."

He fished a pen and paper out of his pocket

and jotted down the address as Eleanor recited it.

"Will you let me know what you find out? That girl is such a treasure, taking care of anyone in town who needs help on a moment's notice. I'd hate for her to be on the needing end with no one to come to the rescue."

"I'll be happy to get back to you as soon as I know what's going on. Talk to you soon." Eric ended the call and tried BJ's number again, sliding behind the wheel as the phone began to ring.

Three rings in, just as he was expecting it to roll to voicemail, someone picked up—but the groggy greeting sounded nothing like the lovely architect.

"BJ?"

"Yes."

"It's Eric. What's wrong?"

Silence.

"BJ?"

"Yes. I . . . I'm here. Is it . . . it's after seven, isn't it? You're at the high school." A tinge of panic colored her words.

"I'm in the parking lot, but don't worry about it. Eleanor said you were sick."

In the background, he could hear a squeak— like someone getting out of a bed. "You talked to Eleanor?"

"Luis told me you were going to stop by there after work. Tell me what's wrong."

"I must have picked up some kind of bug. I was hoping if I laid down for a few minutes I'd feel better."

"Doesn't sound like it worked."

"No—and I slept for a lot longer than a few minutes, unless my watch picked up speed. I'm sorry. I can be there in—"

"Forget it. I'll swing by your place and get the key for the scene shop. Can I bring you anything?"

"No, thanks." Another creak, like she'd sat back on the bed, followed by a sigh. "Of all times to get some crummy virus. I have to finish the sets by Saturday or they won't be ready for tech week."

"You need to get better first. We can deal with the rest later. While you're out of commission, I'll try to make some serious headway on the backdrop. Expect me in a few minutes."

"Don't ring. I don't want to pass on my germs. I'll leave the key under the mat by the front door."

He wasn't going to get even a glimpse of her?

Bummer.

"I don't mind taking my chances with a few germs."

"Uh-uh. I wouldn't wish this on my worst enemy, let alone . . ." Her words trailed off.

His lips curved up. She might not be ready to say the words, but it didn't take a genius to know where she'd been headed with that statement.

"I'll assume that was going to be a compliment."

"It was—but I'm usually more circumspect about my feelings. I'll attribute the lapse to this nasty bug."

"You *could* attribute it to my charm."

"I wouldn't want to give you a swelled head." Humor lurked in her voice . . . until she suddenly started coughing.

Eric's mouth flattened. "Go ahead and put the key out, then get back into bed—and stay there until you feel better. I'll tell Dad you probably won't be at the house tomorrow."

"Stone and Luis will be, though. They're familiar with the plans and know what they're supposed to do."

"Good. That means you can afford to take a day or two off and get better."

"We'll see."

"Cut yourself some slack, BJ."

"Not my style."

No kidding.

"Well, change your style for the next couple of days. Besides, I doubt Stone or Luis—or my dad—would appreciate you filling the house with germs."

"That's a hard argument to counter." She coughed again.

"Don't try. I'll be there soon." He cut off the call so she wouldn't have to attempt to converse between coughs.

Once behind the wheel, he googled directions, and in short order he was turning down Sea Rose Lane.

The street at the far edge of town wasn't one he'd frequented during his growing-up years, and he scanned the small, slightly worn-around-the-edges cottages that lined the dead-end lane. Nothing impressive here—and BJ's house was no exception. In fact, the white clapboard with the tiny front porch was the smallest house on the block.

Odd that an architect with her credentials would choose to live in such a nondescript place.

At least it was better than the squat bungalow on the left with a pitched corrugated roof, a porch suffering from scoliosis, and a For Rent sign stuck in the front yard.

He pulled into the gravel driveway and parked behind her truck. The house she called home might not be much to look at, but the unobstructed view of the sea and Little Gull Island was world-class. Was that what had drawn her to this property?

Tucking the question aside for another day, he strode to the porch and lifted all four corners of the mat.

No key.

He straightened up and rubbed the back of his neck. This was weird. He'd talked to her less than ten minutes ago—and she didn't strike him as the unreliable type.

Was it possible she hadn't followed through because she was a lot sicker than she'd let on?

Pulse accelerating, he knocked on the door. She might not want to see him—but he needed to see her.

Besides, without the key, no work would get done on the backdrop.

Fifteen seconds passed.

He tried again.

Finally a lock clicked on the other side.

He drew a relieved breath . . . only to have it jam in his windpipe after she cracked the door and regarded him with bleary eyes, her usual neat braid askew, cheeks flushed, a sheen of perspiration on her forehead.

She was *really* sick.

"Sorry." The word scratched past her throat as she extended a key, grasping one end gingerly with a tissue. To protect him from germs, no doubt. "I must have fallen asleep again the instant we hung up."

"You look terrible."

He had a feeling the grimace she gave him was supposed to be a smile. "Gee, you sure know how to feed a girl's ego."

"What's your temperature?"

"Higher than normal. You want to take the key?"

No. If he did, she might close the door in his face.

"How much higher?"

She swallowed—an exercise that appeared to be painful. "A hundred and two. It's just a bug—a twenty-four-hour one, I hope. I'll rest and drink plenty of fluids and take aspirin. Do you want the key or not?"

"I'll take it as soon as you promise to call my cell if you get any worse or need anything before morning." He dug a card out of his wallet and held it out. "The number's on here. Trade you."

"I won't need anything. Besides, I'm used to being on my own."

He didn't doubt that, with an absentee father and a brother who was no more than an acquaintance—and both a continent away.

"I know that. But you don't have to be while I'm around."

Her fingers tightened around the edge of the door, and her eyes got watery. From emotion—or the virus?

"You don't have to take responsibility for me."

No, he didn't.

But he wanted to.

And he'd never felt like that about any other woman.

Too soon to share that, though. He didn't want to spook BJ, and based on the little he'd learned about her last romance, it would behoove him to tread carefully.

"Friends take care of friends. Promise you'll call if you need anything, then I'll take the key. The longer we stand here talking, the less work I'll get done on that backdrop."

She swiped her damp upper lip with the back of her wrist. "Fine. I promise."

He took the key; she held on to the tissue and took his card.

"Go back to bed."

"That's my plan. Thanks for coming by to get the key and for . . . for caring. I'll talk to you tomorrow."

She shut the door without giving him a chance to respond.

And perhaps that was for the best.

Because as he turned away, fragments of his part of last night's conversation echoed in his mind.

"I don't want to barge into your life, make a connection—and leave."

"I don't want either of us to get hurt."

"No matter where I end up, we'll still be friends."

Had she lingered at the door, he might very well have been tempted to tell her just how much he'd come to care for her, despite their short acquaintance. And if their relationship heated up, he might not be able to honor the promise he'd made to her.

So for now he'd keep his feelings to himself.

Yet as he returned to his car and gave the tiny cottage one final glance before pulling onto the street, he knew two things with absolute clarity.

He might be able to rein in his feelings enough to protect BJ from hurt if he left, but he wasn't going to be able to protect himself.

And with each day that passed, he was liking the notion of leaving Hope Harbor less and less.

— *14* —

Was someone knocking on her door?

BJ forced her eyelids open and squinted against the late afternoon sun slanting across the water. She must have drifted off. Easy to do any day, stretched out in the comfortable chaise lounge on her patio—and a given if you felt as wrung out as a wet dishrag.

A definitive knock sounded from the front of the house, still muffled . . . but louder now. As if her visitor didn't intend to leave until she responded.

Sighing, she tried to summon up the energy to stand.

Failed.

Oh, well. Whoever had come calling would give up eventually and leave her in peace.

When there were no further knocks, she let herself drift again. She'd rest a few more minutes, build up her strength a bit, then go inside and scrounge up some dinner. As Gram always used to remind her, you couldn't expect a car to run without gas; why expect your body to function without food? And she was operating on fumes at the moment . . .

"So this is where you're hiding."

At the greeting from a familiar male voice, she jerked upright.

"Eric!" She struggled to sit up and swing her feet to the ground.

"Stay put." He strode over to her, set two bags on the patio table beside the chaise lounge, and gestured to one of the empty chairs. "May I?"

"Yes . . . but you better move that several feet away, in case I'm still contagious."

"Too late. I've already been exposed. I drove Luis home earlier after he could barely drag himself to his motorbike, and the germs had free rein in my car."

"Great." To make matters worse, they'd both been at Eleanor's yesterday, spreading the virus around. She grabbed her cell from the table. "I need to see if Eleanor is—"

"Already done. I had the same thought, so I called her an hour ago. She's fine. And I have a strong constitution." He angled the chair toward her and sat.

"I do too—and look at the shape I'm in." She ran her fingers through her hair. Had she bothered to comb out the tangled mess today? Not that she recalled. Nor had she put on a speck of makeup.

Eric appraised her, faint furrows etching his brow. "To use Eleanor's term from yesterday, you *are* a little peaked. More than a little, to be honest. How are you feeling?"

"Better than I did twenty-four hours ago."

"Why do I have a feeling that's not saying much?"

"Because you're a perceptive man? Actually, I *am* improving. My fever broke about two, and other than being wiped out, I feel okay."

"Have you eaten today?"

"Not yet. I was just on the verge of scrounging up some food."

"Then my visit is timely." He opened the brown sack and pulled out a Diet Sprite, a lidded container, and a spoon. "The café had chicken noodle soup on the menu today. Are you up for that?"

Her stomach rumbled, and warmth flooded her cheeks. "I guess that's your answer."

Grinning, he removed the lid from the container and handed it over. "Dig in."

"What's in the white bag?" She nodded toward it while she dipped the spoon in the hearty soup.

"Dessert." He popped the tab on the soda for her. "Stone asked me to tell you not to worry about anything at the house. He said he'll muscle through on his own tomorrow."

"He's not showing any signs of getting sick, is he?" She took another spoonful of soup.

"Not yet . . . but he may be next. My mom always said extra meat on the bones gave a person resistance, and skinny would be a generous term for him."

"He's a lot stronger—and more resilient—than

he looks. I guess spending time behind bars either breaks or hardens a person."

Eric's face went blank.

Whoops.

She'd never told him about Stone's background.

"Um . . . he doesn't like to talk about it, but he served five years for second-degree robbery. Reverend Baker led a Bible study at the prison and recommended him to me. They have a carpentry program at the facility, and he aced it. For the record, your dad knows his history."

"Okay." He linked his fingers over his stomach, his expression guarded. "How long has he been with you?"

"Nine months—and he's a very hard, reliable worker." A note of defensiveness crept into her tone.

He held up his hands, palms out. "I'm not questioning that. I trust your judgment. I was just . . . surprised. Do you only hire people who need a break?"

"No." She stirred her soup. "The first guy I brought on was an experienced construction worker. Two months later, he took a job out of state. The timing with Stone seemed providential, so I hired him. Work kept picking up after that, and I was beginning to think about hiring a second person part time when Reverend Baker approached me about Luis. I had enough work with the Seabird Inn project to take him on full time. In both cases, the decision was a no-brainer."

"It wouldn't have been for a lot of people." A spark of . . . admiration? . . . flickered in his eyes.

Instead of responding, she continued to eat, the silence broken only by the gentle lap of the waves at the far edge of her yard.

As she chased the last noodle around the container, Eric smiled. "I take it the soup was a smart choice."

"Very." She drained the can of Sprite.

"I guess I should have brought two of those."

"No. One's usually more than sufficient. I must be dehydrated from the fever. I'll grab another one from inside." She again attempted to rise.

"Let me get it." He stood and pressed her back with a gentle hand on her shoulder, one side of his mouth hitching up. "I promise not to steal the family silver."

"Since there isn't any, I guess it's safe to let you go in." She sank back. "There are several cans in the door of the fridge. Thanks."

"My pleasure. I'll be right back."

Once he disappeared inside, BJ rested her elbows on the arms of the chaise lounge and let the warmth of the sun soak into her. It was strange, having someone fuss over her. Only Gram and Gramps and Mom had ever done that—and Mom's loving care was nothing more than a faint, distant memory.

However, getting used to this . . . or hoping for

more . . . would be a bad idea. Nice as Eric might be, he was also passing through. In another week or two or three, he'd be gone.

And falling for an itinerant attorney could end up hurting even more than falling for a deceitful architect.

So she'd play this smart and cautious . . . and continue to guard her heart.

No matter how much charm her client's son turned on.

The cans of soda were exactly where BJ had said they'd be, giving him no reason to linger in her kitchen.

Yet Eric didn't rush back out.

Instead, he did a slow sweep of the small room, tucking away the insights it offered into the woman on the patio.

The kitchen was clutter-free. No empty glasses beside the sink, no dirty dishes stacked on the table, no stray boxes of tissue or aspirin bottles. The counters were polished, the glass-fronted cabinets well organized.

Conclusion: She liked her living space neat, clean, and orderly.

A framed prayer of St. Francis hung on the wall, and a Bible-verse-of-the-day flip-over calendar rested near the cell phone charger—along with a solicitation for a children's charity and her checkbook.

Conclusion: The faith she'd talked about to him on the wharf was front and center in her daily life—not just during the hard times she'd mentioned.

The fridge had been stocked with fruit, vegetables, eggs, and some deli turkey. Not a leftover fast-food container in sight.

Conclusion: She ate healthy and took care of herself.

The simple, uncluttered room was painted a warm gray-blue that blended with the view of the sea outside the window. Geometric art prints in bold colors hung on the walls, and her café table was a sleek, modern mix of chrome and glass.

Conclusion: Design was as important in her life as it was in her career.

Resisting the urge to peek into her living room and see what additional clues it might hold about the woman who lived here, he returned to the patio.

As he approached the chaise lounge, however, his pace slowed. BJ was sound asleep again, her long blonde hair spilling onto her shoulders in soft waves.

Whatever bug she'd picked up had really done a number on her.

He stopped a few feet away, taking advantage of this rare chance to study her unobserved. Her head was tipped back, and the descending sun cast a golden glow on her skin. In repose, the charged energy that always radiated from her was gone, and the sometimes taut angles of her face had softened.

Flexing his free hand, he took a slow, deep breath. In this unguarded moment, her defenses down, BJ transcended beautiful. She was stunning . . . exquisite . . . and oh-so-appealing.

Would this be how she looked in the arms of a man she loved—content, relaxed, at peace?

A pang of yearning ricocheted through him, so strong it rocked him back on his heels.

Frowning, Eric tightened his grip on the soda can. Where had *that* come from? It was premature —and dangerous—for such intense feelings . . . especially since he wasn't planning to hang around long. Much as he cherished his childhood in Hope Harbor, living here again wasn't in the cards if he wanted to make partner at a prestigious law firm.

And he did . . . right?

His frown deepened. Yes, of course he did. Hadn't he gone after that goal relentlessly since college? After all the years and effort he'd invested, why would he . . .

BJ's eyes flickered open, forcing him to set aside those troubling thoughts. For now.

"Soda delivery." He held up the can and crossed to her.

"Did I fall asleep again?" She scooted up in the lounger as she took the can.

"Yep. Whatever you had knocked you hard." That was putting it mildly. Close up, even the golden light from the sun couldn't hide her pallor or the faint shadows beneath her lower lashes. "Are you ready for dessert?" He picked up the white bag.

"I don't eat sweets as a rule."

"I think you'll want to make an exception for this." He reclaimed his chair, uncrimped the top of the bag, and dangled it in front of her.

She sniffed as the unmistakable aroma of cinnamon wafted out.

"You went to Sweet Dreams." She took the bag and peeked inside at the giant cinnamon roll.

"Uh-huh."

"I love these." She continued to stare into the bag.

"I know."

She lifted her chin. "How?"

"You wrote your cell number on the back of a receipt for one of these the day we . . . uh . . . ran into each other."

"You mean the day you ran into me."

"Let's not argue the fine points. Go ahead . . . take it out."

After a brief hesitation, she pulled out the gooey roll dripping with icing. "I always buy one of these on Saturday as a weekend splurge. I eat half that day and half on Sunday." She moistened her lips, eyeing the treat. "Tracy got me hooked—but I manage to resist the temptation during the week."

"Are you always so disciplined?"

"I try to be—now."

The caveat didn't escape him. "What does that mean?"

She hesitated. "Let's just say food used to be my nemesis—going all the way back to my childhood." She set the cinnamon roll on the napkin he handed her.

"I don't know if I buy that." He gave her trim figure a swift appraisal. "I see you as a cute little girl with pigtails and freckles and a sunny smile, who charmed everyone she met."

"Not even close. I was an awkward, self-conscious big girl who didn't smile much at all. No one was charmed by me other than Gram and Gramps."

"Hard to believe."

"It's true." She swiped at a blob of icing and sucked it off her finger. "And consuming more food as consolation did not help the problem."

Instead of obsessing over the icing glistening at the corner of her mouth, he shifted his attention to her eyes . . . picked up the lingering hurt in their depths . . . and processed what she'd shared with him.

"Are you saying you were heavy as a child?"

"That would be a kind way of putting it." She

fiddled with the edge of the napkin. "The truth is, I was unpleasantly plump my whole life, until a few years ago."

He tried to conjure up that image.

Couldn't.

"What happened to change that?"

"Tracy—also known as Ms. Outdoors. While we were both in Phoenix, she started dragging me to Sedona on weekends to camp and hike. The first time I went, I was sure I was going to have a heart attack climbing up to Devil's Bridge. I tried to bail after that, but she kept pushing me. Then she convinced me to sign up with her for a healthy cooking class—and got me to join her health club. In a few months . . . voilà." She swept a hand down her body. "A new me began to emerge. And the old one is never coming back."

Based on the resolve in her voice, he didn't doubt that.

"Maybe I better take that away." He reached for the white bag.

She whipped it out of his range. "Not if you value your life. No worries, though. I've learned to consume in moderation. I'll enjoy this over the next couple of days . . . beginning now." She broke off a big chunk of the roll, put the rest back in the bag, and nibbled at the rich confection. "I'd share, but I already touched it and I wouldn't want you to get my germs."

"Thoughtful of you."

"No. Selfish. I could have offered you some before I pulled it out of the bag. But thank you for not pointing that out." She washed down the bite with a swig of soda. "You know, fortified with this and the soup you brought, I might be ready to come back to work tomorrow."

"I don't know about that. If you felt half as bad as Luis looked, you'll need more than thirty-six hours to get your strength back."

"I'll see how I am in the morning."

He folded his arms. "Did anyone ever tell you you're stubborn?"

"I prefer to think of myself as tenacious."

"That too. Listen, I'll make a deal with you. Why don't you rest tomorrow and stop by the scene shop in the evening if you feel up to it? Between the two of us, we ought to be able to get the smokehouse ready for the tech rehearsals."

"I thought you were working on the backdrop?"

"I am. I was there last night and today, and I'm going back after I leave here. It's coming along."

Twin creases dented her forehead. "I didn't expect you to put those kinds of long hours into the project."

"I don't have any other pressing obligations. And to tell you the truth, it's been kind of fun." He tapped her soda can. "Need another one before I leave?"

A flicker of some emotion . . . disappointment, perhaps? . . . clouded her eyes.

Nice to know she might be sorry to see him go.

"No. I'm set. Thanks a lot for stopping by—and for giving Luis a lift home."

"Not a problem. I'll call you in the morning to see how you're doing."

"I might show up for work."

"Don't push it, BJ. If you work all day, you won't be in any shape to go to the scene shop, and if I attempt to work on that set piece without someone directing my every move, it could end up resembling a lopsided outhouse rather than a smokehouse."

She gave him a disgruntled look. "I bet you aced every logic course you took in college and law school."

"Does that mean you'll rest tomorrow during the day?"

"Yes."

"Good."

Silence fell between them.

He should go . . . except he didn't want to. Working on the backdrop was fun—but it was a lot *more* fun when he had company.

However, there was no reason to prolong this visit. BJ was tired, and he'd completed his mission of mercy.

"Well . . ." He dug out his keys. "Take it easy for the rest of the day."

"I will." She leaned toward him and touched his

arm, her features softening. "And thank you again. For everything."

His heart skipped a beat as the warmth from her fingers seeped into his skin. She was close enough for him to see the amber flecks in her green irises. Close enough for him to hear her shallow, unsteady breathing. Close enough for him to reach out . . . trace the gentle sweep of her jaw . . . and claim those—

A loud belch broke the charged silence between them, instantly dispelling the romantic mood.

BJ blinked once . . . again . . . then removed her hand and turned toward the sea. "Casper must have eaten something that didn't agree with him."

Her words sounded as shaky as he felt.

Backing off a few inches, he groped for the edge of the table to steady himself. "Casper?"

"The friendly neighborhood seal." She motioned toward Little Gull Island.

He redirected his attention to the one-acre outcrop of rock a short distance offshore. A silver-white harbor seal stared back at him.

What an inopportune case of indigestion.

Or was it?

Without that rude interruption, he might have been tempted to overstep the bounds he'd set for himself with this woman—and inch closer to breaking the promise he'd made to her about remaining friends.

Clearing his throat, he stood. "The backdrop awaits. I'll talk to you soon."

He hustled toward the front of the house without waiting for a response.

Only after he turned the corner and she was out of sight did he slow his pace . . . fill his lungs with some fresh salt air . . . and give his pulse a chance to drop back into the normal range.

Strange how being in BJ's presence always left him feeling unsettled . . . in a pleasant, almost addictive way. Some of that was due to attraction and electricity, of course—but he'd experienced that kind of fleeting magnetism in the past with a few of the women he'd dated, and this reaction far transcended that.

Why?

You know why, Nash. BJ is nice and smart and talented and compassionate and beautiful and hardworking—just to name a few of her attributes. She's the whole package. You might never have bothered to catalog the traits you'd want in a spouse, but she has all the ones that would end up on your list.

He kicked at a loose rock. Yeah. That was true. And in another time and place, BJ might have been the one for him.

But letting things progress, and expecting her to upend her life again to follow him wherever he ended up if they got serious, was unfair.

And staying in Hope Harbor wasn't an option if

he wanted to pursue the career he'd carefully plotted.

What a mess.

As if to confirm that conclusion, Casper let loose with another loud belch.

Eric swiveled toward the island. With a doleful look in his direction, the seal wriggled clumsily toward the rock ledge and dived into the water. A few moments later, he bobbed to the surface, frolicking with ease.

Funny how seals could be awkward on land, yet nimble and graceful once they were in an environment that played to their strengths.

Kind of like people.

Shoving his hands in his pockets, Eric trudged toward his car. It was a nice analogy—except unlike seals, who simply followed their natural instincts, people had to figure out where they belonged.

And he thought he had.

Yet as he slid behind the wheel of the BMW, he couldn't help wondering if the goal he'd pursued with such single-minded determination was the path God would have chosen for him if he'd asked.

In terms of what that meant for his future . . . he had no idea.

All he knew with absolute certainty was that this visit home, intended to be a relaxing chance to regroup before charging back into the fray of a big-firm partnership track, was beginning to nudge him in a different direction.

One that didn't fit the blueprint he'd laid out for his life.

Fingers not quite steady, he inserted the key, backed out of BJ's driveway, and sent a silent plea heavenward as he rolled down Sea Rose Lane.

I have no idea what you want from me, Lord, so a clue or two would be appreciated. Because for the first time in my life, I'm confused about where I'm supposed to be going.

Not the most eloquent prayer he'd ever said—but it had come straight from his heart.

And he hoped he got an answer.

Soon.

Before he made choices about his future he could live to regret.

— *15* —

The worst might be over.

He hoped.

Luis groaned as he tried in vain to find a more comfortable position in the lumpy bed. How long had it been since he'd been this sick? Maybe . . . ten years? Yes. After working back-to-back shifts in the ER during the island flu epidemic, subsisting on snack foods grabbed on the fly and relying on adrenaline to keep him going, he'd succumbed himself. He'd felt so bad he'd wanted to die.

This bout had been a close second.

Whatever virus BJ had passed on to him was wicked—or else it had hit him harder because he was in his forties instead of his thirties. A decade could make a difference in how a person's body reacted to illness, as could stress . . . and grief.

On a positive note, however, his fever was gone.

He twisted his head toward the nightstand and reached for the glass of water.

Empty.

Again.

He exhaled. That meant he had to get up if he wanted more—and he needed fluids.

His gaze lingered on Elena's photo. She would have taken care of him if she were here. Her nurturing heart had always gone out to those in need . . . especially family members.

Throat clogging, he swung his feet to the floor. It served no purpose to belabor what was lost—and dwelling on the past was dangerous. It might tempt him to take another walk to the cliff.

Not today, though. He could barely totter to the bathroom, let alone hike to the other side of town. And with his motorbike parked at John's house, he was stuck here for now.

Down the road, however? The cliff was still a possibility.

He stood, groping for the chair to steady himself. Once his shaky legs stabilized, he dragged himself toward the sink, refilled his glass, and downed the water in several long gulps.

Better.

Now he needed to eat.

He took a quick inventory of the lean pickings in his small refrigerator. Three eggs, some cheese, apples, leftover quiche from a dish John had made a couple of days ago. Nothing appealed. Nor did the tomato soup or can of beans in the pantry whet his appetite.

What he wouldn't give for a bowl of Elena's *asopao criollo de pollo*!

He closed his eyes, calling up the taste of the rich gumbo, the sauce redolent of green peppers and garlic, the tangy smoked ham adding a burst of extra flavor to the chicken.

His stomach rumbled in misguided anticipation . . . but it would have to settle for John's offering. Quiche might not be a traditional dish from his homeland, but the man was a first-rate cook, and it would be a shame to waste the . . .

A knock sounded, and he arched an eyebrow. Only one person had ever visited him here . . . and there was no reason for Eric to return.

He trudged to the window beside the door and cracked the blinds.

Huh.

It *was* Eric—holding a large brown bag and a six-pack of the Coke he always chose at John's if someone offered him a drink.

Scrubbing a hand down his unshaven face, he unlocked the door and pulled it open.

The other man gave him a quick head-to-toe. "How are you feeling?"

"Not too bad." He waved a hand to the room behind him. "I would ask you in, but I do not want my germs to catch you."

"I've already been exposed. I stopped by BJ's house last night."

"She is doing better?"

"Yes." Eric held out the bag. "With your motorbike at my dad's, I assumed you were stranded out here and might need a few provisions."

The man had made a special trip out here to deliver food?

His vision misted. "You did not have to go to such trouble."

"It was no trouble. And everyone contributed. Dad sent along part of today's breakfast casserole and some orange juice for tomorrow morning. Stone threw in a few of the granola bars he said you like. I ran by Eleanor's at BJ's request, and when I told her you were sick, she added some fudge cake. My last stop was the café. Soup was a hit last night with your boss, so I figured you might like some too. They didn't have chicken noodle today, but the turkey rice sounded like an acceptable alternative."

He took the bag. "You are all very kind."

"I told you . . . this is how things work in Hope Harbor. You have friends here, Luis. Some you've met, and a lot more you haven't. Give the town a chance. You won't be sorry." Eric laid a hand on his shoulder.

He froze. Since the day he'd lost Elena, no one had touched him with warmth or friendship or caring.

Amazing how a simple physical connection could help steady a world.

"I will try." He choked out the words.

"You won't be sorry." Eric tapped the edge of the bag. "The soup's hot, so I won't keep you from it. Do you need anything else before I leave? Would you like me to pick up your mail?"

Mail! There would be two days' worth in the small box by now.

But he never got much, and most of it would be advertisements that could wait until tomorrow.

"It is fine. I cannot ask you to do more."

"You didn't ask. I offered. Are the boxes down by the office?"

"Yes." He hesitated. If Eric was willing, why not let him retrieve it? The walk wasn't far, but even if he waited until tomorrow, he might not have the energy to make it. "Let me get the key."

He retreated to the small counter next to the sink, deposited the bag, and took the key off the peg.

Back at the door, he held it out. "Box five."

"Got it. I'll be right back."

Luis leaned against the frame while he waited. He needed to sit . . . or lie down . . . fast. Just the simple back and forth in the tiny apartment had worn him out.

First, though, he'd have some of the soup Eric had brought.

The man returned faster than he'd expected, clutching a handful of mail that included a bulky envelope.

"I'm glad I checked. The box was crammed. I had to yank to get the big envelope out." He handed it over.

A touch of curiosity in Eric's expression put him on alert, and he examined the package.

The return address said Central Community College.

Luis frowned. This had to be a mistake. He'd had no contact with any college.

Yet it was addressed to him—and the envelope was emblazoned with the words Requested Material.

"This is strange." He hefted the bulky packet. "I did not ask them to send me anything."

"Could be a mistake, I guess. Odd that they had your name and address, though."

Very.

While he puzzled over the peculiar parcel, Eric checked his watch. "I need to run. I'm meeting BJ at the scene shop tonight to work on sets for the show. She says she feels better, but I want to get there first or she'll tackle the heavy stuff without me—and I doubt she's got the energy for that."

"Yes. She pushes on herself too hard. Thank you again for the food."

"No problem. Take care, and let me know if you need anything else." He lifted a hand in farewell and jogged back to his car.

Luis waited until the BMW picked up speed, then closed the door. Curious as he was about the contents of the envelope, he needed food first.

Once he stowed the breakfast casserole and juice in the fridge, he took the soup to the small café table and dived in.

Halfway through, as his energy began to rebound, he opened the envelope from the college and tipped the contents onto the table.

Information about the school's emergency medical services program spilled out.

What in the world . . . ?

He fingered the brochures. Who could have asked the college to send him this?

The list of potential candidates was small. He'd told only John, Stone, BJ, and Father Murphy about his medical background. Perhaps Eric knew too, now that he and BJ had become friends. But the man had appeared to be as surprised by the envelope as he was.

Besides, none of those people were the type to resort to clandestine suggestions.

He continued to sip his soup, skimming through the material while he ate. His English reading vocabulary was limited, but he could pick up the gist—and as he read, a tingle of excitement zipped through him. Being an EMT or paramedic wasn't what he'd hoped for in America, but given the certification hurdles Cuban doctors faced, there was no chance he'd ever practice medicine here. As a paramedic, though, he'd be able to use the skills he'd spent years honing.

His enthusiasm continued to build—until he got to the sheet detailing the cost.

The instant the numbers registered, his budding hope withered.

While the sum wasn't astronomical, it was more than he would be able to accumulate. What extra funds he had went back to Cuba. Even if the time came when Elena's father didn't need the money, he had to work full time to pay his living expenses. He couldn't afford the time or money to be a student.

Spirits sinking, Luis gathered up the material and slid it back in the envelope. Why would someone send him this when he didn't have the funds to take advantage of the program?

The whole thing was beginning to feel like a cruel prank.

He pushed himself to his feet, picked up the envelope, and walked over to the trash can next to the counter. Grasping the lid, he glanced at the bag of food sent by Hope Harbor residents and delivered by a man he'd initially thought might be an enemy.

He'd been wrong about Eric. Instead of ruining what was left of his life, John's son had saved it—and seemed committed to watching over him and bolstering his spirits. Give the town a chance, he'd advised today. And on Sunday, here in this room, he'd promised life would get better. Had suggested Hope Harbor would live up to its name.

Luis fingered the envelope. Perhaps Eric was right about this town. In time, it was possible he'd make friends, build a new life, find—if not happiness—at least a sense of peace.

But putting his medical skills into practice? That was too much to hope for.

He lifted the lid of the trash can and positioned the bulky envelope over it.

Let it go, Luis. This is a dream that can never come true.

Sensible advice.

Yet try as he might, he couldn't unclench his fingers from around the envelope.

For a full thirty seconds, he vacillated . . . but in the end—much to his disgust—he gave up and retracted his hand. Keeping the material was foolish. It would be a continual source of heartache.

And of hope, Luis. Don't forget hope.

No. He shook his head to dislodge that idea. This was not an outcome he could allow himself to wish for. It was possible whoever had requested the college to send the material had good intentions, but it was like dangling a lifeline inches away from the grasp of a drowning man. It tantalized, built up hope—but it didn't change the end result.

Luis opened the door of a bottom cabinet he never used and tucked the envelope out of sight. One day soon he'd throw it away.

But not just yet.

Wow.

BJ came to a dead stop in the doorway of the scene shop.

The backdrop was done—and it was spectacular. All the elements Eric had sketched out leapt from the canvas in life-size, living color. The finished product was even more striking than she'd anticipated.

"What do you think?" He emerged from behind the farmhouse set, wiping his hands on a rag.

"I think you missed your calling." She approached the flats slowly, soaking up the pastoral peace of the scene and his touches of whimsy. "I can almost feel the breeze, smell the fresh air. You've captured the 'Oh What A Beautiful Morning' mood perfectly." She stopped fifteen feet away and propped her hands on her hips. "The audience is going to love it."

He grinned and tossed the rag onto a folding chair. "I have to admit, it turned out better than I expected. I have a few finishing touches to add, but I can wrap it up in an hour or two tomorrow. Tonight, let's work on the smokehouse. Assuming you're game for that."

"Game or not, the clock is ticking. But I do feel better. Staying home today helped." She angled toward him. "I called Luis before I came and told him to do the same tomorrow. He said you dropped off some food. That was very thoughtful."

He shrugged off her compliment. "He doesn't have anyone else—and I still feel bad about jumping all over him the first day. So . . . if you're ready to direct me, I'm ready to wield a hammer and saw."

A man who didn't like to dwell on his good deeds.

Another checkmark in his positive column.

"I'm not an invalid. I can do my share." She started forward, only to have Eric snag her arm as she tried to pass.

"Let me do most of the heavy lifting tonight, okay? If you're planning to put in a full day at the house tomorrow, wearing yourself out tonight could jinx that."

He was right—again.

"Fine. I'll direct and do some of the less strenuous tasks. Let's get rolling."

For the next hour, the sound of hammering and sawing filled the scene shop. Eric took direction well, and with both of them working, they made significant progress. One more night like this, and she'd have only a few final details to deal with on Saturday.

However . . . despite the fact that Eric was doing the bulk of the manual labor, she was beginning to fade.

"Ready for a soda?" He descended the ladder, set his hammer on one of the rungs, and scrutinized her. "Or, on second thought, why don't we call it a night? You've lost some color."

"I'm fine—but I won't veto a short break."

He hesitated, as if debating whether to push for

an early evening, then capitulated. "I'll run over to the vending machine and—"

"Welcome home, stranger."

At the female voice, they both turned.

Lexie Graham stood silhouetted in the doorway, the setting sun adding a luster to her dark hair. Even the genderless police uniform couldn't disguise her womanly curves.

BJ sneaked a peek at Eric. Based on the appreciative perusal he was giving the new arrival, he'd noticed her attributes.

"Hey, Lexie." He gave her a warm, welcoming smile. "What brings you here?"

"I heard you were working on the backdrop for the show. I was passing by on patrol and decided to drop in and say hello since you haven't bothered to come by the station." She strolled toward them.

"I've been busy."

"I can see that." The woman's lips twitched, and BJ shifted her weight as Lexie flicked her a glance. "Anyway, it's nice to have you back."

She crossed to Eric and gave him a hug—which he returned with enthusiasm.

A strange little twinge of some nebulous emotion rippled through BJ.

Could it be . . . jealousy?

". . . know each other?"

She tuned back into the conversation and found

Eric watching her. Waiting for an answer to his question.

"Uh, no. That is, we've never met formally." She wiped her palm on her jeans and held out her hand. "BJ Stevens. Nice to meet you."

The woman took her hand in a strong grip. "Lexie Graham."

"Also known as the chief of police. Who'd have guessed that's where you'd end up back in our days of playing cops and robbers as kids?" Eric grinned at her.

"Yeah. Funny how our lives can take directions we never expected." A shadow flitted across her eyes, so fast BJ couldn't be certain if it had been real or a mere play of light. "I heard about your job. I'm sorry."

"It happens. Everyone's downsizing these days."

The chief cocked her head. "You don't seem nearly as bothered about it as I expected. You had your sights set on a law partnership as far back as I can remember."

Meaning these two had a long history together.

Another piece of bad news . . . for reasons BJ didn't care to examine.

"I was a lot more upset a week ago—but Hope Harbor has a way of restoring perspective."

"No argument there." She rested her hand on the pistol on her belt and scanned the backdrop. "Nice work—but you always did have artistic talent. I thought you might end up doing more with it."

"I needed to pay the bills."

"I hear you. Well, I don't want to hold up your progress. Back to patrol for me."

"Can't police chiefs delegate that duty?"

"Not in a small town. Our department is lean, and if one officer is out . . . guess who fills in? But I don't mind. Keeps me in touch with the street. Nice to meet you, BJ."

"Thanks. You too."

Eric watched the chief stroll out, then turned back to her. "Where were we?"

"Soda."

"Right. Give me a minute."

While he was gone, BJ set up two folding chairs and sank into one. No way was she going to admit she was more than ready to cave, especially after the appearance of the dynamic chief who radiated vim and vigor. Maybe the soda would give her a burst of energy.

Plus, she could use the break to ask a few questions about the ringless woman who knew Eric very well.

Yeah, yeah, she'd noticed the bare fourth finger on her left hand.

What woman wouldn't if she was with a guy who could set off bells and whistles without trying—even if he *was* off-limits? It was a normal female reaction that meant nothing.

Liar, liar.

"A Diet Sprite for the lady."

Squelching the annoying voice in her head, she reached for the ice-cold soda he held out. "Thanks." She popped the tab and took a long swallow.

"I'm surprised you haven't become acquainted with Lexie."

The perfect opening.

"I don't see her around town much when she's off duty. And I haven't broken any laws to attract her attention *on* duty . . . unlike someone I know."

"Ha-ha."

"It's not too late to report your cell phone transgression to the chief . . . but I have a feeling she'd let you off."

Smirking, he swirled his can. "She might. We have a history."

That was what she'd been afraid of.

"I take it you've known her your whole life?"

"Yep. Comes with living in a small town. How come you two haven't gotten acquainted? Don't you see her at church?"

"No. I thought she might go to St. Francis."

"Not when we were kids." His expression grew pensive. "I wonder if she stopped going after she got back from the Middle East."

BJ blinked. "She was in the Middle East?"

"Yeah. A diplomatic security job with the State Department. Apparently she had a rough stretch at the end. According to town scuttlebutt, she got married over there, only to have her husband killed a few weeks later in an attack that left her with some serious injuries. She came back here three years ago with a baby in tow."

So Lexie was a widow with a young child and a traumatic past.

"I wonder if that's why she keeps to herself."

"Could be. But back in the day, she was the outgoing, life-of-the-party type. We had some happy times as kids. In fact, she was my date for the senior prom."

Her stomach knotted.

But he didn't go to see her after he got back, BJ. She had to look him up. That means there aren't any lingering feelings on his part.

Or maybe he simply hadn't gotten around to dropping by the station yet.

And there was no reason they couldn't pick up where they'd left off. The chief appeared to be open to the idea—why else would she seek him out?—and it was obvious Eric liked her.

Her spirits nose-dived.

". . . of their prom date, don't you think?"

Uh-oh. She'd lost the thread of the conversation.

"Sorry. What?" She wrapped both hands around her soda.

"I said, most people have fond memories of their date for senior prom, don't you think?"

A sore subject—and not one she wanted to discuss.

"I don't know." She drained the can and stood. "Ready to go back to work?"

He rose slowly, searching her with that intent, probing look of his. The one that seemed capable of delving deep into her soul.

She snatched his empty can. "I'll get rid of these in the cafeteria."

He grabbed her arm before she could flee. "You didn't go to the prom, did you?"

Pressure built in her throat at his soft, sympathetic question, and her vision blurred.

Good grief! How stupid was this? She was over the prom debacle. Had been for years. Why in heaven's name would she get weepy about some dumb dance for teenagers?

"BJ."

At his soft summons, she lifted her lashes. His eyes were gentle . . . caring . . . encouraging.

Answer the man's question, BJ. Just spit it out and be done with it. It's old news.

"No." The word came out shaky, and she swallowed. "A friend set me up with her cousin, but he called that afternoon and canceled. He said he was sick."

"*Said* he was sick?" A flash of anger hardened his eyes.

"I saw him the next day in town with some buddies." She gave a stiff shrug. "He just didn't want to go with the fat girl. No one did. Let me ditch these and we can get back to work." She pulled free of his grasp and dashed toward the doorway—praying he wouldn't follow.

He didn't.

Once she reached the privacy of the hall, she slumped against the hard, concrete-block wall, tears streaming down her cheeks. Why should a discussion about ancient history set off a deluge of tears? And why hadn't she left her answer at a simple no instead of sharing the whole humiliating explanation?

It made no sense.

And now she had to go back in and face Eric.

Dread congealed in her stomach—but hiding in the hall wasn't going to change reality . . . and they had a set to finish.

Straightening up, BJ lifted her chin and continued toward the cafeteria to dispose of the empty cans. She'd get her unruly emotions under control, wipe away her tears . . . and shore up her defenses.

Because after that dramatic exit, she had a feeling Eric might ask a lot more questions— and if those warm brown eyes of his could coax her to share the story of her disastrous prom date, it was very possible they could also tempt her to reveal the much more recent, and far more crushing, episode that had been the catalyst for her flight from LA.

And if a discussion about the prom could induce tears, talking about LA might trigger a complete meltdown.

On the other hand, it could be healing—and liberating.

Sighing, she tossed the cans in the recycle bin. Who knew how this might play out?

Maybe Eric would make it easy and drop the subject.

But if he didn't, she'd just have to follow her heart—and hope for the best.

— 16 —

Great job, Nash. Making the lady cry is going to earn you a whole lot of brownie points.

Gut twisting, Eric stared at the doorway BJ had fled through moments ago. He shouldn't have pushed about the prom. Shouldn't have pressed her to tell him the painful, humiliating story. The whole high-school-social-event-of-the-year scene might not have been a big deal for him, but stuff like that meant a lot to most girls—especially ones who didn't go on a lot of dates or have a steady boyfriend.

Like BJ.

Inhaling a lungful of the fresh-paint-and-sawdust-laden air, he began to pace. Could he have been any more insensitive? She'd probably spent hours shopping for a dress. Maybe gotten her hair done, had a manicure, purchased new makeup, and spent hours practicing with it.

Then that low-life had ruined her magical night.

She must have been devastated.

And still was, based on the shimmer of tears he'd spotted while she'd relayed the sad story in a few choppy, stilted sentences before fleeing.

If only he could replay that last scene, change the ending.

But this was real life, not theater. He couldn't

rewrite the script. His only recourse was damage control—assuming he could come up with a plan.

Unfortunately, she returned before he'd gotten past the first step.

"Ready to get back to work?" She stopped several feet away, her too-bright smile at odds with the shadows lurking in her eyes.

"Yes—but first I want to apologize." Step one accomplished. He'd have to wing the rest.

Her fake smile seemed as painted on as the images filling the backdrop behind her. "Not necessary. I overreacted. Who cares about what happened sixteen years ago?"

"You do."

"Did."

"I think you still do—and so do I."

Her smile wavered. "I appreciate that. But one teenage disappointment doesn't make or break a life."

"It can leave scars, though." He moved closer, halting when she tensed. "Can I say something?"

"I . . . don't know." A hint of panic wove through her words, and she wrapped her arms around herself.

His throat tightened at the protective move. She seemed so alone, standing there trying to be brave. So in need of a warm, comforting hug . . . a soft caress . . . a gentle touch . . . some gesture that would compensate even in a small way for the unkindness she'd endured at the hands of that high school punk—and the jerk who'd hurt her more recently.

If most of her experiences with the opposite sex had been of the same unpleasant ilk, it was no wonder she was single.

He jammed his hands in his pockets before the temptation to wrap her in his arms became too strong to resist. "I'm going to say it anyway." He locked gazes with her. "I'm getting the impression you haven't had the best experiences in the romance department, and I'm sorry for that. More than I can say. It sounds like you've crossed paths with some real losers—but not all guys are like that."

"I know." Her reply came out in a choked whisper. "Theoretically speaking."

He digested her caveat . . . and came to the obvious conclusion.

BJ had *never* had a pleasant dating experience.

In fact, if she'd been heavy most of her life, she may have had very few dating experiences period. Based on what he'd observed, her earlier comment was true—being plump could put a serious crimp in romance. A lot of guys wouldn't think of asking out someone who was seriously overweight . . . no matter how nice or smart or kind they might be.

Including him.

A wave of guilt washed over him. He'd never considered himself to be prejudiced—or shallow

—but it appeared bigotry could take many forms.

He drew a steadying breath. "Are you telling me you've never dated a nice guy?"

The knuckles gripping her upper arms whitened. "It doesn't matter."

"It does to me."

"Why?"

Good question.

He took his time answering, choosing his words with care. "Because I like you . . . a lot . . . and it bothers me that no one else of my gender has recognized how special you are."

Her eyes widened—then just as quickly shuttered. The wry twist of her lips that followed didn't come close to qualifying as a smile. "That's a great line."

Line?

He clamped his jaw shut, trying to keep his anger—and hurt—in check. Didn't she know him well enough by now to realize he wasn't feeding her a . . .

Wait.

The left side of his brain kicked in as he weighed her comment. Why would she say that unless . . .

As he came to the heartbreaking conclusion, he swallowed past the sudden pressure in his throat, his aggravation evaporating. "That wasn't a line, BJ. I meant every word. But someone less sincere told you the same thing once, didn't he?"

Her nostrils flared, and she glowered at him in silence.

O-kay.

This discussion was over.

But he knew the answer—and he wanted to comfort, to reassure, to ease some of her—

"His name was Todd."

He did a double take at the unexpected revelation—and some quick recalibrating. Her anger had been directed at the jerk, not him. Plus, she'd cracked the door to a discussion . . . and he needed to respond in exactly the right way or she'd slam it shut in his face.

Letting his instincts take over, he crossed to her in three long strides, reached for her cold hand, and twined his fingers with hers. "I've never been in a fistfight in my life, but if he was here right now, I'd punch him out."

A beat passed as BJ scrutinized him. Two. Three. Then some of her stiffness dissolved. "I don't like violence as a rule . . . but thank you."

"You're welcome." He motioned to the chairs. "Want to sit for a few more minutes?"

She hesitated. "What about the set?"

"It's coming along. The rest can wait until tomorrow."

He could read the conflict in her eyes—but pushing wouldn't be wise. If she chose to confide in him, the decision had to be freely made, not coerced. Besides, his behavior since they'd met was a better endorsement of his character than words.

Second after eternal second dragged by . . . but in the end she nodded. "Okay."

The knot in his stomach loosened.

Thank you, God!

Keeping a firm hold on her fingers, he led her back to the chairs, angling his toward her. Their knees were almost touching after he sat.

He waited, letting her set the pace and timing for whatever she was willing to share.

Half a minute ticked by while she picked at a speck of glue on her jeans. Swallowed. Toed some wood shavings on the floor.

"You know . . ." She peeked over at him. "Out in the hall, I was afraid this might happen."

"What?"

"That I'd cave and spill my guts about LA."

"Would that be bad?"

She lifted one shoulder. "Sharing confidences can create . . . bonds. I don't want to start having feelings for a man who won't be around long."

He was tempted to deny her assumptions about his plans—but that would be misleading. At this point, he had no idea what his future held, and they'd promised to be honest with each other.

Better to respond with a question. "What happened to change your mind?"

"You." She homed in on their linked hands.

"You have this ability to make me feel as if you really care."

"I do."

"Why?" Puzzlement etched her features. "Two weeks ago, you didn't know I existed."

"I've been asking myself that same question. All I can come up with is that something clicked between us from the beginning—and I'd like to get to know you a lot better."

She looked down again at their clasped hands. "Todd said almost the same thing on our first date."

He grimaced. "That's not the best news I've ever heard."

"If it makes you feel any better, besides the fact you both drive BMWs and fall into the tall-dark-and-handsome camp, there aren't a lot of other similarities."

"That helps a little. Where did you meet this guy?"

"In LA. Not quite two years ago."

Soon after her grandmother died, when she would have been emotionally wrung out and susceptible to a smooth talker.

A muscle twitched in his cheek. The guy was worse than a jerk. He was a . . . Eric squelched a word that would have shocked his mother—even if it was accurate. "I take it he wasn't the man you thought he was?"

"That would be a kind way of putting it." She

leaned back in her chair, tugging her fingers free.

He let them go—but missed the connection at once. "How did you meet?"

"At a professional dinner. He's an architect too—with a much larger firm than the one where I worked. I'd won a prestigious award for one of my designs, and he came over after the meal to congratulate me. When he called a few days later to ask me out, I couldn't believe it. He was attractive, personable, suave—in other words, miles out of my league."

"You're selling yourself short."

"No. Telling the truth. I'd just reached my ideal weight and was still trying to work up the courage to enter the dating scene. I had zero experience with men . . . and even less confidence . . . but the timing seemed almost like destiny. I was lonely, missing Gram, wondering if I'd ever meet anyone who might be 'the one,' when out of the blue he appeared. It seemed too good to be true—and as it turned out, it was."

All at once, Eric had a feeling he knew where this was heading . . . and it wasn't sitting well.

"Did he take advantage of you?" He forced the question past gritted teeth, the folding chair squeaking beneath him as he leaned forward.

Her mouth twisted again. "Not in the way you mean. He wasn't after . . . that. He had far more ambitious goals."

Not the answer he'd expected. "What do you mean?"

She laced her fingers together in her lap. "He was new in town—and new at his firm. He'd been recruited from a midsized company in the Midwest. Todd had great ambition, and with his glib tongue, he managed to grab the coveted opening. But as I later discovered, he had more charm than talent."

"Meaning he got in over his head?"

"Big-time." She brushed back some soft wisps of hair that had escaped her braid, distress sharpening the angles of her face. "If I hadn't been smitten, I would have seen the red flags. After softening me up with a couple of very nice evenings out, he said he preferred quiet, private dinners to noisy restaurants and began coming over to my condo with takeout. I always brought work home, and he was very interested in my projects. His attention and questions fed my ego—and kept him supplied with the innovative design concepts he couldn't come up with on his own."

"Are you saying he stole your ideas?" Shock rippled through him.

"Yes—but I didn't catch on to his scheme for months. Not until my firm was asked to bid on a high-profile job. It was a huge opportunity for us. We were more of a boutique house, and this would have significantly raised our visibility. My boss—

the owner—was super excited. We all worked our tails off. As I discovered later, Todd's firm was on the bid list too—and Todd was the lead person on the project. Night after night, I talked to him about our design over those cozy dinners at my place . . . and he borrowed all the elements he liked."

Outrage kicked his pulse up another notch. "But . . . but that's unethical—not to mention illegal. There are intellectual property rights at stake. And copyright infringement issues. Your firm could have sued him."

"The design his firm presented wasn't an exact copy of ours."

"Doesn't matter. In a case like that, infringement is based on the presence of substantial similarities. Plus, you'd have had no problem proving he had access to your plans and specifications."

"I know. That's what our firm's attorney said after I told my boss what happened. But she also warned that we could be dealing with a long, expensive court battle. In the end, my boss decided to cut his losses and let it go."

"I assume you figured out Todd's role once you learned who got the job?"

"Yes. After our presentation, the client called my boss to tell him they were going with Todd's firm. That while our ideas were strikingly similar, they felt more comfortable using a larger, more established company. When my boss gathered us together in the conference room to give us the bad news, I almost threw up."

"Did you contact Todd?"

"The minute the meeting ended. He didn't admit to stealing, just made some flippant comment about great minds thinking alike. I hung up on him, went to the ladies' room, and lost my lunch. It was all revoltingly obvious in hindsight. I'd won awards for my innovative designs, and he needed ideas. He looked me over, deduced I was easy prey, and launched his campaign. He used me—and I was too naïve and gullible to realize I was being duped. Needless to say, my shaky self-esteem went straight down the toilet with my lunch."

"Did you get fired because of this?" Eric narrowed his eyes.

"No. Considering the whole mess was my fault, my boss was very gracious. But I'd been rethinking my priorities anyway. After Gram died, the lure of making a name for myself as a big-city architect faded. I'd visited Tracy here and liked Hope Harbor, so I decided to make a fresh start and aim for a better quality of life."

"Did you ever hear from Todd after your phone call?"

"Yes. He sent me an expensive bracelet and a note a few days later, inviting me to dinner to, in his words, 'smooth out the waters.' As if money could fix the problem." Disgust flattened her mouth.

Almost the same words she'd used after his cavalier comment about insurance the day of their fender bender.

Given her history, no wonder she'd been ticked off by his dismissive attitude.

"What did you do with the bracelet?"

"I sold it on eBay and donated the proceeds to Helping Hands after I got here. I like that the gift ended up benefiting a worthy cause."

"Have you ever had any regrets about upending your life and changing direction?"

The tension melted from her features. "Not a one. I love my life here. I like the work, the people, the pace. The circumstances that led me to this decision might not have been pleasant, but I do see God's hand in the outcome. This is where I was meant to be."

Her conviction was indisputable. "I'm sorry for all you went through—with Todd and the guy in high school, not to mention your grandmother's illness—but I envy your contentment . . . and your certainty about your place in the world."

"I thought you were certain about yours too."

"So did I." The chair squeaked again as he shifted position. "But everything's been topsy-turvy since I got home."

"Maybe you just need some time to unwind from that high-stress job of yours."

"Maybe."

A yawn snuck up on her, and she clapped a hand over her mouth. "Sorry."

"Don't be. We ought to close up shop so you can go home and get some rest. You must be exhausted."

"You know, it's kind of weird. I always assumed sharing that story would be draining, but I actually feel better."

At least one of them did.

"Sometimes talking things through can help clarify and add perspective."

"Assuming you do it with the right person—and I did." She stifled another yawn, inched her chair back, and stood. "If you'll get the lights, I'll grab my tools and meet you at the door." She hurried toward the smokehouse without giving him a chance to respond.

He rose more slowly and wandered toward the door. When she joined him thirty seconds later, he was still trying to sort through everything she'd told him . . . his own feelings . . . and the ramifications of both.

After locking up, she scanned the western sky, where banks of clouds were massing on the horizon. "I have a feeling we're in for a beautiful sunset."

"Yeah." And any other time, he'd like nothing better than to share it with the woman beside him, sitting on a cozy bench on the wharf, boats bobbing in the foreground, Floyd and Gladys pecking at scraps of food around their feet.

But not tonight. She might have found her confession cathartic, but it had left him with a myriad of disconcerting emotions and questions.

"You seem deep in thought." She looked over as they strolled toward their vehicles.

"You gave me a lot to think about."

"Too much?"

"No." His reply was immediate—and emphatic. He did *not* want her to regret baring her heart. "But it makes me feel guilty. I haven't faced nearly as many challenges as you—and people like Luis—have."

"Don't even put me in the same category as Luis. Next to what he's gone through, my life's been a cakewalk." She stopped beside her car. "Thanks for listening tonight."

"Thanks for trusting me with the story."

There was nothing more to say, but walking away with a casual "see you around" didn't feel right, either. Not after she'd shared so many intimate details about her life.

Would she be receptive to what his instincts were urging him to do?

Only one way to find out.

He conjured up a smile. "You know, after our little hand-holding session in the scene shop, don't you think we ought to say good-bye with a hug?"

She crossed her arms.

Not a positive sign.

"Like the one you gave the chief?"

He squinted at her. What did Lexie have to do with this? Unless . . . did BJ think he had feelings for the chief?

Better clear that up. Pronto. "You mean the one she gave *me?*"

"It looked pretty consensual to me." Her teasing inflection sounded forced.

"Let me set the record straight. My high school crush on Lexie ended long ago. She's a great gal, but our lives went very different directions. I expect we'll always be friends—but that's it. So . . . about that hug."

She slowly uncrossed her arms. "I guess that would be okay—as long as it's a just-friends hug."

"I'm good with that."

For now.

Scrubbing her hands on her thighs, she stepped toward him.

He met her halfway.

Keep it simple . . . supportive . . . straight-forward.

He let that mantra loop through his mind—but when she lifted her chin to look up at him, the air whooshed out of his lungs. Her jade irises, that faint sprinkling of freckles across her nose, the graceful curve of her cheek, those lush, perfectly shaped lips . . .

Her breath hitched.

Uh-oh.

She must have realized he didn't have friendship on his mind.

Watch it, Nash, or you're going to blow this.

Before she could back off, he pulled her into his arms.

She stiffened—but when he did nothing more than hold her, she began to relax, her soft curves melting against him.

He gave her a tentative squeeze . . . and she squeezed back, the silky strands of hair that had worked free of her soft braid brushing his jaw.

She felt perfect in his arms. So perfect he wished he could hold her for hours, until the sun set over the sea and stars lit the night sky.

But the instant she made a move to pull back, he let her go.

"Well . . ." Her respiration seemed as ragged as his while she groped for her keys. Dropped them.

He bent to retrieve them, but she beat him. After scooping them up, she turned aside to open the truck door, hiding her face from his view. "I'll see you tomorrow, I guess."

"Count on it. I can pick up Luis in the morning, if he's planning to come to work."

"He is . . . but you've done enough. I'll swing by and get him." She put on a pair of sunglasses she didn't need and climbed behind the wheel.

He waited while she put the truck in gear and pulled away with a final wave, then meandered back to his car.

If BJ had felt so right in his arms during a mere hug, what would it be like to . . .

No.

He'd promised her friendship, and he'd keep that promise—unless both of them decided to venture into deeper waters, no matter the compromises that might entail.

However . . . he, for one, wasn't there yet.

Keys in hand, he slid behind the wheel of the BMW. It was possible BJ might be thinking about exploring more than friendship too—but even if she gave him the green light, he needed to make some decisions about his future before he got in too deep. He was *not* going to hurt this woman who'd already endured more than her share of trauma. She didn't need another broken romance, and he didn't need a broken heart.

Which was exactly what he'd get if he let himself fall for the lovely architect, only to leave Hope Harbor—and her—behind in the end.

Oh. My. Word.

This was where Luis lived?

BJ gaped at the dilapidated motel-turned-apartment-complex, her stomach roiling as she maneuvered around a rut in the crumbling asphalt drive. No one had told her the place was a dump —and she'd had no occasion to drive down this road. The well-maintained sign on 101 certainly offered no hint of the disrepair beyond.

They ought to change the name from Sea Haven to Sea Hovel.

Why in heaven's name hadn't the town or the county condemned this place long ago?

And why had Luis chosen to live here? She paid him enough to afford better accommodations.

Except if he upgraded his lodgings, he wouldn't be able to send as much money back to Cuba.

Of course he'd apply the frugal rationale that guided his choices on all necessities—food, transportation, clothing—to his living quarters too.

But this wasn't right.

Scanning the faded numbers on the doors, she spotted unit five just as Luis emerged. He lifted a hand in greeting, twisted the key in the lock, and crossed to the truck.

"Thank you for picking me up." He slid in and buckled up.

"No problem. How are you feeling?"

"Much better."

That might be true—but he looked as if he'd lost ten shades of color and several pounds while battling the nasty bug.

"If you need another day to recuperate, that's not a problem. I don't dock employees for being sick."

"I will be fine. I am stronger today—and I do not take money for work I have not done."

The very opening she needed.

"Luis . . ." Her fingers contracted on the wheel. *Be careful, BJ. Don't offend him.* "Look, this is my first visit here." She swept a hand down the length of the apartment units. "It isn't a . . . uh . . . great place."

"It is okay. The door has a lock and the roof does not leak." He flashed her a quick, dismissive smile.

This was going to be a tough sell.

"I understand the need to have lower expectations in a new country—and I know money can be tight when you're starting over—but government assistance is available to Cuban immigrants. Why don't you apply for some . . . just until you get your feet under you?"

He was shaking his head even before she finished. "No. America . . . she has given me safeness and freedom. It is enough. I cannot take more."

The same thing he'd told Father Kevin. Almost verbatim, based on the conversation the St. Francis priest had shared with her.

"I admire your attitude—but it wouldn't be forever. And other refugees take the aid."

"That is their choice. How is the work going?"

Subject closed.

If she was going to win this argument, she'd have to come up with another strategy.

BJ put the truck back in gear, and as they trundled over the rough pavement toward 101, she filled him in on what had taken place at the job site in his absence.

But she wasn't letting this go. If the decaying apartment complex was half as bad on the inside as it was on the outside, the place wasn't fit for human habitation . . . and she had a feeling it might be worse.

At least she had a source for that information. Eric had surely been inside—or gotten a peek—during one of his visits. At the first opportunity, she'd corner him and ask some questions.

And if the accommodations were as bad as she expected, she was going to get Luis out of here.

Fast.

Whatever it took.

Because a man who'd left everything he knew

behind, who'd endured a harrowing sea voyage, who'd watched the woman he loved die a tragic death, and who'd traded his skilled career as a doctor for a life of freedom as a carpenter deserved—at the very least—a decent place to rest his head at night.

It was still here.

Eric gripped the easel, gave it a yank . . . and released a cloud of dust from the pile of stuff stacked under the basement stairs.

A sneeze tickled his nose, and he waved a hand in front of his face to clear the air. Obviously his dad hadn't rummaged around down here in a while.

He braced the pile with one hand and tugged the easel again with the other. It came out on his second attempt—along with a bunch of other junk that clattered to the floor.

Muttering a few choice words, Eric propped the easel against the wall and began to gather up the old TV trays, unmarked boxes sealed shut with yellowed tape, and almost-empty paint cans.

"Everything okay down there?"

As his father's voice echoed down the stairs, he accelerated his pace. "Fine. I'll be up in a minute."

"You need some help?" His father began to descend the stairs.

"I've got it." A thread of desperation wove through his reply.

"Another set of hands can't hurt." His father clumped closer.

He picked up the last TV tray and shoved it into place as his father rounded the bottom of the stairs.

"You were making as much commotion as my rehab crew." His dad swatted at the dust motes floating through the air. "Guess I ought to clean up down here every year or two."

"Couldn't hurt." Eric shifted in front of the easel and leaned against the steps.

"What were you looking for?"

"Nothing. I was . . . uh . . . poking around." Not a lie. He hadn't been looking for the easel; he'd known exactly where he'd left it.

"Oh." His father leaned sideways. "I thought you might be pulling your easel out of mothballs."

So much for his clandestine mission. He'd never been able to get anything past his father as a kid; why should that change now?

"Okay. Guilty as charged." He turned and pulled out the dusty easel. "I wasn't certain it would still be here."

"No reason to move it—or get rid of it. I always hoped you'd take up painting again one day."

"Listen, Dad." It was important to be clear about his intentions up front. "I'm just fooling around with this while I'm here. Don't get the wrong idea."

"Which would be . . . ?"

"That I'm going to start painting again."

"You're already doing that—at the high school."

"A one-time project is different. This kind of painting"—he tapped the easel—"is more serious."

"It doesn't have to be. Some people paint for fun. As a hobby."

"I don't have time for hobbies. When I leave Hope Harbor, the easel will stay here. Doing that backdrop simply gave me the itch to work on a real painting. That's all."

"Besides, what's wrong with being serious about painting?"

Eric narrowed his eyes. Had his dad heard a word he'd said?

"Painting isn't a reliable occupation."

"Who said anything about making it an occupation? You can be serious about painting and have another career too."

"Not if the other career is the partner track at a law firm."

"You still set on going back to that?"

"Haven't I said that all along?"

"Yes. But I thought being back in Hope Harbor might change your perspective. That, and meeting BJ." His father grinned. "You two seem very chummy."

Warmth crept up his neck. "She's a nice woman."

"At the very least."

"She's also building a business here."

"True."

"Long-distance relationships are problematic—assuming I was interested."

"Also true. I wouldn't recommend it . . . assuming you were interested."

He frowned. "Then what are you saying?"

"Just throwing out ideas." He eyed the stuff piled in the stairwell. "It appears you took care of the landslide down here without me. Guess I'll head back up. Breakfast is ready. Sounds like the whole crew will be here today. You joining us?"

"Yeah. I'll be up in a minute."

He waited while his father ascended the stairs, then grabbed a stray rag from a pile in the corner and dusted off the easel, his hands busy cleaning up one mess while his mind wrestled with a bunch of others.

Why had almost every conversation since he'd arrived home left him with more questions than answers?

How had he managed to get himself so involved in the life of this town—and the lives of several of its citizens—in less than ten days?

What was he supposed to do about BJ and his growing feelings for her?

Should he let all that had happened on this trip sway him from the path he'd laid out during his senior year of high school?

Why, after all these years, were those sixty-plus-hour weeks beginning to lose their appeal?

He wadded up the grimy rag and hurled it back into the corner as the questions strobed across his brain.

Flexing his fingers, he forced the taut muscles in his shoulders to relax.

Chill, Nash. You're getting too worked up about this. There's no rush here. No lives—or major court cases—are hanging in the balance.

All that was true. He'd allotted himself three weeks of downtime before diving into an intensive job search, and he wasn't even at the halfway point of that.

So why not take one day at a time and pray the answers he needed would come?

Preferably sooner rather than later.

BJ swung the hammer, secured a nail in the smokehouse set, and glanced toward the scene shop door.

Again.

Of all nights for Eric to be late.

Huffing out a breath, she picked up another nail. Ever since her visit to that cruddy apartment complex this morning, she'd been chomping at the bit to talk to him about Luis. How frustrating to sit right across from him at breakfast and have to remain mute on the subject. But with Luis on her left, there'd been no other option. Besides,

Eric had seemed distracted—and once the meal wrapped up, he'd disappeared for the entire day. There'd been no opportunity for a discreet discussion.

Her only direct communication from him had been a text message telling her he'd be here tonight.

But he wasn't—yet.

If he'd been delayed, or was going to cancel, why hadn't he . . .

"Sorry I'm late."

She swiveled around as he pushed through the doorway, relief coursing through her. "I was about to give up on you."

"No excuses. I lost track of time this afternoon and got home late for dinner." He picked up the other hammer from the bench and canvassed the set. "You've made some progress without me."

"A little. You must have been seriously distracted if you forgot about dinner."

"Yeah. What would you like me to tackle here?"

He didn't want to discuss his day.

Fine.

She had other subjects to talk about, anyway.

"We're down to the details. I need that stuff over there tacked to the inside walls. The director left a diagram of where it all should go. But first, I have a question. Have you been inside Luis's apartment?"

"Yes. Why?" He picked up the diagram.

"Is it as bad inside as it is outside?"

He hiked up an eyebrow. "Haven't you ever been there?"

"No. I've never had a reason to drop by. The outside is awful."

Eric's face grew grim. "The inside's no better."

"That's what I was afraid of." She shoved the nail back in the pouch on her tool belt and exhaled. "He can't stay there."

"Are there any other nearby options that offer better value for the price?"

"I doubt it. I called the manager today to ask about the rent. It's dirt cheap—validating the old adage that you get what you pay for."

"If that's the least expensive housing around, how do you propose we get him to move?"

"I don't know." She began to pace, tapping the hammer against her palm. "But he deserves better."

Eric set the layout down. "Did you discuss this with him?"

"I tried—but he wasn't receptive. He said the place was acceptable. I suggested he apply for government assistance, but that went over like a lead balloon."

"Do you think Father Kevin might be able to intercede?"

"He's already tried. The problem is, Luis is adamant about not taking anything he views as charity. I have a feeling he won't even let me pay him for the sick days he . . ." Her phone began to vibrate, and she pulled it out. Skimmed the screen. "Give me a minute." She tapped the talk button and walked a few feet away. "Hi, Eleanor."

"Hello, dear. I'm not interrupting anything, am I?"

"Nothing that can't wait a few minutes. Eric and I are working on the set for the Helping Hands benefit."

"How nice! He's a delightful young man. We had a nice conversation when he dropped by while you were sick. I gave him some fudge cake . . . and I sent some to your friend, Luis, too. Eric told me he'd caught the same bug you had. I wanted to see how you both were doing."

BJ stared at the nest of hungry hatchlings Eric had painted in the willow tree, so in need of loving care, her mind whirring as several seemingly unrelated pieces of information began to connect.

Eleanor needed someone to help her with daily chores.

Luis needed to escape from the rat hole he called home.

They were both alone—and lonely.

And she needed a test case for Helping Hands before the board would approve her companion program.

It was a heaven-sent opportunity—but could she convince both parties to give it a shot?

"BJ? Are you there?"

"Yes. Yes, I'm here." She tried to tamp down her growing excitement. "Luis and I are both much better. How are *you* doing?"

"Fine. None the worse for wear after my silly tumble. I won't keep you from your work, my dear—or from that fine young man. If you want to stop by in the next day or two, I saved you a piece of fudge cake. Methuselah and I are always happy to see you."

"I may do that."

"Wonderful. Take care and stay well until I see you."

As Eleanor ended the call, BJ lowered the cell, mind racing. Were Eleanor and Luis the solution to her dilemma with Helping Hands, or was she grasping at straws? After all, she hadn't envisioned the program catering to their exact situation. Nevertheless, why not . . .

"What's up?"

She angled toward Eric. "That was Eleanor."

"So I gathered."

"While I was talking to her, I had an idea about my Helping Hands project."

"Yeah?" He set down his hammer. "What is it?"

She gave him the gist in a few sentences. "I mean, it's not exactly the scenario I envisioned. I assumed we'd pair up same-gender companions—but Luis and Eleanor would both

308

benefit from the arrangement . . . and I can't see why it wouldn't work. What do you think?"

"I think it's a brilliant idea."

His smile warmed her all the way to the tips of her toes.

"The only question is, will they go for it? And will the Helping Hands board consider it a sufficient test case?" She began to pace.

"That's easy enough to check."

"Right." She tried to keep a lid on her burgeoning hope. Rushing would be a mistake. There were details to work through, documents to draw up, feelers to put out. "Maybe I'll corner Reverend Baker on Sunday after church and get a quick read from him before I take this any further."

"Not a bad idea. And if he's receptive, you could run it past Michael too." He propped a shoulder against the smokehouse and folded his arms. "I don't want to barge in on your party, but if you'd like some moral support for any of those discus-sions, I'll be happy to provide it. That, and whatever legal documents you need to make this happen."

"I accept on both counts, with thanks." She stopped in front of him. "Which reminds me— did you ever manage to contact that former colleague of yours from Coos Bay? We'll need ongoing legal help if this pans out."

"As a matter of fact, he texted me today. I was

going to let you know after we finished up here tonight. It seems he's too busy with *important* work to forward a few names of attorneys there who might be willing to help out with your program." Sarcasm scored Eric's words. "However, I'm not giving up. I can reach out to some other contacts."

"Any help is gratefully accepted . . . and appreciated." She laid her hand on his arm. "Thank you for everything you've done."

All at once, his brown irises darkened, and a current of electricity sizzled between them.

Mercy.

Any second now he was going to pull her into another one of those delectable hugs.

Instead, with an abrupt move, he pushed off from the smokehouse, breaking the connection between them. "I think we have a set to finish."

Whoops.

She must have misread his cues.

"Right." She circled around him and got back to work.

For the rest of the evening, loud hammering eliminated the possibility of extended conversation —but by the time they wound down, the set was done. And although her mind had kept wandering to the man working at her side, she'd also managed to put together a mental checklist of all the issues that needed to be addressed before she could launch her test case.

"I think it's a wrap." Eric drew back a few feet from the smokehouse and sized it up. "Is this what you envisioned?"

"Exactly." She began to gather up her tools. "And I'm glad it's over, aren't you?"

When he didn't respond, she looked over at him.

"To be honest, I kind of enjoyed working on it."

"I guess that makes sense from your perspective." She went back to collecting her tools. "The project did give you a chance to use your artistic talent."

"True . . . but that's not the only reason I enjoyed it."

She turned back to him—and her pulse stuttered at the appreciative gleam in his eyes.

No question about it this time.

The man was flirting with her.

And if she responded to his cue, if he hugged her good-bye tonight, she had a feeling he'd have a lot more on his mind than a friendly squeeze.

Scary thought, despite the delicious tingle that raced down her spine. Playful flirting was one thing; flirting with danger was another.

Remember your rule, BJ—be cautious and prudent and measured. Your heart's at stake here.

Check.

"So . . . I'll meet you at the door, okay?" Her words came out shaky.

He hesitated for a moment, then nodded.

She finished stowing her tools, keeping tabs on him in her peripheral vision. But he simply walked to the exit and waited.

Getting to her car without a hug, however, could be tricky if he had a clinch on his mind— and if he did pull her into his arms, she wasn't certain she'd have the willpower to resist.

After easing aside to let her precede him out the door, he pulled it firmly shut behind them and tested the lock. It rattled but held.

"Our work is safe and secure." He dropped his hand from the knob.

"Good. We wouldn't want any scenery stealers to walk off with our masterpieces." She gripped her car keys in her hand and started for her truck, trying with limited success to match his teasing manner.

He fell in beside her. The sun had set, and vast swaths of intense color spanned the horizon. It was a beautiful evening. The kind featured in a lot of happy-ending-type books. The kind that was conducive to hand-holding . . . and hugs . . . and romance.

Stay strong, BJ.

She picked up her pace.

Eric did too.

"So what does BJ stand for?"

At the out-of-the-blue question, her step faltered. "What?"

"Your initials. What do they stand for?" His tone was relaxed, conversational, chitchatty.

It was too dim to detect his expression, but from all indications he'd switched emotional gears.

"Um . . . you won't laugh, will you?"

"Why would I laugh?"

"It's a very southern and old-fashioned name. My mom's choice. But it never fit. It seemed to belong to someone slender and graceful, who'd look great wearing a hoop skirt—and that wasn't me."

"It is now."

"Thank you for that. However, I hated the name. After I went to live with Gram and Gramps, I asked them to call me BJ instead—and it stuck."

"Instead of what?"

He wasn't going to let her off the hook.

She sighed. "Belinda June."

"Belinda June." He said the name slowly, giving it a musical cadence. "Pretty. I like it."

"Sorry. I'm BJ now . . . and for always." She stopped beside her truck. "Will I . . . uh . . . see you at church Sunday?"

"Yep. Dad and I will be there. I'll join you afterward and we'll corner Reverend Baker." He pulled her door open for her. "Drive safe."

It appeared all her worries about a hug had been for naught.

Quashing an inappropriate pang of disappointment, she slid behind the wheel. "Have a nice Saturday—and thanks for lending your talent to the scenery and sets."

"My pleasure." He shut her door and stepped back.

Well.

That, apparently, was that.

BJ rammed the key into the lock, started the engine, and drove away. When she glanced in the rearview mirror, he was already striding toward his own car.

Had she imagined those romantic vibes wafting around the scene shop—or had he picked up her nervousness and gallantly backed off?

Not that it mattered. The result had been what she'd sought—a clean escape, with no emotional entanglements.

Yet hard as she tried to suppress it, all at once she foolishly wished she'd sent the tempting, dark-eyed attorney a whole different set of signals.

The waves lapped gently against the sand in the sheltered cove, while seals frolicked on the sea stack a hundred yards offshore and the sun shone in a cloudless blue sky.

Best of all, he had a paintbrush in his hand and hours to kill.

Eric gave a contented sigh.

It was a perfect Saturday.

Or as perfect as it could be when you were out of a job, trying to decide what to do with the rest of your life . . . and fantasizing about a beautiful architect who'd kept you tossing half the night.

He rolled his shoulders and let out a slow breath. He'd come close yesterday at the scene shop to breaking every rule he'd made about BJ. If she hadn't started telegraphing some serious anxiety signals he'd have given her another parting hug.

One that could easily have morphed into an embrace that went way beyond friendship.

Taking a break today, removing himself from temptation, had been wise—even if he'd have preferred to spend the day in her company.

But he'd see her in church tomorrow . . . and until then, a whole glorious day of painting stretched before him.

From his spot beside the sheer rock face, in the shadow of majestic fir trees, he surveyed the deserted cove that had been his favorite fair-weather painting spot since the day he'd found it as a teen. Although the small, crescent-shaped beach was accessible from Shore Acres State Park, few visitors bothered to hike down and explore it—or dip their toes in the turquoise water.

Their loss.

Shifting his attention to the easel, he examined the composition he'd roughed in yesterday with diluted burnt umber paint. The scene had nothing to do with this cove, which served as studio, not subject—and it was very sketchy. Yet he could see the finished piece in his mind.

A small, placid river. A bright summer day. A woman knee-deep in the water, holding the side of a rowboat with one hand, the other extended in a silent, tempting invitation toward the viewer. But what lay ahead, beyond the gentle curve of the river? Were there beautiful vistas and smooth sailing—or rough water and dangerous rapids? Would the trip be fun . . . or frightening?

The finished painting would offer no answer to those questions. Viewers would have to decide whether to accept the invitation to adventure based on their own tolerance for risk and their life experience.

It was a piece that would make people think

about more than a simple excursion on a river . . .
he hoped.

"That could have some potential."

Eric jerked and spun around.

"Sorry. I didn't mean to startle you." Charley
strolled toward him across the sand.

"How did you . . . what are you doing here?"

"I like to visit the gardens in the park. The roses
are always spectacular in July. I often swing by
this cove while I'm here. Pretty spot." He gave it
a leisurely sweep. "As I recall, you used to be
partial to it."

"Yeah." But why had Charley picked today of
all days to pay this off-the-beaten-path a visit?

What a bizarre coincidence.

"Nice to see you at an easel again." Charley
slipped his fingers in the back pockets of his
jeans as he perused the canvas. "I was at the high
school yesterday and peeked into the scene shop.
Great work on the backdrop."

"Thanks—but you would have done a better job
if you hadn't hurt your . . ." Eric stopped.

The bandage was gone.

He folded his arms. "How's the wrist?"

"Much better."

Convenient.

"Nice ploy."

"What's that supposed to mean?"

"I'm beginning to think you faked an injury so
I'd take on the backdrop—and you hoped that

would nudge me back into this kind of painting." He tapped the edge of the canvas.

"You always did have a vivid imagination. I expect that's why you excelled at art. When did you start that?" He inclined his head toward the roughed-in canvas.

"You're dodging my question."

"I didn't hear one—but I did ask one."

Charley could be as slippery as a slime eel when it suited him . . . and trying to pin him down if he didn't want to answer a question was an exercise in futility.

"Yesterday. I don't know how far I'll get with it before I leave."

"You beating the bushes for a new job?"

He busied himself straightening the canvas on the easel. "I thought I'd take a short break first."

"Seems reasonable. I'm sure you won't have any trouble connecting somewhere once you're ready. Every town needs a good lawyer."

Including Hope Harbor.

The man didn't have to say the words for Eric to get the message . . . and he wasn't going to pretend he'd missed the implication.

"Not every town can offer a lawyer a decent living, though."

"Depends on how you define decent—but big-city jobs come with lots of perks you wouldn't find in a small practice, I expect."

"Not to mention generous salaries, bonuses, benefits . . ."

"And long hours that don't leave much time for activities like that." Charley gestured to the easel. "Or for people either, I imagine. But I suppose if you're always at the office until the wee hours, you might not notice what's missing at home."

"Like what?"

"Love, for one thing."

Eric stiffened. "You seem to have survived just fine without romance . . . or marriage . . . or a significant other."

The man smiled gently, crinkles radiating from the corners of his eyes. "Love comes in many forms." He leaned close to the painting and touched the figure of the woman. "Check your perspective here. Given the composition, I think she needs to be a bit bigger. Good luck."

With that he swiveled around and strolled back toward the path that led to the bluff overlooking the cove.

Eric waited until he was out of sight, then evaluated the roughed-in figure. Charley's assessment was sound. It did need to be bigger.

As for the rest of their conversation . . . sometimes the man talked in riddles—and Eric wasn't going to waste this beautiful day trying to solve them.

Nor was he going to let Charley's insinuations bother him. Practicing law in Hope Harbor was a ridiculous idea. There wasn't enough legal work in the town to keep food on the table, let alone provide him with the kind of upscale life he'd led in Portland.

As for love . . . he was working on figuring that out now, thanks to BJ.

In the meantime, he'd do what he—not the town's taco-master artist—thought was best for his life.

As soon as he figured out what that was.

She had to make her move . . . with or without Eric.

BJ rose from her pew and scanned the emptying church. He'd been here for services; she'd seen him and John enter. But there was no sign of either now.

Had he forgotten his promise to provide moral support while she broached her test-case idea to Reverend Baker?

Tamping down her nerves, she brushed a hand down her skirt. No matter. It was her idea, and she didn't need a man to . . .

Eric emerged from the shadows in the back of church, lifted a hand in greeting, and strode toward her.

"Sorry. Dad insisted on introducing me to a guy who's planning to open a business here. Between you and me, I think he wanted to mooch some free legal advice." He wrinkled his brow and scrutinized her. "You weren't worried I'd stood you up, were you?"

"I . . . uh . . . didn't think you were the type to do that." Warmth crept onto her cheeks at the obvious hedge.

"But once—or twice—burned, thrice shy. I understand." He touched her arm. "And I'm sorry if my delay upset you. I hope you'll eventually realize I keep my word. Always. Now . . . are you ready to talk to Reverend Baker? He's still greeting people out front, but the line is dwindling. Everyone's making a beeline for the doughnuts."

"Ready as I'll ever be."

"I think he's going to be 100 percent on board with your idea." Eric stepped aside as she left the pew, then fell in beside her, his hand on the small of her back as they skirted a small cluster of congregants lingering in the aisle.

She had to fight the temptation to lean back into his touch.

A few gray clouds had gathered during the service, and the sun was hiding as they joined the end of the line to greet the minister.

"BJ—nice to see you." Reverend Baker cocooned her hand in a warm clasp when she drew close. "You too, Eric. Are you enjoying your visit home?"

"Yes, although it's been busier than I expected."

"I heard about the fine work you've done on the backdrop for our fundraising show. Helping Hands is grateful."

"It was my pleasure."

"Speaking of Helping Hands . . ." BJ tried to quash the flutter in her stomach. "If you have a minute, I'd like to run an idea by you related to the program I proposed."

"Of course. Let me greet these last few stragglers, and we'll go back inside."

BJ eased out of the line of traffic while the minister shook a few more hands . . . but as he was wrapping up, Father Kevin pulled into the parking lot and got out of his car.

"He's early." Reverend Baker planted his hands on his hips. "He may be tardy for meetings, but he never misses a tee time."

"I thought you two played golf on Thursdays." As the priest retrieved his clubs from the trunk, BJ returned Tracy's wave across the lawn, where members of the congregation were chatting in small groups.

"We do, but Kevin had an unexpected sick call at the hospital in Coos Bay this week and we had to reschedule."

The priest raised a hand in greeting as he trotted across the lawn to join them, clubs slung over his shoulder. "Good morning, all."

"Let me guess . . . you came early to filch some of our doughnuts." Reverend Baker gave him a stern look.

"I think I'm insulted." The priest huffed, but there was no missing the twinkle in his merry eyes. "I assumed the service would be long over and that everyone would be gone."

"We aren't like Catholics here, you know. No one in this church leaves before the end of the service—and we actually like to linger afterward and enjoy some food and fellowship."

"Hmph." The priest sniffed. "Our people come to pray, not eat and socialize. There isn't one mention in the Bible about stuffing your face after going to church." He extended his hand to Eric. "I don't believe we've met—and since my fellow cleric appears to be more worried about his doughnut supply than decorum, I'll do the honors myself. Kevin Murphy."

Eric took his hand, and BJ tried not to chuckle as his uncertain gaze flicked from one man to the other. No one must have clued him in to the notorious and good-natured jibing between the two clerics.

"Nice to meet you," Eric said.

"Given the early arrival of my golfing partner" —Reverend Baker turned to her—"would you like to defer our discussion?"

BJ glanced back toward Tracy and Michael, who continued to chat on the lawn with another couple. "As a matter of fact . . . if we can corral Michael, it might be better if all three of you heard this. Let me run over and see if he has a minute."

"I'll fill Kevin in on the reason for this impromptu meeting while you're gone." Reverend

Baker launched into the explanation as she hurried across the grass.

By the time she returned with Michael in tow and they all moved into the back of church, her pulse was hammering. As if sensing her nervousness, Eric edged in close. So close she could feel his breath on her temple. As if he wanted her to know he was on her side.

Strange.

For a woman who'd always taken pride in standing on her own two feet and meeting every challenge without the need for hand-holding, it felt surprisingly nice to have Eric in her corner.

She squeezed the strap of her purse and plunged in. "I know you all have other plans for the day, so I'll keep this short. Michael passed on the board's concerns about my proposal, and I believe we can overcome quite a few of them. Eric has agreed to develop a boilerplate agreement while he's here and perhaps line us up with continuing legal assistance. One of the other major hurdles appears to be lack of a model program—but I think I may have a solution for that."

As she laid out her plan, it was difficult to judge the reaction of the three men. They were attentive, and their expressions were encouraging and receptive . . . but she wasn't going to draw any conclusions until they voiced their opinions.

Once she wrapped up, Michael was the first to speak.

"I think that's a great suggestion. If the test goes smoothly with those two subjects, I can't imagine the board will drag its feet about proceeding."

"I concur. It's an excellent idea, BJ." Reverend Baker beamed at her. "What do you think, Kevin?"

"That I wish I'd thought of it myself. I don't know Eleanor very well, but I do know Luis—and the man is due for a break. I've tried and tried to persuade him to apply for government assistance or to take some of our St. Vincent de Paul funds for food and housing, but accepting charity is anathema to him. The question is . . . will we be able to convince him this isn't charity?"

"I have a few arguments up my sleeve—and I may call on you for backup with Luis if necessary." BJ turned to Reverend Baker. "And yours with Eleanor."

"Happy to assist."

Father Kevin peeked at his watch and adjusted the golf clubs on his shoulder. "If that wraps things up for now . . ."

"You have a tee time." BJ smiled. "I won't keep you any longer. Enjoy your game."

"Always."

"Kevin, I'll change, grab my clubs, and meet you at my car. Give me ten minutes." The minister walked them to the door.

"Don't hurry on my account. I'll mosey over to the fellowship hall and have a doughnut or two."

"Aha. I knew that was why you came early."

"Hey, I don't want them to go to waste. Waste not, want not, you know."

Reverend Baker rolled his eyes. "Leave it to a Catholic to quote Ben Franklin instead of the Bible."

Father Kevin bristled. "Don't start with that Catholics-don't-read-the-Bible bit again. 'Judge not, that ye be not judged.' "

"Is that the best you can do? Even nonbelievers know that one."

"What is this, Bible *Jeopardy*?" When the minister began to speak, Father Kevin held up his hand. "I have just one more comment on this subject: 'Do not envy those who are wrong. Like grass, they wither quickly.' Psalms, in case that didn't ring a bell."

"I'm impressed."

"I'd rather impress you with my golf game."

"On that note, I believe I'll rejoin my lovely wife." Lips twitching, Michael angled away from the clerics. "BJ, I'll look forward to hearing a report on your progress. Keep me informed— and let me know if I can help."

"I will. Thanks for being receptive to my experiment."

"And I'm off to the fellowship hall." Father Kevin motioned toward it. "Would you two like to join me while my golfing companion gets ready for our game?"

"I think I'll pass, padre." Eric pulled out his keys. "I need to round up my dad."

"And I have Helping Hands plans to make." BJ retrieved her own keys.

"Remember, let me know if you need help persuading Luis." The priest took off for the fellowship hall.

Reverend Baker shook his head as his friend departed. "I better hurry or he'll scarf down half a dozen doughnuts—and his cholesterol is too high already. Talk to you both soon."

As the minister closed the door, Eric smiled. "It took me a minute to catch on, but to use an old cliché, I take it those two are peas in a pod."

"They are. According to Tracy, when Reverend Baker moved here eight years ago and took the helm of Grace Christian after his wife died, Father Kevin sent him a pack of expensive golf balls and an invitation to the links. That was the beginning of a beautiful friendship. But their bantering is a stitch." She played with her keys. "You know, I think I'll swing by Eleanor's and claim that piece of fudge cake she offered. Would you like to join me? I have a feeling she'd be willing to part with two pieces."

"I wish I could, but I promised Dad I'd join him for a belated welcome-home breakfast at the café this morning. I could go later."

That wasn't going to work. Much as she'd like his company, she was too impatient to wait.

"That's okay. I might need backup with Luis, but talking with Eleanor shouldn't be an issue."

"Maybe I could swing by your house later for an update . . . if you'll be home."

Her spirits took a decided uptick. "That would be great."

"For now, let me walk you to your truck at least." He rested his hand on the small of her back again and guided her toward the parking lot. "So you think Eleanor will be an easy sell?"

"Yes. She's such a kind, sweet, caring woman. Given Luis's history, and the fact that the entire program could hinge on her participation, I think she'd be receptive even if there wasn't anything in it for her. But in light of her own situation—and her recent fall—I can't imagine she won't welcome an opportunity to have a very skilled person on hand who can help with both home maintenance and any medical issues that might crop up. I'm more worried about convincing Luis."

"Count on me for that discussion. And if we both strike out, we can enlist Father Kevin."

"Trust me, I'm keeping that as an option." She pressed the auto lock button on her key chain.

Eric pulled open the driver-side door, and she slid behind the wheel.

"Think positive." He winked and closed the door.

BJ started the engine, waved good-bye, and followed his advice as she accelerated toward Eleanor's.

Because to make this program fly, they needed both her and Luis on their side.

BJ wanted her to let a stranger live in her house.

A stranger from *Cuba*.

A man who spoke with a foreign accent and was still adjusting to American customs.

As Eleanor tried to grapple with the request her visitor had just dropped in her lap, she tightened her grip on Methuselah. The old feline let out a yowl of protest, wriggled out of her grasp, and scurried across the kitchen with a sulky glare.

"Mercy! Methuselah isn't in the best of moods today, is he?" Her hand fluttered to her chest as she tried to summon up a smile for BJ, but her lips refused to cooperate.

Creases appeared on the young woman's forehead. "I think I might have thrown too much at you at once, Eleanor." She moved her half-eaten piece of fudge cake aside. "This project has been near and dear to my heart for months, and I tend to assume everyone will jump on board the minute they hear about it. I probably ran through the details too fast. You must have a lot of questions."

No, as a matter of fact, she didn't. She understood both the proposal and the benefits to herself and Luis.

But despite the heartbreaking tale BJ had told

her about the man's background, she knew little else about him, or the country he came from, or the culture that had shaped him, or his moral character. BJ and Father Kevin might think he was a fine person—but they weren't being asked to live under the same roof with him, either.

Heavens . . . didn't they have drug smuggling and corruption and crime and . . . and *communism* . . . down in Cuba, with those shady Castro brothers in charge? Living in an environment like that could have a negative effect even on a well-educated person like Luis—couldn't it?

However, suggesting that to the sweet girl sitting across the kitchen table from her, who no doubt believed the best of everyone, might not be appropriate.

"I can't think of a single question. You took me by surprise, my dear. My brain hasn't quite caught up. What does your friend Luis have to say about this?"

"I haven't mentioned it to him yet. I thought it would be easier to talk with you first." She swallowed, as if the fallacy of that assumption had left a bad taste in her mouth. "He's opposed to taking charity of any kind, so I need to think about how to present it to him in a way he'll find acceptable."

"I see."

BJ laced her fingers on the table, knuckles whitening as she leaned closer. "Luis is very quiet and agreeable, Eleanor. I'm certain he'd be happy to abide by whatever parameters you set—assuming I can convince him to give the arrangement a try. And we could begin with a limited trial period, if you like. At that point you could both reevaluate and decide whether you want to continue."

"Would any of this be in writing?" Not that a contract would clear up her uneasiness—but extending the discussion would buy her a few minutes to come up with a response.

"Yes. I should have mentioned that up front. Eric is planning to draw up a legal agreement. Liability issues would be covered and responsibilities laid out. Also, since no cash will exchange hands, there aren't any tax implications."

Eleanor touched a paper napkin to the corner of her mouth. Everything BJ had said made sense—and Lord knew she needed some help.

Yet she couldn't summon up an ounce of enthusiasm for the idea. The hard knot of fear lodged in her chest got in the way.

But why was she afraid? From what she'd seen and heard, Luis didn't appear to be a menace to anyone—and he'd endured more than his share of suffering and loss. If anyone deserved a second chance, it was him. Plus, he'd come to her aid in her moment of need.

As far as she could see, her fear had no basis.

Nevertheless, she couldn't shake it.

And until—unless—she managed to do that, she couldn't give this sweet girl the answer she wanted.

"I do appreciate all the effort you've put into this program, BJ. It's a fine idea, and I can see how it will benefit Hope Harbor residents. However, I must admit that the notion of having someone live under my roof is a bit . . . unsettling. Why don't you let me think about it for a day or two?"

"Of course." BJ swallowed and picked up her fork. Set it down again. "Um . . . do you think I could take the rest of this with me? I guess I ate too much breakfast."

Being too full wasn't the reason for her sudden loss of appetite.

Disappointment was written all over the girl's face.

Eleanor crumpled her napkin into a tight ball. Much as she hated to stand in the way of BJ's plan, it couldn't be helped. She wasn't going to agree to this sort of arrangement without a lot of thought and soul-searching.

"There's plastic wrap in the third drawer. You know where it is. And take a piece for that nice young man of yours too."

"Eric?" BJ shot her a startled look.

"Yes."

"He's not my . . . we're not . . . involved."

"No? Ah, well. This old romantic heart of mine has a tendency to get carried away."

In silence, BJ rose, wrapped up the remains of her treat and a piece for Eric, then offered a smile that seemed forced. "If you have any questions as you think about this, don't hesitate to call."

"I won't."

Eleanor started to rise, but BJ placed a gentle hand on her shoulder. "Don't bother to get up. I'll see myself out."

She sank back without protest. "Give my best to that nice young man—and enjoy the rest of your day, my dear."

"Thanks. You too."

BJ bent and gave her a quick hug. Half a minute later, the front door clicked shut.

Eleanor eyed Methuselah, who continued to keep his distance.

"I won't squeeze you hard again, my friend. Want to come back and curl up in my lap?"

He sniffed and, nose in the air, stalked into the living room and his favorite sunny spot on the carpet.

At least one of the occupants of this house had no ambiguity about his feelings.

Eleanor pushed herself to her feet, giving her stiff knees a few seconds to loosen up while she placed her empty iced-tea glass on the tray on the front of the walker. Once she got a refill, she'd settle into her chair in the living room and mull over BJ's proposal.

At the refrigerator, she paused to examine her collage of photos, as usual. Such happy memories. All those exciting trips with Stan by her side, plus the activities that had brought her fulfillment back in the days when she'd made a difference in the lives of others.

Except . . .

She frowned, her gaze skipping from photo to photo. Birthright . . . food pantry . . . church mission work. All worthwhile activities—but her work had been done at arm's length, from behind the scenes, insulated from those she was helping.

Come to think of it, had she *ever* directly touched the life of someone in need, person-to-person?

Hard as she tried, she couldn't come up with one instance where she had left her comfort zone to get personally involved. All her life she'd played it safe.

In fact, the biggest risk she'd ever taken was marrying Stan and moving away from the town where she'd grown up.

Yet once he died, she'd scurried back here as fast as she could, to the comfort of familiar surroundings.

She examined the photos again, one by one. Was it possible she was being too hard on herself about her hands-off role? Wasn't it okay to support charities from . . . a distance? After all, people who worked behind the scenes, removed from the actual beneficiaries, produced lots of positive results.

But if you were asked to help one person specifically . . . wasn't there an obligation to do so if you had the ability?

Yes, Eleanor, there is.

As the gentle chide echoed softly in her mind, fear bubbled up inside her again—along with denial.

I can't do this, Lord. Most of the people I helped years ago . . . they weren't like me. They were a different color, or spoke a different language, or lived in a family situation or a degree of poverty I can't begin to understand. We had nothing in common.

Or did they?

The lesson Charley had passed on from his grandmother the day he'd brought her those tacos replayed in her mind. The notion that, while looks and language and traditions might differ, all hearts feel the same emotions.

The woman might have lived thousands of miles away in a foreign country, but she'd been wise.

As was her grandson.

A man whose skin was a different color and who had come from a culture that was foreign to her.

A man she'd known for two decades and had never once invited into her home, though she'd befriended other merchants in town.

Truth be told, she'd often included people she knew far less well than Charley on the guest list for the annual Christmas open house she'd held until her arthritis finally forced her to give up the tradition.

Eleanor tightened her grip on the walker to steady herself as the truth smacked her in the face.

She was prejudiced.

"Dear Lord." The whispered words reverberated in the silent kitchen as she locked onto the photo of herself mugging for the camera in the back room of the food pantry.

She'd never dealt with the people lining up for the food, because deep inside, she'd considered herself better than them.

Her vision blurred, the photos on the refrigerator melding together in a sea of shame. She might have done worthwhile work—but always with a holier-than-thou attitude. Never had she reached out a hand directly to a stranger in need or made a personal investment in an individual life.

But she had the chance to do that now.

With Luis.

If she could muster the courage to let go of fear and self-righteousness.

Instead of refilling her glass, she trundled into the living room, lowered herself into her chair, and picked up the Bible from its place on the table beside her. Perhaps the Good Book—and prayer —would offer her guidance . . . and answers.

Yet she didn't open the dog-eared pages.

Because she already knew what she should do. She had the means to add a touch of joy and comfort to a life sorely in need of it, and to help ensure that BJ's worthwhile program was given a chance to succeed so others in her situation would be able to stay in the homes they loved.

Eleanor leaned her head against the upholstered back of the chair, smoothing a finger over the worn cover on the book, the weight of it familiar and comforting in her hands.

Forgive me, Lord, for being afraid of people who are different than me. Help me find the courage to do what the good Samaritan did that day on the roadside. Give me grace and compassion to overcome my narrow-mindedness and bigotry. Help me drive out any feelings of superiority. Let me see everyone as an equal and a worthy brother and sister—and act accordingly.

A soft meow sounded at her feet, and Methuselah put one paw on her leg. She leaned down to give him an assist into her lap, where the cat curled into a ball and turned those intelligent amber eyes on her.

"What would you think about having another person live here with us, my friend?" She stroked his soft fur.

He adjusted his position, one paw draped over the Bible—as if pointing her toward Scripture for her answer.

Eleanor scratched behind his ear. "Excellent advice."

Easing the book from beneath his paw, she opened it. Some reading . . . some prayer . . . some thinking . . . some sleep. She'd do all those things before she made a decision. In all of her eighty-eight years, no one had ever accused her of being rash—and she wasn't about to become impulsive at this late date.

But no matter how long she deliberated or dragged her feet, she knew where the process would lead.

The real question was, would she be brave enough in the end to follow the direction she received and take the leap into unknown—and daunting—territory?

The meeting with Eleanor hadn't gone well.

As Eric rounded the corner of BJ's house after the doorbell went unanswered, he took a moment to study her unobserved. She was sitting at the patio table, staring out to sea, distress carved into every line of her features.

His first instinct was to pull her into a hug . . . but he tempered the impulse. Later, that might be appropriate. First, he needed to let her tell him what had happened.

She turned as he drew close, as if sensing his presence, and gave him a shaky smile. "Hi."

"Hi back." He took the chair beside her. "You don't look happy."

Her throat worked as she swallowed. "I should have waited for you."

"What happened?"

He listened as she recounted her visit with Eleanor, resting his elbows on the arms of his chair and steepling his fingers.

"I have a feeling it wouldn't have mattered whether I was there or not."

"You could be right." She sighed. "I guess it seemed like such a perfect solution for her and Luis that it didn't occur to me she'd see any negatives in it."

"Maybe she just needs to get used to the idea of having someone else living under her roof. That would be a big adjustment for her."

"I don't think that was the stumbling block. It was more like she was . . ." BJ shrugged. "I don't even know how to describe it. From the beginning I got the feeling she was unreceptive." She kneaded the bridge of her nose. "I guess I totally misread this."

"Did she say no?"

"Not in words, but her body language spoke volumes. She asked for some time to think about it."

"You want to pay her another visit tomorrow? I could go with you. Strength in numbers and all that."

"I guess it might be worth a try. You made quite an impression on her, in case you didn't know."

He flashed her a grin. "She must be easy to impress. I only paid her one very brief visit."

"Sometimes it doesn't take long to discern a person's character." She locked gazes with him.

He studied her. "Are we still talking about Eleanor?"

"No."

The soft breeze ruffled her hair, which was loose and full today. She hadn't changed out of the slim skirt and soft blouse she'd worn to church this morning, and the hue of the shimmering silk was a perfect match for her jade irises.

Lovely.

And hard to resist.

He tried to satisfy his yearning by reaching for her hand. "I'm trying very hard to remember my promise to you, BJ." He cleared the huskiness out of his voice. "However, you're making it difficult."

Her throat contracted. "Maybe I don't want you to remember it."

Eric forced himself to take a slow, deep breath. BJ was disappointed in the outcome of today's meeting. Her emotions were in turmoil. Comfort, not romance, was what was called for—no matter how tempting her implied invitation.

"I promised you we'd be friends when I leave."

"We're already friends."

"I want to keep it that way."

"What about what I want?"

"Which is . . . ?"

She didn't miss a beat. "You. Holding me. Like you did that night at the scene shop."

"A friendly hug?"

She hesitated . . . then gave a slow nod. "Yes."

That's not what her eyes were saying—but he'd try his best to honor her verbal request.

"I can do that." He rose and tugged her to her feet, giving Little Gull Island a quick sweep. "Casper's not around, is he?"

A smile tweaked the corners of her mouth. "I haven't seen him."

"Good. I don't want another rude interruption."

He pulled her into his arms, tucked her against him, and dipped his head to inhale the fresh scent of her hair. Her heart thudded against his chest as he rested his cheek against her temple, and he had to work hard to convince his lungs to keep inflating and deflating.

Just like the last time he'd held her, this felt right . . . and meant to be . . . and better than any—

All at once the cell phone in his pocket began to vibrate.

She jerked back, breaking the connection . . . and let out a shaky laugh. "That was a weird sensation."

"Sorry. I'll turn it off." He pulled it out.

"Don't you want to see who it is first?"

Not really.

What he wanted was to go back to that hug.

He gave the screen a quick scan, trying to place the vaguely familiar name. Oh yeah. The guy his father had introduced him to after church today.

Huh.

He'd assumed the man's request for contact info was mere politeness to make up for picking his brain for ten minutes.

"Go ahead and take it." BJ eased back and retook her seat.

No reason not to now. The romantic mood was gone—through no fault of Casper's.

As soon as Eric said hello, the man got down to business.

"I enjoyed meeting you earlier today. After I got home, I did some googling—and I'm impressed with your background. Your father said you're visiting between jobs, but I wondered if you were planning to be around long enough to draw up some incorporation paperwork for the new business I mentioned. It appears you've had plenty of corporate legal experience. I could find an attorney in Coos Bay, but I'd rather work with someone from Hope Harbor."

Eric focused on the horizon, where a large ship traveling to places unknown hovered in the mist between land and sea. How should he respond to the out-of-the-blue request?

When the silence lengthened, the man spoke

again. "I understand you're here on a vacation of sorts, and I don't mean to infringe on that. But based on your experience, I don't think this would be a major commitment. Unless you're planning to leave within the next week or two."

"No. I'll be around for a while." He glanced over at BJ, who'd retaken her seat at the table.

"In that case, could we get together tomorrow to discuss this? If you decide to pass after that, I'll understand."

Why not? The only other item on his Monday agenda was working on his painting.

"Sure. I can do that."

After arranging to meet at the café for a late breakfast, they said their good-byes.

"That sounded interesting." BJ crossed her legs.

Eric tried to ignore her shapely calf as he sat beside her. "Yeah. That was the . . . uh . . . guy who cornered me at church this morning. He needs some legal assistance."

"I guess he wasn't mooching after all."

"I guess not."

"Are you going to help him out?"

"I didn't come down here to work—but it sounds like a simple incorporation, which wouldn't take long. I'll have to research fees for that sort of job, though. I have a few law school friends I can contact who are single practitioners in smaller towns. They should be able to give me what I need—if I decide to let work interrupt my time off."

"Mmm." She looked out over the sea. "Speaking of work infringing on play—I'm curious about something."

Her tone was casual, but some subtle undercurrent put him on alert. "What's that?"

She transferred her attention to him. "I know you put in long hours in Portland, but how come you're not married . . . or involved . . . with someone? You're a well-educated, accomplished man who also happens to be a nice guy. I would have pegged you as a chick magnet."

His neck warmed. "That was direct."

"We agreed to be honest with each other. And since you know my whole dismal dating history, I didn't think that question was out of line."

No, it wasn't. He did owe her some relationship background—except there wasn't much to tell.

"I've never been serious about anyone. I date on occasion, but my job has always been my focal point. I was never willing to invest the time required for a long-term relationship."

"And you never got lonely?"

The wistfulness in her inflection tugged at his heart, and he thought back to Charley's comment in the cove yesterday. The man had nailed it.

"With my grueling work schedule, I didn't have a chance to get lonely."

"Maybe it was a blessing in disguise, then."

A few weeks ago he might have agreed with her. But since he'd been home . . . since she'd entered his life . . . he was all too aware of what he'd been missing.

And if he went back to that lifestyle—no, *when* he went back to that lifestyle—he had a feeling it was going to be a lot harder to keep the loneliness at bay, no matter how many hours a day he worked. "It might have been."

"I bet you never had a problem getting a date if you wanted one, though."

"No." Why play coy?

"Lucky you."

"Dating isn't all it's cracked up to be, BJ. Noisy bars, crowded restaurants, making small talk, discovering fifteen minutes into the date that you have no desire to spend the next three or four hours with someone and then having to endure the rest of the evening."

"You never met anyone whose company you enjoyed for a whole evening?"

"Once in a while. But never anyone I was willing to sacrifice billable hours for."

She gave a soft laugh. "That is utterly unromantic."

"Until now."

At his caveat, her laugh died. "What . . . what do you mean?"

He had no idea.

"I . . . uh . . . meant that if we'd met in Portland, I would have found time to see you."

"Oh."

That was all she said—but it was obvious from her subdued tone she'd hoped for more. That she'd wanted him to say he liked her enough to think about reconsidering the future he'd carefully laid out.

But he wasn't there yet. Might never be. Changing direction after the years of effort he'd plowed into his career was a decision that required a lot of careful thought.

And until he was ready to make it, the wise course was to steer clear of the subject.

"So are you going to pay Eleanor another visit tomorrow? I could go with you after you finish at the house for the day, if you like."

"I think I'll wait until she gets back to me. If she says no, I can give it one more try."

I, not we.

She was pulling back.

And who could blame her? She'd been very clear about her interest in him, and he hadn't responded the way she'd hoped. After all the hurt she'd endured in previous dating experiences, she was wise to protect herself.

He needed to protect her too—by maintaining the just-friends status quo until he knew what he wanted to do with the rest of his life.

"I guess I'll be going." He rose.

"Eleanor sent you some fudge cake. Let me get it for you."

She stood, skirted the far side of the patio table, and disappeared into the house. Fifteen seconds later, she was back, a plastic-wrapped wedge in hand.

"Thanks." He took it from her.

"I'm only the delivery person. You need to thank the baker."

"I'll do that."

Behind him, a loud belch sounded.

"Casper's back." BJ folded her arms tight against her chest, her smile strained around the edges as she turned toward Little Gull Island. "He may not be polite, but he's predictable. The little guy never fails to show up when I need to see a friendly face."

"I have a friendly face too."

She angled back toward him, no trace of humor in her demeanor now. And though her words were soft, they packed a punch. "But you might not always show up. I can't take that risk, Eric."

It wasn't an ultimatum. BJ wasn't the type to resort to that. She was simply stating a fact.

But ultimatum or not, he knew as he said good-bye that they would share no more hugs unless he found a long-term-potential way to incorporate her into his life.

The persistent ring of the phone pulled Eleanor from sleep, and as her location registered, her jaw dropped.

Good heavens—she'd spent the night in her recliner!

The phone trilled again, and she fumbled in the pocket of her slacks while Methuselah gave her a puzzled look. As if he couldn't figure out why she'd never gone to bed.

"Because I was up late thinking about BJ's visit, if you must know, and fell asleep in my chair."

The cat yawned . . . stretched . . . and moseyed out to the kitchen—in search of breakfast, no doubt.

She finally put the phone to her ear and said hello.

"Good morning, Eleanor. How are you today?" Rose's cheery voice came over the line. The woman sounded awake and alert, as if she'd been up for hours.

What time was it anyway?

Eleanor peered at her watch. Eight o'clock. Past her usual rising time.

"I'm fine. Thanks." She smothered a yawn with her free hand.

"Oh dear . . . I didn't wake you, did I?"

"You know I never sleep late, Rose." A true statement—even if today happened to be an exception to that rule.

"I know. That's why I didn't think you'd mind an early call. I heard you had a fall, and I wanted to see how you were doing."

"It wasn't a fall. It was a . . . misstep. And how did you find out about it?"

"I happened to overhear Charley ask that nice BJ about you at the taco stand last evening. I wasn't eavesdropping, mind you."

No, that wouldn't be Rose's style. They'd been friends too long for her to doubt the other woman's honesty or genuine concern.

"I'm right as rain. Nothing more than a bruise or two."

"Well, I'm glad to hear that. Falls can be serious for these old bones of ours. Did you hear about Martha?"

"Martha who?"

"Atwood. I believe you've met her at a few church functions. She lives in Coos Bay but has a number of friends in town who invite her to special events."

A vague image formed in her mind of a tall, thin woman with silver hair.

"I think I know who you mean."

"I'm sure you'd recognize her if you saw her. To make a long story short, she fell off a step stool in her kitchen while changing a lightbulb.

Broke her pelvis and arm and a couple of ribs." Rose tut-tutted. "Now she's in rehab and has had all kinds of complications. She lives alone, so there's some doubt about whether she'll be able to return home. It's such a shame."

"Yes, it is." A cloud of doom settled over her. That could be her future someday.

"Well, on to cheerier subjects. Besides checking on you, I was hoping to convince you to have lunch with me at the café tomorrow. We haven't done that in ages. And afterward, if you're up to it, we could stop in at the grocery store. I'd be happy to get anything you need, but I know you enjoy trips to the market."

Her spirits took an uptick. "That would be lovely. I was beginning to get cabin fever."

"Wonderful. I'll pick you up about eleven. Take care."

Methuselah wandered back in as she ended the call. After sitting on his haunches, he gave her an annoyed stare.

"You're hungry, aren't you?"

He meowed.

"So am I." She set her Bible on the table, juggled her walker into position, and hoisted herself to her feet. "Let's see what we can round up for breakfast."

The tabby rose too and did a U-turn toward the kitchen.

She followed, slowing as she passed the bulging

rack of cookbooks. In the old days, she'd been a whiz in the kitchen. Stan had liked to brag about her skills to his friends. At least in that one area of her life, she'd been bold and adventuresome.

Resting one hand on the walker, she skimmed her fingers over the spines of the books. When had she last made any of these recipes? Her final Christmas open house, perhaps—several years ago. The layer of dust on top told the story.

She started to move on . . . but stopped as one title caught her eye.

International Favorites Made Easy.

That had been a fun book to page through—and Stan had enjoyed the recipes she'd tried from it. He'd always said the dishes made him feel like he was dining in exotic locations without ever leaving the comforts of his home.

She touched the book as an idea began to take shape in her mind.

Hmm.

She pulled it out, continued toward the table, and set it down. Reading material for breakfast.

And potentially something more.

"Come on in out of the rain, Eric."

Knuckles poised over the studio door, Eric froze. Once again, Charley had somehow known not only that he had a visitor but who the visitor was.

The man must have some kind of security system he kept under wraps.

Eric lowered his hand, twisted the knob, and ducked in out of the soupy weather.

Charley swiveled toward him on his painting stool as strains of Vivaldi filled the studio. "What brings you all the way out here on such a dreary day?"

He gave the space a quick sweep. No visible security monitor—but that was meaningless. Knowing Charley's aversion to all things electronic, he had it tucked in some unobtrusive—

"Eric?"

He snapped his head back to the artist. "I, uh, was hoping to get in some painting today, but my favorite spot is out of the question in this weather, and the house is noisy and dusty." Besides, no one other than his dad and Charley knew he'd started painting again—and he wanted to keep it that way for now.

"Your easel's still in the closet." Charley went back to his work-in-progress. "Help yourself and let me know if you need any other supplies."

The same greeting he used to give him in the old days.

It was like rewinding the clock twenty years.

After retrieving his painting gear from the car and getting situated, Eric went to work. Within minutes, he was lost in the creative process.

Only when he paused to rotate the kinks out of his neck did Charley speak. "Want a soda?"

"Yeah. Thanks." He glanced at his watch.

Blinked. Where had the past two hours gone?

Charley sauntered over and handed him a Dr Pepper, swigging his Coke as he examined the painting that was beginning to come to life.

As the artist took his sweet time perusing it, sweat began to bead on both the can and Eric's forehead.

When he couldn't stand it any longer, he popped the tab and spoke. "Well?"

"You haven't lost your talent." Charley swirled his soda and scrutinized the painting. "I see you fixed the proportion on the woman."

"Yeah."

"Better. The hint of gray in the distant sky is a clever touch too. Adds to the subtle tension, the sense of the unknown. A dash of Permanent Violet Dark might enhance that mood. I have some if you need it." He wandered over to the turntable and changed out Vivaldi for Gershwin.

Eric stood and stretched. "You opening the taco stand today?"

"Maybe later." The strains of *Rhapsody in Blue* filled the room. "How'd your meeting at the diner go this morning?"

Eric almost choked on his soda. "How did you know about that?"

"I stopped in for an omelet and saw you."

"How come I didn't see *you?*"

"Guess you were too engrossed in that intense discussion you were having. Seemed serious."

Eric swigged his soda. It had been—and he had some decisions to make—but he'd forgotten all about them once he began painting.

"It was. The guy I was with wants me to do some legal work for him while I'm here."

"You interested?" Charley wandered back to his easel.

"I don't know. It's an easy job—and the pay's not bad." Better than he'd expected, actually, based on the fee schedules forwarded to him by his law school colleagues who'd gone into small-town practice.

"Sounds like a no-brainer."

Eric retook his seat. "You want the truth? I'd rather paint while I'm here."

"A person can't paint sixteen hours a day. Not without going crazy. Look what happened to poor Van Gogh. That's why I have the taco stand. Variety is the spice of life. Too much of anything can warp your viewpoint."

"I practiced law sixteen hours a day in Portland."

"I rest my case."

"Very funny."

Charley drained his can of Coke and settled back on his stool. "That wasn't a joke. How's life been since you left those kinds of hours behind?"

Better. Happier. More interesting.

But he kept that to himself.

"Different."

"You enjoying yourself?"

"For the most part."

"Then why not work a little law back in? Sounds like this legal job would leave you plenty of time for other pursuits, and it would help keep your skills sharp."

"I'm considering it."

Charley picked up his paintbrush. "Makes sense to me."

As the other man went back to painting, Eric finished his own soda and set the empty can on the floor beside him. Charley's advice—about painting and life—tended to be sound. Maybe he ought to take the job. If nothing else, it would ease him back into law so returning to the rat race wouldn't be a total shock.

Rat race.

Bad choice of words.

Partner track had a better ring to it.

But as the driving beat of the Gershwin classic filled the room, he knew they were one and the same.

And he was less and less certain that reaching the finish line he'd always planned to cross was going to bring him the kind of joy and satisfaction he'd expected.

"Stone, would you grab that piece of crown molding and . . . hang on a sec." Holding on to the ladder with one hand, BJ pulled her vibrating cell out of her pocket with the other and skimmed the screen.

Eleanor.

The woman must be ready to give her an answer . . . and BJ had a sinking feeling she knew what it was going to be.

If her intuition was correct, she might have to take Eric up on his offer to accompany her while she paid the woman a second visit—even if it would be safer to walk a wide circle around him after their parting last night. Anything that gave her companion program a fighting chance would be worth some personal risk.

The phone vibrated again, and she descended the ladder. "You guys can go ahead and put up that section of crown molding. I'll be back in a minute."

As Stone and Luis went to work, she exited the suite, moved down the upstairs hall of what would soon be the Seabird Inn, and greeted her caller.

"I hope I'm not interrupting anything." Eleanor sounded a bit breathless.

"I have a few minutes to spare." Hammering began to reverberate in the empty room beside her, and she continued down the hall. It would be quieter on the first floor.

"Well, I've been thinking about your proposal ever since you stopped by yesterday. I have to admit the notion of having a stranger under my roof takes me outside my comfort zone. But after a lot of thought and prayer, I've decided to explore the possibility. I believe it might help me make a decision if I got to know Luis better." The woman cleared her throat. "So if he's interested in the idea, I'd like to invite him to have dinner with me here at the house tomorrow night."

BJ stopped halfway down the stairs. Sank onto a step. Leaned a shoulder against the wall.

Eleanor hadn't said no.

"BJ . . . are you there?"

"Yes." She did her best to regroup. It appeared she didn't need to muster any of the arguments she'd been marshalling. Nor did she need to tap into Eric's powers of persuasion. At least not yet. "I'm here—and that's great news. I'm glad you're open to the idea."

"Why don't you check with Luis, see what he says? I know you thought he might have some reservations too. If you could let me know by this evening whether I should expect him for dinner, I'd appreciate it."

"Of course. I'll talk to him this afternoon and get back to you as soon as I have an answer."

"I'll be waiting to hear, sweet child. Don't work too hard, now."

Once they ended the call, BJ remained sitting on the steps while the hammering continued above her. One hurdle passed. Eleanor hadn't said yes yet, but her willingness to explore the idea was heartening. And once she got to know Luis, she'd be impressed. The man was the perfect solution to all the problems she faced living alone—and she was the perfect solution for him too.

Now all she had to do was convince Luis that her proposal had nothing to do with charity and everything to do with helping those in need—and that he could play a key role in making life better for older Hope Harbor residents.

No small challenge.

But if she succeeded, her Helping Hands companion program might get off the launching pad after all.

BJ was nervous.

Luis watched her surreptitiously as she guided the truck toward 101. The unplanned trip to the building supply store wasn't all that unusual, but in general she didn't take either him or Stone along. Even Stone had raised an eyebrow when she'd tagged Luis to accompany her.

And her white-knuckled grip on the wheel was unsettling.

It couldn't have anything to do with his work, though. He put in a full day and never scrimped on effort. She'd complimented him often.

Was it possible the green card issue had come up again?

He fought back a sudden wave of panic. Tamed it. No. There was no reason to be afraid on that front. He was legal—and he'd done nothing to endanger his status here.

That left just one possibility, as far as he could see . . . and it churned his stomach.

She'd told him from the beginning that her business wasn't yet able to support two permanent full-time workers, but that his place was secure until the Seabird Inn renovation was completed.

That job, however, would be winding down in two weeks. Unless there was another big project in the offing, someone would have to be let go—and Stone had seniority.

But how would he survive without a job?

An image of the paramedic course materials arrayed on his table materialized in his mind, but he erased it. That would be a perfect job—but it wasn't an option. Even if the tuition was free, he needed money to live on. He had to have a job *now*.

Maybe Father Murphy could help him if . . .

". . . repercussions of that bug we had?"

As the end of BJ's question registered, he tuned back in. "I am sorry. I did not hear what you asked."

She shot him a quick, concerned glance. "You okay?"

"Yes. Much better. The flu is gone." That must be what she'd asked about.

"No. I meant . . . you seem a little tense."

He seemed tense? Did she realize she was taut as a plumb line?

Perhaps he should make this easy for her. She'd done more than enough for him as it was. He couldn't expect her to keep him on the payroll if there wasn't sufficient work—nor should she feel guilty if she had to let him go.

"I was thinking that the job . . . it is almost finished. I understand if you do not need me after that."

Her face went blank for a moment . . . and then understanding dawned in her eyes.

She muttered a few unintelligible words under her breath, checked her rearview mirror, and swung into one of the scenic pullouts that lined this picturesque stretch of highway. From here, on a clear afternoon, they'd have a panoramic vista of the ocean and the sea stacks that today were shrouded in gray mist.

Like his heart.

BJ shut off the engine and angled toward him. "I'm sorry, Luis. I didn't mean to worry you. Your job with me is secure for the foreseeable future. I have some big projects coming up. Grace Christian wants us to remodel their offices as soon as we finish at John's, and after that I'll be doing a single-family home out at Harbor Point Cranberries."

"Then . . . why do you look worried?"

"I'm not worried, exactly." Her death grip on the wheel, however, said otherwise. "It's just that a program that means a lot to me is . . . it's hanging in the balance, and I need your help to make it happen."

If there was anything he could do for this woman who'd given him a job when he desperately needed one, he would. "Tell me how."

He listened as she laid out the proposal she'd presented to the Helping Hands board members, outlined their reservations, and described the model program she wanted him to participate in.

"Eleanor thinks it would be helpful if you two got to know each other better before either of you commit, and she wanted me to extend an invitation from her for dinner tomorrow night at her house."

As she concluded, he turned toward the window. The somber haze hid the beauty of the landscape, but the splendor was there nonetheless, ready to emerge as soon as the sun returned.

Was this his chance to brighten his own world, while brightening others' as well?

Perhaps.

Moisture clouded his vision as the potential impact of her request began to compute, and he swiped the back of his hand across his eyes.

"You don't have to commit to anything now except dinner." Tension wove through BJ's words.

"I would be happy to eat with Eleanor."

Her face went blank again, as if she was shocked by his answer. Finally she exhaled . . .

and the strain in her features eased. "Excellent. I'll let her know you're coming." She reached over and touched his arm. "Thank you for considering this, Luis. The program means a lot to me."

"It could mean a lot to many people. And I should thank *you*. Eleanor seems like a nice woman, and her house would be a fine place to live."

"Well, let's hope you feel the same after sharing dinner with her tomorrow night." She put the truck in gear and pulled back onto the highway just as a ray of sun managed to peek through the obfuscating fog swirling around them.

And as they continued along the winding road, he hoped that was a positive omen for the future . . . beginning with dinner tomorrow.

— *21* —

Luis having dinner w/El 2morrow nite. Fingers XXed. BJ

Propping one elbow on the mattress of his sofa-sleeper bed, Eric reread the text that had been sent late yesterday afternoon. Funny. In his old life he'd checked his messages constantly. Here, he often forgot about the phone.

And he'd sure forgotten about it at the studio. Once Charley had left to go open the taco stand for a few hours, he'd lost track of time. Only the dimming light had finally pushed him out. He'd gone straight home, foraged for dinner in the fridge, and crashed—as exhausted as if he'd spent a full day in court.

It had been a better type of exhaustion, though. The kind that comes from pouring your soul into your passion.

But he should have skimmed his messages once he got home. BJ must be wondering why he hadn't responded.

He also owed his potential client a response, based on the follow-up email the man had sent pressing for an answer.

The banging overhead that had awakened him

started up again. He could respond to BJ in person. An email acceptance would suffice for the client.

At least his conversation with Charley had clarified that decision. He did have time for both art and law in his present circumstances, and the two might balance each other. He couldn't paint intensely sixteen hours a day or he *would* end up like Van Gogh. Yesterday's marathon had been invigorating—but draining.

He tapped in a response to the client, pulled on his jeans, ran a comb through his hair, and left his makeshift living room suite to track down BJ.

"We missed you at breakfast." His father turned from the dining room table across the foyer, where he was sorting through what looked like Mom's collection of napkin rings.

"Sorry. I slept like a rock until the noise kicked in." He strolled toward his father. "What are|you doing?"

"I thought I'd pull these out of mothballs and put them to use. I think the guests will enjoy them, don't you?" He held up one ring with an enameled hummingbird attached and another fashioned from a seashell.

"The women will."

"Since they're the ones who usually choose this kind of place, their approval is what matters. One of the lessons I've learned through the years is that as long as you keep the ladies happy, it's smooth sailing."

Speaking of ladies . . .

"I hear you. Have fun with that." Eric waved a hand toward the collection. "I'm going to run up and talk to BJ for a minute."

"She's not here."

He halted and swung back. Not the news he wanted to hear. "Where is she?"

"On her way to Coos Bay. It seems the plumbing subcontractor is dragging his feet. She said she was going to light a fire under him—and based on the fire in her eyes, I expect she'll succeed. Hey . . . remember this one?" His father held up a seagull made of feathers.

He grimaced. "How could I forget? Mom almost scalped me after I used those for target practice in the backyard the year you guys gave me the BB gun for my birthday. I didn't know there were any survivors."

"This one must have escaped the firing squad." His dad chuckled. "Want it as a souvenir?"

"I'll pass. It does *not* evoke happy memories."

"I bet my guests will appreciate it, though—and the story behind it."

"Going for laughs at my expense, huh?"

"Anything to keep my patrons entertained." His dad winked and put the ring back in the pile. "There's a message from Rose Marshall on the kitchen counter for you. She wants to know if you'll review her personal documents—will, power of attorney, that sort of thing—to ensure they're up-to-date. Apparently some acquaintance just had a major accident, and she wants to get her house in order."

Good grief. Clients were coming out of the woodwork.

"What did you tell her?"

"That I'd pass on the message. I didn't make any promises. What did you decide to do about our friend from church?"

"I'm going to take the job. I could do it in my sleep, and the pay rate is higher than I expected for small-town legal work."

"High enough to tempt you?"

"To do what?"

"Stay."

Eric shoved his hands in his pockets. "That's not in my plan, Dad."

"Plans can change."

"I've put a lot of years into mine. It's not easy to alter your course midstream."

"No one ever said life was easy. Besides, taking the easy route doesn't always lead to the best views."

"That sounds like something Charley would say."

"I'm flattered. He's a smart man." He gingerly picked up a froufrou woodland fairy napkin ring and dangled it from his finger at arm's length. "What's your verdict on this one?"

Eric pretended to gag.

"Yeah. I'm with you. What was your mother thinking?" He shook his head and set it down. "I left some quiche in the oven for you. Help yourself."

"Thanks."

Eric wandered into the kitchen and picked up the message his dad had left on the counter. If work like this kept falling into his lap, it would almost be a job.

Almost.

But even if there was sufficient work to sustain him, practicing law in Hope Harbor wouldn't lead to the kind of success he'd envisioned. Only a big-city partner track job would do that.

Hope Harbor, however, *would* provide a better quality of life—and allow him to deepen his relationship with BJ.

Too bad the two options were mutually exclusive.

While he retrieved his breakfast from the oven, the hammering upstairs resumed at full force.

Fitting.

It matched the sudden pounding in his head as he struggled with the choices before him.

Because the direction he chose in the coming days could change his life forever.

Was that . . . ?

Luis stopped on Eleanor's front porch and sniffed the aroma wafting through the open windows.

No.

It couldn't be *moros y christianos*.

Could it?

He sniffed again, the distinctive aroma transporting him back to the land of his birth. To happy times spent with family and friends.

But how would Eleanor know about that?

And where would she have learned to cook such a dish?

All at once, the door opened—as if she'd been watching for him through the sidelight windows.

"Good evening, Luis." She gave him a tentative smile. "Please come in."

"Good evening." He stepped inside, skirting Methuselah as he held out the small box of chocolate truffles he'd purchased. "For you."

"My." Her hand fluttered to her chest. "What a thoughtful gesture. These are my favorites." She took the box.

"I know. I asked BJ what you might like."

"You didn't have to do this. They're very pricey—a special-occasion splurge."

"A guest always brings a gift. My mother taught me this when I was a young boy."

"She must have had admirable manners."

"Yes. We were not rich, but she was a lady."

"Well . . ." She motioned him toward the back of the house. "Why don't we visit in the kitchen while I finish dinner?" After setting the box of candy on the tray attached to the front of her walker, she led the way.

He followed, pausing on the threshold of the room. A bright yellow cloth draped the table, which had been set with china, cloth napkins, and gleaming silver. Cut-crystal glasses filled with water were at each place, and fresh flowers over-flowed from a vase in the center.

His throat tightened. "You have gone to much trouble."

"Not at all." She waved a hand and continued toward the stove. "I like to cook. Your visit gave me an excuse to prepare a real meal again. I hope you like black beans and rice."

Bendiga mi alma!

That aroma *was* moros y christianos!

"It is one of my favored foods." He choked out the words, steadying himself on the back of a chair.

"I've never made it until today, but I understand it's a popular dish in your country. I hope it's edible." She smoothed a hand down her slacks. "If it's not, I also have . . . *pulpeta Cubana*. With hard-boiled eggs and olives."

Her pronunciation was off, but Luis had no problem understanding what she'd said.

"I also like meatloaf. My mother cooked it on special days. You are very kind."

A flush rose on her cheeks. "I try to please my guests. If you'll help me set out the food, we're ready to eat."

Luis carried the dishes to the table under Eleanor's direction, then assisted her as she took her seat.

Once he was in his chair, she folded her hands. "I know we come from different religious backgrounds, but I always pray before meals."

"It is good to give thanks. And while we do not go to the same church, we honor the same God. I do not think he will mind if we share a simple prayer." He bowed his head and made the sign of the cross.

After a moment, Eleanor spoke. "Thank you, Lord, for this food and this opportunity for Luis and me to get acquainted. Open our hearts to your will and help us make the right decision about BJ's proposal. Please bless us with health and abundant grace. Amen."

"Amen." Luis echoed her as he crossed himself again.

"Help yourself. Don't be shy. There's enough here to feed an army." Eleanor swept a hand over the food and took a slice of meatloaf. "So tell me how you're liking Hope Harbor now that you've been here a few months."

"It is a beautiful place, and I have been shown much kindness." He spooned out a hearty helping of the black beans and rice, inhaling the savory scent of garlic.

"It must be very different than your home-land."

"The weather and plants and customs are different, yes. But I am . . . adopting." He frowned. "That is the proper word?"

"I think you mean adapting."

"Yes. I am adapting." He shoveled in a mouthful of rice and beans, the salty flavor of ham, the kick of onions and green peppers, the earthy tang of cumin exploding on his tongue.

He closed his eyes, savoring the taste of home.

"Is it good?"

At the anxious note in Eleanor's voice, he met her gaze. "It is better than good. It is . . . *maravilloso*."

"I'm glad you like it." She took a helping herself. "BJ told me about your medical background and the barriers to practicing medicine here. I'm sorry. That must be a disappointment."

It was . . . but even that heartache couldn't ruin his enjoyment of this wonderful meal.

"I miss medicine, yes. I studied very long to help the sick. But I see the need for passing many tests to get a license. I was lucky to have another skill to earn money."

"You passed many tests in Cuba to be a doctor, didn't you?"

"Yes." But they meant nothing here.

"I hope someday you can practice medicine again."

"No. Being a doctor here . . . it is too hard. But there is a paramedic program at the college, and . . ." Luis pressed his lips together. Why had he brought that up? No one but Eric—and whoever had requested the material—knew about the information he'd received. Talking about unrealistic dreams was foolish.

"Go on." Eleanor leaned forward encouragingly.

"No." He pushed it from his mind and took another helping of beans and rice. "It will not be possible for many years—and only if it is in God's plan. Now I work in construction." He lifted his heaping fork in salute. "The food is *delicioso*."

Taking his cue, she let the subject drop.

She did ask many more questions during the meal, though—and he asked a few of his own. By the time she retrieved a plate of homemade *pastelitos* for dessert, he had no qualms about signing on for the pilot program BJ wanted to run.

Yet as he bit into one of the flaky, jam-filled turnover pastries, he was less certain about Eleanor. She'd gone above and beyond in her efforts to welcome him to her home, and she couldn't have been more hospitable during the meal.

But there was a certain . . . restraint . . . in her manner that suggested she harbored doubts.

That did not bode well for the outcome.

When they finished, however, she surprised him.

"While I load the dishwasher, why don't you

go upstairs and take a look at the two rooms that would be yours if we decide to pursue BJ's proposal? I haven't been up there since I've been saddled with that nuisance"—she flicked a hand at the walker, an expression of disgust contorting her face—"so ignore the dust."

"I will help you first."

"No. You're a guest tonight. There are many chores I can't do these days, but kitchen duties aren't a problem. Besides, I enjoy puttering around out here, especially when I have the chance to cook a real meal. Go on up and poke around. No need to hurry. This will take me a few minutes. I'll meet you in the living room once I finish."

He acquiesced with a nod. Although he'd prefer to help with the cleanup, it was also important to respect turf—and preserve pride.

After making his way back through the living room, he ascended the stairs to the second floor of the cozy Cape Cod house. The two rooms off the small landing were each about nine-by-twelve. There was also a full bath. Both rooms were furnished, one featuring a queen-sized bed, the other a couch. All the furniture was covered with sheets, and while the rooms were as dusty as Eleanor had warned, this was a palace compared to Sea Haven Apartments.

No matter what Eleanor expected of him in return, no matter how much maintenance and caregiving work she required, he was ready to sign on the dotted line.

But was she?

He lingered in the rooms, as she'd requested, trying to figure out which way this might go.

In the end, however, all he could do was put the outcome in God's hands—and hope for the best.

He was every bit as nice as BJ had said he was.

Eleanor stacked the dishes in the dishwasher, rinsing by rote as she tried without success to find one negative about the man who'd shared her table. As far as she could see, he would be a dream companion. He was considerate, respectful, polite, articulate, and imbued with a quiet dignity.

She finished loading the dishes and ran a finger over the small box of truffles on the counter. Based on the frugal life BJ said he led, this had been a huge extravagance.

He must be very interested in moving in with her.

And who could blame him, based on the dismal, bare-bones accommodations BJ had described? Anything would be a step up from that. He would reap huge benefits from this arrangement.

But she would too.

She gave the room a critical sweep. A piece of wallpaper was beginning to peel in the corner, and the baseboards could do with a fresh coat of paint. Another door had begun to stick. The outside needed work too. Old houses required constant attention—and more energy than she had these days. The place was getting away from her. But with Luis's assistance, she ought to be able to stay on top of things.

Plus, having someone on hand to fetch and carry and run errands would be a godsend. You could only impose on friends so long before the friendship began to wear thin. Rose was an angel —but she had other obligations too.

Best of all, though? If Luis were here, she would no longer have to eat dinner alone, with just Methuselah for company. He was a great cat—but not much of a conversationalist.

Eleanor gripped her walker, shifted it toward the living room, and pushed toward her chair, decision made.

As she settled in, Luis appeared in the doorway. "The rooms are nice."

"Have a seat." She waved him toward the couch at a right angle to her chair.

In silence, he crossed the room, perched on the edge of the sofa—and waited.

"If we can come to an agreement about expectations, duties, and responsibilities, I'm willing to give this a try. What do you think?"

The emotions parading across his face weren't difficult to read—disbelief . . . relief . . . gratitude . . . and hope.

"I think . . ." His words scraped out, and he swallowed. "I think I would like to try this too."

"You realize I'll expect help with household chores, maintenance, errands—those kinds of duties?"

"Yes. BJ told me how it would work. I would be happy to do all those things for a nice place to live and home-cooked meals."

"I can provide both of those." She played with a loose thread on the arm of her chair, debating how much more to say. How much risk to take. But in the end, she spoke what was in her heart. "I can also provide friendship, Luis, if all of this works out as I hope. Living a solitary life can be lonely."

"Yes." He focused on his clasped hands. "I, too, have been lonely."

More than she, no doubt, given all he'd lost and his new life among strangers.

"If we're in agreement, I'll call BJ tonight and let her know we want to proceed. I believe Eric will draw up some paperwork for us to sign. Do you have any other questions for me?"

"No. I cannot think of any. I am too . . . my heart is too full."

Pressure built behind her eyes, and she blinked it away. "It's been a long day of cooking for me, and I know you put in a full day of physical labor. Shall we call it a night?"

He rose at once. "Yes. Of course."

"I put together a package of leftovers for you to take home. You'll find it in the refrigerator."

"You do not have to—"

She held up a hand. "No protests. I'll be eating the remains of our meal for a week as it is. There's plenty for both of us."

After a brief hesitation, he retreated to the kitchen.

While he was gone, she pushed herself to her feet and trundled over to the front door.

Once he joined her in the hall, he stopped beside the door, cradling the leftovers in his hands as if they were as fragile and precious as her Waterford Christmas tree ornaments. "May I speak from here?" He placed his hand on his heart.

She gripped her walker and dipped her head.

"When I came to this town, I did not think life would ever be happy again. I knew no one, and my soul was heavy with grief. That sadness has not gone away, but the kindness you and others have shown me has made it smaller. May God bless you for all you have done to help BJ with her program—and for sharing your home with me."

She nodded, unwilling to trust her voice.

With a slight bow, he let himself out.

As the door closed behind him, Methuselah wandered over to rub against her leg.

She swallowed and slowly exhaled. "What do you think of all this, my friend?"

He purred and trotted over to his favorite rug, a new spring in his step—or was she imagining things?

Probably.

But as she returned to the kitchen to close up the house for the night, she wasn't imagining the new spring in *her* step.

It was possible, of course, that once they were living under the same roof, one or both of them would decide the arrangement wasn't working and end it after the trial period.

Yet deep inside, she couldn't help hoping that tonight was the beginning of a long and beautiful friendship.

— 22 —

Yes!

Fingers trembling, BJ pressed the off button on her cell and clutched it to her chest.

Eleanor and Luis were in!

Sparing Tracy and Michael's in-progress house plans no more than a distracted glance, she left them behind and headed for the kitchen. If this news didn't merit the rest of that fudge cake she'd saved when she'd met with Eleanor, nothing did.

After removing the treat from the freezer and nuking it to take the chill off, she poured herself a tall glass of milk, retrieved a fork, and sat down at the kitchen table to indulge.

Halfway through the rich confection, a niggle of guilt prodded her conscience as she eyed the phone on the table beside her. She owed Eric a call in response to the text and voicemail messages he'd left during the past twelve hours while he'd been MIA.

Where had he been all day, anyway?

Not that she *wanted* their paths to cross. After their exchange on the patio Sunday afternoon, it was much safer if their orbits didn't intersect.

Warmth flooded her cheeks just thinking about how close she'd come to crossing a dangerous line that day . . . and inviting *him* to cross it.

Thank goodness an incoming call had interrupted the charged scene. Sharing hugs that might end up going far beyond friendly would put her heart at major risk.

However . . . ignoring his messages was rude. The man deserved an update on the Eleanor/Luis situation—especially since he'd volunteered to put together the necessary paperwork.

She finished her cake, picked up her cell, and tapped in his number.

Halfway through the first ring, he picked up.

"I was beginning to think we were never going to connect." He sounded tired but happy to hear from her.

"I'm not the one who disappeared all day."

"I . . . uh . . . had some things to do. And *you* were gone this morning. How did you fare with the plumbers?"

He didn't intend to tell her where he'd been.

Fine. She could deal with that—even if it rankled for some reason.

"They'll be at the house Friday morning. Early."

A chuckle came over the line. "Dad said you'd get action."

"I've dealt with plenty of contractors. I know most of their stall tactics—and how to circumvent them. But I didn't call to talk about plumbing. I have good news."

"Eleanor and Luis hit it off."

"Yes. They're ready to sign on the dotted line."

"I'm glad I got a head start on the boilerplate agreement."

No surprise that a go-getter like him would take the initiative and dive in.

"How close is it to being ready?"

"Very. I'll make a few final tweaks tonight and email it over for your review. Let me know if you have any questions or comments. Once it's finalized, all we'll need to do is personalize it for their situation. I could meet with them tomorrow night, after Luis gets off work, if that fits with everyone's schedule."

"I'll talk to both of them, but I can't imagine either has a pressing commitment. Why don't you plan on seven, and if anything changes, I can let you know tomorrow at the house."

"I may not be around much, but you can text or call me."

Another disappearing act.

What could he be up to?

"Sounds like you have a busy schedule."

"Yeah. Um . . . another legal job came up."

She had no reason to doubt that—but she had a feeling there was more to his absences than legal chores.

"Must be nice to have work fall into your lap."

"I guess . . . if you're in the market for work. That wasn't the purpose of my visit. However, I'm learning to go with the flow. You'll be there tomorrow night, right?"

"Yes. If the program gets the nod, future paperwork will be overseen by Helping Hands, but this is my baby for now."

"That's what I assumed. I'll see you there."

No offer to swing by and pick her up.

It's safer this way, BJ.

True.

But that didn't mitigate her twinge of disappointment.

"Okay. Enjoy the rest of your evening." She prepared to hang up.

"Wait. I have a question for you. After all your work on the sets for the musical, you're going to one of the shows this weekend, aren't you?"

"Yes—and I almost forgot to tell you. There'll be a comp ticket at the door for you, usable for any of the performances."

"Which night are you going?"

"Friday, unless I get hung up at your dad's with the plumber."

"Want to go together?"

Despite a surge of pulse-elevating adrenaline, she hesitated. The more time she spent in his company, the more difficult it would be to cope after he left. But he might show up Friday night anyway. It was silly not to sit together—and it would be a safe environment. What could happen in an auditorium full of people?

"Why don't I meet you there? Whoever gets

there first can save a seat." That seemed like a reasonable compromise.

"I suppose that will work." He didn't sound happy about it, however. "Maybe I'll see you tomorrow at breakfast."

"I doubt it. I need to stop in at Grace Christian and take some detailed measurements for the remodel job that's next on the schedule. Breakfast will be over before I arrive."

A beat of silence passed.

"Are you avoiding me, BJ?"

He *would* ask a direct question like that.

"I told you. I have a meeting at Grace Christian."

"I mean in general."

Of course he did.

"I lead a busy life, Eric."

He muttered some phrase she didn't catch. "Look, I'm a lawyer, remember? Trained to spot evasive maneuvers. I thought we agreed to be honest with each other."

She pressed a finger against one of the chocolate crumbs on her plate and popped it in her mouth—but it didn't help sweeten what she needed to say.

"We did." She took a deep breath and plunged in. "The truth is, I like you a lot. Too much, in view of the high probability that one day soon, you're going to leave Hope Harbor—and me— behind. I don't want another broken heart . . . and that would be a given if our relationship escalates."

"Even if I leave, there might be a way to—"

"No." She swallowed, clamped her fingers around the edge of the table, and said what she had to say. "I don't want to fall for a man who puts career above everything else. I know what the partner track demands, and it doesn't leave time or energy for much else. That's not the kind of life—or relationship—I want."

A sigh came over the line. "I figured that's how you felt after our . . . on Sunday. There's one thing you need to know, though. Your heart isn't the only one in danger here."

Nice to hear . . . even if it wasn't likely to change the outcome.

"But your career is more important."

"I didn't say that. The truth is, I want it all."

"That's not how life plays out for most people. We have to make choices, let go of things that aren't as important to get the things we want most."

"Assuming you know what those are."

"You'll work it out, Eric—sooner or later."

"I'd prefer sooner."

"Patience is a virtue."

"I haven't mastered that one yet, but I've got diligence down pat—and I'm not bad at humility." Although his teasing tone seemed forced, it lightened up the conversation.

Better. She didn't want to end this exchange on a heavy note.

"Speaking of diligence . . . I'll let you get to those boilerplate tweaks you mentioned."

"Check for the document in about an hour. See you tomorrow night—and sleep well."

"You too."

But as she ended the call and cleared the table, she had a feeling that during the long night to come, restful slumber was going to prove as capricious—and elusive—as true love.

BJ looked exhausted.

As the lights went up for the intermission of *Oklahoma*, Eric examined her profile. Since their meeting at Eleanor's on Wednesday night to finalize all the paperwork, faint shadows had appeared beneath her lower lashes, and the fine creases at the corners of her eyes had deepened.

If he hadn't been spending every spare moment at Charley's studio, he'd have noticed her fatigue sooner.

"So what held you up?" He angled toward her. All she'd offered as she'd slid into her seat while the lights dimmed for the overture was a murmured "Sorry I'm late."

She shifted her attention from the program to him. "I had an errand after work that ran long."

"You feeling okay?"

"Yes. Why?"

"You look like you've been working too hard— or are toying with a relapse of whatever bug you had."

"No relapse." She closed the program. "It's been

busy, though. I spent last night after work at Eleanor's, cleaning the upstairs so Luis won't have to contend with layers of dust before he can go to bed tomorrow night."

"That wasn't part of the deal."

"I didn't mind." She shrugged off the frown he aimed at her. "And I don't have any plans to repeat it. They'll be on their own once he moves in. I just want this to get off on the right foot."

"You take on too much."

"I could have tapped you to help me clean the bathroom, I guess. I bet you'd have loved that." She shot him a teasing grin.

"If you'd asked, I might have volunteered."

"I haven't seen you to ask."

"I've been busy."

"So you've been saying."

She waited, giving him a chance to expound . . . but he wasn't ready to admit he'd been doing some serious painting. Fortunately, several members of the audience interrupted their exchange to compliment him on the backdrop.

He stood to greet them, and as he chatted, BJ rose and wandered off.

His spirits nose-dived.

Could she be leaving? Would she text him in a few minutes to say she was tired and had decided to go home?

Before he could call out to her, she disappeared into the milling throng.

Short of being rude, he couldn't ignore the cluster of people around him . . . but as the group thinned at last, she reappeared juggling two disposable cups and a napkin-wrapped packet.

Relief flooded through him—and when another guy stepped up, he prepared to dispense with him quickly. At this rate, the lights would go down again and he'd have no chance to talk to BJ.

"Steve Davis. Nice job on the backdrop." The man extended his hand, and Eric returned his firm clasp.

"Thanks." He sent a pointed glance toward BJ, who was edging down the row past a brigade of knees toward their seats. If the guy had any people skills, he'd get the hint.

Steve followed his line of sight. "I won't keep you—but I do have a favor to ask. I'm on the city council, and I heard through the grapevine that you've temporarily hung out a shingle. We've got some urgent zoning proposals that need a legal review, and we'd appreciate your input. We used to have Rick Jenson on retainer for this kind of work, but after he retired we never got around to lining up a new contact."

It was raining work in this town.

At this rate, he wasn't going to have a chance to finish his painting before he left.

"I understand you're here on vacation, so if it's an imposition . . ."

"I'll tell you what." No reason to leave ill will

387

behind, and it sounded like the council was in a bind. "Why don't I swing by city hall and see what you have? If it's not too involved, I'm sure I can fit it in."

"That would be great. And thanks again for pitching in behind the scenes here." Steve waved toward the stage in the packed auditorium. "You have real talent."

While the man returned to his seat, BJ sank back into hers, holding up a cup. "Lemonade was the only beverage at the concession stand."

"Perfect." He sat too and sipped the tangy drink.

"Take your pick." She opened the napkin to display several cookies.

"You choose first."

"Not necessary. I like them all."

He selected an oatmeal raisin. "What's on your agenda for tomorrow?"

"I told Luis I'd haul his stuff over to Eleanor's." She set the bundle in her lap and picked up a chocolate chip cookie.

"He's not wasting any time, is he?"

"Would you, if you lived in that dump?"

"True. You need some help?"

"I don't think so. He said he only had a few boxes. Mostly clothes." She broke off a piece of cookie, her expression troubled. "It's sad how little he has to show for his life, considering all he's done. I can't imagine how difficult it must be to face every new day knowing the people and work you love are gone forever. How does a person cope with that kind of loss?"

Sometimes by taking desperate measures—or trying to.

But that secret would remain between Luis and him.

"Having a decent place to live might lift his spirits."

"I hope so. Let's pray the four-week trial period works out well for both of them."

The lights blinked, signaling the end of the too-short intermission.

"You need to help me finish these." She handed him another cookie.

"I never turn down cookies." He gave her a smile.

She returned it . . . but the curve of her lips was perfunctory rather than sincere.

Understandable.

She'd warned him she didn't want to get involved. Had been honest about her feelings— and her fears. Keeping him at arm's length was the prudent course.

Too bad he couldn't reach for her hand, twine his fingers with hers, and offer her the assurance she needed to feel comfortable about moving forward.

Instead, as the lights went out and the orchestra launched into the entr'acte, he kept his hands occupied with lemonade and cookies.

Because despite the doubts that had begun to surface with alarming regularity, he wasn't yet ready to admit that maybe . . . just maybe . . . it might be time to change the course he'd set on the day he'd applied to law school fourteen long years ago.

She needed a taco.

She also needed a shower.

BJ braked at the intersection in downtown Hope Harbor. Straight would take her home; a left would take her to the wharf.

Her stomach growled.

Decision made.

She flipped on her blinker and hung a left.

Five minutes later, after finding a parking spot near Charley's despite the Saturday tourist rush, she joined the queue at his stand. Inching toward the window, she inhaled the aroma of sizzling fish and savory spices.

"Morning . . . or should I say afternoon?" Charley smiled as she approached the window. No matter the crowd, he never appeared to be in a rush. Yet for some odd reason, the line always advanced at a reasonable pace.

"It's definitely afternoon—and I'm hungry."

"One order coming up . . . or is someone else joining you?"

"Nope. I'm having a solo lunch." By choice. Eleanor had invited her to stay and eat after all of Luis's boxes had been hauled in, but it was better to let the two of them settle in without a third party hanging around.

"Well, Floyd and Gladys will keep you company." He waved a spatula toward two seagulls perched on the boulders that sloped down to the water.

She peered at the two birds. As near as she could tell, they were identical to the dozen others in the vicinity.

But if he said so . . .

"I think I'll take the food home and enjoy it on my patio."

"Not a bad idea. Maybe Casper will join you."

She blinked. Had she ever mentioned Casper during their chats? Not that she recalled . . . but it could have slipped out somewhere along the way. How else would he know her pet name for the companionable seal on Little Gull Island?

"He might."

"Did you get Luis set up in his new digs at Eleanor's?"

"You heard about that already?"

He flashed his white teeth. "You wouldn't believe how much I hear—and see—from this counter."

"I don't doubt that. I bet you could write a book."

"Not on my bucket list. Now Luis, he could write a book."

"Yeah. I hope this arrangement works out for both of them."

"I have a feeling it will. Those two will be good for each other." He gave a pan of onions and peppers a shake. "What's Eric up to, now that he's done with the backdrop?"

She dipped her chin and pulled some bills out of her pocket. "I haven't seen a lot of him since then."

"I heard he's taken on some legal work." He flipped the fish and began to line up the corn tortillas.

"Yes." But not enough to account for his long absences from the house.

If he was making himself scarce, however, she had no one to blame but herself. He was simply respecting the boundaries she'd set.

"It would be nice if he stayed on in Hope Harbor." Charley sprinkled some kind of seasoning on the sizzling vegetables in the pan.

Wouldn't it, though?

"I don't think that's in his plans."

"Might be, if there was sufficient motivation." He piled the tortillas high with filling, added a dollop of sauce to each, and deftly folded them over.

"Like what?" She laid her money on the counter and sent him a wary look.

"Oh, I don't know." He wrapped the tacos in white paper and slipped them in a brown bag. "I suppose it would help if he had a personal reason to stay." He met her gaze as he slid the bag across the counter and picked up the money.

Sheesh.

Now Charley was playing matchmaker.

Should she pretend she didn't know what he meant . . . or take advantage of the man's counsel, which had proven wise in the past?

She checked over her shoulder. For once there was no line behind her.

Why not see what he had to say?

"I tried to give him one." She kept her voice low, in case someone appeared. "But I don't want to put too much pressure on him. I'd rather he make his decision based on what *he* wants rather than what I want."

"Do you think he's clear about what you want, though?"

She opened her mouth to reply in the affirmative.

Closed it.

Maybe not.

Yes, she'd been upfront about her attraction to him, but she'd never admitted that the notion of marriage had begun to creep into her thoughts— assuming all continued to go well.

Nor had she admitted it to herself . . . until now. Marriage was a gigantic step—and it was much too soon to suggest to him that was where she hoped they might be heading.

Besides, you could scare a man off by bringing up the M word this early in a relationship.

"Because a man would have to have a powerful reason to rethink the dream of his youth. And there's nothing as powerful as a human connection." Charley picked up on his previous comment as if there'd been no gap in the conversation, then eased sideways to greet some new arrivals. "Be with you in a minute, folks."

BJ grabbed the bag and her change and took a step back. "Thanks for the food . . . and the food for thought."

He offered her a mock salute, his grin back in place. "No charge for the latter."

Bag in hand, BJ wandered back to her truck and swung up into the driver's seat. A lot of what Charley had said made sense—but what if she told Eric she was thinking long term about them, he changed his life for her . . . and the relationship fell apart?

That would add to the boatload of guilt she already carried.

Dodging the traffic on Dockside Drive, she kept a firm grip on the wheel—and her emotions. She needed to make the correct call on this . . . whatever that turned out to be.

And since she was clueless about how to proceed, she'd better put some heavy-duty prayer at the top of her priority list until she got the direction she needed.

"What's going on with you and BJ?"

Eric set his laptop on the kitchen table and plugged it in while he responded to his father. "What do you mean?"

"She's skipped out on my breakfasts three days in a row." He pushed a button on the dishwasher, folded his arms, and leaned back against the counter. "I don't think my culinary skills are the culprit. Luis and Stone haven't had a problem polishing off any of the food I've made."

"Why do you think it has anything to do with me? I haven't even seen her for five days." Eric busied himself powering up the laptop.

Silence.

When he slid a glance toward the sink, his father was watching him with the let's-cut-the-bull look he'd employed whenever his wayward son had tried to finagle out of responsibility for some transgression. The look that said he knew exactly what was going on whether Eric admitted it or not.

Not.

He turned his attention to his email. "After I finish with this, I'm going to go over to . . ."

His phone began to vibrate.

Saved by the buzz!

He pulled out the cell . . . hesitated over the

unfamiliar name on the screen . . . pressed talk. Better to converse with a stranger than play bob-and-weave with his dad.

"Eric Nash?"

"Yes."

"Carol Richter."

As she named the company she represented, his eyebrows rose. Everyone in the legal business had heard of that top-notch recruiting firm.

"If you have a few minutes, I'd like to discuss an opportunity with you. I spoke with an attorney at your previous firm who wasn't interested in making a move, but he gave me your name and number."

"Yes. I have time." He checked on his father, who'd gone back to puttering around the kitchen.

He listened as she described a partner-track position at one of the premier law firms in Seattle. A firm larger and more prestigious than the one he'd been affiliated with in Portland.

"Only top-tier candidates are being considered. I can tell you that the salary and benefits are commensurate with or better than those at your previous firm—and this is a fast-track position. The expectation is that whoever is put in this job will be made partner in six to twelve months."

As she concluded, Eric leaned back in his chair, nerves thrumming. This was exactly what he'd worked to achieve all these years. "I'm interested."

"Excellent. I'll email you some additional

information. They'd like to fill this ASAP. Assuming you find the material to your liking, would you be available to interview on Monday?"

That *was* fast.

But he had no commitments that would prevent him from taking a trip to Seattle.

"Yes."

"Good. Expect my email in the next twenty minutes. If you could get back to me by noon tomorrow, I'd appreciate it."

"No problem."

After they said their good-byes, Eric slipped the phone back in his pocket.

"That was a very one-sided conversation."

Keeping his face averted, Eric tapped a finger against the polished oak table. Unless the information the woman sent contained some unacceptable fine print, he was going on this interview. Since his dad would soon find that out anyway, why keep it a secret?

He swiveled around. "It was a recruiter."

"Ah." His father strolled over, mug of coffee in hand, and took a seat. "I'm not surprised. Someone with your experience and skill wasn't going to languish for long. Is the job a fit?"

"Yeah." He told him about the firm and the fast track to partner.

"Sounds like everything you always wanted." His father sipped his coffee, watching him with that discerning gaze of his.

Eric tried not to squirm. His dad was right about this job dovetailing perfectly with his goals, but now that the initial ego-boost excitement was dissipating, he wasn't as thrilled as he should be. As he *wanted* to be.

Which was more than a little disconcerting.

"I think it has potential." He tried to inject a healthy dose of enthusiasm into his response.

"I guess you'll be doing the interview."

"Yes—unless I find a deal breaker in the material she's sending, which is doubtful."

"Well . . ." His father rose. "It's been nice having you around, even if the visit was shorter than I hoped."

"I haven't been offered the job yet."

"You will be. They'd be crazy not to grab you —and that's not just your father talking. You're smart and practical and articulate, you have excellent credentials and experience, and your work ethic is second to none. My guess is, by this time next week you'll have an offer."

"That might be ambitious."

"I don't think so." He smiled, but there was a touch of melancholy in it. "At least Seattle isn't as far away as New York or Chicago, where you could have ended up. Maybe you can get home a little more often in the future. There will always be a room for you at Seabird Inn."

"Dad . . . it's not a done deal." He fought back an odd surge of panic.

"Only a matter of time." He rinsed his mug and set it in the sink. "I need to run a few errands. Will you be home this afternoon?"

"No." If his stay here was coming to a close, he needed to put as many hours as possible into his painting or he wouldn't finish it before he left.

"I'll see you later this evening, then." His father headed for the attached garage.

Once he left, silence descended in the house . . . until the usual commotion began upstairs.

No wonder his dad ran a lot of errands during the day.

He powered down his laptop, closed the lid, and carried it toward the living room to stow with the rest of his stuff.

At the foot of the stairs, however, he paused. BJ would be up there by now. Should he tell her about the call?

No. Why not wait until he reviewed the material the recruiter sent . . . in case this fell through?

Fat chance, Nash.

Yeah, yeah. He knew that.

Nevertheless, he continued to the living room, grabbed his jacket, and ducked out to spend the day painting. Later, after the house was quiet and BJ was gone, he'd tackle some of the legal work he'd taken on and review the material the recruiter was sending. He could tell BJ about the interview in a day or two.

Coward.

He slid behind the wheel of the BMW and jabbed the key in the ignition.

Okay, fine. He didn't want to have a discussion that would prove her fears were valid . . . and cause her to back off even farther. Besides, a lot of pieces had to fall into place before he walked away from Hope Harbor. An excellent interview. A firm offer on the table. Agreeable terms, including a definitive timeline for partner. Only then would he have to make a decision about whether to accept the job.

And until that moment arrived, he wanted to hold on to the pipe dream that he could have it all.

No matter how foolish or unrealistic that was.

"Let's call it a wrap for today, guys." BJ pulled off her baseball cap and swiped the sleeve of her T-shirt across her forehead. It was downright stuffy in John's upstairs—and she had places to go on this sunny Friday afternoon.

Stone and Luis began to collect their tools and clean up while she evaluated the status of the job. All that remained were a few finishing touches. They ought to wrap up by the end of next week, assuming the plumber stuck to the schedule he'd laid out. The painters could move in after that, still allowing John ample time to decorate and furnish the rooms in advance of his projected opening.

"It's coming along nice." Stone gave the room a cursory sweep, picked up his lunch pail, and headed for the door.

"Yeah, it is."

"See you Monday." He lifted a hand in farewell.

She waited until his footsteps sounded on the stairs, then crossed to Luis. "Everything going okay at Eleanor's?"

"So far, so well." He twisted his wrist to check his watch. "Do you need me to do anything else?"

"No. We're done. You in a hurry?"

"Eleanor . . . she is making *arroz con pollo*—rice and chicken—tonight. She goes to much trouble for our meals. I do not want to be late, and I promise to stop at the market on the way home. She needs groceries, and there is some medicine to pick up."

It appeared they were both trying hard to make a success of their new living arrangement.

If the setup continued to work well, she should have no problem convincing the Helping Hands board that the companion program would be an excellent addition to the organization's services.

"I won't keep you. Go ahead and enjoy your dinner."

"I am sure I will."

He took off too, leaving her alone in the suite.

She wandered over to the window that offered a panoramic view of the harbor and distant horizon, thanks to the house's hilltop location. John's guests would enjoy their stay here. It was a perfect setting for relaxation, rejuvenation—and romance.

Sighing, she turned away from the picturesque vista.

As far as she could see, there was no romance on *her* horizon. She'd been clear about the kind of relationship she wanted—and didn't want— and Eric had apparently decided the demanding partner track was more appealing than a less-stressful life in Hope Harbor . . . and an architect who called the town home.

On the other hand, she'd never told him directly about the depth of her feelings.

"A man would have to have a powerful reason to rethink the dream of his youth. And there's nothing as powerful as a human connection."

As Charley's words echoed in her mind, she massaged the sudden throb above the bridge of her nose.

Maybe she ought to be honest. Tell him that despite their short acquaintance, she was falling in love with him. That she wanted to give their relationship a chance, to tap the potential she was certain it held.

But what if he gave up everything and the two of them fizzled?

She was back to square one.

Huffing out a breath, she flipped off the light in

the suite and trudged down the corridor. Perhaps the brief, spur-of-the-moment getaway she'd planned would bring her some clarity—and help her build up the courage to bare her heart. Besides, why rush the process?

After all, what could happen to change the status quo in a mere handful of days?

"You want to tell me what's going on?"

At the out-of-the-blue question, Eric angled away from his easel to find Charley watching him, paintbrush in hand. He had a feeling the man had been observing him for a while. "What are you talking about?"

"You've been painting like you're in some kind of race for the past two days. What gives?"

"What time is it?"

"Close to four-thirty. I'm getting ready to mosey over to the wharf and cook for the Friday night crowd. Where's your watch?"

"I took it off last night and forgot to put it back on."

"That doesn't sound like you."

"I have a lot on my mind."

"I'm picking that up. I'll repeat my earlier question. What gives?"

Steeling himself, he set his brush in the container of solvent beside him. He couldn't put off telling Charley about his trip any longer.

"I have an interview Monday with a law firm in

Seattle. I'll be leaving early tomorrow morning, driving to my condo in Portland, and continuing to Seattle Sunday."

"You apply for this job?"

"No." He gave Charley a condensed version of how it had come about. "On paper, the position appears to be tailor-made. I was trying to finish this by today"—he tapped the edge of his canvas —"but I'm not going to make it."

"Hmm." His mentor twirled his brush between his fingers. "You planning to leave another unfinished painting to clutter up my studio?"

"I don't have the job yet."

"You will."

"I wish I was as certain of that as you and my dad are."

"Are you?"

He furrowed his brow. "What's that supposed to mean?"

"Think about it." He stood. "So are you going to finish that or not?" He waved toward the canvas.

"I hope so."

"Me too." He cleaned his brush in some solvent. "I'm going to take a shower and go feed some folks. If I don't see you before you leave, have a safe trip."

"Aren't you going to wish me luck?"

Charley ambled over to the turntable and lifted the needle, shutting off the mellow jazz strains of Stan Getz. "Luck is an overrated commodity. I'll wish you success at finding your destiny instead. Turn off the lights and lock up as usual when you leave."

Without waiting for a reply, he walked out of the studio, closing the door with a soft click behind him.

Silence descended—and all at once the air in the studio felt flat, as if every volt of energy had been sucked out of the room.

Eric examined his painting again . . . picked up the brush . . . put it back. The motivation to finish was gone. Besides, he wouldn't be able to manage that, no matter how late he worked tonight—and he had a lot of driving ahead of him in the next two days, plus some prep work for the Seattle meetings. Better reserve some stamina for that.

And for breaking the news to BJ about the interview.

He couldn't put it off any longer.

Perhaps he could catch her at the house before she closed up shop for the day.

But by the time he cleaned up at the studio and got home, her truck was already gone from the street in front. So was Stone's rattletrap car. He did manage to snag Luis as the man was climbing on his motorbike.

"Hey, Luis!" He opened his window and waved at him as he pulled up.

"Hello, Eric." He left the bike and crossed to the car.

"How's it going?" Based on appearances, Eric could guess the answer. In the week he'd been at Eleanor's, Luis's eyes had lost some of their sadness. He'd also been upbeat in the exchanges Eric had initiated every couple of days.

"Things are . . . better."

"I'm glad to hear that." Not unexpected—but it was reassuring to have it affirmed. "I take it everyone's gone for the day?" He motioned toward the house.

"Yes—but I forget my wallet and had to come back." He patted his back pocket. "I think BJ had someplace to go. She said we should all get an early start on our weekend."

That was out-of-pattern behavior. As far as he could tell on the days he'd been around at quitting time, she was always the last one out the door.

"Thanks. Tell Eleanor I said hello."

"I will be happy to." With a wave, he hurried back to his motorbike.

Resting his hands on the steering wheel, Eric watched Luis rev the engine and roll down the street. Why not swing by BJ's, see if he could catch her at home? She might have stopped there before setting out for wherever she was going this evening—and the news he had was best delivered in person.

He put the car in gear and wove through the town toward Sea Rose Lane . . . but a hundred yards down her street he slowed.

Her truck wasn't in the driveway.

She must already be gone . . . or might she have swung by Charley's for dinner?

Reversing direction, he returned to the center of town and drove down Dockside Drive, scanning the parked vehicles.

BJ's truck wasn't among them.

As he passed the taco stand, the aroma of grilling fish wafted into the car, and his stomach rumbled. No surprise, since he'd painted through lunch instead of stopping to eat.

But he wasn't up for another go-round with Charley, much as he loved the man's tacos.

Too bad his dad was meeting a friend for dinner. Otherwise, the two of them could have shared a pizza.

He turned the corner and accelerated toward Main Street. The café wasn't a bad option for solo dining. After he grabbed a bite, he'd swing by BJ's again.

Unfortunately, when he once again rolled down Sea Rose Lane an hour later, there was still no sign of her truck.

He pulled into her driveway, letting the engine idle while he tapped her number into his cell. If he could find out when she'd be home, they might be able to . . .

The call rolled to voicemail.

It figured.

"BJ, it's Eric. I'd like to see you tonight . . . or first thing in the morning. Let me know which would work better for you."

Message sent, he pocketed the phone, backed out of her driveway, and steered the BMW toward home. Only if they couldn't connect before he left town would he resort to passing on his news by phone.

But he'd rather see her face, touch her hand, reassure her that . . . what? He wasn't getting ready to leave Hope Harbor behind?

Frowning, he stopped at the end of the street, verified there was no traffic either direction, and pulled out. What *was* he going to tell her, beyond the fact that he'd scheduled a promising interview? That was no reassurance. She'd made her position clear. The life he was pursuing was the kind of life she'd left behind and no longer wanted.

Nor did she want to get involved with a man who did.

However, this whole trip north could be a bust, no matter what his dad or Charley thought. He might have excellent credentials, but it was a given that everyone else Carol Richter had tapped for interviews did too. It was possible he'd be back in a few days with nothing on his agenda except finishing up the legal work he'd taken on and completing the painting waiting for him in Charley's studio.

And that was fine with him.

While the job in Seattle sounded perfect, the timing wasn't. If his hand hadn't been forced, he'd have taken another week or two to think about what he wanted to do with the rest of his life. To weigh his options. So no matter what happened in the next few days, this was *not* a done deal. He still had decisions to make.

All of which he needed to tell BJ before he left—or he had a feeling one of the options he was weighing might no longer exist.

— 24 —

Getting away for twenty-four hours had been an inspired idea.

BJ stepped out of the yurt she'd managed to snag in Sunset Bay State Park thanks to a last-minute cancellation and lifted her face to the sunny blue sky above. The small, domed, canvas-wrapped structure might be spartan, but how better to disconnect from the world and clear the clutter from your mind than to spend a peaceful night nestled among old-growth forest?

She strolled down the short path from the campground to a sandy beach protected by towering sea cliffs, energy bar in one hand, bottle of water in the other. One last look at the view and she'd be ready to dive back into the real world.

But her day off the grid had been profitable.

With no electronics or house chores or work obligations or calls from Helping Hands to field, she'd had plenty of uninterrupted hours to think . . . and pray . . . and reflect on what Charley had said to her last Saturday about Eric.

And the counsel of Hope Harbor's resident sage had been wise, as always.

If a certain handsome attorney was searching

for a compelling reason to stay, why not give him one?

While she might not be able to offer any guarantees their friendship would blossom into something deeper, every instinct in her body told her it was headed that direction. He needed to factor her conviction into his decision . . . assuming he returned her feelings.

Given the warmth that filled his sable brown eyes whenever they were together, plus that comment he'd made about her heart not being the only one at risk, she was confident he did.

Emerging onto the beach, she scanned the expanse of sea and sky and forest, letting the tranquility seep into her. She'd promised Eric honesty, and she'd keep that promise, trusting that if they were meant to be together, God would pave the way.

After soaking up the calm for a few minutes and washing down the energy bar with her water, she returned to her yurt, packed up her sleeping bag and the few other items she'd brought, and pointed her car toward home . . . and Eric . . . feeling more relaxed than she had in weeks.

Unfortunately, her newfound serenity was short-lived.

Less than five minutes after she drove out of the park and powered up her cell, it rang—and a quick glance at the screen on the passenger seat goosed her pulse.

Why was Eleanor calling?

She let the call roll to voicemail as she maneuvered a curve on the two-lane road. Should she return the call now or wait until she got home?

Now.

If there was an issue with her prototype companion arrangement, better to deal with it than worry for the whole drive.

As soon as she found a spot to pull off, she called Eleanor, who gave her a cheery greeting.

That was a positive sign.

She hoped.

"Hi, Eleanor. What's up?"

"I'm not interrupting anything, am I?"

"No. I was out of town last night, but I'm on my way back now. What can I do for you?"

"Luis and I were wondering if you might have a few minutes to stop by this afternoon. We have a matter to discuss with you."

Her stomach clenched. "Is there a problem?"

"I don't think so . . . but we'd like to talk with you in person."

That wasn't too comforting.

"I should be back in town in about forty minutes. Why don't I swing by your place before I go home?"

"That would be perfect. We'll see you then."

The line went dead.

BJ blew out a breath.

So much for her peace of mind.

And since it was evaporating as rapidly as the cloud of billowing mist that had enveloped her car a few moments ago, she might as well check the rest of her voicemails in case anything else urgent had come up.

When she tapped the icon, half a dozen messages popped up.

Four of them were from Eric.

The knot in her stomach tightened. Why had he been trying so hard to reach her?

More negative vibes began to swirl around her as she listened to the first message.

He'd wanted to see her last night . . . or first thing this morning.

The next two messages, one left much later last night, one early this morning, were similar.

The fourth message explained the reason for his calls.

He'd left this morning for a job interview in Seattle. Not one he'd sought, but the position met every criteria he'd hoped to find at a new firm.

And no matter how much he'd downplayed his chances in the message, no matter his assurance he'd be back soon, he was going to get the job.

Meaning his return to Hope Harbor would be brief.

She gripped the top of the steering wheel, rested her forehead against her knuckles, and slowly exhaled. This was the outcome she'd expected all along. It was what he'd said from the beginning he was going to do. Hope Harbor's many charms might have caused him to waffle a bit while he was home, but the fact that he'd bolted for Seattle the instant he had a made-to-order opportunity told her everything she needed to know about his priorities.

Swallowing past the lump in her throat, she sent him a quick text, tossed the phone back on the seat, and tried to prepare for whatever crisis awaited her at Eleanor's.

Just got your messages. Good luck.

Eric toweled his hair dry and frowned at the cryptic text from BJ that had come in while he was in the shower. Why hadn't she seen his messages until now—almost twenty-four hours after he'd sent the first one?

Whatever the reason, they needed to talk, not exchange texts.

Pressing his lips together, he called her number.

It rolled to voicemail—again.

Was she tied up . . . or avoiding him?

Cell in hand, he prowled barefoot through the condo, eyeing the beige-toned contemporary furnishings that had once seemed stylish but now struck him as bland and anonymous. There wasn't one item in this place that reflected his personality—perhaps because he'd spent too little time here to ever put his stamp on it.

He crossed the granite and steel kitchen, the tile chilling his bare feet as he set his cell on the counter. Nothing in this room was warm or welcoming, either. It was night and day from BJ's kitchen, with its geometric art prints, framed prayer of St. Francis, and warm gray-blue walls that coordinated with the view of the sea out the window. Nor was it anything like the house where he'd grown up, filled with touches that reflected the people who lived there . . . like woodland fairy napkin rings.

If he got the job in Seattle, he'd be leaving this place—but not the lifestyle it represented—behind.

Was that what he wanted?

Sighing, he grasped the handle of the refrigerator, where he'd stowed the takeout meal he'd picked up from his favorite . . .

His phone began to vibrate against the granite on the countertop across the room.

Another text from BJ?

He raced over . . . snatched it up . . . and stared at the name of the sender.

Charley was texting him?

The man who eschewed all modern electronics? Major disconnect.

Last he'd heard, the Hope Harbor artist was still using one of those throwaway, pay-by-the-minute cell phones. Archaic—but consistent with his preference for face-to-face social interactions.

If he'd resorted to texting, the message must be important.

Eric scrolled through the short paragraph.

I sent a photo of your work-in-progress to one of my galleries yesterday. They'd like to see the piece when (if) it's finished. They get big bucks for paintings.

Eric's jaw dropped.

A high-end gallery wanted to see—and attempt to sell—his painting?

He read Charley's note again to verify his eyes hadn't been playing tricks on him.

They hadn't.

Wow.

He stood there open-mouthed until the cold permeating the bottom of his feet became uncomfortable. Setting the phone on the counter, he snapped his jaw closed and gave the room a blank scan. Why had he come out to the kitchen again?

Oh yeah.

He was going to nuke the takeout he'd picked up at his favorite Chinese place and prep for Monday's interview while he ate.

But he wasn't hungry anymore.

After grabbing his laptop, he moved into the

living room, dropped into the leather chair in front of the TV where he reviewed case files during the rare waking hours he wasn't in the office, and powered up.

He needed to forget about Charley's text and focus on the interview.

Except no matter how hard he tried, he couldn't.

A high-end gallery wanted to see his painting—*if* he finished it, as Charley had been quick to point out.

Wouldn't it be a kick if they offered to display it?

And if they liked this one . . . if they sold it . . . might they be interested in others?

He entered his password at the prompt and went back to daydreaming.

An appropriate term.

Because that's all this was. Selling art was a hit-or-miss proposition. There was zero security in it . . . even for an accomplished and respected artist like Charley, if the confidences his mentor had shared about his income were true. He might make enough from his painting to provide the kind of life he wanted, but he had the taco stand to supplement those earnings, and that business was steady and reliable.

A law practice in Hope Harbor could be too.

Eric tapped a finger against the keyboard as that thought flashed through his mind.

Could it?

Perhaps.

If the gallery did take his paintings and made an occasional sale, there might be sufficient legal work in Hope Harbor to pick up the slack in income. Not that any of the jobs he'd done in his hometown had generated the kind of money he was used to—but if he had enough of them, the revenue could add up to a tidy sum.

Plus, according to Steve Davis, the town's previous attorney had been on retainer with the city. It was possible he could negotiate a similar arrange-ment. A few of the law firms in Coos Bay and Eugene might be interested in sending overflow jobs to an attorney with his credentials too.

It would be a balancing act, but it might work.

There wouldn't be any high-profile cases or huge settlements in a Hope Harbor practice, but working one-on-one with the residents these past couple of weeks had been a lot more enjoyable than most of what he'd done in the world of corporate law.

The cursor blinked at him, and he summoned up all of his powers of concentration. Despite the intriguing dual-career option beginning to take shape in his mind, he *was* going on the interview. A life-altering decision like this shouldn't be made on the fly.

Besides, the whole gallery thing could fall through. They might hate the finished piece. Or they could take it, only to have it languish.

Yet if that happened, there were other galleries —and life in Hope Harbor had a lot to recommend it.

Not the least of which was a lovely architect who was fast stealing his heart.

Luis had been busy.

After shutting off the engine of her truck, BJ examined the walkway leading to Eleanor's front door.

The once-rippling stepping-stones had been reset to provide a flat path for visitors instead of an ankle-threatening obstacle course. There was some new wood on the front steps too, where rotted boards had been replaced.

And if the sound of hammering in the back was any indication, Luis was busy on another project this Saturday afternoon.

She climbed out of the car, dusting off some grains of sand clinging to the hem of her jeans. It would have been better to detour to the house first and shower, but waiting any longer to find out what was going on wasn't an option. Another half hour would have pushed her blood pressure into the danger zone.

Pulse picking up, she climbed the refurbished steps and sent a silent plea heavenward.

Please, Lord, if this is a glitch, help me find a way to smooth it out.

It took two rings to summon Eleanor, who cracked the door a mere three inches.

"Hello, my dear. Methuselah is being a nuisance today, and I'm afraid if I open the door any farther he'll scoot out. Hang on while I divert his attention." She shut the door.

Half a minute later, her muffled voice came through the wood. "The coast is clear, but make it fast."

BJ inched open the door, sidled through, and clicked it shut behind her.

Somehow Eleanor had herded the headstrong cat into the living room, and when BJ entered, he arched his back and gave her an indignant glare.

"Sorry, Methuselah." BJ bent down to ruffle his ear. "But we can't have you roaming the streets."

The cat turned his back, padded to his favorite rug in the sun, and coiled into a ball.

"Goodness. What rude behavior. He's been out of sorts all week. I think he's miffed about having to share me with Luis."

"Is that a problem?" Eleanor couldn't be rethinking the agreement based on her cat's disposition—could she?

"Maybe for him. Not for me. Have a seat and I'll let Luis know you're here. He's building a ramp from the back door to the patio so I can get out there more easily with my walker. He's a treasure."

BJ's spirits lifted. If the arrangement wasn't working out, Eleanor wouldn't be praising the man—would she?

Seconds after the older woman disappeared, the hammering outside stopped.

Less than a minute later, both of them joined her in the living room.

"I'm sure you're wondering why we asked you to come here today." A flush rose on Eleanor's cheeks as she lowered herself into her recliner.

"Yes." The word hitched slightly.

Eleanor looked over at Luis, who perched on the edge of a chair and gestured for her to continue.

"Well . . ." She folded her hands in her lap. "As anyone in town will tell you, I'm not an impulsive person. And as Luis and I have discussed, he isn't, either. But during dinner last night, we both agreed our first week together has far surpassed our expectations. He has been a great blessing in my life already."

"And Eleanor in mine." Luis gave the older woman a gentle smile. "She has made me feel very welcome . . . and needed."

His hostess's color deepened. "I've felt needed too . . . for the first time in a very long while. So we wanted you to know that even though we've only been at this a week, we'd like to adjust the legal agreement to make our arrangement permanent—or as permanent as anything can be when one of the parties is eighty-eight years old."

Methuselah lifted his head and gave a loud meow that sounded like a protest.

"I will win him over yet." Luis rose to stroke the grumpy feline's back.

"I have no doubt of that. You won me over by day two." A twinkle sparked in Eleanor's blue irises. "So what do you think, BJ?"

Think?

She was still trying to come to grips with this unexpected turn of events. Best case, she'd hoped they'd agree to an extension at the end of four weeks. The Helping Hands board wouldn't be satisfied with a model that didn't last several months, since the companion arrangements weren't intended to be short-term.

But this . . . this was a gift from heaven.

"I think . . . I don't know what to think. I'm stunned—but also thrilled. This has worked out better than I could ever have imagined."

"We feel the same, don't we, Luis?"

"Yes. God has been good."

Eleanor pulled her walker close and stood. "I think this calls for a celebration. BJ, will you stay and have some fudge cake—or *pastelitos*—or both?"

"Both." She rose too. No counting calories today.

Half an hour later, after sharing laughter and hugs, she said her good-byes, patted a still-sulking

Methuselah, and retraced her route down the pristine pathway to her truck.

Yet as she climbed behind the wheel and waved to the two people in the doorway who'd found renewed purpose in life, a wave of melancholy washed over her.

This had been a day of surprises.

Some good.

Some bad.

But she wasn't going to let the bad dim her joy for Eleanor and Luis. Their story appeared to be on track for a happy ending.

Even if hers wasn't.

Man, was he beat.

Rotating his shoulders, Eric exited the high-rise Seattle office building where he'd just spent six intense hours. All he wanted to do after the grueling day of back-to-back interviews was return to Portland as fast as possible and crash at his condo.

Instead, he was stuck here for two more nights.

Clenching the handle of the overnight bag he'd retrieved from his car in the underground parking garage, he moved toward the curb. What could he have done except agree when one of the senior partners asked him to stay in town and meet with the head honcho over dinner tomorrow night, after the man returned from meetings on the East Coast?

As it was now, best case, he'd pull into Hope Harbor Wednesday afternoon—unless he wanted to drive straight through for eight hours after the dinner.

Not a smart idea.

He peered through the fog, searching for a cab as he tried to get a handle on his unsettled emotions. He should be elated. Exhilarated. Euphoric. The request to extend his stay meant he'd aced the interview.

But disappointment trumped all those positive emotions—for one simple reason.

He didn't want to delay his return to Hope Harbor . . . and BJ.

A cab emerged from the mist, veering to the curb after he lifted his hand. He slid into the backseat, gave the address of the nearby hotel where the firm was putting him up, and leaned back against the cushions to check his messages. Maybe doing a routine chore would take the edge off his frustration.

There were only two texts. One from his dad, and one from BJ, sent midafternoon.

Pulse picking up, he clicked on hers.

I miss you. A lot.

His throat tightened. In light of her recent withdrawal—and reticence—those five words spoke volumes.

Mood brightening, he tapped in a reply.

Ditto. Home Wednesday.

Finger poised over the send button, he zoomed in on the word *home*. An interesting choice. He could have said *back*. Or *will return*. Or *see you on*. But he'd instinctively chosen *home*.

Telling.

And food for thought.

The cab braked, and he braced himself as the car stopped inches short of clipping a bus that was pulling out from the curb.

Close call.

And the very reason he'd left his car in the office building garage instead of trying to drive through pea soup in an unfamiliar town.

While the cabbie muttered under his breath, swerved around the bus, and picked up speed, Eric leaned back again.

Brakes were a valuable asset—on cars and in life.

Was it time to put the brakes on a career that had taken on a life of its own, leading him to a destination that no longer held the appeal it once had?

Perhaps.

Being plunged back into the frenetic world of high-stakes law for even one day had been a potent reminder of what awaited him if he was offered—and took—this job. Was that how he wanted to spend his days . . . and evenings . . . and weekends . . . and holidays for the foreseeable future?

The cab pulled up in front of the hotel six blocks from the law offices. After paying the bill, he stepped into the swirling fog that hid the tops of the high-rises around him and reduced street visibility. It was impossible to see very far ahead.

He could relate.

But that was no excuse for procrastination. Life didn't guarantee outcomes. In the end, you had to make your choices based on the information at hand . . . and trust your heart.

Ducking inside, he crossed the elegant lobby toward the registration desk, fingered the cell containing BJ's message—and made a decision.

No matter the outcome of tomorrow's dinner, before he returned to Hope Harbor on Wednesday he was going to sweep away the fog hanging over his future.

And by the time he passed the welcome sign at the edge of town, he would know exactly what road he intended to follow in the days—and years—to come.

Still no message from Eric.

His three-word response to her text two days ago had been reassuring, but she'd hoped for more.

Quashing her disappointment, BJ tucked her phone back in her pocket and descended the stairs in John's house.

Her client met her at the bottom.

"I peeked into the suites while you were loading some stuff in your truck. They look ready to decorate."

"Close. We'll be out of your hair by the end of the week, taking our mess with us."

"The mess has been worth the payoff. And to tell you the truth, I'm going to miss you and the crew. You livened things up around here."

"We'll miss you too—not to mention your gourmet breakfasts. That was a great perk."

"You have an open invitation to drop by for breakfast any morning."

"Thanks." She fiddled with a hammer on her tool belt. Would John have any idea about the timing of Eric's return today? His son *was* staying here, after all—and the day was winding down. "Um . . . I guess it's been quiet around the house, with Eric gone." Not the smoothest transition—but it was the best she could come up with.

"Yes . . . after you all leave for the day, anyway." He grinned. "But I've gotten used to being on my own. Besides, I don't expect he'll be around much longer."

So they were on the same page in their assumptions: Eric would be offered—and accept—the position in Seattle.

No need for further discussion.

"Well . . ." She pulled out her keys. "I'll see you in the morning."

"Eggs Florentine are on the menu. Don't be late."

"I won't. See you then."

She pushed through the front door into a heavy gray overcast that was a perfect match for her mood.

But letting the weather get her down was ridiculous. Had she really expected her five-word message to change Eric's mind? Maybe the *three*-word message she'd been tempted to write would have had an impact . . . but it was too soon to throw the L word around—no matter what Charley might think.

Once behind the wheel, she switched on the wipers . . . for all the good they did in this soup. Visibility maxed out at fifty feet, with or without them. Fortunately, she didn't have far to go. And once she got home, she was going to put on some mellow music, change into her sweats, and try to chill.

At the main intersection in town, however, she hesitated. Her cupboards needed restocking, and she wasn't in the mood to grocery shop or prepare a meal. Tacos would be tasty—but there wasn't much chance Charley's would be open. The man was a literal fair-weather chef; if the sun didn't shine, he didn't cook.

She continued straight on, toward home. A can of soup or a scrambled egg would have to suffice—and either would satisfy her meager appetite . . . fallout from Eric's voicemail Saturday about the interview.

Eight minutes later, after pulling onto Sea Rose Lane, she slowed as she guided the truck through the thick fog. This was the biggest downside to her seaside cottage; it might be sunny half a mile inland, but shore property tended to catch all the clouds.

On the flip side, there was nowhere else she'd rather be on a sunny day—and the fog often passed over quickly. In another few minutes it might—

She jammed on her brakes.

Why was there a car in the driveway of the vacant house next to hers?

And why did it remind her of Eric's BMW?

Hard as she tried, she couldn't get a clear read on the car through the swirling mist. No way could it be his, however. If he'd come to see her, his car would be parked at *her* house.

She accelerated again and pulled into her driveway, the house and car next door vanishing into the mist. The owner of the house must have finally found someone to . . .

All at once, a person cradling a huge bouquet of red roses in one arm and gripping a white shopping bag in his other hand materialized out of the fog.

It *was* Eric.

Ten feet from the truck, he stopped and smiled.

Heart racing, she fumbled with the handle, pushed the door open, and slid to the ground, clinging to the edge for support.

"Hi." His smiled broadened.

"W-what are you doing here?"

"Is that any way to greet your new neighbor?"

Her voice deserted her.

"A 'welcome to Sea Rose Lane' would be nice."

"You . . ." The word wobbled, and she tried again. "You rented that house?" She waved toward the structure, one corner of which was now visible through the evaporating mist.

"Uh-huh."

"Why?"

"I like the location. It has excellent proximity."

"To what?"

"You." He closed the distance between them and held out the vase of flowers. "If I'm going to court the most beautiful woman in Hope Harbor, I figured I'd keep the commute short."

She stared into the mass of perfect crimson buds, trying to digest his news.

"The florist removed the thorns. You won't get hurt if you take them. I promise."

A ray of sun peeked through the mist, illuminating the bouquet as she looked at him across the velvet expanse.

His husky promise was for more than roses.

"Does this mean . . . are you staying?"

"Yes."

Joy bubbled up inside her, so intense her heart began to ache.

She took the flowers, burying her face in the sweet fragrance, trying to stem the tears brimming on her lower lashes.

"Hey." He nudged aside the blossoms and lifted her chin with a gentle finger. "I didn't intend to make you cry."

"Th-they're happy tears." More wisps of fog dissipated, and a few patches of blue sky appeared as she swiped her eyes on the sleeve of her T-shirt. "When did you . . . what made you decide?"

"Aside from the text you sent, about missing me?"

She blinked. "You mean . . . that's part of the reason?"

"A big part. I've gotten pretty proficient at reading between the lines during my legal career, and it wasn't hard to translate your message. But there are other reasons." He scanned the rapidly clearing sky. "Why don't we continue this on the patio? I picked up a picnic dinner for us at a gourmet shop in Coos Bay on my way in. I can't think of a better place to enjoy it." Without waiting for her to respond, he took her hand, closed the truck door, and led her around the side of the house.

"Everything will be wet from the mist."

He stopped beside the table, pulled a huge handful of paper napkins from the bag, and dried the table and chairs.

The man had thought of everything.

She sat, placing the bouquet on the far side of the table as he scooted his chair closer to hers and set the bag beside him.

"Would you like to eat or talk? I know you put in a full day of physical labor, and I'm sure you're starving."

Was he kidding?

Food was at the bottom of her priority list.

"I can wait to eat. Tell me . . . everything."

"Okay . . . but I'll start with the most important thing." He wove his fingers through hers, his touch strong but gentle. "After a lot of thought and prayer—and more sleepless nights than I care to count—I realized that losing my job was a blessing, not a disaster. It brought me back to this town, to the roots and values that shaped me. It showed me how messed up my priorities had become, and reminded me of all I've given up in pursuit of my career goals. Most importantly, it led me to you."

"But . . ." BJ took a steadying breath and forced herself to voice her greatest fear. "What if we . . . if we fizzle? Will you still be happy here? Will you regret changing course?"

"I have great confidence our future will be rosy—but if I happen to be wrong, I'm not leaving. I was overdue for a course correction . . . and this is where I belong."

She scrutinized him, searching for any sign of uncertainty, but his eyes were steady and filled with conviction.

The kink in her stomach loosened. "So you're going to practice law here?"

"Yes."

She listened as he outlined his plans for expanding the scope of his legal work beyond Hope Harbor.

"And the best part about my new law career is that it will leave me time for my passion. Correction . . . my *other* passion." He winked at her. "I haven't told anyone except my dad and Charley, but I started painting again after I came back. I have one piece almost finished—and Charley took it upon himself to send a photo of it to a gallery that handles some of his work. They're interested."

Joy bubbled up inside her. "That's wonderful, Eric!"

"Yeah. It is, isn't it?"

"So what will you do if the firm in Seattle offers you the position?"

"I turned it down."

Past tense?

"You mean . . . they already made a decision?"

"The recruiter called on the drive down here today. I didn't expect it to happen that fast, but I'd already made up my mind. Saying no was so easy I knew it was the right decision. But here's the thing, BJ." He angled toward her and took both her hands, his expression solemn. "I'm not going to be making big bucks anymore. I have a nest egg from my years in Portland, but I'll be living a modest life from now on. No glamour or glitz. And unless my art takes off, I'll never be rich or have the kind of financial security I once had."

She squeezed his hands and met his gaze. "If I'd been after glamour or glitz or wealth, I'd have stayed in a big city. A nice little cottage to call home . . . work that feeds my soul . . . and someone to love is all the security I need."

"Then I may be your man." He rose, pulling her to her feet—and into his arms. "Now that I'm back in town, I'm going to try and adopt the slower-paced Hope Harbor vibe. But there's one part of my life I want to rev into high gear—if the lady's willing."

The last tendrils of mist evaporated, and the sun warmed her face as she lifted it to smile at him. "She's very willing."

He tightened his grip and bent down.

Her eyelids fluttered closed, and she rose on tiptoe.

Just as his lips touched hers, a loud belch echoed across the water.

Oh, for pity's sake!

Eric rested his forehead against hers, a chuckle rumbling deep in his chest. "Casper needs to work on his timing."

"I'll say." This was so not funny.

At least Eric was being a good sport about it.

He backed off slightly until he could look down at her. "Since we're going to be doing a lot of this on your patio, I guess we'd better get used to his rude interruptions."

"It's not a problem for me if I'm distracted." She snuggled closer and draped her arms around his neck.

"In that case . . . get ready for some serious distracting."

Once more, Eric bent to claim her lips—and the instant he did, the rest of the world faded away. If Casper was still trying to ruin their moment, he was getting nowhere.

For here in Eric's arms, nothing mattered except them—and the bright and shining future they would create together here in Hope Harbor.

— *Epilogue* —

"Get ready for an early Christmas present—the Helping Hands board just approved the companion program."

As Michael's words came over the line, tears pricked BJ's eyes. Maybe she hadn't been there for Gram, but at least she'd helped give older residents in Hope Harbor an option to stay in their own home.

Thank you, Lord.

"Everything okay?" A warm hand clasped hers.

She nodded, squeezing Eric's fingers as he swung onto Eleanor's street and guided the BMW toward the older woman's house. "Thank you for letting me know right away, Michael."

"No problem. I knew you'd be waiting to hear. Will we see you at Eleanor's open house?"

"I doubt it. Eric and I are pulling up now and we're not staying long." She perused the car-lined street. "Be prepared, though. Parking is at a premium. I think half the town is here."

"I'll alert Tracy to wear her walking shoes."

"Not a bad idea. Tell her I said hi."

"Will do. Talk to you soon."

As she tucked her phone back in her purse, Eric

437

wedged the BMW into a tiny vacant space. "I take it the program's a go?"

"Yes."

"Christmas is coming early this year."

"Really early." She rested her fingers on the back of his hand as he shifted into park. "I got my first present the day you told me you were staying in Hope Harbor. You haven't had any second thoughts, have you?" Hard as she tried to shake it, a touch of doubt nipped at her peace of mind now and then.

"Nope. A very wise woman once told me that to get the things we want most, we sometimes have to let go of things that aren't as important. And what I want most is here in Hope Harbor."

"Even though you haven't sold any paintings yet?"

"Painting was only part of what I wanted. The one-on-one legal work has turned out to be a lot more satisfying than I expected. I like dealing with people versus conglomerates. Plus, the thing I wanted most of all is sitting inches away and planning to spend Christmas with me. My cup is full."

Moisture clouded her vision. "For the record, mine is too."

"Nice to know." He cupped her cheek with his palm, then motioned toward the house behind them. "Shall we go in before all the food is gone?"

"Are you hungry?"

"Always. But we also have another stop on our agenda this afternoon."

"What is this mystery destination, anyway?"

"It wouldn't be a mystery if I told you. Sit tight and I'll get your door."

While he circled the car, she took a quick peek in the visor mirror. Her hair was behaving, no lipstick was stuck to her teeth, and no mascara had smudged under her lashes.

But hair and makeup weren't responsible for the glow on her face or the sparkle in her eyes. Those were produced by love—not L'Oreal.

And one of these days, if all went as she expected, that love was going to lead to the M word they'd both been dancing around for weeks.

It couldn't happen soon enough for her.

Her door opened, and Eric took her hand. Once she was on her feet, he looped his arms around her waist. "In case I haven't told you, you look especially beautiful today. Radiant . . . and very kissable." His breath was a whisper of warmth against her lips.

"Actions speak louder than words." She gave him a playful nudge.

Another car drove by, searching for a parking spot.

"Hold that thought for later—when we have more privacy."

"How much later?"

"Depends on how long you want to stay at the party."

"Forty-five minutes?"

"Half an hour?"

"Sold."

Grinning, he took her hand and led her up Eleanor's walk to the front porch, where a COME IN AND JOIN THE PARTY sign was taped to the front door.

Eric twisted the knob, and laughter, Christmas music, and enticing aromas greeted them as they entered—so different from the silence and solitude that had permeated the house in pre-Luis days.

After passing through the foyer, BJ paused on the threshold of the living room. The walls gleamed with a fresh coat of paint, the scuffs in the hard-wood floor had been buffed out, and a beautiful spruce tree laden with lights and crystal ornaments occupied one corner, where Methuselah held court from under the boughs.

The door opened again behind them, and BJ turned. Charley entered, a box of Eleanor's favorite truffles in hand.

"Merry Christmas, you two. I hoped I'd run into you. I have news." He angled away from the crowd milling about in the living room and lowered his voice. "The gallery called me an hour ago, since you asked me to handle all dealings with them. They sold the painting of the woman by the river."

BJ's breath hitched, and she groped for Eric's hand. The price the gallery had put on the painting had been far beyond what either of them deemed reasonable, despite Charley's assurance that the owner knew how to value art.

"Is this . . . are you sure?" A tremor rippled through Eric's fingers.

"Yes. The check will be in the mail shortly. I always knew you had talent. Not that you need to sell to prove that . . . but it's a nice ego boost."

"And a boost for the bank account."

"Uh-huh. I figured that would make you happy . . . considering." The artist's eyes began to twinkle.

BJ looked from him to Eric. Some kind of silent message passed between them, but before she could try to decipher it, Eleanor trundled over.

"Welcome, everyone."

"Thank you—and Merry Christmas." Charley handed her the candy.

She took it in one hand and touched his arm with the other. "I'm glad you could come, Charley. This invitation was long overdue."

"To everything there is a season." He rested his hand over hers for a moment, then motioned toward the dining room. "Everything smells delicious. You must have been cooking for days."

"And loving every minute of it. But I couldn't have done it without Luis. I don't know how many times I sent the poor man to the grocery store, or asked him to help me dice and chop and mix dough. Go on in and sample the results."

"I never pass up home cooking."

As Charley wandered toward the dining room, greeting his taco customers along the way, Eleanor set the candy on the tray of her walker and leaned in close to the two of them. "I gave Luis his Christmas present this morning."

"What did he say?" BJ tightened her grip on Eric's hand.

"He cried. And his first concern was about leaving you in the lurch with all the new construction business that's been landing on your plate."

BJ's throat thickened. That sounded like Luis. But finding a new full-time employee and allowing Luis to work part time when his schedule permitted was a small contribution to his Christmas gift compared to the older woman's generosity. "Did he accept?"

"Yes. We'll finish the registration process on Monday so he can begin classes in January. After I explained his background to the nice woman at the college, I think they may waive some of the rudimentary courses. He's going to meet with them next week to discuss it."

BJ spotted Luis over Eleanor's shoulder, weaving through the crowd toward them. "Here he comes."

"And I have some new guests to greet." Eleanor

patted Eric's arm. "Take this young man into the dining room and feed him after you talk with Luis."

As Eleanor pushed her walker toward the foyer, Luis joined them.

"I hear Christmas came early for someone." BJ smiled at him.

"Yes. Eleanor . . . she is a wonderful woman. Much like my grandmother. I tell her the gift is too big, but she says the tuition cost is small compared to all I have done for her. Yet she has done just as much for me." His words wavered, and he swallowed. "I have you both to thank too." He took her hand and gave a slight bow.

"I'm happy to accommodate your class schedule, Luis. I wish you could practice medicine full time, but you'll be a wonderful paramedic."

"I am grateful to have the chance to put my medical training to use again in any way I can. I never thought it could happen." He turned toward Eric. "You were right, *mi amigo*. I did make friends. Life did get better. And Hope Harbor is a special place. Thank you for helping me see that."

As the two men shook hands, some silent communication passed between them.

Interesting.

They must have bonded somewhere along the way.

Once Luis moved on, Eric tapped his watch.

"You want to grab some food so we can head out?"

"Eat and run, hmm?"

"I have plans for the rest of the day." He propelled her toward the dining room.

They nibbled at the buffet; chatted with Reverend Baker and Father Kevin, who arrived together; spoke briefly to a few other residents as they worked their way back toward the front door; and said their good-byes to Eleanor and Luis.

Once outside, Eric took her hand. "Nice party."

"Not that we stayed long." She waved to Lexie, who was approaching Eleanor's house from across the street. "She looks a lot different in civvies, doesn't she?"

"Yeah." Eric spared the striking woman no more than a distracted glance and kept walking.

"What's with you today?"

"What do you mean?" He hit the auto lock button on his keychain, hurrying her along.

"You seem kind of on edge."

"I'm . . . uh . . . still thinking about the news from the gallery. That came out of the blue."

"I knew it was only a matter of time. Those first sketches you did for the backdrop were proof you had talent." She waited beside the car while he opened her door. "This has been a day for great news, hasn't it? The companion program was approved, you sold your first painting, and Luis is back on track to work in the

444

medical field again." She slid inside and smiled up at him. "How could this holiday season get any better?"

T minus ten and counting.

As Eric flipped on the BMW blinker, BJ's earlier comment echoed in his mind.

If everything went the way he hoped, this holiday season was about to get *much* better.

"Is there a road here?" BJ leaned forward in the passenger seat and inspected the wooded shoulder.

"Yes. Barely." Eric swung onto a faint, two-lane gravel track that led into the woods.

Two hundred feet in, the trees thinned to reveal a spectacular view of the coast, the tall grass at the edge of the bluff dancing in the wind.

"Wow." BJ leaned forward to take in the scene.

Once he stopped the car, she jumped out without waiting for him to open her door and jogged toward the view.

"What a gorgeous panorama! How did you find this spot?"

"Charley's house isn't far from here." Eric strolled up beside her. "He told me about it."

"If we hadn't already eaten, this would be a great spot for a private picnic."

Or something more.

He fingered the small, square box in the pocket of his slacks.

T minus five and counting.

"Take a look at this." He drew her to the far side of the bluff, where a trail wound down to a small private beach.

"How cool is that? Should we go down?"

"That was my plan." Part of it, anyway.

They descended the rocky, forested incline, emerging onto the sand in a tiny, sheltered cove. Here, the wind that had buffeted them on the bluff was nothing more than a gentle breeze.

BJ crossed the sand to where the water lapped gently against the shore, scanned the long expanse of horizon, and sighed. "I think I could live here."

The perfect opening.

Heart pounding, he dug out the box, flipped up the lid, and moved beside her. "I was hoping you'd feel that way—because this land is for sale . . . and I'd like to build a house on it to share with you."

She swung toward him, eyes rounding when she spotted the ring. "Is this . . . are you proposing?"

"I'm getting ready to."

"Yes."

He blinked. "I didn't ask yet."

"Whoops." She clapped a hand over her mouth. "I didn't mean to steal your thunder. Go ahead."

"It's kind of irrelevant now." He grinned and

pulled the marquise-shaped stone out of the box.

"No way." She hooked her hands together behind her back and shook her head. "I want to hear your proposal. Most women only get this chance once, and I intend to savor every minute of it."

She wasn't letting him off the hook.

His pulse picked up speed again. Putting your heart on the line was way tougher than presenting a high-stakes closing argument—even when you already knew the outcome.

But he had his speech prepared.

If he could remember it.

"Okay. Here goes." He took her hand . . . twined their fingers together . . . and held on tight as he plunged in. "During my career in law, I've learned to present facts in a way that sways the judge and jury to my position. So here are the facts in this case. Since the moment we met, every day has brought new questions—and new doubts—about the path I'd laid out for myself and the priorities I'd set. But through it all, one thing became more and more clear: I didn't want to live my life without the most wonderful woman I'd ever met."

He stroked his thumb over the back of her hand and focused on her beautiful face. "I'm not the best bargain, BJ. Hope Harbor has a mellowing effect, but I'm a type A personality and will probably always work too hard, whether it be at law or painting. On the flip side, I'll also work hard to be a great husband. I may not be able to offer you trips to Paris every year, or designer clothes and expensive jewelry on your birthday, but I *can* offer you my love for the rest of my life." He positioned the ring at the tip of her finger. "So will you do me the honor of becoming my wife?"

She opened her mouth . . . but when no words came out, she resorted to a nod.

He slipped the ring over her finger and gestured to the land around them. "Welcome home, BJ."

All at once, faint creases dented her brow. "But . . . isn't this property outrageously expensive?"

"It's on the pricey side. However, Charley knows the owner and got me an excellent deal. It will eat up most of the nest egg I accumulated— but as Charley pointed out, coastal property at a moderate price is always a smart investment. As for the house . . . I know a talented architect who could design an amazing one with a studio for me and an office for her. She might even waive the fee if there are fringe benefits."

"What kind of fringe benefits?" A teasing light began to dance in her eyes, chasing away her frown.

"Shall I demonstrate?"

"By all means. But first . . . can I tell you something?"

"Always."

"I think I'm the one coming out ahead on this deal."

"How so?"

"I get *you*. A swoon-worthy guy who's generous, kind, smart, funny, caring, romantic, and trustworthy. Who pitches in whenever and wherever he's needed. Who walked—or should I say crashed?—into my life one day and changed it forever . . . for the better. Who makes me feel like the sun is shining even on cloudy days."

Her final words quivered with emotion, and pressure built in his throat. "Thank you."

"You're welcome. Now"—she cuddled closer—"about that demonstration . . ."

"Coming right—"

A loud belch offshore.

He groaned. "Don't tell me."

BJ squinted at the silver-white seal perched on a small outcrop of rock. "Do you think . . . could that possibly be Casper?"

"Stranger things have happened, I guess. And to tell you the truth, at this point it would feel dd if he *didn't* show up at amorous moments."

"Maybe he's lonely and our romance gives him a vicarious thrill."

"In that case, let's give him the thrill of a lifetime. Unless you have any objection?"

"Nope. The defense rests."

Smiling, he tugged her close again, this woman who'd managed to transform his world. Who'd shown him that love trumped high-profile

449

litigation any day. Whose caring heart and compassionate nature added grace and beauty and joy to his days.

And as their lips melded . . . as the world around them melted away . . . he gave thanks for happy endings—and for Hope Harbor's everyday miracles that made life good and sweet.

— Author's Note —

I've always believed milestones should be celebrated—and you're holding one in your hands.

Sea Rose Lane is my fiftieth published novel.

I'm still trying to wrap my mind around that number.

I've also been trying to figure out how I managed to reach this landmark . . . and I have to conclude it's a God thing. Writing, like any other talent, is a gift—and while I did work hard to develop the gift, the real credit for this achievement belongs to the giver. He gave me the stories . . . and the words to tell them. It's been an amazing blessing that has graced my life in countless ways.

Many people have also played a role in my writing journey, and to them, too, I owe a huge debt of gratitude. Family, friends, teachers, publishing colleagues—there are too many to name here, but most have had a book dedicated to them somewhere along the way.

I do want to offer a special thank-you, however, to the following:

My husband, Tom—my real-life hero—who understands that writing is hard, demanding work and who does everything he can to keep our life running smoothly so I can lock myself away in my office and tell stories.

My parents, James and Dorothy Hannon, who gave me roots . . . and wings—and who created a home where unconditional love was never out of stock.

My brother Jim, who noticed and passed on the tiny news article that led to the sale of my first book.

My publishing partners at Revell—a talented, savvy, professional, conscientious, and committed group. I feel privileged to work with you.

And finally, my readers, who have made this milestone possible. Please know that I treasure you—and give thanks for your support every single day.

Sea Rose Lane is special to me not only because it's a milestone book but because I've fallen in love with Hope Harbor. I hope you have too. And I invite you to return next spring for another visit to this charming Oregon seaside town, where hearts heal . . . and love blooms.

— *About the Author* —

Irene Hannon is a bestselling, award-winning author who took the publishing world by storm at the tender age of ten with a sparkling piece of fiction that received national attention.

Okay . . . maybe that's a slight exaggeration. But she *was* one of the honorees in a complete-the-story contest conducted by a national children's magazine. And she likes to think of that as her "official" fiction-writing debut!

Since then, she has written more than fifty contemporary romance and romantic suspense novels. Irene is a seven-time finalist and three-time winner of the RITA Award—the "Oscar" of romantic fiction—from Romance Writers of America. She is also a member of that organization's elite Hall of Fame. Her books have been honored with a National Readers' Choice Award, three HOLT Medallions, a Daphne du Maurier Award, a Retailers' Choice Award, two Booksellers' Best Awards, two Carol Awards, and two Reviewers' Choice Awards from *RT Book Reviews* magazine. In addition, she is a two-time Christy Award finalist. Finally, she is the recipient of a prestigious Career Achievement Award from *RT Book Reviews* for her entire body of work.

Irene, who holds a BA in psychology and an MA in journalism, juggled two careers for many years until she gave up her executive corporate communications position with a Fortune 500 company to write full-time. She is happy to say she has no regrets! As she points out, leaving behind the rush-hour commute, corporate politics, and a relentless BlackBerry that never slept was no sacrifice.

A trained vocalist, Irene has sung the leading role in numerous community theater productions and is also a soloist at her church.

When not otherwise occupied, she and her husband enjoy traveling, Saturday mornings at their favorite coffee shop, and spending time with family. They make their home in Missouri.

To learn more about Irene and her books, visit www.irenehannon.com. She is also active on Facebook and Twitter.

Center Point Large Print
600 Brooks Road / PO Box 1
Thorndike, ME 04986-0001 USA

(207) 568-3717

US & Canada:
1 800 929-9108
www.centerpointlargeprint.com